Eden, Dorothy

An important family

DATE DUE

AUG 17 1994			

An Important Family

An Important Family

DOROTHY EDEN

WILLIAM MORROW AND COMPANY, INC.

New York 1982

Library of Congress Cataloging in Publication Data

Eden, Dorothy, 1912–
    An important family.

    I. Title.
PR9639.3.E38I45   1982   823   81-19026
ISBN   0-688-01148-9   AACR2

Printed in the United States of America

First U. S. Edition

1   2   3   4   5   6   7   8   9   10

BOOK DESIGN BY MICHAEL MAUCERI

Fic.

FOR
NANCY
AND
HARVEY HACKMAN

Supposing there should be going to the Canterbury colonies a large number of families of the gentry class, all being truly respectable or worthy of respect, to found an important family in one part of the British Empire...

—EDWARD GIBBON WAKEFIELD

1

When she arrived on the doorstep, Kate couldn't bring herself to ring the doorbell. The house was too grand and she was uncertain as to whether she should have gone to the servants' entrance. But the advertisement had said "to live as family." Families used the front door. Would there be a servants' entrance in a colonial house? She doubted it. Therefore, to live as family meant little since there could scarcely be an alternative.

"And is it cannibal country you're planning to go to?" Cousin Mabel had asked in great alarm.

"A bonny tender young thing like Kate," her husband, Cousin Giles, hidden behind *The Times* newspaper, had murmured. "She'll be served as the *plat du jour* at the Big Chief's table."

Cousin Mabel was English and didn't appreciate Irish humour. Kate didn't always appreciate it herself, and particularly not today when she had such an ordeal ahead of her.

But it wasn't cannibalism she was afraid of, it was what the advertisement had candidly stated about isolation and loneliness. Was she strong enough to face those things?

Of course she was. They couldn't be worse than the loneliness and grief she had suffered for the last two years, the hatred of Ireland and the longing, since Dermot's death at the hands of an ill-tempered British sergeant, to get away from that sad, weeping country for ever.

The familiar wrench of pain and anger stiffened her resolve. Kate set her finger on the doorbell and waited in the grey spacious London square, austere and orderly and exuding wealth and power. A thought puzzled her. Why did the people who lived in this grand house, apparently lacking nothing, want to travel so far away? Were they also escaping from grief?

The door opened. A majestic butler appeared. His lofty gaze took in Kate's modest appearance. His expression said that she should have gone to the servants' entrance.

"Yes, miss. What do you want?"

The newspaper containing the advertisement, which she had outlined in black ink, trembled in Kate's hand.

Wanted—for titled family emigrating to the colony of New Zealand, young woman of pleasant disposition and resourcefulness. To be companion to two ladies and to live as family. A knowledge of music, art and literature an advantage, also needlework and care of the ladies' wardrobes. The post will inevitably represent some isolation from society, so nobody who has not the strength to contemplate partings from family and friends should consider it. Apply with references to 3 Belgrave Square, London.

Kate indicated the column to the butler. She spoke with as much confidence as she could manage.

"I have come to see somebody about this. I'm afraid I don't know your employers' names."

"Sir John and Lady Devenish, miss. I'll see if the master is available. Will you step inside?"

A black-and-white tiled hall, good furniture, mirrors, the curve of a well-polished staircase. Why should Sir John and Lady Devenish be travelling into the unknown? Why did they need to seek a new life? Intrigued, Kate forgot her nervousness. She must have caught the scent of adventure for suddenly she knew that she terribly wanted to accompany them, no matter what kind of people they were.

"Will you come this way, miss?" The butler had returned and was indicating that Kate should follow him down the hall into a darkish book-lined room.

"The young lady, my lord."

"Ah, yes, Parker. Has she told you her name? Never mind, you may leave us. Come and introduce yourself, madam."

"I'm Miss O'Connor. Kate O'Connor, sir."

"Irish," he said at once.

It was impossible to tell from his voice whether he was prejudiced or not. So many English people, especially since the Great Hunger, seemed to hate and despise the Irish. Their own consciences were guilty, that was the trouble.

But this man, strong-looking and youngish, surely not more than forty, seemed impartial, almost a little absent in his manner, as if the irritating Irish were minuscule compared with his own private concerns.

He was well groomed, from his glossy waving brown hair, to his sparkling white shirt-cuffs, his polished fingernails, the heavy, gold watch chain across his stomach. When Kate dared to raise her eyes and look into his face, she saw that he was looking at her with deep-set observant eyes. He was not perfectly handsome because his high-bridged nose was very slightly crooked as if it had once been broken. A fall in the hunting field, perhaps. This slight fault, to Kate's mind, was attractive. His colour had a healthy ruddiness, as if from an outdoor life, he was clean shaven, his mouth was unsmiling and had a look of intolerance, his jaw strong.

A formidable figure, Kate decided. But who would want a meek and polite gentleman to be in charge of three ladies sailing into an unknown world?

Kate's heart was beating hard. "Anglo-Irish, sir," she said in her soft voice. "I was brought up in Mallow by two aunts. My father was thrown from a horse and killed when I was a child. He was Irish and reckless. My mother was English." She saw him watching her. "She grieved too much, and soon followed him."

"And now you want to leave your aunts and your country? Why? Are you penniless? In trouble? Are you running away from something?"

I don't think I care for that inflexible mouth, Kate was thinking. If I could see him smile...

"Does one have to be running away from something, sir?"

"I should explain that I'm a great admirer of the writings of Edward Gibbon Wakefield, the coloniser. Have you heard of him? He has a dream about the ideal colony. A utopia, in fact. He says that emigrants to empty lands should not be in flight from disgrace or crime or starvation or other desperate ills. He was referring to the unfortunate convict settlements in Australia, of course."

Kate was interested and forgot her nervousness.

"And so the emigrants should all be respectable people with no blemish on their characters?"

"In Wakefield's Canterbury settlement in New Zealand, this is his intention. He wants large numbers of families of both the gentry and the working classes to settle there. There must also be members of the professions such as law and medicine. A bishop would be an excellent idea."

There was the shadow of a smile on that serious mouth.

"And of course a fair measure of craftsmen such as carpenters, bricklayers, shopkeepers, shepherds and ploughmen. A perfectly constructed and balanced society, in other words. It's a concept that I find tremendously exciting. Surely a promising new country like New Zealand gives enterprising people the opportunity to create it."

"And everyone is to be perfectly happy?" Kate heard herself saying. "But what about human nature?"

"Human nature?"

"I mean the usual components of love and hate, greed, envy, bad tempers, craftiness, guile. Even stupidity. Your perfect colony can't banish the things that we all carry on our backs."

Sir John Devenish was looking at her with some impatience. Had he expected nothing but romantic idealism from a woman? How could he, an intelligent and thinking man, be so gullible himself? Yet the concept was exciting, and how could such a society become a fact if people didn't believe in it?

"I apologise, sir—"

"What are you apologising about?"

"I think I was impertinent."

"To express your opinion? No, I welcome an intelligent opinion. Although I had hardly expected such a quickly formed one." His eyes remained hard and unfriendly. He didn't like his dream being pricked even in the smallest way. It obviously meant a very great deal to him.

"At least I don't need to enquire about your education, Miss O'Connor," he commented. "That's apparent. Although you have a woman's way of looking at things. Perhaps you should answer the question that led up to this."

"Am I running away? From Ireland, certainly. My fiancé was killed there." Kate bit her lip, and tried to keep her voice calm. "He wasn't an important person, just a schoolmaster, who was too compassionate. He tried to stop the military from evicting a family from their cottage. There was a young mother and two small children. He acted impulsively, I know, and he would never have succeeded, even if he had been given a chance. But the sergeant, a big brutal fellow, struck him down. Killed him, sir. Although unintentionally," she added fairly.

"That's terrible," Sir John Devenish said with sincerity. "It's understandable you should want to leave that unhappy country. Have you overcome your grief?"

"I will not be a weeping female, sir."

Sir John's mouth gave a twitch. Almost, he had been about to smile.

"Your family?"

"I have only two aunts in Mallow and a cousin in London. They agree with my aspirations."

They didn't. At least Aunt Dolly, the younger of the two elderly sisters in Mallow may secretly have done so. She still had the light of the dreamer in her soft blue eyes. But she was accustomed to letting her sister, Esmeralda, be the spokesman, so it was officially known in Mallow that the Misses O'Connor were puzzled and grieved by their niece's extraordinary decision. They should not have been. Their troubled country had seen many departures from its shores, and the letters and the small packages of gold had come trickling back. Even Aunt Esmeralda and Aunt Dolly would not scorn the gold, if Kate could send it. Their rambling old house was shabby and their tangled demesne had shrunk from ten acres to two since Paddy Dowell had taken the other eight to graze his cows. The money had been most useful while it lasted. But it had quickly gone, and the house was again falling into disrepair. What future did it have for Kate? Even Cousin Mabel in London had been unable to make any suggestions save that Kate, so clever in her brain, should open a small private school for girls—without apparently money or pupils!

"And the other requirements in the advertisement?" Sir John was saying.

Kate was on firmer ground now. "Oh, they'll be no bother to me. I can do them all, and other things, too."

"What other things?"

"Speaking French. Riding."

"French won't be necessary in New Zealand, I fancy. Maori, more likely. I hear it is a musical language. Riding will indeed be useful as it is the only way to get about, except for bullock waggons. And coaches on the roads, but there are few roads."

"Does Lady Devenish ride, sir?"

"Not much. My daughter does, but doesn't care for it. They're what I call drawing-room women."

He spoke with a certain pride, as if this was the kind of woman he admired. But in a new settlement? As pioneers? One supposed the ornamental would be necessary, as well as the practical, if they were to have a balanced society.

Kate found she had been enjoying their conversation. It had been much more an exchange of ideas than an interrogation of herself. It was possible that there would be more discussions of this kind, on the long tedious voyage, when good conversationalists would probably be scarce. A stirring of excitement made her eyes brighten. She watched Sir John pull the bell rope, and nodded when he said that he thought it time for her to make the acquaintance of his wife.

"Since she must make the ultimate decision. You will be con-

stantly in her company. And my daughter's, of course. Parker"—
the butler had appeared—"ask Lady Devenish if she is able to
come down. You understand," he went on to Kate, "that no
decision can be made today. You are the first applicant and I
daresay there will be others."

"I understand, sir." For all her confused feelings the excitement stirring in her told Kate that she very much wanted this
position, and infinitely more now than when she had been standing nervously on the doorstep. She guessed that Sir John Devenish would be a forthright man, perhaps an intolerant one,
and not easily knowable. If he deferred to his wife so meticu-
lously, what could she be like?

Don't let her spoil my hopes, Kate prayed silently. If she is
a dragon, can I live for three months in the confined space of
a ship with her, and then in the isolation of a lonely house? And
with the daughter, too, who may be just as domineering as her
parents...

Her tumbled thoughts scattered as the door opened and a
small fragile woman, like a moth, or a white mouse, came in.

"You wanted me, John? Oh, you have an applicant." There
was surprise and apprehension in Lady Devenish's sigh. "So
soon."

"It can't be too soon, my dear. This is Miss Kate O'Connor
who seems eager to join us in our new life. I know you will have
a long list of matters to discuss with her, so I'll leave you."

Lady Devenish made a groping movement towards her husband. She was dressed in pale grey and her face had almost the
same sad colour. Her eyes were downcast as if she were too
diffident or too nervous to look at Kate. Or was it her alarming
future which she was refusing to face? Kate was amused at her
own apprehension. Was this the woman who was going to dom-
inate the ship's poky cabin? Poor thing, what she needed was
a mousehole.

How could someone so urbane and confident as Sir John
Devenish have married a timid woman like this? Or had marriage to him developed the timidity? Once Lady Devenish must
have been delicately pretty, like a harebell. If one liked the frail
short-lived flowers.

The door closed. The two women were alone and unexpectedly Lady Devenish raised her eyes and gave Kate a surprisingly sharp scrutiny. She was not entirely colourless, after all.

"How old are you, Miss O'Connor?"

"I'm twenty-three."

"And are you good with young girls, Miss O'Connor? Have you a kind and sympathetic manner?"

"I haven't had much experience, Lady Devenish. But I would be kind, of course."

"Celina has an extremely nervous disposition. She inherits it from me. Her father, I am afraid, doesn't always understand a young girl's vapours."

"May I ask how old your daughter is, Lady Devenish?"

"How old? Were you not told? She is eighteen."

"Oh! I had imagined—"

"What?" The sharpness was in Lady Devenish's voice now. Brittle. Like glass breaking.

"I don't know why I imagined that she wasn't out of the schoolroom."

"That's because her father babies her. We both do, I'm afraid. She has always been so sensitive, so easily upset. She lives on her nerves. Oh, Miss O'Connor—"

"Yes?"

"Do you believe that the natives of New Zealand are cannibals?"

One could not lie. Kate had heard the same stories herself.

"I believe some of the tribes did practise cannibalism. But not since the coming of the white man, and the missionaries. There is a Bishop Selwyn who has made himself famous for teaching the savages Christian ways."

"I am relieved to hear it." Lady Devenish had brightened a little. "Of course, with decent British rule, those horrible practices must disappear. Anyway, Sir John says that our property is not in a native area. It is too far from the sea. The natives live on fish a great deal. Avalon is quite a fine place, Miss O'Connor. We are not going to live in mud huts. Sir John bought the property from a settler who is returning to England. He has seen sketches of the house and outbuildings. It has verandahs and gabled windows. It is nothing like Leyte Manor, of course. That is our home in the Cotswolds that we are leaving. But it has a romantic name, hasn't it? Avalon."

"Perhaps it will be romantic, Lady Devenish."

"With those snowy mountains as a backdrop." Lady Devenish was clasping her hands tightly. "Cold," she muttered. "Cold, cold." She seemed to be shivering. Presently, however, she composed herself.

"Forgive me, Miss O'Connor. It's my wretched nerves, which Celina has, too. We have both been having ridiculous dreams about sheep. Oh, dear Miss O'Connor, you will come with us, won't you? And help us to be brave."

"Am I to come?" Kate cried.

She wanted to throw her arms round the little quivering figure and reassure her, as one would a child. Why was she so suddenly taken up with this family? In half an hour she was identifying with them, the adventurous husband with his ideals about a new colony, a utopia on earth, and now this slender thread of a woman with the fearfulness coming and going in her eyes.

What about the daughter?

"Oh, yes, I think you are to come, my dear. My husband wouldn't have allowed me to waste my time on someone unsuitable. But naturally we will have long discussions and we will want to see you again. Celina must see you. Have we your address so that we can send you a message?"

"I have it here," said Kate, handing her one of Cousin Mabel's cards. "I shall need to reflect, too, of course."

"If my husband decides in your favour," Lady Devenish said, "he will allow you no time for reflection."

After the young woman, Miss O'Connor, had gone, Lady Devenish retired to her bedroom, shutting the door and drawing the curtains although it was still daylight. She liked gloom. No one could watch her in semi-darkness. People watched her too much. She had first known this when she was quite a small child. She had never been left alone. They had seemed to be watching her for something but what it was she didn't know. She had learned not to meet their eyes. Painfully shy, she was always more comfortable with her gaze averted.

"Hold your head up, child," Mama had used to say. "You have pretty blue eyes. Let people see them." But Mama had disappeared before her daughter was ten years old, and she had not seen her again. Nobody could, or would, tell her where Mama was, and only some years later had she learned that the sharp-voiced little person who had scolded her was dead, for the house had been in mourning, the blinds drawn, the servants in black, and a new grave dug in the churchyard.

"Poor thing, like a wild bird come to rest," Nanny had said.

"Why wasn't I told? Why did I never see her?" she asked.

"Your Papa thought it better not. Now don't ask questions that I can't answer, Miss Iris. Your Papa expects you to grow up into a charming young lady and find a good husband, so that is what you must set about doing."

"Me?" she faltered.

"Who else, for goodness sake? You're fifteen years old and you're quite passably pretty. Some men like the quiet ones. And your fortune will help. We must be practical in this life."

Sir John Devenish, that handsome young man with the dark bright penetrating eyes, had liked her quietness and her prettiness. More or less than her fortune? He had obviously liked that, too. She had married him when she was seventeen, and she had been terrified of him.

When her baby had been born he had been enchanted with its silvery head and his own dark eyes. Celina was a little witch, an other-worldish creature, but with all the lively vociferousness her mother lacked. All the same, John had hoped for a son.

He never understood why his wife always stiffened in his arms, but he supposed that was the prerogative of a highly sensitive woman. She never conceived again.

It had seemed to be always cold at Leyte Manor in the dark-panelled rooms with the diamond-paned windows. She had never felt at home there. But now, in comparison with the wastes of an almost uninhabited country, it seemed infinitely desirable, even though she was sure it was haunted. There had been that long moan she had heard one night. No one else had heard it. Yet it was soon after that that her husband had announced their impending departure for the colonies. Partly because he wanted an invigorating change, partly because his pretty doll child, Celina, was moping and pining and not pleasing him. Lady Devenish had always thought of Celina as a doll, albeit often a cross and disagreeable one. Recently the doctor had diagnosed a nervous debility and recommended a complete change of scene and climate.

So here she was, Lady Devenish thought, wringing her hands in her despairing fashion. Caught between the two of them, her alarming husband and her perplexing daughter. But at least New Zealand would not have old haunted houses, with sad moaning in the night.

2

They were like a group out of a painting, standing at the crossroads overlooking the gentle rolling landscape of the Cotswolds.

Pa wore his shabby tweed cape over his best Sunday jacket and trousers, Mam her Sunday bonnet and the warm shawl Granny had finished knitting just in time for the departure. Emily was in her much treasured blue velvet cape and bonnet. Granny hadn't thought it at all suitable for travelling, not warm enough and fripperish. But Emily, in tears, had pleaded to wear it because it always made her feel good, and she needed desperately to feel good on this strange, sad morning. She had polished her buttoned boots to a brave shine, and then had done the same for the little boys. Her brothers, Jonnie and Willie, had their tweed overcoats and tweed caps on, making them look like little men. Jonnie was eleven, Willie five. Jonnie was looking bright-eyed and excited about the journey ahead, but Willie's face was smudged with tears. He had cried about leaving his ferret. There was a small bulge beneath his overcoat, but this came, not from the ferret, but from the shabby wooden doll that he still cherished furtively, for he felt he should have grown out of dolls.

The two boys were younger than the boy who had been the last to hang on the gibbet at the roadside a little way ahead. Although that poor lad had been child enough, not quite thirteen, a starved skinny form like a paper doll swinging in the breeze. Mam hadn't let any of them near that evil spot on the roadside until the sparrow bones had been cut down and laid to rest. What had the poor boy done, Emily asked over and over again, not believing that he could have been hanged for stealing a trussed fowl from the poulterer in Burford. His Mam and his six younger brothers and sisters had been starving, Mam had explained to Emily. He had done wrong, of course, but the punishment had been far too cruel. It was things like that that made you want to leave the old country and hope for true justice in the colonies.

Mam herself was staring at the sinister outline of the gibbet in the distance, imagining the poor doll hanging there. Making it give her courage, perhaps. Emily understood that because she was in need of courage, too. No matter what dreadful things happened now and then, this green part of England was their home and it was terrible to leave it. Granny and Grandpa were left in the little cottage that was one of a circle of cottages round the village pond, a cottage that had been bursting at the sides when they were all there. Granny and Grandpa in one small low-ceilinged upstairs bedroom, Aunt Annie, who had a crippled leg and walked with a tilt, and would never marry, in the other. Mam and Pa in the tiny downstairs parlour where Grandpa kept his books and the children in the wall bed in the kitchen where the fire winked cosily in the stove until after midnight and the world was safe.

From the pond, in the early summer, there had come the croaking of frogs, and on Sundays the ringing of church bells. The small grey church up the hillside was where squire and his wife and daughter went every Sunday when they were in residence at the manor. Grandpa rang the bells. He was also the parish clerk and recorded, in beautiful script, the births, marriages and deaths in the parish register. He was a very clever man. He had taught his grandchildren to read and to write. He believed that that knowledge was of far greater value than money.

Pa didn't agree, neither did Mam, otherwise they wouldn't be standing here on this chilly morning surrounded by their baggage waiting for the London coach. They were going to find gold in the colonies. The boys were going to be rich and Emily was going to get a fine, hard-working, healthy husband. They would all own their own houses and land. There was plenty for everybody and there would be no more masters and mistresses. Everyone would be equal.

Not that Squire was a bad master. If he had been, Pa wouldn't have agreed to go to New Zealand with him. Nor was the mistress unkind or thoughtless, though Mam had a certain contempt for her. A poor anxious lady, she called her, whom one had to protect. Especially when there was trouble in the house.

But Emily had never been told what the trouble was.

She only knew that it was unlikely she would ever love a house as much as Leyte Manor. She would take the memory of it with her over the seas and keep it in her head for ever.

Mam had given way to her pleading and let her have a last look over the lovely old rooms after the Squire and Lady Devenish and Miss Celina had gone to London.

"You won't like it," Mam said. "Everything's under covers. It's sad, ghostly. It's as if the old house was ready for burial."

"Oh, no, Mam!"

But Mam was right. For the two large drawing rooms, the library, the tapestry room, the mistress's sitting room and all the bedrooms were shrouded in sheets. There were faded squares and oblongs on the damask wallpaper where pictures had been removed, and all the fascinating porcelain figures that Emily had loved but never dared to touch had disappeared.

"Packed away," said Mam briefly.

Emily looked sadly for her most admired painting, that of a child in Elizabethan dress, a tiny, slender creature with a pinched white face and suspicious, slightly crooked eyes.

"A mean, spoiled little lass," Mam had used to say. "Wasn't long for this world, I'll be bound."

22   /

Emily had once had a doll with a cracked china face and sharp eyes. She had loved it dearly, mostly because of its defects. They had made it seem real and human. But it had been broken. Now the painted child with her long-ago sorrows had disappeared, too. And the plants in the conservatory had been given away, Mam said, since there would be no one to care for them. There was a smell of damp and decay in that once green world.

The mistress had kept a parrot. It was said to be sixty years old, as old as Grandpa, and it had used to whistle cheekily at Emily and wish her good night, although it was only mid-morning. It had gone, too. There would be no more fires burning in the huge stone fireplace in the hall, or in the living rooms and bedrooms. Drawing the heavy curtains at all the windows would be her last task, Mam said. Then Jem Watts who lived in the lodge at the gates would pull all the outside doors shut and turn keys in the locks. The garden would become overgrown because he couldn't manage it alone, not ten acres of lawns and flower beds and woodland.

"What will happen to the roses?" Emily asked.

"They'll bloom every summer until Squire comes home," Mam said, blowing her nose. She had been crying, Emily noticed with anguish. "If he ever does come home. If any of us ever comes home."

"But, Mam, you told us it was to be a great adventure." Emily was in dire need of reassurance.

"That's what your Pa says. And Squire. We women weren't particularly asked what we thought."

Emily had never before heard her mother speak with that kind of bitterness. She had thought that women were happy always to do as their husbands wanted.

"Didn't the mistress want to go, Mam? Is she afraid of cannibals? I'm not. Nor is Jonnie. I don't think Willie knows what cannibals are."

"The mistress is afraid of most things," Mam said shortly. "Poor creature."

"Miss Celina, too?"

Mam gave Emily a sideways look. No one ever seemed to speak out honestly about Miss Celina.

"Oh, no, she's not afraid. But she don't want to go, nevertheless. Where will she ever be able to wear her fine clothes, she
says. That's more on her mind than anything else. And will there
be any man good enough for her to marry. She's angry with her
Papa. But then—"

"What, Mam?" Emily begged. She had always longed to know
more about Miss Celina, what she thought, what were her favourite things, but nobody would tell her. She had been sent to
a school in Switzerland last year, although for some reason she
had soon been home again. It was whispered among the servants
that she was sometimes locked in her room. She could be heard
screaming, especially in the night. Eerie...

There had been a very bad night not long before Squire had
astonished and appalled everybody by saying that he was shutting up the manor and going on a voyage to New Zealand.
(Where *was* New Zealand? Over the edge of the earth?) But the
news had apparently upset Miss Celina a great deal, and Doctor
Woodstock had been called to give her a calming draught. After
that, although she was seen out in the garden or perhaps in the
village, she had never been alone. Even in the seclusion of the
garden she had been in the company of her maid.

"Sad," the servants has whispered inexplicably.

"A nervous disposition," Emily had heard Mam saying to Pa.
"And strong-willed with it. Not like her mother who couldn't
hurt a fly."

Emily had thought of the picture in the gallery, the little girl
borne down by her heavy finery. Miss Celina often had the same
look of frustration and bad temper.

"She's right pretty when she smiles," Mam said loyally and
added under her breath, "poor Squire."

Everyone said, after that night when the doctor had had to
be called, that Squire had begun to look like a man with a heavy
burden on his shoulders. It was then that the talk of New Zealand had begun. Squire went several times to London and saw
members of the New Zealand Company as well as members of
Parliament. Quite fortuitously (this was the gossip that went
round the village) he had met a returning settler, a rich and
bored young man who had tried many things and grown tired

of them all. His latest venture had been as a station owner in the Canterbury settlement of New Zealand. He had built a fine house, probably the finest in the province, and imported live-stock, to stock his farm. The venture had prospered, but—quite abruptly—the young gentleman had given it all up and returned to England. Eventually, he had told Sir John, the isolation from the world had begun to drive him mad. He was surfeited with the company of shepherds, a Chinese cook, some Maori la-bourers, and the rare visit of a passing stranger. Besides, being alone, he wanted to come back to England to find a suitable wife and raise a family.

Squire already had a wife and a daughter, and he looked forward to the isolation from the world. Or so he said. He had always been a friendly man, genial and jolly when in a good temper, who had enjoyed hunting and shooting and giving elab-orate dinner parties and visiting his club in London. Why should he suddenly declare that he longed for solitude? And how would his wife and daughter fare in such a strange, quiet place? Splen-didly, he had declared. It would do their health all the good in the world. The wind from the mountains was unbelievably pure. And the house was no mean pioneer cottage but a capacious building, with ample room for as many guests as could be found. They would have balls. The grand piano must go, and a good selection of furniture and fine rugs and silver. The best Spode dinner service and some favourite pictures and ornaments. They would give style to pioneer life. Also, it would be diverting to become a sheep farmer.

At least that was what Squire was reputed to have said. When he told Pa, however, and asked him if he would be prepared to transport his family to such a promising land, with a great future for himself and his sons, Pa said there had been a strange look of torment in his eyes.

"Some sort of secret torment, Mary," he said to Mam, at night when the children were supposed to be asleep in the wall bed. The boys were asleep but Emily lay awake, alternately fascinated and fearful of Pa's revelations. "I don't know what it is, but he's been a good employer. I'd like to stick by him. And the mistress refuses to go unless she had you along. Or so Squire says."

"She's a poor creature," Mam said.

"Aye. But you can manage her. And think of the opportunity for Jonnie and Willie. By the time they're grown they can be landowners. Here they'll never be anything but labourers, and lucky to be that. Think of the hanging boy."

Mam was silent, not needing to be reminded of that pathetic scarecrow swinging from the gibbet.

Then she said, "You mean to go, don't you, Jonas."

"I do. And I hope you do, too."

"No!" said Mam with sudden violence. "I'd lief not."

"But you'll have to, Mary. You must do as I decide."

"It's not fair, Jonas Lodden. I didn't marry you for this. To be taken out of my country like a transported convict."

"No, no, New Zealand doesn't have convicts. Squire has explained it to me. There's an ordered society with all the right kind of people in it. A utop—something."

"Utopia," said Mam, who had always read books.

"That's it. A kind of paradise."

"In this world! Paradise! You have to get to heaven for that."

"No, it should be here if people acted right. Squire's been talking to learned people. There's a band of settlers called the Canterbury Pilgrims gone out. Respectable people who haven't got guilty secrets or haven't committed crimes or aren't half-starved. People who are honest and hard working, educated ones and the labourers, judges and schoolmasters and carpenters and shepherds. Enough decent single women for the men to marry so there won't be trafficking with the natives. There's even to be a bishop, Squire says. Now what do you think, Mary? Squire goes and we don't, we'll be left without jobs because he's shutting up the manor."

"You're mightily talkative tonight, Jonas," Mam said. "I've never heard you use such big words."

"It's listening to Squire. He never talked to me like this before. As man to man. It's the beginning of what he says will happen. We're all to be equal. But I won't go without you, Mary. You're my wife. Where I go you go. Isn't that what the Bible says?" There was a brief silence. "We'll take the family Bible," Pa said.

"We'll need our forbears in that lonely land," he added in a less certain voice.

"Jonas, you're a good man." Emily knew that Mam was crying again. "But I can't bear the thought of leaving our home. Granny and Grandpa. The church. All the things we love. And just for a wild dream of Squire's. He'll get tired of it like that young fellow whose farm he's bought."

"I don't fancy he will, Mary."

"Why not?"

"There's something deeper. Something I don't rightly understand."

"Something to do with Miss Celina?"

"Could be. Though it hardly seems likely. She's only a lass, albeit a wayward one."

Mam's voice was sharp.

"I can't decide all at once. Why must it be so quick?"

"The *Albatross* sails on the fifth day of February. Squire has accommodation paid for. I'll take care of the stock. Two milking cows, two sows, some speckled hens and a rooster. We may get fresh eggs on the voyage. The name of the place is Avalon."

"What place?"

"Where we be going, of course. It's near the mountains."

"Is it a castle?" asked Mam unbelievingly.

"Course it's not a castle. What an idea."

"A dream castle," Mam murmured. "That's what it's called in fairy tales."

"Oh, you and your book learning."

"We'll need that if we're to live on the edge of the world." Mam said, and then began to cry again. "Oh, Jonas love, I can't bear it. All the goodbyes. Leaving the old ones. It isn't right. It'll break my heart."

"Nonsense, lass, your heart's a deal stronger than that. I don't like to leave the old ones, neither, but it's the young you have to think of."

"It's not our young that Squire's thinking of," Mam said resentfully. "Nor his own. If you ask me, he's taken leave of his senses."

* * *

So here they were, Mary Lodden thought, the manor shut up, the drawn curtains closing out the light and bringing a quiet death to the rooms, the trunks packed and strapped, and good-byes said, the choking sobs stifled. The early morning wind sweeping across the low hills made them shiver. Would the pure wind from the New Zealand Alps make them shiver more?

Emily scuffed her boots in the dirt road, then remembered how carefully she had cleaned them, and desisted. The little boys were hopping about and swinging their arms to keep warm. Jonnie was sturdy, with a stiff thatch of brown hair and red cheeks, like his father's. Willie was shy and skinny, little more than a bag of bones, with big anxious eyes. It was always Willie who got the coughs and colds, the sore throats and the fevers. The sea voyage would set him up into a strong little lad, Jonas said. The churchyard at Little Shipton held too many children, dead from unexplained illnesses. Some said the cause was the bad humours from the scummy village pond, some the lack of proper drains to the picturesque row of cottages. Whatever the cause, the little boys and Emily, who was thirteen and inclined to outgrow her strength, would be much healthier in the wide, free spaces of an almost empty country. Grandpa had always dreaded having to take up his quill pen and make an entry in the church register concerning the demise of one or more of his grandchildren. Now he was to be spared that great misfortune.

Mary lifted her chin. The farewells had been terrible, both with her parents and lame sister, and with Jonas's brother who had ridden over from Burford. But now they were over, and although Mary thought she would never again in her life feel so desolate, a sensation of pride was easing the grief. She was a strong responsible woman obediently accompanying her mate on his chosen way. She had stopped complaining, and had resolved to accept cheerfully whatever lay ahead. They were a small family, complete in themselves. And God would accompany them because they had the shabby family Bible packed in the wooden trunk.

They were so much more fortunate in their serenity and hardiness of spirit than poor Lady Devenish, a prey to nervous anxieties, and her wilful difficult daughter...

As a shaft of pale sunlight slanted over the brow of the hill, the peaceful scene became etched on Mary's mind for ever. She slid one hand into her husband's and one into her own good little daughter's. Both hands were squeezed hard in return. Jonas didn't look at her, and she guessed he was embarrassed by sudden tears because he sniffed mightily. Emily took one last swift, compassionate glance at the distant gibbet and said boldly, "Goodbye, poor hanging boy. We're going to be luckier than you. Aren't we, Ma? Pa?"

"For a certainty we are," Pa said.

And then the coach lumbered into view. Pa stepped into the road beckoning it to stop. Had it room for a new complement of five passengers heading for London and the East India docks?

Heads looked out. The driver leaped down, and cheerfully stowed the trunks and baggage on board. Mary and Jonas and Emily fitted themselves into the stuffy interior. The boys, to their great delight, were squeezed on top beside the driver.

"You be telling us where you're going, young sirs," he said.

A sudden flight of seagulls over the ploughed land, swooping on their immaculate white wings, crying with the hopeless pain of lost mariners, seemed symbolic. Mary pulled Emily against her and made herself smile cheerfully at the curious faces of her travelling companions. Jonas didn't need to pretend cheerfulness. Now that he was on his way the adventure had completely captivated him. He was his own man at last. He was a pioneer.

3

Kate O'Connor was the successful applicant for the post of companion to Sir John Devenish's wife and daughter. The other applicants had been impossible, Sir John said. One, he vowed, was a petty criminal, guilty of pilfering from shops and other mean offences. Another did nothing but fidget nervously with her bonnet ribbons, her reticule, her gloves, and could not raise her eyes to look him full in the face. The third had been a bold enough young woman, but an eyesore, poor creature. To look at that deplorably plain visage all the way across the ocean to Lyttelton harbour would be a penance no one should be expected to make.

So Miss O'Connor it was, if she had not changed her mind.

"I haven't changed my mind," Kate said steadily. They were sitting in Cousin Mabel's parlour, for Sir John had done them the honour of driving out to see not only Kate but her family. It was only fair to them as well as to himself he said.

Cousin Mabel was in a rare fluster and could hardly get out a word. Cousin Giles did a lot of silent staring at the handsome caller, so it was left to Kate to make conversation.

She was not flustered as Cousin Mabel was. She had got over her nervousness, and was contemplating her future with equanimity.

"You do realise, sir, that I haven't yet met the young lady who is to be my charge."

"That's the reason for my visit. You are bidden to take tea with us tomorrow at four thirty. Celina is as eager to meet you as you are to meet her."

He smiled, and Kate was suddenly aware of his charm. The groove of anxiety or bad temper between his eyes seemed to disappear and his face became youthful. He must have been a light-hearted young man once, she realised. And why not? We have all had times when we were happy and carefree, she thought. And I am not too old to be unable to have them again, she added to herself, in optimism and excitement.

"Thank you, sir. I will be delighted to come to tea."

"So you are taking our Kate away from us!" Cousin Mabel had got herself into a state of indignation and was speaking up to her grand visitor. "Will it be for ever?"

"Not if she doesn't wish it."

Cousin Giles was more puzzled than indignant.

"But you, sir, you intend to make this savage country your home? Why, if I may ask?"

Sir John's deep-set eyes held a boyish sparkle.

"Oh, for change. Adventure. A testing of a man's skills. And being a loyal Englishman serving the interests of my Queen."

"Now, come, sir, the Queen is acquiring more colonies than she can keep count of." Kate winced. Cousin Giles was not always respectful to his monarch. But Sir John continued to look good-humoured, even amused.

"I can assure you that her new brown-skinned subjects occasionally remind her of their existence. They send messages of loyalty to their Great White Mother. Don't doubt it, my dear fellow, New Zealand will be of some moment one day, even so far away as it is."

"Damn near at the South Pole, isn't it?"

"Not quite. It has a temperate climate, and being virgin soil it is splendidly productive."

"So you mean to make it your permanent home, sir?"

"Perhaps. Perhaps not. I shall certainly be making visits home. I still have my property in the Cotswolds. It will need an inspection from time to time. But since it has already stood for two centuries I don't imagine its owner's absence for a few years will harm it."

"This property is for your daughter to inherit?"

Kate winced again. How could Cousin Giles be so impertinent?

"Perhaps. Perhaps since I have no son, her husband as well."

"A New Zealand husband?"

Sir John smiled easily, but this time his eyes remained dark and inward.

"Not a brown one, I assure you. There are many young men from good families emigrating. Some of them are cadets on the big sheep runs. They learn their trade, and have every chance of becoming rich. Quite apart from my daughter acquiring a husband, I shall live in fear of Miss Kate doing the same thing. We won't want to lose her too quickly."

"Oh dear!" Cousin Mabel exclaimed. "Then we will never see you again, Kate. What will your aunts in Mallow say?"

"There are people who stay at home, and people who do things," Kate murmured, and saw Sir John looking at her with approval.

"Well put, Miss O'Connor. The world is here to be discovered, surely. I have been asked by a friend in Parliament to write articles for *The Times* on the new colony. You must watch for them, madam, and learn about the Maoris, and the white settlers. Now I must be off." He bowed to Cousin Mabel, "A pleasure meeting you, madam." And then a brief nod to Cousin Giles. "And you, sir. Don't forget to look for my articles."

It was a very formal tea party, with Lady Devenish presiding over the silver teapot, the hot water urn, the silver bowl of sugar lumps and the silver milk jug, the delicate fluted cups and saucers, the plate of thinly cut bread and butter, the muffins in their silver warming dish, the rich brown fruitcake.

Would she ever be able to give a tea party like this in her

colonial home? No doubt exactly that thought was going through her mind for her head was bent in a subdued fashion, her expression sad. Very different from her daughter's. That young lady, Miss Celina Devenish, was a fascinating enigma. Dressed in a childish fashion in a sprigged muslin with a sash round her infinitely slim waist, she looked no more than twelve years old. She had come into the room meekly, her eyes downcast, the dark lashes lying on her pale cheeks. She had seemed almost as gentle and colourless as her mother, sketching a curtsy to Kate, and then sitting down in a huddled fashion, as if she were modestly trying to conceal her budding breasts.

The first thing I will have to do, thought Kate, is correct that young lady's posture. The second will be to instruct her in polite conversation, since she had not yet deigned to speak a word. Her looks didn't seem to be anything to be vain about, and she did curl up as if she would like to be invisible. But her hair was striking, an extremely pale blonde, almost silver, and luxuriant. That would make men look at her, even if her face promised little.

But Kate discovered that she was already underestimating the young lady. For Sir John Devenish, apologising for his lateness, had just come into the room, and his daughter's head had shot up, her dark eyes now opened wide, transforming her insignificant face, making it brilliant with feeling. One didn't know what the feeling was, joy or love or—could it be, startlingly, a flashing message of hate? Sir John, taking her hand as if she were indeed the child she had looked a moment ago, sat beside her and continued to hold her hand tenderly.

"So now you are all acquainted," he said genially. "What do you think of my little witch, Miss O'Connor?"

"Don't call her that," Lady Devenish protested. "She is no more a witch than I am. Are you, Celina? I hope you won't spoil her with absurd compliments, Miss O'Connor. You will find her a perfectly ordinary young woman with little learning, in spite of all her expensive schooling."

Celina seemed only half to listen, her huge eyes fixed on one, then the other parent. Finally they were turned to Kate, and she spoke in a high, insipid voice.

"I find study so tedious. I think my new governess ought to know that I am much too old for books."

Sir John smiled, as if she had made some profound statement. Nevertheless he spoke firmly. "Your education has a great many gaps, and these I expect to be filled on the long voyage. You will be glad of an occupation."

"Education, for a cannibal country!" Celina said scornfully. Then her face changed, and turning abruptly to her father she cried, "Papa, why must we do this crazy thing? I never really believed you would. Why must we? Mama cries all the time, and so do I. What am I to do there, in the dust and wind? Where am I to wear my best gowns? Who am I to talk to? Papa, you are so cruel to us, wanting to turn us into savages."

"Cruel to be kind." Kate wasn't sure whether she had heard Sir John's words correctly. For a second his eyes had gone dark, as if with thoughts he preferred to keep private.

Then Lady Devenish spoke with some weariness.

"Celina, it's too late to talk in this way. Your father has decided, and we women must obey." She gave a brave smile. "And indeed enjoy our new life as much as possible. Isn't that so, my dear?" She directed the smile at her husband. "You did promise that it would be enjoyable, didn't you, John?"

Sir John's face was lively and cheerful again.

"Infinitely so. There will certainly be balls to which this minx can wear her finery. Not perhaps equal to our own balls at home, but the greatest fun. And there'll be no doubt Celina will be the best-dressed young lady present. I'm sure you'll enjoy that, my dear."

Celina, however, had lost what had been only a temporary animation, and was huddled in her chair again, limp and silent. This was obviously an argument they had had many times, and always the two women must have been defeated. Yet Sir John seemed to be very concerned for them. So what kind of a man was he, to go so determinedly against their wishes?

"I hope we are not frightening you with our domestic frankness, Miss O'Connor." He gave Kate that sudden persuasive smile that already she was finding hard to resist. "You are not going to beg to stay at home, too?"

"No, sir. I have already promised. I keep my promises."

He nodded approvingly. Lady Devenish was busy with the tea cups. She was murmuring to herself absently, "We must take this silver tea service with us. And the china, of course." Celina had stirred and was watching her father. For one moment her large dark eyes were lambent with some unreadable thoughts. Then, as if the effort of emotion was too much, they dulled and went blank.

A curious, unknowable young woman, Kate thought, with a touch of uneasiness. She made herself dismiss her anxiety. If ever she were to know Celina Devenish she would do so on the three months' voyage. Neither one would be able to escape the other. And, since she was to be in charge, she knew who must win the arguments.

Cousin Mabel helped Kate pack her trunks. Neither of them knew all the necessary articles of clothing to take. There must be at least three morning dresses and three afternoon dresses, and one dinner gown, Cousin Mabel opined.

"And a ball gown," Kate said.

"But aren't you a servant?"

"To live as family. That's what they promised me."

"Is Sir John the kind of man to keep promises? He looked very arrogant, very self-interested, to me."

"He's a gentleman, Cousin Mabel."

"And the daughter? You've told me so little about her."

"It's because I don't understand her yet. I hardly know how to describe her. She has a strange sort of beauty that seems flawed."

"How flawed?"

"I can't explain. It's in her expression, I think. She has a small pale face, with eyes far too big for it. Dark eyes that burn when she's aroused or upset."

"Has she a short temper?"

"I don't know. She spoke so little. I think she may have melancholy spells."

"You mean sulky ones, more like. Her father has obviously ruined her by spoiling. You'll have your hands full, Kate."

"I know that."

"You'd better keep your Irish temper in check."

"I can do that, too."

"But don't let them crush the spirit out of you. Not that I think anyone could do that. Oh, dear me, Kate, I shall miss you. I'm much older than you, but we have always seemed like sisters."

"Write to me often, Cousin Mabel. And tell me about everything. Not only fashions and the weather, but what is happening in Parliament, what the Foreign Secretary says about this new colony."

Cousin Mabel gave a h-r-r-umph. "So far he only says that emigrants needn't be afraid of being eaten by the natives. All very fine for him, living in luxury and safety here."

Kate laughed and said, "He's perfectly right. The Maori wars are over. Tell me other things in your letters, Cousin Mabel. The court gossip, who the princesses are to marry, if the Queen is still in mourning. We shall be so far away from the world. And of course I want all the news of Aunt Dolly and Aunt Esmeralda as I'm afraid they won't be reliable correspondents. But just now let's get on with our packing. What do I need? Boots and riding clothes, at least six bonnets—they say bonnets are inclined to be lost overboard when the wind blows too strongly. And I'll need a warm cape, and a woollen shawl as well as a silk one. And plenty of petticoats and under linen. And handkerchiefs and stockings, and a workbox with needles and pins and buttons and thread and scissors and crochet hooks. And some lengths of muslin and alpaca to make new gowns. And of course books. Books, books, books."

"Your head seems to be capable of holding a deal more than your boxes can. How are we to pack so much in so short a time?"

"We'll manage. But it will require some shopping expeditions. I shall spend the last of Mama's legacy, and after that I will have my salary. Isn't it wonderful to be a working girl?"

Kate saw the moisture in Cousin Mabel's eyes and impulsively flung her arms round the small plump body of the cousin who all her life had been like an elder sister to her.

"Now don't cry. Tears are not allowed. This is the beginning

of my new life. Death is over for me. Mama, Papa, Dermot—"
For a moment her lips quivered. Then she went on vigorously,
"All that tragedy is in the past, and now I intend to be happy.
As well as to live for ever."

"Then you had better keep away from the Maori cannibals,"
Cousin Mabel said drily, and suddenly they were both laughing
wildly as if there were nothing but joy in the future.

Neither Cousin Mabel nor her rather dour but infinitely kind
husband, Giles, looked distressed in Kate's sight again.

It was Kate who shed tears in the night when nostalgia overcame her, and her past life became too vivid. She saw Aunt
Dolly pottering in the rose garden, smelt the syringa and the
stocks and sweet william and honeysuckle after a rainy afternoon, saw the ragged lawns, the cows in the distance, grazing
in the soft blue haze of an Irish evening, wandered in her mind
through the rooms of the old house, looking at the shabby wallpaper, the faded chintzes, the Irish Chippendale chairs and the
long mahogany dining table, the Waterford glass chandelier in
need of a good polishing, but beyond the reach of elderly Bridget
who had never been able to mount stepladders, the silver
epergne and the silver candlesticks on the sideboard, the ancient
grand piano draped with an Indian silk shawl, the badly executed
portraits of Grandmother and Grandfather O'Connor, ruddy Irish
faces with severe blue eyes and unsmiling mouths. Her own
bedroom with worn carpet, faded patchwork quilt, dressing table
holding her modest toilet equipment, a silver-backed brush and
mirror, a cut-glass scent bottle. Ah, the scent of clover blossom
through the open window on a warm night—the bathroom with
a bath big enough to accommodate the portly figure of King George
the Fourth of England, or any large Irish person. The whinny
of old Betty from the stables, lonely because she was the one
surviving horse on the estate. The cry of a pair of mating barn
owls, perhaps furtive footsteps and low voices in the garden.
Fenians? There was a portrait of Uncle Rory consigned to the
attic because there had been the terrible shame of his being a
Fenian. Later, in the dawn, there would be the clanking as
Danny left the pail of milk on the back doorstep, the spreading

sunlight, the birds singing as merrily and hopefully as if there had never been a tragedy in a country constantly marked by grief.

Oh, it was all unbearably lovely and heartbreaking, and Kate, crying softly into her pillow, wondered how many months or years it would take for memories to grow less painful. She wanted to remember Mallow Lodge as a green and peaceful dream, a soft background to the possible harshness and loneliness ahead. Something to escape into if there were too much adversity.

But the remembered vision must shut out the stark picture of Papa carried home on a five-barred gate, by Paddy and Danny who both sobbed audibly. And who were followed, with dreadful poignancy, by the unharmed horse who had thrown him. And a year later of standing beside Mama's grave and smelling the bitter ivy and the damp mould. And still another year later of Dermot lying face downwards at the roadside, his blond curly hair streaked with blood, blood on his face...

These memories, as she had firmly told Cousin Mabel, were to be wiped out of her mind. She would cling only to the gentle loving ones, and take them with her to the new country. She was full of enthusiasm and excitement and hope. No one should see her weeping.

4

I t was the 5th of February 1862. A grey day, grey sea, grey sky, and wind coming surely from the northern arctic.

The cold added to the misery of the little crowd, already affected by the pain of farewells, standing on the dock. The ladies' hands were tucked in muffs, or inside woollen shawls, the gentlemen had ruddy wind-bitten cheeks and eyes red-rimmed with cold. Or they could blame the cold if anyone accused them of unmanly tears. The women could weep if they wished. And they did wish, for frequently handkerchiefs came up to mop tears.

There was a half-hearted cheer when the Bishop of Southwark, his vestments blowing about him, climbed the gangway. He had come to bless another band of pilgrims about to embark on their long journey to the other side of the world, carrying with them the shield of the Christian religion, and all the stalwart honest and hard-working characteristics of the British people. There were no disgraceful elements among this shipload of emigrants, no sour and hardened criminals being tipped on to the human refuse heaps at Botany Bay and Van Dieman's Land, only decent, open-faced, enterprising travellers deserving God's blessing.

Perhaps it was due to the cold, or the competition of the wind in the rigging and the shrill crying of sea-birds, but the bishop made his sermon brief. He ended with the words, "I salute you brave pioneers setting out to tame the savage and ignorant native and to serve your Heavenly Father in the uttermost reaches of the earth. I pray to God to accompany you, to preserve you from the dangers of the deep, and to keep you safe. The grace of the Lord Jesus Christ and the love of God and the communion of the Holy Ghost be with you all. Amen."

The brave words of the hymn lifted and floated away on the wind. *All people that on earth do dwell, Sing to the Lord with cheerful voice...*

Emily Lodden suddenly burst into sobs, and was dreadfully ashamed. She tucked her chin into the collar of her coat and tried not to let her tears stain the precious blue velvet. She was frozen cold, and Mam was holding Willie's and Jonnie's hands, so she had to be grown up. But it was all so terribly sad, the white faces of the people on shore gazing up, the white sea-birds sobbing, the ship giving strange, long drawn-out creaks as the deck rose and fell ever so slightly beneath their feet, and the gap of water between ship and shore threatened every minute to become too wide.

Funny if the bishop had to jump ashore...

Emily gave a sob that turned into a giggle, and a hand as cold as her own seized hers and held it tight. She looked up and saw the beautiful blue eyes of the lady looking down at her.

"I'm Kate O'Connor, and I'm scared, too. Who are you?"

"Emily Lodden, ma'am."

"And that's your mother, and your brothers?"

"Yes, ma'am. Jonnie and Willie. Willie's only five."

"I can see. Well, then I think we all ought to get to know each other because I think you're travelling with the Devenishes."

"Oh, yes, ma'am." Emily was feeling warmer and much more cheerful. If this lady was with them they would be safe, she was sure.

"Mam and Pa is their servants, ma'am."

"I know. You must call me Kate."

"You're to look after the mistress?"

"Yes. And Miss Celina. We haven't begun to unpack yet. Why don't you introduce me to your mother?"

Emily responded shyly, tugging at her mother's arm.

"Mam, this lady wants to meet you."

"I'm Miss Celina's companion," Kate said. "I'm sure we'll all get on well together."

Mary Lodden's wan face became distinctly more cheerful.

"I'm sure we will. I'm pleased to meet you, miss. My husband's down in the hold seeing to the animals. They have to be kept fit, so the cows will give milk, and the hens lay. We'll be needing fresh food."

"Cows and chickens," cried Kate. "How splendid."

"Oh, yes. And some pigs which might have to be slaughtered on the voyage, and Squire's favourite mare. Though horses get seasick, Jonas says. Squire has been studying books on emigration. He's got flower seeds, too, for the mistress's garden, so she won't miss the manor too much. And of course all manner of furniture, even the grand piano. Jonas says you wouldn't believe folks' possessions down in the hold. There's even a church bell. But how is the mistress, miss? And Miss Celina?"

"Both in low spirits, I'm afraid. But we'll manage between us, won't we?"

"I'm sure we will, miss."

"Call me Kate, won't you? I'm a servant, too."

"Why, if you wish." Mary looked gratified. "I'm Mary Lodden, and these three are Emily, Jonnie and Willie. We're in steerage, but I have permission to come up each day to tend to the mistress and Miss Celina. Do the laundry and see to the food if they don't want to eat in the saloon. And the captain says the children can come on deck for fresh air now and then. It'll be hot in steerage in the tropics. But it's quite well-arranged and clean down there. The children think the bunks are great fun. Jonnie and Willie share one and Emily has her own because she's a big girl. We're all in one corner together. If the sea's rough it'll be a bit uncomfortable for a while, but we'll get over it."

"They tell me the Bay of Biscay is the worst," Kate said. "When we've navigated that we'll all be happier."

Mary Lodden was looking at Kate curiously.

"Can I ask—why are you going on such a perilous voyage, miss?"

"Perilous? I hope it isn't. And why am I going? We'll have weeks to talk about our lives. But one of the reasons," Kate's eyes twinkled, "is to teach Miss Emily grammar and spelling and maybe a little French to impress the natives of New Zealand. How about that, Emily?"

Emily gave a pleased nod.

"I don't think that's what Squire and Lady Devenish expect, miss," said her mother. "You're here to take care of Miss Celina, not my girl."

"Will Miss Celina take all my time?"

The question was serious. Mary Lodden must know a great deal more about Celina than she did.

"Well—" Mary's expression was guarded. "Depends."

"Depends on what?"

"On what mood takes her. I shouldn't say more. But as for Emily—"·now she was on safer ground.

"Oh, I'm sure Sir John won't object. After all, he keeps talking about Mr. Wakefield's equal society, doesn't he?"

"It's one thing talking, and another doing," Mary said shrewdly. "Can you think of a man like Squire ever not giving orders? Or ever taking orders himself?"

"Yes, that would be surprising, I admit. But who knows? I fancy we're all going to change." She was distracted by movements about her. "Look, everyone's going on shore. And the tug seems to be ready. So we must be about to sail. I had better go and see how Miss Celina is. We're sharing a cabin. It's going to be rather cramped, but I'm sure we'll manage very well."

The cabin certainly was awfully small and claustrophobic with its one small window and its sloping walls. Kate had viewed it with dismay, especially after the furniture had been arranged, the writing desk and the dressing table, two chairs, a washstand and a chest of drawers. Not to mention Celina's extravagant array of boxes and bags. Most of the luggage had gone to be stored in the hold, but Celina had insisted on keeping an ample wardrobe in case of shipboard festivities. There was a fixed bed and a swinging cot, the latter no doubt being Kate's.

Sir John and Lady Devenish had brought their own double bed and had it riveted to the floor in their more spacious cabin. They also had a small table on which to take meals, two comfortable wing chairs, a horsehair couch, and a cheerfully bright Turkey rug for the floor. Their cabin was altogether more comfortable and even had two windows hung with dimity curtains. It was fairly certain that Celina would begin grumbling about the superiority of her parents' quarters, but since she would be spending a good deal of time with her mother the difference in the cabins hardly mattered.

The next three months were going to be awfully long, Kate thought, with a suddenly sinking heart. And where was she to hang her clothes and arrange her books and write her letters?

The deck would be the best place for the latter activity. She would find a sheltered corner and take her writing materials there. How often this would be possible she didn't know. But she would need some respite from the sulky young lady with whom she was to be closeted. Celina hadn't said a word to her, or indeed to anybody, since departing from Belgrave Square that morning. She had been white-faced and withdrawn, huddled into a corner of the carriage, and resisting all requests to sit up straight, to take an interest in her surroundings, to show at least a little enthusiasm for the great adventure ahead. Kate was beginning to fear that her charge was either mentally sick or just plain contrary. She did notice that when her father attempted to pat her hand reassuringly she snatched it away as if she couldn't bear his touch. And that strange expression of pain came and went in his eyes.

In the cabin, surrounded by baggage, Celina had given one look of horrified disbelief, then burst through the communicating door to her mother and demanded in high dudgeon, "Where am I to bathe? Where am I to dress? This is no better than a jail!"

"Mr. Wakefield spent several years in Newgate jail," Kate heard Sir John saying. "That is where he wrote his treatise on the ideal community. Think of that, Celina my dear, when you feel cramped and uncomfortable on this very fine ship."

"Why was the great Mr. Wakefield in jail?" Celina asked pointedly, showing that there was nothing wrong with her mental powers.

"Oh—some long ago trouble." Her father's voice was deliberately vague. "Some young man's recklessness. Perhaps he was lucky not to be hanged, as so many innocent people are in our very imperfect society."

"Papa, you're getting to be a bore, always preaching sermons," Celina said.

"Celina, that's impertinent," Lady Devenish murmured in her defeated voice.

"Perhaps she's right, my dear." Sir John's voice had an unfamiliar humility. "But we're none of us perfect. Now go back to Miss O'Connor, Celina, and endeavour to be polite to her."

"Papa, you treat me like a child! I hate Miss O'Connor! I hate you, too! I hate absolutely everybody! I'd like to be dead."

"Iris?" Sir John queried.

"Yes, I think a little of her medicine," Lady Devenish answered. "Just a teaspoonful. It will stop her worrying and getting homesick. You know, Celina darling, that the doctor gave us specific instructions for your care until we get to New Zealand. There, of course, we can throw all your medicines away because you will be strong and happy. Isn't that so, John?"

"Oh, undoubtedly."

It was while Lady Devenish was administering the medicine, obviously a palliative of some kind, that Sir John knocked, and came into Kate's cabin.

"What about a little blow on deck, Miss O'Connor? Just briefly before we get out to sea and less stable conditions. Put on a wrap. The wind will be fresh."

And there, in the blowing sea wind among the bustle of departure, where there was too much noise for anyone but Kate to hear his words, Sir John gave startling orders. Celina was never to be left alone unless her cabin door was locked, she was never to walk on deck alone. If Kate were not with her, then he or Mary Lodden would be.

"What I am saying, Miss O'Connor, is that she is never to be left to her own devices. You must keep her occupied as much as possible, and when she gets restless you or I must walk her up and down the deck until she is tired. She and her mother will probably take their meals in their cabins, but if she is to come to the saloon in the evening, where no doubt there will be a little entertainment, then you must be at her side all the time. All the time, I repeat."

"But why, sir?"

"Because she is young and impetuous, and inclined to behave recklessly. And because she is a beautiful creature."

Kate didn't dare to voice her suspicion. Was Sir John afraid of men making advances to his precious daughter? Perhaps rough seamen? Surely he was over-protective and over-possessive. They were not on a pirate ship, after all. And in Kate's opinion Celina wasn't at all beautiful. No doubt her silvery hair would have an attraction, but not that white sulky face.

"You will remember my instructions, Miss O'Connor?"

"Why—yes, sir."

"Good. I'm sure I can rely on you." He pressed her arm, suddenly. The intimacy of the gesture made a shaft of nervous excitement shoot through her body. Her colour rose and she moved a little away. Sir John was so persuasively charming, any woman would like to be near him. But not her. If she were to fall in love again she would make sure it was with someone who was free. She had enough common sense for that.

All the same that hard masculine touch had made her shiver. Am I getting to be an old spinster? she wondered.

"Sir John, may I ask a question?"

"Of course."

"What is the medicine you give your daughter?"

"Just a soothing draught. She is to have it when she is overwrought. As I explained to you, she has a nervous temperament and is inclined to hysterics. A spoonful makes her quiet and a little drowsy. But of course all these remedies have their dangers. Lady Devenish and I restrict the doses as much as possible. We will expect you to use your discretion. Have I made everything clear to you?"

"Did you have a reason for not telling me these things in London?" Kate asked bluntly.

He gave his deliberately attractive smile. "Of course. You might have got nervous, too, and decided not to come." His intense eyes regarded her. "And I very much wanted you." Then, giving her no time to reply, if indeed she had known what to say, he threw up his head and regarded the darkening horizon.

"Tomorrow we will be some miles out to sea. Isn't that an invigorating thought?"

"If the weather is kind."

"Ah. You're a prey to seasickness? Surely not."

"Never on the crossing from Ireland. But this is different. The Bay of Biscay."

"Yes. Immensely exciting, is it not?"

The weather was not kind. No doubt the strong winds, reaching gale force, were of no great discomfort to seasoned sailors, but to the inexperienced passengers they were devastating. There was no need to think of Celina's medicine for she would never have been able to hold it in her stomach. She was, in any case, far too ill to indulge in even the slightest tantrum. Kate, in between her own miserable bouts of sickness, spent her time between Celina and Lady Devenish who was equally prostrate. She was helped by Mary Lodden who, thankfully, was quite unaffected by the ship's tossing.

"Jonas is looking after the children," she said. "They're in a bit of misery, but they'll get over it quickly and he'll bring them up on deck. You ought to get out on deck yourself, Kate. The fresh air will do you good.

"What about Squire?"

"Oh, he's like you. The picture of health. Striding up and down. Talking to anyone who is able to converse." Dizziness swept over Kate again. The ship was bucking like a horse. It was difficult to stand upright. Celina moaned from her bunk. Mary hastened to her side, saying over her shoulder, "Now, off you go, Kate. Get some fresh air into your lungs."

The remedial effect of the fresh air was remarkable. Almost

immediately Kate's head cleared and she had a feeling of exhilaration. She walked carefully along the tilting deck, stopping now and then to hold the rail and look up at the splendid spread of sail cracking in the wind. The sea, a murky green tipped with feathery white waves, stretched into infinity. She seemed to be alone in this wild world. No, there were two seamen aloft attending to the sails. And in a corner out of the wind two passengers were sitting deep in conversation.

As Kate approached them she saw that one of them was Sir John Devenish. His companion was a younger man, in tweeds and a deerstalker cap who happened to turn and see Kate at the rail. He stared interestedly, and made a comment to Sir John who at once sprang up exclaiming, "Why, it's Miss O'Connor. Kate!"

He was calling her Kate! And she recalled that firm pressure of his hand on her arm.

"Come here and meet Captain Oxford. This young lady is my daughter's companion, captain. Miss Kate O'Connor, Captain Oxford, late of the Royal Hussars, recently stationed in Meerut. Isn't that so, captain?"

"That's so." The young man was looking at Kate with blue eyes narrowed against the wind. He was still brown from the Indian sun. He could not have been back in the fogs of England for long. He looked very fit, and his smile was pleasant.

"Farmer Oxford from now on," he was saying. "I've sold my commission. I intend starting a new life."

"Isn't that what we're all doing?" Sir John said. "Kate, how are the ladies?"

"Mary's with them, sir. I came out for a little while to recover from my own slight indisposition. But I'm better now." She turned her face into the wind, letting the fresh air fill her lungs. "Isn't it absolutely wonderful out here?"

"You're obviously a good sailor, Miss O'Connor," Captain Oxford said.

"And you, too."

"Oh, I've had a great deal of experiences. Voyages to the Baltic, to India, the China seas."

"And now you mean to stay in one place?"

"If I like the look of New Zealand and can acquire some land."

"Oh, you'll do that all right," Sir John said confidently. "You're just the kind of settler Mr. Wakefield has in mind. You know his thesis, don't you? I can quote it for you. 'Supposing there should be going to the Canterbury colonies a large number of families of the gentry class, all being truly respectable or worthy of respect, to found an important family in one part of the British Empire, to be leading colonists in the projected settlement at Canterbury.'"

Captain Oxford had a quizzical look.

"And are we all so respectable?"

"Oh, emphatically," said Sir John. "I am told that on this ship there is a parson, a surgeon, a schoolmaster, a bank manager and some missionaries. As well as a complement of craftsmen, dairymen, shepherds, and so on."

Captain Oxford was regarding Sir John with some amusement.

"I've talked to one passenger on his way back to New Zealand after buying some pedigree stock. He's met your Mr. Wakefield and he says the gentleman has a large stock of brass and impudence. He thinks he's another Napoleon Buonaparte, putting his brothers into high positions, without, I am told, much success. One brother is reputed to be a rum drinker and a womaniser. Native women at that."

Sir John looked put out.

"Every man has flaws, of course. Even a man of vision."

"And his utopia will have flaws, too, I have no doubt," Captain Oxford said cheerfully. "But here we are, all prepared to try it out. I am told I can buy wasteland at thirty shillings an acre."

"Wasteland?" Kate queried. It sounded desolate.

"Unoccupied lands, belonging to the natives, of course. But they have been persuaded to sell nine-tenths to the white men. The *pakeha,* as they call them."

"For what price?"

"You may well ask. For gee gaws, sealing wax and beads and pocket knives and blankets and cooking pots. Unfortunately, for muskets, too, and gunpowder, and tomahawks. And rum. Those things make a deadly combination. I must say one wonders at the white man and his folly."

"The natives let the land go to waste," Sir John said sharply. "They leave it untouched, covered with tussocks and snow grass and manuka."

"They're not farmers, Sir John," Captain Oxford said. "But one day they're going to find they've lost an area where they fished in the lakes, or found their cherished greenstone deposits. Or even just wanted to take their war canoes down a river to fight a hostile tribe. Then we will find what the combination of muskets and rum does. I've seen it all with the tribes in India, Sir John."

"The Maori wars are over. I have been assured of it."

"One hopes so. But one has to reflect that Mr. Wakefield's utopia is only to come into existence for the white man."

Sir John's voice had become distant.

"You are an admirer of the native, Captain Oxford?"

"I admire fair play. I also admire life. I don't like killing, although I've been trained to do it." He gave a philosophical shrug. "I'm simply looking for a change of direction, just as I imagine you are. We all have our reasons. Although I doubt if they'll all come up to Mr. Wakefield's high standards."

"What do you mean by that?" Sir John's voice was now distinctly chilly. He had taken a dislike to Captain Oxford for having the temerity to criticise his cherished dreams. This was a pity, for Kate liked the captain's honest directness.

"Just a generalisation. I'm referring to the disease from which we all suffer. The imperfection of human nature."

"Well, we can do something about that," Sir John said briskly. "Discipline. Plenty of hard work. Freedom. Now, Miss O'Connor, isn't it time you went and saw to my wife and daughter. Frail creatures, Captain Oxford."

"Yes, I'll go back to the cabin," Kate said obediently. She had enjoyed listening to the conversation. It was entirely different from what one might hear in a London drawing room, much less an Irish one. Although there were vague connotations of the plight of the Irish peasant under the same imperial British.

"My, that blow on deck did you good," Mary Lodden commented, looking at Kate's pink cheeks. "You look ever so lively now." She lowered her voice. "A pity we can't persuade our patients to do the same. But I'm feared they're going to keep to their beds for some time. The mistress did manage to sup a little gruel, but Miss Celina won't look at a thing."

5

The middle-aged lady, Miss Tabitha Pugh, who had not been stricken by seasickness and seemed impervious to all weathers, spent every morning sitting in her canvas chair placed in the most sheltered and strategic part of the deck. She wore a knitted woollen cap that came down over her ears, a voluminous Scottish tweed cape, and stout buttoned boots. She always had with her a wicker basket holding all the items she required for a morning spent on deck in the brisk sea wind, a warm scarf, spectacles, books, knitting wool and needles, and a diary. When she wasn't knitting she was making entries in her diary, which would be read avidly by her sister May in the vicarage, and in time to come, she hoped, by nieces and great-nieces interested in the life of a pioneer lady.

Miss Pugh did not consciously look as far ahead as the existence of great-nieces. She was anxious only to keep May fully informed of the pleasures and discomforts of this novel way of life. She was also a very observant lady with a shrewd and kindly interest in her fellow travellers. She had taught twenty pupils

DOROTHY EDEN

in the vicarage school and would still be teaching there had it
not been for the tragic deaths by drowning of her brother and
his wife while crossing a flooded river in far away New Zealand,
and the consequent orphaning of their only child, a boy aged
fifteen years. Rather than have him abandon his parents' dream
of a promising future on the fertile plains of Canterbury, she
had volunteered to go out and take charge of his affairs until he
was grown.

It was what her brother Matthew would have wished. So,
after a sensible but painful farewell to May and their elderly
father, the vicar of All Souls, Axminster, she had gathered together her boxes, climbed on the stage coach, and left her familiar and much loved home and village for several years, if not
for ever.

It did no good to grieve. Miss Pugh's motto was to make the
best of any situation in which it might please the Lord to place
her. So now, escaping from her tiny cubby hole of a cabin, she
spent most of her day on deck observing her fellow passengers.
Now that they were reaching milder climes people she had not
seen before were appearing on deck. It would shortly be like
Blackpool in the summer, she observed in her diary.

Dear May,

How interested you would be in our "aristocratic" family.
They stand out prominently among a rather battered-look-
ing collection of lawyers and clerks and shopkeepers and
their wan-faced wives, the latter recovering from severe
cases of seasickness and homesickness. Lady Devenish, it
is true, is a retiring kind of gentlewoman in spite of her
expensive clothes. She seems a timid creature, and it must
have cost her a great deal of courage to make this journey.
Her husband, Sir John, however, is a fine-looking person,
tall and commanding, with a noble brow and an easy manner. He smiles and nods in a friendly fashion to all and
sundry, almost as if he is making too much of being popular
and well-liked. I have caught an uneasy look in his eyes as
if something troubles him. He converses a great deal with
the ship's captain, Captain Brighthouse, as if he is interested
in learning how to sail a ship over thirteen thousand miles
of ocean, although it would be more practical if he talked

to the sheep-farmers on board, since that is what he avows he is to be himself.

I am giving an unfair amount of space to the Devenish family, but they do interest me greatly. I sense a mystery about them. They have left behind a manor house in the Cotswolds and also a London house, and I cannot feel that this can be solely for love of adventure. The daughter is an enigma. She did not appear for two weeks after sailing, and then only on the arm of her father, or of her companion, an attractive young woman in her early twenties who is partly Irish with an open face and very fine dark blue eyes. I am afraid she (the companion) will be snapped up quickly by some marriageable young man, which will not please her employers since they have brought her on this long journey for their own purposes.

However, she looks an honest young woman and perhaps has promised to remain unmarried for a certain time. One thing that is certain is that the Devenish daughter needs her. She looks delicate, and has a strangely wild look as if queer thoughts occupy her head. She has been one of the greatest sufferers from seasickness, and has not yet regained her strength. Her cheeks are white, and she has a mass of pale hair that is inclined to come loose and fly about her head like a flock of feathers. She seldom raises her eyes. I have caught only two or three glimpses of them and they are dark, with a strange trapped look.

You might think from this description that she is nondescript, being so thin and pale, but I have a feeling that in the right clothes and the right setting—and the right mood, of course—Miss Celina Devenish would be well worth looking at.

What disturbs me is why she is never allowed to be alone, and why she never smiles. Is she melancholy? Queer in the head? She is guarded too closely for anyone to guess. But we all look at her on the brief occasions when she appears. She and her mother and the companion, Miss O'Connor, take all their meals in their cabins, while Sir John enjoys the saloon and the boisterous talk there.

I am not finished with this family yet, for they have servants in steerage, a good solid fellow, Jonas Lodden, who tends the animals they are transporting to New Zealand, his wife, Mary, who is a decent neat-looking person, and their three children. I intend to teach them, along with other children, before the voyage is over. The eldest, Emily, looks shy, intelligent and biddable, the two younger boys, Jonnie, named for his father, I presume, and Willie, who is only five and has a slightly crooked foot, also look bright and alert. Are these the new generation of New Zealanders? One would like to think so.

Steerage is tolerable at present, in spite of the seasickness during the gale, but it is overcrowded as I gather these places always are. There are 106 souls on board this ship, not counting the crew. I hesitate to think what steerage will be like when we run into hot weather and are perhaps becalmed in equatorial waters. Then it will be fetid and airless, and there are sure to be outbreaks of disease, measles or mumps or worse. And the food, which is still fresh and plentiful, will get worse. This, I am told, is unavoidable on such a long sea journey. The cows will give milk so long as they can be fed. A few eggs are laid by Sir John Devenish's poultry. Some sheep and pigs have been brought for the purpose of slaughtering for fresh meat. We will have to take on water at the Azores, and other suitable ports. But we seem to have a good experienced captain, thank God.

Now this epic must come to an end for today, dear sister. I think of you constantly, and would like nothing more, at this moment, than to be sitting down to tea in our comfortable parlour. Freshly made tea, out of a silver pot, and some of Bertha's new-made scones. Ah me!

I have just remembered your request to hear of flirtations and such on board. We have not yet reached the balmy tropical nights which are reputed to enhance these affairs, but I can report that a certain young army captain, recently stationed in India, has eyes for no one but Miss Kate O'Connor. He is a pleasant young fellow, cheerful and good-humoured and not without brains, and Miss Kate does not seem averse to his attentions. The young couple have little time together, however, as Sir John has an uncanny habit of stumbling on their tête-à-têtes. Sir John has said that he finds Captain Oxford too opinionated, and poor Kate feels guilty about her neglected duties. Not neglected often, I might say. One wonders how she tolerates the confinement of the cabins with that white mouse of a woman Lady Devenish in one, and sulky Miss Celina in the other. I personally would like to give them both a good shaking.

Again au revoir, dear sister

* * *

If Kate had been permitted to read Miss Pugh's diary, she would have agreed with most of that astute lady's observations. Celina was sulky and unco-operative and completely self-absorbed. And her mother, although mildly disapproving of her manners, did nothing to correct them.

Half the trouble was Sir John's strictures on his daughter's freedom. It was absurd that a grown girl should be so constantly chaperoned. Captain Oxford certainly thought so.

"Is her father intending her to be a settler's wife?" he marvelled. "If so, she will have to stir herself. Those women make bread in camp ovens and turn a sod cottage into a home, and have their babies without the help of a doctor. Can you imagine your delicate plant, Miss Celina, doing that?"

"Can you imagine me doing it?" Kate asked.

"Indeed, yes. I can see you overcoming anything. You and Celina are exactly like the two different types of memsahibs in an army garrison. One will wilt and faint and demand endless attention, and the other like you will face any kind of emergency with serenity."

"What kind of emergency?"

"Oh, fevers, childbirth, dishonest servants, isolation, homesickness, attacks by hostile natives."

Kate had flushed with pleasure. That was the sort of honest compliment she appreciated. Though she would like to be told, as well, that she was vastly attractive.

It almost seemed, from Captain Oxford's intent gaze, that he was about to make such a statement. Some instinct made her abruptly change the conversation.

"You haven't really seen Celina, captain. She has been so downcast and low-spirited. But when she is animated—"

"She is different? I can hardly believe it. She looks exactly like a drooping Welsh leek to me."

Kate couldn't help giggling, which gave Captain Oxford the courage to ask, "Why have you never married, Miss Kate?"

Her amusement vanished.

"Am I so far advanced in spinsterhood?"

"Spinsterhood! You! Never!"

"Then what about yourself?"

"Easily answered. The army doesn't encourage early marriages. Besides, I would have had to make do with one of the memsahibs I told you about, and I decided they were not for me."

Kate hesitated a moment, then said abruptly, "My fiancé was killed."

"Ah! I'm sorry. Ireland, of course."

"Yes, Ireland. It was two years ago. I've long stopped crying. And now"—she had to escape his too interested gaze—"I must leave you. The ladies will be waiting for their tea."

"I am beginning to heartily dislike your ladies."

"That's a pity."

"Why is it a pity?"

"I fancy you'll have to put up with their proximity for some time to come. That is if we are to remain friends."

"I see your point." Captain Oxford called after her, "But at least call me Henry."

"Of course. Of course, Henry. I'll be delighted to."

The small cabin she shared with Celina had truly become a prison, and not only for Celina who spent most of the day on her bed, fretful, bored and spiritless. Kate found the four walls, and her constant companion, terribly oppressive. But eventually the time would pass, she told herself. And at least so far there had been none of the disasters at which Sir John had hinted.

Quiet, capable Mary Lodden was of great assistance, and when they were all in the larger cabin with Lady Devenish it could be quite pleasant. Kate read aloud, insisting on the ladies doing their needlework as they listened, while Mary boiled water over the spirit lamp and made tea, and talked of that strange but kind lady, Miss Pugh, who had started morning lessons with a handful of the children who were eager to learn.

"It keeps them out of mischief," Mary said. "Emily's a bright child. Jonnie would rather be with his father tending the animals."

"And Willie?" Kate asked.

"Willie's a dreamer. He looks up at the sky for hours, and when you ask him what he's thinking he says he's riding on the clouds." Mary frowned slightly. "He's a bit peaked lately. Off his food. Not that that's surprising considering how uninteresting the food is. There's been a bit of sickness among the little ones. Oh, nothing serious, ma'am," she added, seeing Lady Devenish's alarm. "It's getting hot below. There isn't much air. I think of the wind blowing over the home hills."

Celina suddenly clenched her small white hands.

"Don't, Mary. I can't stand it. I shall die!"

"We were beginning chapter six," Kate said calmly. "Shall I continue?" As far as she was aware, Celina had needed no more than a daily teaspoon of her medicine. This had kept her calm, and perpetually a little drowsy. That sudden flash like lightning in her eyes just now had been surprising. Was it a warning of incipient storms?

Afterwards Kate knew that she should have interpreted it as a warning, and increased Celina's medicine. Or at least mentioned it to her father.

She did neither of those things. That night, long after all the passengers, even the most bibulous, were in bed, Kate was awakened by a breeze on her face. The cabin door was swinging open. It took only an appalled moment to discover that Celina's bed was empty.

She slid out of her swinging cot, snatched her dressing gown, thrust her feet into slippers, and was out on the deck.

A half moon made a shimmering path across the sea. The night breeze was deliciously fresh with a hint of tropical mildness. The sails billowed gently and the ship slid sweetly through the hissing water. The empty deck could be a rendezvous for lovers, but there was no sign of anybody. Kate walked swiftly over the scrubbed boards, calling softly, "Celina! Are you out here, Celina?"

Had that strange wilful girl come out here to escape her jailers? For that must be how she regarded Kate and her father.

She called again, "Celina!"

And then she heard the high-pitched feminine giggle, followed by a common, lecherous voice saying, "And where have you been hiding all this time, my little dear? Eh, but we've got to catch up on things, ain't we?"

"What's your name, sailor?"

That was Celina's voice, suddenly almost as common as her companion's.

"Names don't matter, do they, dearie? Just—Who in hell is that?"

Kate had ripped back the canvas overhanging the ship's long-boat, and exposed the two of them. She could hardly believe her eyes, Celina in her nightclothes displaying a slim white leg and allowing this nameless sailor, a brawny fellow with a glint of gold in his ears, to fondle it.

"Celina!" Kate exclaimed in horror. "What *are* you doing? Come out of there at once!"

Afterwards Kate was to wonder if Celina would have obeyed her if the man she was so shamefully embracing had not wriggled out of the shelter and taken to his heels.

Her eyes, huge and dark, glared at Kate.

"You spy!" she hissed. "You horrid spoil-sport. Why can't I have some fun? I'm dying of boredom. I'll jump overboard!"

"Don't be a silly child!"

"I'm not a child, Kate."

And that indeed, Kate realised with foreboding, was all too true. Those luminous eyes looking at her were far from childish. Nor was that flat statement made by a child. It had an adult weariness that was disturbing.

Kate was nonplussed and deeply upset. Had she stumbled on the truth about Celina, and the reason for her parents' exaggerated watchfulness?

She didn't know, but she had to get the wretched girl back to their cabin before anyone else discovered her.

"Come on! At once, miss!"

"Will you tell Papa, Kate?"

Kate regarded the strange, luminous, threatening gaze and felt deepening apprehension.

"If I promise not to do so this time will you come at once?"

Celina stirred in a leisurely fashion.

"Not telling Papa will save an awful lot of trouble. Anyway, I didn't care very much for that sailor. He smelled terribly."

Kate took the frail white arm and pulled it hard, dragging the girl out.

"I'll tell you something, Miss Celina. If you ever attempt to play a trick like this again I will see that your Papa and everyone on the ship knows. I don't imagine you will enjoy being the subject of a scandal. It would completely ruin your chance in New Zealand society."

"New Zealand society!" said Celina contemptuously.

"Oh, yes. In Canterbury. The elite society. And you the daughter of a baronet could be the centre of it. There won't be many titled people there. And after all, what did you bring that elegant wardrobe for? You meant to make an impression. What sort of an impression would a young woman who was known to flirt with common sailors make? Tell me!"

"Kate, you're hurting my arm."

"I mean to. You haven't been fair to me, either. Now come on, back to bed. And the door of our cabin will be locked in future. I will keep the key."

Celina came slowly, sobbing. Her moods were so mercurial. Her wild rebellion seemed already to have died. Kate prayed that it had. She infinitely preferred the sulky, silent girl to this disturbing creature roused by strong and shameful desires.

Shameful? Hadn't Kate felt those desires herself when with Dermot? When she was young and reckless and full of hope.

But Dermot had been a loved and loving friend. She was to have married him. Celina, who was so fastidious regarding her own person, had allowed a strange and lustful sailor to touch her. How disturbing. No wonder Sir John kept her under such strict surveillance. He must hope she would marry, respectably, as soon as possible, her reputation untarnished. Something of this nature must have happened before. She wondered if Mary Lodden knew anything. She would ask her, tactfully.

But this delicate conversation had to be postponed, for the next day Mary Lodden came up to the cabin to ask to be excused her day's duties. Willie, her youngest, was sick. She wanted to be with him, if the mistress permitted.

"Of course, Mary," Lady Devenish said sympathetically. "I hope the boy hasn't anything serious."

"Oh, no, ma'am. It's just the fever the children have been getting."

"If it's infectious, Mary"—now Lady Devenish was alarmed—"you'd better not come up here again until the boy's well. My husband would be upset if Celina were to catch anything. Or me, either, I expect." Her voice was less sure. She had little confidence where her husband's affections were concerned. "You go down, Mary. Kate will look after us."

The fever infecting the children, however, was more serious than Mary had suspected. That day it came as a deep shock to the ship's passengers to hear that a child had died. A little girl, Annie Dobson, six years old. The illness spreading among the children already weakened by a bad diet and too little fresh air proved to be measles. A deadly disease under these conditions.

The body of the little girl was sewn into a canvas bag and slid overboard, scarcely making a splash in the shining blue sea. The ship's captain read some verses from the scriptures, in a somewhat perfunctory manner, Kate thought, and soon the small group of mourners dispersed. It was all over so quickly.

Miss Tabitha Pugh was there. She took Emily Lodden's hand and held it comfortingly. Emily was hypnotised by the way the sea had rippled over the offering it had received.

"Will the Lord ever find Annie down there?" she asked.

"Of course He will. She's bigger than a sparrow, and He always knows when a sparrow falls."

Emily was only partly reassured.

"Willie's sick. Mam wouldn't leave him to come to the funeral." She looked at Miss Pugh with fearful eyes. "Will he die, Miss Pugh?"

"Not if we can help it," Miss Pugh said emphatically. Her lively eyes were sharp with determination. Perhaps anger, too. Children should never be allowed to travel in such unhygienic conditions. "Now I'm going down to help your Mam. You stay here in the fresh air. Breathe it deep into you. It's the best medicine."

"When's Mary coming again?" Lady Devenish asked fretfully. "It's very tiresome. I seem to have no clean nightgowns."

"I'll launder them for you," Kate said. "We can manage very well. Poor Mary is so worried about Willie. He's a frail child."

"I hope you're not going down to steerage, Kate," Lady Devenish said suspiciously. "You know that my husband would be very angry if infection were carried."

And what was so valuable about these two pampered women's lives? Kate wondered angrily. Sometimes she thought she couldn't bear them for another minute, Lady Devenish fussing about freshly laundered linen, Celina trying on dresses and bonnets, then pettishly throwing them down and declaring it was all a waste of time, Papa would never allow her to make anybody's acquaintance. She was a prisoner.

"Only because of your wild ways," Kate said unsympathetically. She had never allowed Celina to forget her behaviour the other night, and found that, fortuitously, the threat to tell her father was a method of subduing her more difficult moods.

But it was all unnerving, and the sooner they reached their destination the better.

The sooner the better for the Lodden family, too. Now not only Willie, but both Emily and Jonnie were sickening with the same disease. Miss Pugh brought this information. More than ever, Mary Lodden was unable to leave the side of her sick children.

The weather was growing hotter and more oppressive. Jonas Lodden, bringing up a little fresh milk for the ladies, said that soon there would be no more. His cows were going dry. They got no exercise or good green grass. They were skin and bone, he said sadly. "I doubt I'll get them to land alive, Miss Kate."

"Oh, how sad, Jonas."

Jonas, the previously healthy, sun-browned countryman, looked gaunt and hollow-cheeked, as if he too were partially starving. Although he was not, of course. It was only that the food for steerage passengers was so unpalatable.

Then he said what Kate dreaded to hear.

"I'm afeared Willie isn't going to get well, Miss Kate. Mary holds him in her arms all day. He's like a sick sparrow, poor lad."

"What about Emily and Jonnie?"

"I think they'll come through. They're stronger. Willie always was a weak little fellow. I shouldn't have brought him, Miss Kate. None of us should have come on this journey."

"You weren't to know, Jonas." Although he must have known about the perils of ship journeys to the Antipodes. "We must just pray."

Jonas, a canny countryman, who lived by the weather and the stars, knew his premonitions were correct. For that night, in the darkest hour, the heat like a damp suffocating blanket, Willie died.

He was rapidly sewn into the narrow canvas bag, his cherished wooden doll tucked beside him.

Emily, just recovered herself from the nasty spotty illness, cried bitterly. "Is his doll to go into the water, too? The paint will wash off its face. Willie won't care for that. He loves that doll, he do, even though he's a boy. How will Jesus know he's a boy if he has a doll?" she sobbed, distraught.

"Jesus will know," Miss Pugh said comforting. "And the doll's company for such a little lad, travelling alone."

It was Miss Pugh who had to comfort Emily and Jonnie, for now Mary, her bleak eyes staring into dark distances, was sick. Measles were dangerous enough for children, but for adults, under these conditions, they could be deadly.

The ship's doctor had too much fondness for rum, and few medicines. It was almost certain that Mary was going to die. When she was conscious she asked repeatedly for Willie. "Where is he? He can't be lost. He's my youngest," she explained earnestly to faces she no longer recognised. Then she became conscious less and less, and early on a Sunday morning, when the *Albatross* was becalmed in silken blue tropical waters, she closed her eyes and didn't open them again.

Emily wondered if Willie would be waiting for Mam at the bottom of the ocean. It surely wasn't a bit like heaven. She stood at the ship's rail staring for long hours at the dazzling sea. No one could persuade her to come out of the hot sunshine into the shade until Sir John Devenish, tall and commanding and immaculately dressed, stood over her and ordered her to do as she was told. She stared up at him, dazed, wanting to obey because one always obeyed Squire, but not being able to move.

Then a strange thing happened. Kate saw it, as she came towards the two. Sir John gave an infinitely warm and tender smile, and held out his arms. In a moment Emily was in them, her skinny arms were tightly round his neck, her face pressed into his chest, her hair, which no one had brushed, blowing across his eyes. He held her like that for what seemed a long time. Then, with great care, he moved across to his familiar chair on the deck, and sat down, still holding the silent child.

When he looked up at Kate she saw not only the tenderness but that old look of desolation in his eyes.

"It was my fault, Kate. I shouldn't have persuaded them to come. That good woman gone and her husband walking about like a shadow." He thought a moment, then he said with determination, "I will be responsible for this child and her brother. It's the very least I can do. I'll talk to their father about them." He attempted to smooth Emily's tangled hair and she quivered sharply. "She's a pretty thing, isn't she? She'll grow up to be like her mother. Will you help me, Kate?"

Kate agreed wholeheartedly, not even beginning to think of the extra commitment she was taking on. What about Captain Oxford? He was becoming more ardent in his attentions, and she was not averse to them. But just now all she could see was Emily's thin distraught figure, and Sir John looking at her with that surprising, almost womanly tenderness.

"It's a terrible thing, Kate, having power over other people," he was saying. "One should always use it responsibly. Do I? I always imagined I did." He mused a moment, then said more cheerfully, "However, out of it I seem to have got myself another daughter, and I must do my best by her, for her mother's sake."

Kate pondered over the strange situation. Was Sir John so

disappointed with his own daughter that he would find Emily a welcome substitute? No, that couldn't be so, for under his anger and his anxiety about Celina, there were glimpses of what must have once been adoration for her. Emily, a working man's daughter, could never take Celina's place.

Two days after the tragedy of Mary's death, land was sighted. They were able to draw near a palm-fringed island with a ramshackle jetty, the ship's boat was manned and sent in search of food and fresh water. Both these immensely valuable commodities were obtained. They sailed at sunset, and soon the days became cooler. The ladies put on wraps to walk on deck. The children grew stronger from their illnesses, and there were no more deaths.

Even Lady Devenish became more animated. She was enormously relieved that the voyage was over without more mishaps. She was not thinking so much of poor Mary Lodden's death but of Celina, her doll child, and the strange animosity between her and her father which Lady Devenish was powerless to overcome. She didn't know what caused it nor why it had lasted so long. Celina had become secretive and John too overbearing. She was unhappy about the sedative the doctor had prescribed and hated the way it dulled Celina's liveliness. But at least it had avoided scenes.

She herself had taken a spoonful now and then to calm her apprehensions. Then, thinking that Kate looked at her oddly, she had had to plunge into trivial conversation, talking of the characters in the book they had been reading, and sewing feverishly. Life, always difficult, now weighed on her too heavily. Her face became pinched, her small fine hands developed a tremor. She had great difficulty in threading her needle with the bright-coloured silks of the tapestry she was working.

"We must have covers for the chairs," she said vaguely. "Like the ones in the hall at home. It will be a long task and we may not be in New Zealand sufficient time. But perhaps I can leave them for some other lady who will appreciate the culture we have left."

"You are bringing it with you, Lady Devenish," Kate said.

"Yes, but without much purpose," Lady Devenish replied. "It is only my husband who has a purpose. And I don't know what that is."

Then the voyage really was ended. One cloudy morning with a brisk southerly breeze blowing, someone shouted, "Land." It was difficult to believe that they had sailed through that wilderness of seas and found their destination.

"Aotearoa," Captain Oxford said to Kate. "The land of the long white cloud."

"What is that?"

"New Zealand, my dear young lady. The name the Maoris call it."

"Why, you're a romantic," Kate exclaimed.

He grinned. "Sometimes. And always to my disadvantage."

The relief and the excitement among the passengers that land was sighted were intense.

Captain Oxford walked beside Kate on the deck. Across the stretch of white-tipped breakers the surprisingly brown and barren hills of Lyttelton harbour rose against a windy sky.

"May I have permission to call on you in Christchurch, Miss Kate?"

Kate coloured with pleasure and hoped he didn't notice her emotion. Increasingly she had grown to enjoy the company of this sober, serious man, and to lean on him. She hoped their ways were not to part now that land was in sight.

"Oh, I hope you will. I believe Lady Devenish and Celina and I are to wait in Christchurch while Sir John goes to look at his property, and see if it is fit for habitation. He'll take Jonas, and the livestock that has survived the journey. Emily and Jonnie are to be in our care. I believe Miss Pugh, too, for we are all going in the same direction and she has grown fond of the children. They call her Aunt Tab. Of course Emily is fond of Sir John, too, and he is remarkably gentle with her. I don't know why he can't be so with his own daughter. I am sure she would behave better if she were shown more affection."

"Will you stop babbling about other people, Kate, and talk about us?"

Kate blushed again, infuriatingly. He would think she was a seventeen year old.

"We are invited to stay with the bank manager, Mr. Collins, who is said to have quite a mansion on the borders of the River Avon. I expect I won't be required all the time—if you should wish to call."

"Isn't that what I've just asked you?" He took her hand and squeezed it hard. "I have to make my land purchase and acquire horses and other livestock. And find a cadet willing to travel with me, and to teach me. These young men come out to New Zealand to learn about running sheep stations. I'll try to engage one with some experience."

"And you'll need household goods," Kate said practically.

"That's for a woman to arrange. When my house is built." Captain Oxford looked at her with some intensity. She could read his thoughts, and her own became increasingly confused. She was committed to the Devenish family for at least a year. She had promised this in London, an immensely long time ago. If Captain Oxford should want to make her his wife in the near future she would be in honour bound to refuse.

He seemed to be reading her thoughts, for he gave a half smile, his eyes tender.

"As I said, I shall have to build a house before I acquire a wife. Isn't patience a devilishly difficult virtue?"

"I don't believe it's a virtue at all," Kate said emphatically. "It's just tiresome. But nevertheless we have to learn it."

She didn't say that she had learned a great deal of it during the long voyage. But now that was over and they were going ashore. Lady Devenish had a scarf tied round her bonnet to prevent it sailing away in the strong wind, and Celina, who took so little interest in her appearance, letting her hair fall in a straggling unkempt way round her peaky face, didn't care whether she had her bonnet securely tied by its ribbons or not. Kate had tried to button her cape, and her boots. She had seemed strangely frightened.

"To be on land—all the people—all strangers," she had murmured once, and Kate wondered guiltily what they had done to her in her long confinement. However, her eyes did flash with some emotion when she saw her father with Emily clinging confidently to his hand. Was it jealousy?

"Ah!" Sir John exclaimed, holding out his other hand to her. "Now here are my two daughters."

Celina tucked her hands inside her muff.

"Take Mama's arm, Papa," she said coldly. "She needs more support than I do."

6

Not for the first time, Kate looked round her room with pleasure. It was not large, but in comparison with the cramped cabin on board the *Albatross* it was spacious, and completely civilised. None of the roughness of pioneer life existed here. The bed had a spotless white crocheted spread, the floor was carpeted, the chair at the little davenport was in the Hepplewhite style, if not a genuine Hepplewhite piece. On the dressing table there was a pottery mug containing a posy of real English flowers, late roses and carnations and old-fashioned pinks. The dressing-table mirror in its mahogany frame reflected the rosebud wallpaper and the snowy muslin curtains.

Mr. and Mrs. Hubert Collins appeared to be comfortably rich, and their house was a work of art in such a raw though rapidly growing town as Christchurch in the Canterbury province of New Zealand. On the first morning Kate thought that it had been like waking up in England, until she had heard the strange melodious, unidentifiable bird calls, and seen the unfamiliar shrubs in the garden, the waving feathery *toi toi,* a large flax bush with clacking fronds, and other glossy-leaved evergreens whose names she did not know. But at the end of the garden that ran down to a muddy stream called the River Avon, a fringe of young willow trees, their autumn leaves whirling away in the strong wind, were completely English.

There was so much to do, so much to explore, but the imperative thing at the moment was to write to Cousin Mabel and the two aunts in Mallow. With an hour of blessed privacy at her disposal, since Mrs. Collins had taken her other guests, Lady Devenish and Celina, on morning calls, Kate was able to sit at the davenport with her writing materials.

Dearest Cousin Mabel,

How can I describe the bliss of being safely arrived and living on dry land again. And in most congenial surroundings. We, Lady Devenish, Celina, poor orphaned Emily Lodden, and kind Miss Pugh are the guests of the bank manager and his wife, Mr. and Mrs. Hubert Collins, while Sir John, Jonas Lodden and little Jonnie go to look over Avalon. If it is habitable Jonas will stay there with Jonnie, while Sir John comes back to escort the ladies. It is quite a long journey by Cobb's stage coach to Ashburton, there will be a night in Mr. Turton's hotel, and then on to Timaru where one exchanges the coach for a very primitive conveyance, a bullock cart!

Christchurch is, as yet, a straggling town following the course of the river. But it has a surprising number of shops, mostly round the square of land where the cathedral is to be built. Mrs. Collins and I have walked up the dusty road to do the day's marketing, and to gaze at the surprising range of goods offered, sacks of seed wheat and seed potatoes, farming implements, hoes, rakes, ploughs etc., freshly baked bread and pastries, rosy apples and pears, large brown eggs (my mouth still waters at the sight of good fresh food after the *Albatross*), as well as non-edible goods, such as rolls of good sensible cloth for ladies' gowns (most women here are hard-working and have no servants), blankets and bedding, household furniture, even some surprisingly fashionable bonnets! There are, of course, too many bars selling alcohol, but I am told this is a feature of colonial towns. There is quite a lot of drunkenness at night, but we do not go abroad then, so we do not see it.

Celina's spirits, I am happy to tell you, have improved markedly, although she still has moments of outrage at this "wilderness" her Papa has brought her to. Nevertheless, both she and her mother were agreeably surprised by the comfort of the Collins's house. Of course the Collins have been here for some years and are well settled. They, at least Mrs. Collins, enjoy being leaders of society! It is said that she was an heiress (her father was a button manufacturer!) and it is her money that is responsible for the house and its furnishings. Understandably, with the dread stamp of trade on her, she could never have been a leader of society in England, so she is enjoying to the full what has probably been her dream. I'm awfully afraid, in spite of Mr. Wakefield's ideals, that money is going to be the criteria of importance here.

Nevertheless, Ada Collins is a nice, kind body although a great rattle, and is being *very* important about her titled guests. Sir John impressed her greatly, he was all courtesy and charm, but I fancy she is disappointed that Lady Devenish is so retiring, and she thinks that Celina should come out of herself more.

Well, perhaps Celina will surprise her and do that at the dinner party Ada is planning for Sir John's return. There is a great deal of fuss going on about that function already, and I have been asked to name any other of the *Albatross*'s passengers who might be invited. I have suggested Captain Oxford, whom I found such an agreeable companion on board ship.

Indeed, dear cousin, you have probably gathered from my previous letter that Captain Oxford and I are not likely to lose touch with one another. He is more than a dear friend. But of course my private plans for my life must be postponed until I have kept my promise to the Devenishs.

They say it snows a great deal at Avalon in the winter months. Strange as it must seem to you, we are now enjoying late autumn weather in May! Sunny days, great rolling clouds, and always the wind coming from the everlasting snowpeaks that hang over the Canterbury plains like a shining wall.

I am wondering how Celina will endure the lonely life in the country. She may think she is back on board the *Albatross,* but I do hope we are not forced to have recourse to her medicine again. She has been able to cease it since being here, and is consequently considerably more alert. I must create many occupations for her at Avalon.

They say there is a lake, and a little village with a school-room and a church not too far away. After a sojourn at Avalon perhaps, I, too, will share Mrs. Collins's view that Christchurch is a metropolis!

Most of the ladies out here, if asked what they want from home, say pictures of the latest fashions and the materials, taffetas and laces, to have them created into gowns by the very clever little dressmakers and milliners who have some-how wafted on to these shores. Ada Collins tells me that there are a surprising number of balls and other gatherings.

However, I have a large enough wardrobe to accommo-date me for some time, and so has Celina. That young lady is unlikely to wear out all her gowns in her lifetime.

So I would beg you to send me books and periodicals, novels, biographies, everything. For it will be a long long time before this country has literature of its own. And I am thinking of the long frosty or snowbound nights round the fire at Avalon.

How exasperating it is that you will not receive this letter for three or four months. But I am hoping that news of you and of the Mallow aunts will arrive on an incoming vessel before too long. Although that news, perforce, will be several months old. Ah me, patience! Captain Oxford and I have both decided that that is a necessary but very dull virtue.

I must close this letter now, and go and see if Ada (you see already I am adopting informal New Zealand ways) requires my help. She has two good respectable servants, Maggie and Martha, sisters from Bristol, and a Maori girl whom she is attempting to train. Far from all that talk about cannibals, the Maoris in these parts who come up from the bay round Lyttelton harbour are friendly, docile and rather amusingly fascinated by white households. I believe Rata thinks she is in heaven. Except that she has no concept of our heaven. She continually rolls her big brown eyes and says "What for?"—almost her only English words. This question applies to dishes, brooms, shopping baskets, a pound of sausages, the unfamiliar English vegetables like carrots and cabbages, everything. She is slow but biddable, and extremely good-tempered. Her family, wrapped in dirty old blankets, spend a great deal of their time sitting at the Collins's garden gate, hoping for hand-outs. Any trifle pleases them. The mother, the *wahine*, smokes a pipe!

Ada Collins says it is our duty to civilise the Maori and turn them into Christians. I wonder if this is wise.

In the days that followed, Kate had ample time to write to the Mallow aunts and to other friends, as well as to attend to her charges, Lady Devenish and Celina. She supervised their clothes, took them on walks (which Celina found dusty and dull—the wind constantly exasperating her, since she would insist on being elegant and holding up her parasol), and read them the next chapter from *The Vicar of Wakefield,* or encouraged them to take their needlework down to Mrs. Collins's pretty drawing room. Mrs. Collins was never at a loss for a topic of conversation, blissfully unaware of what might or might not interest titled ladies, and even eventually persuaded Celina to sing at the piano. Kate was surprised by the purity of her voice. With her back to the audience and her halo of pale hair she looked like an angel.

Then, at last, a message from Avalon by post, no less, the postman riding his horses in stages over the long miles, arrived. Sir John expected to be back the following week. He had found everything to his satisfaction, the house completely habitable, indeed, he said, quite charming in its colonial fashion, and equipped with a Chinese cook. And did they know that Captain Oxford had been looking at land not twenty miles away? Wasn't that a coincidence? He was returning to Christchurch at the same time as Sir John.

Kate tried to conceal her elation. She had missed Henry when he had left on his explorations, and had tried not to think of him too much. But it was delightful that he was returning, and also that he might live so near to Avalon. Twenty miles was considered nothing in this country.

So in a great flurry of excitement invitations were issued and the dinner party arranged.

As soon as the party had been discussed a month ago, Mr. Collins, a small pale-faced businessman, scarcely half the size of his wife, but with shrewd steely eyes dominating his otherwise insignificant face (money eyes, Henry had called them), had had the idea of persuading Mr. Wakefield to sail across the Straits from Wellington and attend. He had written telling him that an English gentleman, a great admirer of Wakefield and his colonising genius, would be overcome with joy if a meeting could be arranged.

However, it was not possible. Mr. Wakefield replied that his health was very poor. He lived like a hermit, his only companion his niece Alice and his bulldogs, Powder and Blucher. New Zealand, he concluded mournfully, was going to be too liberally furnished with Wakefield graves, first his brothers', William and Arthur, and before too long his own.

This seemed a sad, solitary end to a man who had inspired so many people. But Mr. Collins commented in his dry manner that the habit of being a recluse had probably begun when he had had his enforced stay in a cell in Newgate jail. He had been imprisoned for abducting a schoolgirl heiress. Such a strange crime for such a clever man!

Mrs. Collins said, "Tch! Tch! We don't talk of those old things. Mr. Wakefield was a headstrong young man. But now he's a hero. No doubt he'll have a statue erected to him one day."

Captain Henry Oxford, back from his explorations in the tussocky foothills of the Mackenzie country (named after a crazy, sheep-stealing Scotsman) found it interesting to view the Southern Alps from the vantage point of Christchurch, the aspiring city at the head of the Plains. The sky in the evening had opened into a yellow window, clear and bright, hanging over the long magnificent range of snowpeaks. This was a phenomenon that followed a day of raging wind, the vicious nor'-wester that hurled itself across the endless flatness of the Canterbury Plains, uprooting trees, lifting whole acres of ploughed soil and distributing it miles away, tearing the corrugated roofs off settlers' cottages, even sending unacclimatised sheep headlong into ditches.

The daylong wind was hard to endure, but when it stopped there was such a purity to the sky and the shining mountain tops, such radiance catching the dusty wool of grazing sheep and flattened tussock, such long, quiet shadows across the autumn grass, that it was like a benediction.

Captain Oxford was well content with what he had learned of this unique land. On one side it was lapped by the warm waters of the Pacific, on the other by the turbulent Tasman Sea leading to the arctic wastes explored only by whalers. A combination of mountains and lakes and snowy foothills, volcanoes and glaciers, and, so he had been told, of boiling mud pools in which one could cook an egg, it was so much more worth colonising than an uninterested and penny-pinching Parliament in London thought. And not for the utopian reasons of an idealistic Mr. Wakefield.

Did Mr. Wakefield really think that the usual human components of love and hate, greed, envy, melancholy, bad humours and guile could be washed away on the long voyage from East India Docks? Had he considered what homesickness combined with isolation, lack of medical care, loneliness and fear could do to the spirit? No place could be perfect whatever Mr. Wakefield, or that strange fellow, Sir John Devenish, thought. But with enthusiasm and optimism and hard work Captain Oxford had decided that life here could well be better than in most places.

He had decided on the land he would buy in those remote foothills scarcely yet trodden by man. He had already been to the Land Office to make his claim. There was a lake scarcely more than a pool like a blue diamond, some clumps of trees, and scree slopes, and endless grazing land. Kate would like it, he was sure. She would make an ideal wife, strong, resourceful, capable, and immensely charming, too. He had never met a more suitable young woman and could scarcely believe his luck. Of course he would have to wait until she had worked out her time with the Devenish family, but in that period he could have his house built and his sheep station established. By fortunate chance he had chosen land which was scarcely twenty miles distant from Avalon, so there could be frequent meetings. Kate could ride over to see the progress of the house, he would be invited to festivities at Avalon. The time would go quickly. He and Kate were both people who would plan their future sensibly.

At least so he thought, but at this moment, as he walked back to his lodgings at the Golden Fleece to change for the dinner party at the Collins's he was bursting with impatience to see Kate again. How long had they been parted? Less than a month. He hoped she was as eager for their reunion as he was. What would she be wearing? Would her dark blue eyes light up with pleasure when she saw him?

How splendid it was to be young and with such opportunities ahead. He longed to write to his parents in their quiet Norfolk farmhouse that he was at last planning to settle down. No more roving army life, no more self-centred bachelor ways. His mother would be delighted. She had always wanted grandchildren, even though it seemed that they would be born on the other side of the world. Perhaps when they were grown up they would decide to make the long journey to England, turning affairs full circle.

Suddenly tired of such musing, Captain Oxford quickened his pace. He couldn't wait for the festive evening and his reunion with Kate.

In one of the attic bedrooms of Mrs. Collins's fine house, Emily was aware of the first real excitement and happiness that she had experienced since the day beloved Mam's body, wrapped in its horrible canvas shroud, had been tipped almost carelessly into the sea.

There were two reasons for her emotion. One was the beautifully starched and ironed muslin dress spread out on the bed. For her. A real party dress, like a lady!

The other was that yesterday Squire had come back from the wilderness. He had looked tanned and fit and he had smiled and talked a lot. He had been on the best of terms with everybody, including Lady Devenish to whom he was sometimes curt and unkind. He had kissed Celina on the cheek, asking tenderly after her health, and then had bent his bright gaze on Emily, standing against the wall, too shy to be noticed.

Perhaps because Celina had stiffened in his embrace, and pulled back, complaining fretfully that Papa was crushing her dress, he had swooped forward and gathered Emily into his arms, lifting her high as if she were feather weight.

"And how is my second daughter?" he demanded.

"John!" Lady Devenish protested. "The girl is much too big for that sort of thing. Put her down."

"What sort of thing, my dear? A harmless embrace? Doesn't the child need affection?" He nuzzled his lips against Emily's cheek before putting her down. He was still smiling. "And I have to tell you, Emily, that your father and brother are in fine health and have stayed on at Avalon to get it in order for us. Jonnie already says he never wants to leave. He and Jonas are sharing quarters with a Chinese cook and a Maori shepherd. They're all trying hard to understand each other's language. It'll make you laugh when you hear them." He looked up. "You, too, Kate. You're looking very well. And did you know that Captain Oxford is back? Yes, I see you did, by your blush. What's this, Mrs. Collins, about a big dinner party tomorrow night? As if you haven't been hospitable enough to us already. And what about my daughter? How does she like the Antipodes?"

Celina pouted. "It's always so windy, Papa. I can never hold up my parasol."

Sir John laughed genially. His good temper was not going to be ruffled.

"You'll have to get used to the wind. Wait until you see the Southern Alps close to. Wait until you watch the sun set on the peak of Mount Cook. That's real grandeur. We have nothing like it in England. I declare it humbles a mere human traveller like me."

He was in such high good humour that the loneliness began to seep out of Emily and warmth to take its place. She adored Squire, this handsome god of a man who gave orders so easily and was always obeyed, who had so much affection to give. Just being held in his arms shut out all the cold nightmares.

Mam and Pa had always said Squire was a good man, but beset by mysterious troubles. She would like to comfort him. Could she ever?

It was on Squire's insistence that she was to sit at the dinner table the next night. Surely she was old enough. Nearly fourteen.

Pioneer women had to grow up young. Perhaps Kate or Miss Pugh could contrive a dress for her to wear.

"She mustn't be left to brood over her mother and her little brother at the bottom of the sea," he said in a voice she was not intended to hear. "This new country is for living and happiness."

Emily noticed that he didn't suggest Lady Devenish or Celina find a dress for her. She was glad of that. They would always think of her as a servant, she knew.

Miss Pugh arranged the dress, and the petticoats, and some black velvet slippers, and a ribbon for her hair.

"You mustn't be too dressed up, Emily," she said in her sharp kind voice. "It isn't your place. And you mustn't let Squire spoil you. Your Mama wouldn't care for that. You and Jonnie are bred to be useful citizens. Remember that and don't get ideas. Though you're a pretty lass. You'll be finding a husband before you know it."

Emily had ideas about that, too.

"To live in a cob house?" she asked, wrinkling her nose. "I always think of the manor. I dream about it all the time."

Miss Pugh's eyes were sharp.

"Now don't you get airs because Sir John has been making a fuss of you. It's just a passing whim, you know. He has a kind heart."

"I'm not getting ideas, Miss Pugh. I only remember—" Emily blinked back tears and said in a too grown-up voice. "Yes, I expect you're right, Miss Pugh. It's silly to think of the manor. It's so far away. I really will be good, and learn to cook, and do things. I can do a lot already. Mam taught me. Will it be all right if I just think of the manor in my sleep?"

"I should think it would be splendid," Miss Pugh said, keeping her voice steady.

There was, however, a suitable companion for Emily, for Sir John had brought back Miss Pugh's orphaned nephew, Daniel. He was nearly sixteen, a gangling freckle-faced lad with eyes that were already narrowed, like a sailor's, against vast horizons and the constant wind. He could hardly be persuaded to say a word. He was still recovering from the shock of his parents' death, Miss Pugh said, and was also unused to company. Emily must talk to him and draw him out.

Emily was put out. Apart from only wanting to be in the same room as Squire, all the time, so that she could gaze at his magnificence, she found an inarticulate boy who blushed whenever spoken to a desperate bore. However, as Miss Pugh kept reminding her, they had a tragedy in common, both having lost parents. So they must sympathise with each other, and clever young women could always persuade young men to talk.

He was only a boy, Emily thought disgustedly, not much older than Jonnie. But he had blond hair that stood up in funny stiff tufts and she began to tease him about it. At first he was angry, blushing furiously, then he retorted that if she didn't stop he would pull her hair ribbons out, and her silly plaits as well. Didn't she know that he was becoming one of the best shepherds in South Canterbury. He could tell at once when a sheep developed scab, or ate the poisonous *tutu* grass, or when a ewe needed help in lambing.

"You wouldn't even know how lambs are born," he said scornfully.

Emily couldn't help a furtive interest.

"How?"

"They come out of their mother's belly, just like you did."

"I! Out of Mam's belly! Don't be so rude!"

"But it's true," Daniel said earnestly. "You'll have to learn the facts about birth and death if you're going to be a pioneer."

"My Mam would never have told me such things," Emily said, although she couldn't help being fascinated. "The angels brought me. I expect they brought you, too, though that's hard to believe, I must say."

Daniel turned his back on her, and she was afraid she had hurt him. She didn't really want to do that.

"I'm supposed to be like my father," he said stiffly. "He was big—good-looking—" the adolescent voice quivered.

"I expect you've got quite a lot of growing to do," Emily conceded. "Like me."

When he turned back to face her they both smiled tentatively.

"What's my Aunt Tab like?" he asked.

"Aunt Tab! Is that what you call her? It sounds like a cat."

Then their smiles turned into giggles, and Emily supposed that Daniel, with his tufty hair and long skinny wrists, wasn't too bad. But she was to sit next to him at the dinner party, and that really was a bore.

7

The party had begun by the time Captain Oxford arrived. The yellow light in the sky had been abruptly blown out as the wind rose again. Candles and lamps were burning in the downstairs rooms, in the wide hall with its fine oak staircase, and the pleasant drawing room where people were gathered, and the dining room opposite with its long table laid with silver and crystal.

The Collins must have travelled from England with all their possessions. Their house was full of good furniture, rugs and pictures.

Captain Oxford was intrigued by the scene that met his eye. Seeing the group of ladies in slightly old-fashioned but charming gowns with low-cut bosoms and crinoline skirts, he was glad he had worn evening dress himself. The gathering was civilised enough to be taking place somewhere in England. There were even servants, a butler carrying a silver tray with sherry or whisky for the gentlemen, and two maid servants in starched caps and aprons bearing crystal glasses of fruit cup for the ladies.

Captain Oxford helped himself to a whisky, and looked round

eagerly for Kate. Instead, he saw Lady Devenish elegantly dressed in cream lace. She wore good jewellery, too, diamond ear rings and a diamond and pearl pendant. But none of this finery had enabled her to lose her tentative manner, as if there were too many things of which she was nervous. Her skin was like rice paper that would disintegrate in strong sunlight. Why had Sir John brought such a delicate woman to this new country? Not to mention the daughter whom Captain Oxford remembered from the *Albatross,* a shrinking, pale-faced creature who seemed to shun the daylight.

Lady Devenish was holding out a narrow hand. "Captain Oxford, how nice to see you again. How are you finding this new country?"

"Very much to my liking. Is it not to yours?"

"I've scarcely decided yet. I must admit there are certain things that disturb me."

"Are you thinking of hostile natives?"

"Oh no, they're peaceable enough here. Rather a nuisance, though. They sit outside the gate in smelly blankets, and smoke their pipes, and let their children run about naked. No, I'm thinking of the wind howling and the tremendous empty spaces. The way the dust gets in everything." Her pale blue eyes had a forlorn look. She attempted a smile. "I hope I can get used to it. My husband finds it all tremendously exciting."

"And Miss Celina?" Captain Oxford made an effort to remember the shadowy young lady. "She's with us tonight?"

"She will be." The nervous eyes swivelled round. "She's a little late coming down. Kate is with her. Oh, here is Kate. You're alone, my dear? Where is Celina?"

But Kate had eyes only for Captain Oxford, and answered Lady Devenish briefly. "She told me to go ahead. She wouldn't be hurried."

"She is coming down?" The permanent anxiety flickered in Lady Devenish's eyes.

"Yes, of course. She was dressed and almost ready." Kate could no longer keep from welcoming Captain Oxford. "Captain Oxford, I believe?" she said with mock formality, sketching a curtsy.

"And you are Miss O'Connor?" He took up her game.

"Kate."

"Ah—a charming name."

"We are to sit next to one another at dinner. So you will have the opportunity to tell me all about your journey into the wastelands."

"Bleak and lonely and awe-inspiring and tremendously challenging," he said enthusiastically. "And I learned that you must build a house near water and cabbage trees, because cabbage trees are a sign of good land."

She smiled a little. "So you have no regrets about leaving the army to become a sheep man?"

"None at all. After all, my father and grandfather were Norfolk farmers. It's in my blood much more than cavalry charges and spit and polish. Though if there were any more trouble with the Maori I should, of course, join the militia. I've heard that some of the tribes still resent the *pakeha*."

"Only because they think their land is being stolen. I am sure the Land Societies have meant to be honourable but they haven't been able to resist grabbing. When you think of a million acres for the price of a consignment of muskets and swords and bottles of rum, it really is taking advantage of the natives' ignorance." Kate had stopped joking and was very serious. "I know Governor Grey has tried to be fair but this can't be said of all the people concerned."

"You seem to have become a very political young lady since we last met," Captain Oxford teased.

"One can't help becoming so. The Collins are very well-informed, especially Mr. Collins. He's very astute." Then her eyes danced, her cheeks dimpled. "Henry, I'm so happy to see you again. I'm only talking stupidly like this because I was afraid of showing my pleasure too much."

"Would that matter?"

Kate saw Sir John Devenish watching them from across the room.

"I think a little circumspection is wise." She touched his arm. "In company, at least. This is going to be quite a memorable party. That tall, good-looking gentleman over there is the famous

Bishop Selwyn who does so much good work with the Maori. His wife is here, too. But unfortunately Mr. Wakefield was unable to come. Mrs. Collins so much wanted Sir John to meet him. I know you have reservations about his theories."

"About their practicability. Perhaps it's a good thing he isn't here. I might have crossed swords with him."

In a short time with another of the excellent whiskies beneath his belt, and some conversation with his host and hostess, and the spare, handsome bishop and his rather dowdy wife, Captain Oxford was beginning to enjoy himself. This warm, lighted room was a far cry from the wind whistling down the gullies of the Mackenzie country, and the bleak grandeur of the Alps. It made a stimulating contrast. The women were surprisingly well-dressed and attractive, Kate most of all. He found himself pleasantly contented with her good looks and her intelligence, reflecting again on his unbelievably good luck in finding just the kind of wife he had been seeking, even though their marriage would have to be delayed for some time.

However, if a husband could be found for the sulky Miss Celina—and they said bachelors here were so starved for brides that they would take even the cross-eyed or the hare-lipped— perhaps Kate could be released from her duties much sooner.

There was a stirring on the staircase and Captain Oxford looked up idly. The next moment he was staring in fascination.

"Who is that?" he whispered to Kate.

"Why, Celina, of course. Surely you recognise her."

"I never saw her looking like that," he murmured.

Kate tugged his arm a little impatiently. "Don't stare like a goose. When Celina chooses to, she can look very well."

"I believe," he said slowly as if in a dream, "she is the most beautiful thing I have ever seen."

"Oh, you men, you're so gullible. Blonde hair and a pair of large eyes and you think you're seeing an angel. I can tell you, Celina is very far from that."

But Captain Oxford continued to stare. He had met many good-looking women, not excluding Kate, but he had never before been conscious of such instant fascination as he watched this slim girl, her amber skirts billowing out from her tiny waist, her long neck held gracefully, her strange pale hair making an aureole round her head, her eyes dark and luminous. He truthfully couldn't stop looking at her. He was bemused and bewildered. He had always been a level-headed fellow, not subject to wild emotions. Perhaps he had been too cautious, too sensible, for now his repressed feelings were turning into irresistible desire. He believed this was the strangest moment of his life.

At the dinner table Kate sat on the left of Captain Oxford, Celina on the right. Opposite them was the handsome, silver-haired bishop and his brown wren of a wife. Sir John was on his hostess's right, Lady Devenish similarly placed on the right of Hubert Collins. In between were eminent citizens of Christchurch, including a husky young man down from the North Island and his wife, a sallow woman with nervousness jumping out of her skin. It seemed she had been leading a lonely life in the bush and it had left her in this state of nerves and shyness. The two children, Emily and Daniel, sat silently, not daring to venture a word, either to their neighbours or each other. Although Emily would gladly have spoken had Squire turned to her.

At first conversation was conducted in low voices with one's immediate neighbour. It was all very correct. Ada Collins might never have been able to give an important party in England, but here she was in her element, managing her guests and the two maids waiting on table, with a mixture of bossiness and transparent pleasure. Her husband was less genial. His clever, sharp-eyed face must look entirely right behind the counter of a bank. But he was obviously not an expert at small talk and was finding Lady Devenish distinctly hard work.

No harder, Kate thought resentfully, than her own attempts at conversation with Henry. He simply could not take his eyes off Celina. And she, for her part, knew exactly what she was doing. She had waited for a suitable occasion to display her dramatic and deliberate transformation from waif to witch. For a witch was what she must seem to a susceptible man, a seductive, clinging creature with her small, high voice and the sudden burning of her eyes.

To Kate she was simply sly and wicked, angling for attention, or withdrawing if it bored her. A strange unpredictable, unsound person who surely could never make such a sensible man as Henry permanently lose his wits. Kate was remembering the episode with the sailor on board the *Albatross*. She began to understand more clearly why Celina's parents had kept her sedated with laudanum or whatever her medicine had been. A pity they had not thought to administer some tonight. In society in England, Kate thought, Celina must have had a flawed reputation. So flawed that her parents were prepared to transport her across the world to find an innocent and gullible husband for her, before there had been some great scandal.

And now her favourable glances had fallen on Henry. Was she just flirting, or was there a deeper motive beneath her attentiveness? Whatever she was doing, Henry was completely smitten.

She got his attention at last, and said, "Tell me more about your plans, Henry. You've said so little. Only that you intend to build a house in that lonely country. I personally think that's a splendid challenge, but all women wouldn't."

"What do you mean, Kate?"

"There would be just sheep and hills. Maybe childbirth without a doctor. Illness. Accidents. A bad snowstorm."

Henry laughed heartily.

"I had never thought you such a pessimist."

"*I'm* not pessimistic," she said crossly.

"And certainly I am not." He lowered his voice, "Kate, what have you done to Celina? Or what has this new environment done? She's completely come out of her shell."

"Safer in it," Kate murmured.

She became less patient. Her own hurt feelings made her speak frankly. "Have you never met a siren before?"

"That's what you call her? Why, how right you are."

She is poison, Kate wanted to say. Like belladonna or henbane. She is secretive and aloof, and I don't think she cares for anybody except perhaps her father, although I also think she hates him. But when she wants to dazzle, vulnerable men, like you, poor Captain Oxford, become moonstruck.

/   85

She returned hopefully to her first question.

"So you have decided on this land in the foothills?"

Before Henry could answer, a handsome military-looking gentleman sitting opposite leaned across the table.

"I believe you, sir, are an army officer."

"Retired," said Henry. "I decided to have a change of occupation. This country I was told was badly in need of farmers, tillers of the soil, sheep men."

"You have experience in these things?"

"My father manages an estate in Norfolk. I was brought up in the country."

"But you chose the army as a career?"

"My mother did that for me. Her father was colonel of an Irish Foot Regiment. Her brother fell at Waterloo."

The man introduced himself. "Colonel Rawlinson, sir. I have Irish connections myself. I'm sure you'll make a capital station holder, but may I suggest the land in the Taranaki province. We could do with a settler like you in that area."

"Because I can fire a gun?" Henry asked.

"Partly. I was in the Sixty-fifth during the Maori wars. We thought we had made lasting peace with the natives, but they still have grievances. Some of the tribes are extremely warlike. Uprisings may have to be put down. Which grieves my friend here, the bishop, who calls them his brothers. Don't you, bishop?"

The bishop turned his benevolent face.

"Indeed. They are children of God as much as you or me."

"Are they good fighters?" Henry asked.

"Clever, crafty, brave and honourable," the colonel answered concisely, and suddenly the whole table was listening.

"They're splendid fellows and many of them are now Christians," Bishop Selwyn said. "I've tended their wounded after a battle, and I've witnessed their care of fallen enemies."

"And fought in battles yourself," commented the colonel.

"With my tongue, not with a sword."

Bishop Selwyn's wife, the thin, dark-haired woman leaned forward.

"My husband doesn't tell you how foolhardy he is on occasions. I wait with our children in our house in Auckland and think he will never come home again. He travels so many miles, and mostly on foot."

"I have a large parish," the bishop said serenely. "And I can tell you, I feel ashamed when I travel with my Maori deacons, who behave like gentlemen, and yet I can't take them into public rooms where a tipsy carter would be considered perfectly good society."

Hubert Collins spoke for the first time. "But what about that story of the old chief who wouldn't allow a white man to climb Mount Tongariro because it was the backbone of his ancestor and was therefore *tapu*? Can such a savage be converted?"

Captain Oxford thought how fortunate such a young country was to get a man of the calibre of the bishop. But Mrs. Selwyn was adding words perhaps not intended to be heard.

"He knows how desperately I worry. It rains a great deal in Auckland in the winter, and our roof leaks, as does everyone else's. The children get fevers..."

The bishop gave his sunny smile.

"My dear, you mustn't dwell only on miseries." He had been going to add something else, but suddenly, shockingly, the nervous woman from Hawkes Bay began to weep loudly. The painful sound of her sobs was shattering. Mrs. Collins sprang up.

"Mrs. Thomas! Are you ill?"

The distraught woman began to babble hysterically.

"You say the Maoris are gentlemen, bishop, but you haven't had a child murdered. You haven't seen his poor little bleeding face and his limp body, like a dead puppy. You haven't had your house burned down and your stock driven off, and your husband near demented. You haven't heard their war cry in the early dawn." She took a deep breath and became composed enough to say in a quiet, chilling voice, "They're howling, murdering savages. Don't try to make them Christians, bishop. God wouldn't want them."

"Mrs. Thomas!" Ada Collins begged. "Come upstairs and lie down. You're still ill from your shocking experiences. Oh, Mrs. Selwyn, how kind of you. Will you take her upstairs? Persuade her to take a little brandy?"

"I'll never live in the bush again!" Mrs. Thomas cried, as she was led from the room. "It isn't fair of James to expect me to."

"A dreadful ordeal," murmured the bishop. "Poor woman. You are come to Canterbury then, Mr. Thomas?"

The husband, a ruddy-faced young man answered, "For the present. Until Ruth forgets a bit. I had a nice piece of land in Hawkes Bay. It hurt to leave it. But we'll go back. You have to, don't you? You can't let the savages win."

"But you can't expect a woman to forget the death of her child, either," Ada Collins said. "A man doesn't feel quite the same emotion. Don't you agree, Lady Devenish?"

Lady Devenish seemed alarmed at being brought into such a grim discussion, and it was Celina who suddenly began to laugh. Kate recognised that light ripple, with its underlying hysteria.

"Goodness, what dreadful things we're talking about. But none of that can happen to us, can it? Not in Canterbury. Papa, you promised Canterbury was safe." It was her father to whom she spoke, but her limpid eyes sought Henry's, and he answered.

"Assuredly not, Miss Devenish. As long as one stays in safe areas."

Celina dropped her eyes. She sighed.

"Yet that could be boring, too. Couldn't it?"

"I shouldn't think life could ever be boring for you, young lady," Colonel Rawlinson said gallantly.

Kate could stand no more of it. She pushed back her chair, excusing herself.

"May I just slip upstairs and see how Mrs. Thomas is?" she asked Ada Collins.

"How kind of you, Kate. Tell Mrs. Selwyn to come down. Now, I do pray that no one lets this spoil his dinner. The pudding is just coming in."

"When are you going to get a bishop for Canterbury?" Sir John asked. "Mr. Wakefield says it would increase the respectability of colonisation."

"I see you are a follower of Wakefield's, Sir John."

"Indeed I am. I share his dream of a perfect society. It's a fascinating concept."

Ada Collins fluttered her eyelashes at him coquettishly, "And you think we are all suitable for this society, Sir John?"

"Oh, certainly. Especially you, dear lady."

The voices followed Kate upstairs. She heard Celina's light laughter again. She imagined her turning those huge, luminous eyes on Henry, and her blood boiled. Surely he couldn't remain so stupidly bemused.

Ruth Thomas lay on the bed in one of the guest rooms. This room was furnished like the others with pleasant English furniture and chintzes, but tonight, more than ever before, Kate was conscious of the atmosphere of an English house stopping within the four walls. Outside the spears of the flax bushes clack-clacking in the wind made a harsh foreign sound. Dim lights in the distance were too feeble to suggest anything but goblins or will-o'-the-wisps. They trembled in the darkness. The whole immensity of the dark, empty plain seemed to loom around the small oasis of this warm, comfortable house.

Moving away from the window, looking at the still figure on the bed, for Mrs. Thomas's hysteria had left her exhausted and looking like a child with her tumbled hair, Kate could vividly imagine the loneliness of an isolated homestead in the bush. Every rustle, every slapping branch or snapping twig could mean danger. Of what? Hostile natives who could move as silently as smoke, wild pigs rooting and grunting in the undergrowth? Or just the unknown, which could be the most terrifying of all.

It was not a place for nervous women, most of whom had come from well-populated towns. Yet, being here, they must endeavour to make the best of it. Kate was eager to do so herself. She was impatient to get out of the artificial comfort of this house and begin to live as a true pioneer woman. With Henry, of course. She had been so certain of that until tonight. The fact that he had been so easily and so ridiculously smitten by Celina had shaken her confidence.

Henry had seemed the most steady and honest of men, yet there he was turned to a jelly by Celina's strange beauty. He hadn't had to live with her day and night for three months, enduring her sulks and silences, her melancholy, her sudden hysterical outbreaks and, most disturbing of all, her sexual aberration. Tonight, Henry was seeing a fragile butterfly whom he suddenly had a passion to possess. But didn't he know that butterflies lived only a day? And that they could not cook or sew or spin or make a garden in the wilderness? They probably could not even give birth to healthy children, or certainly not without an immense amount of fuss. And what on earth would they be like under the circumstances Ruth Thomas had endured?

Kate pressed her forehead against the window pane. Was her jealousy unwarranted? Or was her instinct that Henry would be haunted by Celina for weeks, even months, correct? She had none of Celina's deliberate seductiveness. She had thought Henry wanted a practical sensible wife, good-looking, but with no wild glamour. Now she was not at all sure. She was terribly afraid the damage had been done. He was like a sailor who had heard the sirens singing, and his senses had left him.

"What are you thinking about so seriously?" Ruth Thomas had stirred. "Are you wondering what kind of country you have come to?"

"Men," Kate said involuntarily.

The unexpected answer made Ruth smile.

"Oh, I know. I get mad with them, too. They tell you you can get over bad things, that you can go on hoeing and washing and cooking and keeping the fire burning and nursing sick children and never seeing another soul. And when you start crying they get angry with you, because the truth is, I think, they're a little frightened, too." She looked at Kate. "Could you do those things I said, all those practical things, Miss—"

"Kate O'Connor. Yes, I could." Kate's voice was hard and definite. "But not everyone could."

"Wait until you have a sick child and no doctor within twenty miles. Wait until—" the horror touched the woman's eyes again. "I am forgetting it. Really I am. It was only the talk at dinner that brought it back. Listen! I can hear someone singing. Do go down, Kate. I'm all right now. I'll just rest a little longer. To tell the truth I don't want to show my face again. My husband will be so ashamed of me."

Celina's high, clear voice floated up the stairs. *She is far from the land where her young lover sleeps*... Kate winced. She would like to have stayed up here in the company of the sad woman on the bed, yet she knew she had to go down and observe people's reaction to Celina's youthful purity. Henry's reaction.

As she descended the stairs she saw Celina seated at the piano, her pale face as serene as an angel's. Everyone's eyes were on her. Sir John's gaze was fond, hostility gone. Lady Devenish would never quite lose her anxiety, but she was quietly composed, her hands folded in her lap. Ada Collins was smiling happily, the success of her party, after the unfortunate episode at dinner, established. Her husband tapped his fingers and waited for the sentimental song to finish so that he could get back to serious conversation. The bishop was benign, his wife's eyes were bright with a hint of tears. Captain Henry Oxford sat upright, totally absorbed. Kate badly wanted to put her hands round his throat and shake him back to common sense.

The song finished and Celina rose. She gave a small bow, then passed her hand over her brow and sighed.

"Could I be excused please, Mrs. Collins? Mama? I am suddenly so tired. But it has been the nicest party."

Lady Devenish looked at Kate, then, apparently seeing some lack of sympathy in Kate's expression, said, "I'll go up with her." She turned to the company at large. "My daughter is a little highly strung. We take great care of her."

There was some enthusiastic clapping and murmured expressions of admiration. Kate crossed over to Henry.

"I see you applauding, too, captain."

"She was delightful. You never told me she could sing like that."

"Because she has never deigned to do so in company."

"She has a charming voice."

"A sweet voice, I agree."

"You sound so critical, Kate."

"Ah, but I'm not a besotted male." She tried to speak lightly. Then she turned to face him with great earnestness. "Henry, you know what that young woman can be."

"No, actually I don't. I've never been permitted to know. You've kept her hidden away."

"I didn't," Kate denied. "On board ship it was her parents'

express instructions that she be kept quiet. She's so highly excitable. She has a very strange nature." She saw that he was scarcely listening, his eyes directed to the now empty staircase.

Kate took a deep breath and told herself to be sensible.

"I see that the bishop is leaving. His schooner *Undine* is in harbour. He travels round the coast of New Zealand on her. Henry, I don't believe you've talked to the bishop at all. Nor to the Land Commissioner." She saw his face and sighed. "Perhaps there wasn't much opportunity. When shall I see you again?"

"When? Oh, tomorrow. I shall call on Mrs. Collins to pay my respects."

"And catch a glimpse of the little witch upstairs?"

"Kate, you're mocking me. A glimpse of you, too, of course."

"Really, Henry?" She was angry that she could not keep the too-revealing wistfulness out of her voice.

8

Lady Devenish, weary to the bone, lay back on the plump pillows and watched her husband undressing. There was no dressing room in this wretched colonial house. While everyone else seemed to think it a remarkably luxurious building, she thought it vulgar and tasteless, not at all the kind of home to which she had been accustomed. Imagine having to watch one's husband undress.

Still, he remained a fine figure of a man whom many women would admire. They would envy her having that well-kept body stretched beside her in the double bed. She, privately, found it a great ordeal. She was used to her own room, her own bed. John had never come to her frequently, and over the last few years scarcely at all. She didn't want to know where he satisfied his desires. She trusted him to be discreet and to leave her reluctant body in peace. She suspected that now there was no hope of a son he had been glad of the excuse not to trouble her. This, too, was galling in its way.

But in this uncivilised country they were forced temporarily together. It would be different at Avalon. She would see to that.

At least sharing a bed gave him no alternative but to listen to her complaints.

"John, I do wish you wouldn't make such a fuss of Emily. She's only the daughter of your cowman and you're turning her head."

"Turning her head!" He gave his laugh, with its ever so slightly contemptuous edge. "Not now she's got young Daniel. That boy has as much charm as his aunt, which isn't saying much. But the young aren't critical. Emily will dote on him. He's bigger and older than she is. She'll think him a man."

"Don't be so blind, John. Can't you see that it's you she dotes on?"

"Like a father, I'm happy to say. The way I had always wanted my own daughter to do."

"You must always be admired, mustn't you, John? Even by children." Lady Devenish was surprised at her temerity. But weariness and her vast sense of desolation and unhappiness made her bold. "Celina takes after you in that respect."

"In that respect only. I'm fearful for her. You know the reason She must be married as soon as possible."

"But not to Captain Oxford. He belongs to Kate. You must not encourage that infatuation."

"I don't even like the fellow. He's a typical soldier. No subtlety. No, I won't actively encourage him to be my son-in-law." The look Sir John gave his wife was troubled, and held its familiar hint of accusation. He was blaming her again for Celina's difficult nature. Her flawed nature, he called it. She had inherited her mother's genes, he was saying again silently. Then why had he married her? Had her fortune not been sufficient compensation?

"But it may be that we can't be choosers, my dear."

"Oh!" Lady Devenish's voice was a small cry. She buried her face in her narrow white hands. "Why did you bring us here, John? Why? I don't know how I shall stand it."

He got into bed beside her, carefully, so that no part of their bodies touched. He lay his head on the pillow so that his long nose pointed at the ceiling.

"I don't believe you have realised the sacrifice it was for me,

Iris. Leaving my family home, my friends, my whole way of life."

She lay still in surprise.

"But you wanted to come. You said it was to be a great adventure, a great enterprise while you were still young enough. Mr. Wakefield's theories—"

"I am not in the mood for Mr. Wakefield!" he interrupted with sudden violence. "I've discovered that he, too, was once nothing but a common criminal."

"Too?" she faltered.

"As so many of the Australian immigrants are," he said tiredly. "Oh, go to sleep, Iris. I'm tired, and I daresay you are also. Tomorrow we will both be enthusiastic settlers again. The crème de la crème of antipodean society."

Lady Devenish was frightened. Her husband had never before admitted to weakness, to faltering. What was wrong? Tears lay on her cheeks as she tried to sleep.

Ada Collins took her husband's arm to begin the trudge home. The coach had racketed away, and the long road leading to nowhere was empty. There was a dusting of frost on the grass, a sharp chill in the air. Winter was coming rapidly.

"You're walking too fast, Hubert," Ada said crossly. She had short, plump legs and took two steps to his one.

"I have to be at the bank. I've wasted enough time." Hubert turned his pale, solemn face to her. "I hope we are now to have a rest from social activities. I couldn't understand why you had to house all those people, Ada. Sir John and Lady Devenish and the daughter would have been enough. Not all the followers."

Ada panted and sighed.

"Yes, it was too many. But it seemed hospitable. Thank goodness they've gone."

"The titles went to your head," her husband grumbled.

"Well, it was an elevation to our community."

"Didn't see much elevating about those two. The wife is a mouse and the husband far too full of his own importance to make a good settler in this country."

"But handsome and charming, Hubert. The very epitome of a gentleman."

"If you want my opinion he should have stayed in his London clubs. I can't think what he is doing here."

"Adventure, Hubert. And admiration for Mr. Wakefield's concepts—"

"Nonsense. He's neither a true adventurer nor an idealist. However, it's no business of ours. I hope they were grateful for the hospitality they had, though I've no doubt they'll take it as their due. The person I'm sorry for is that nice young woman, Miss O'Connor."

"Kate. Oh dear, yes. The captain's going to jilt her. He's besotted with the daughter. Now, there's an odd one, Hubert. I've never met her like before."

"Over-breeding," Hubert said succinctly. "Plenty of that in the gentry."

Ada giggled, with a touch of malice.

"Poor Captain Oxford. He'll be quite out of his depth. Imagine Miss Celina cooking a meal in a camp oven. Oh dear, oh dear." Ada giggled more, and held her husband's arm possessively. "We do better than that, don't we, my dear? We understand each other."

At last the exhausting journey by coach was over. Kate was never so thankful to get out of a vehicle that had rocked precariously over dry land and plunged dangerously through streams and river fords. Lady Devenish had shut her eyes tightly at the worst moments. She hadn't uttered a sound but her small white hands had clung like birds' claws to Kate's arm. Celina had been less controlled; she had screamed half in panic, half in fearful excitement. Miss Pugh, with Emily on one side of her and her nephew Daniel on the other, had remained stoical. She was a great support, Kate thought, practical, unflappable, even-tempered, although not to be taken advantage of. The round, little figure wrapped in the good tweed cloak, with a curious tweed bonnet to match, was stability in this insecure rocking world. Kate was sunk far enough in her own misery without wanting hysterical companions.

Sir John and Captain Oxford had elected to ride their own

horses, and kept regularly in touch with the coach, especially at river crossings. Kate felt a stirring of pride whenever the two handsome figures came in sight. Celina behaved in an irritating fashion, waving and laughing and shouting to Henry. It amused her to think she was being a true pioneer woman. But she would tire of it, Kate thought cynically. She would tire of good, sober Henry, too, which was the tragedy. When was Henry going to come to his senses? Kate blinked away tears. Miss Pugh's sharp eyes were watching.

By the time they reached Timaru, after a night's stay at a roadside inn in Ashburton where the horses were changed, they were all bone-sore from the jolting and too weary for politeness. Their eyes were tired from gazing at the endless flat country, rabbit brown, glistening in the sun, then fading to a depressing faded beige as the sun sank. There was nothing out there, Lady Devenish cried in desperation. It was an empty and limitless wilderness. Daniel pointed out pale blobs of sheep, and once or twice a thin waver of smoke from a homestead. But the landscape was virtually empty, Lady Devenish insisted. And the wind howled from the dazzling mountains. Whatever were they all doing there?

They were lucky to have each other, Kate said stoutly, as they jolted along in that most primitive of vehicles, a bullock cart. Miss Pugh and Daniel would be leaving them for the Pugh homestead, but fortunately it was no more than five or six miles from Avalon. Or so Daniel said, and he, with his solemn face and steady eyes, was the expert among them. The oldest, too, in a strange way.

"You must ride over for dinner," Lady Devenish said, conjuring up a vision of silver and lighted candles and napery as snowy as the peaks of the mountains. Such a scene was surely impossible in this desolation. "My husband said we would have frequent dinner parties," and added, less certainly, "though who is to come—"

"People call at well-known homesteads," Daniel said. "Cadets, shepherds, sometimes a whole family in a bullock waggon."

"Without being invited?" Lady Devenish exclaimed.

"You couldn't invite them, ma'am. They just turn up. My mother and father always said that you must offer hospitality to travellers."

Lady Devenish put her handkerchief to her face, as if she could smell the ripe odour of unwashed intruders. Celina gave her high-pitched laugh.

"How interesting, Mama. Like a lucky box."

"What about the village?" Kate asked. "There must be a minister. A schoolmaster. And others." She couldn't bring herself to say tradesmen for fear of shocking Lady Devenish further. But who else could there be?

"Who lives in the village, Daniel?" Miss Pugh asked comfortably.

"It's like Miss O'Connor said. There's the Reverend Hope and the schoolteacher, Miss Morrison. And Pat O'Brien who keeps the pub."

"Pub?" said Lady Devenish faintly.

"The public house, ma'am. The inn. Then there are four or five cottages where farm labourers live with their families. There's a blacksmith and a baker and a dry goods store. The church has a steeple, and a window you can look through and see the lake."

"Thank you, Daniel, that was interesting," Miss Pugh said. "It all sounds very cosy."

"A complete metropolis," Lady Devenish murmured, her voice too weary for sarcasm.

"Imagine a church with a steeple," Celina said. "That's where I'll be married."

It was starlight when they at last reached Avalon, although the stars, trembling in the dark sky, were almost eclipsed by the luminous snowpeaks, as cold as death, that rose ahead of them. It was from them that the wind came, bending the tops of the black fir trees and rustling the coarse snow grass and tussocks. It carried the chill of the snow. Kate had been shivering ever since the sun had set and the strange landscape had darkened, and especially since Sir John and Captain Oxford had ridden ahead to warn the household of their arrival.

What household? Kate wondered miserably. She had been so

unhappy since leaving Christchurch and the warmth of Ada Collins's house, and now, in this dark melancholy landscape, she was acutely lonely. The last lights of cottages had long since vanished. Miss Pugh and Daniel had been dropped at a tumbledown gate leading to a vaguely glimpsed low house among trees. It had looked to be little more than a cabin, but Miss Pugh had set off bravely, her cape flying in the wind.

After that the hideously uncomfortable bullock cart had seemed empty and far too draughty. Emily had fallen asleep, her head on Kate's shoulder. Opposite, Lady Devenish was a slim crouched shadow, her face pressed down into her collar. Celina's hair had become unpinned and tossed about her face in uncontrolled skeins. The driver sat up on his box, a solid figure, though diminished in the immense landscape. He occasionally cracked his whip but never spoke. Now that Miss Pugh had gone and the men had ridden ahead no one spoke. Emily mercifully slept, the three women were too weary and appalled to say a word.

They were all in a freezing, aching wilderness. It had been a terrible journey. Could there be a house with welcome lights at the end of this bumpy, rock-strewn road?

I should have been riding beside Henry, thought Kate. Then my spirits would have been undefeatable.

"Ha!" The sudden eruption of sound from the driver made them all jump. "Ahead, missus. Avalon."

Kate could make out a thin avenue of leafless trees, a glimpse of steel—lake water?—then some outbuildings, and beyond them the sprawling shape of the house, windows dimly alight. Dogs were barking. A horse neighed. The night was no longer empty of living creatures. The driver cracked his whip, and the cart lurched.

"Are we home?" asked Emily, stirring.

"Home!" whispered Lady Devenish unbelievingly. "Where is home?"

Two slim forms came leaping down the track.

"Emily!" shouted Jonnie. "Are you there, Em?"

Emily leaned excitedly over the side of the cart.

"Jonnie! Who's that with you?"

"That's Honi. He's my friend."

"What a funny name."

"He's a Maori. He helps Pa and Lee Fong and me. Squire's here, Em. And Captain Oxford. We've got fires lit. It's ever so grand indoors. Lee Fong has cooked supper. It's nice here. Pa and me like it. Excuse me, ma'am, you have to get out here." He was speaking to Lady Devenish. "Honi and I will show you the way up to the house. Don't stumble on rocks. There are a lot of rocks about. Volcanic, Pa says. Isn't it interesting? There's an awful lot to learn. But Honi knows. He's always lived here. It's his country, really."

There was a log fire burning in the dining room and in the large sitting room. Fires were lit in the bedrooms upstairs, too, Sir John said, welcoming his shivering wife and daughter, smiling at Kate and giving Emily an affectionate embrace.

He seemed very pleased with himself. He hoped the long journey hadn't been too much for the ladies, but now they were here they would appreciate the comfort of the house.

Lee Fong had made plenty of hot soup, which would be followed by mutton chops, Chinese style, with plenty of rice.

"Where is Henry?" Celina asked. She looked wan and spiritless and sulky.

Surely if Henry saw her like this he would realise that she was far from being a goddess, Kate thought.

"He's rubbing down the horses. The army's taught him to attend to his mount before himself. An admirable practice in a country where we wouldn't get far without horses."

"We had bullocks today," Emily said excitedly. "They were as slow as snails."

"But they brought you safely here. The driver can have a meal in the kitchen. Jonas will see he gets a bed for the night. Iris, my dear, you haven't noticed that our furniture has arrived. Don't you see the Chinese cabinet, your favourite piece?"

Lady Devenish glanced indifferently at the beautiful red lacquer cabinet, so strangely come to rest in this colonial drawing room.

"Oh, how wrong it is here," she murmured fretfully, and

added, "John, I'm completely exhausted. Celina is, too. Will someone show us to our rooms?"

Sir John gave a jovial laugh.

"This isn't a house full of servants, Iris. We'll do what's possible about engaging them later. In the meantime perhaps Kate would like to explore and decide which rooms you are to have. Kate, you haven't said a word."

Indeed Kate had not, for Henry had just come in, and she had seen that once more his gaze was only for Celina. He looked concerned and anxious. It was no use encouraging that young lady to think she was being martyred. If she was going to live in this country and make somebody a good wife she had to get used to enduring hardships cheerfully, and not stand there looking like a dying duck.

With her usual honesty Kate thought that she must be doing the same herself, although her present hardship was not physical but mental. She had a very badly bruised heart.

"I'm longing to see the house, Sir John," she said. "I think we'd all like to go upstairs and take off our coats, and wash. Do we take lamps or candles?"

"Candles. They're on the hall table in enamel candlesticks, just as in an English house, eh? There are seven bedrooms. I think Lady Devenish should have the big front one, it has a superb view of the Alps. You can decide the other ones among yourselves. We have plenty of fires, but I'm afraid no hot water at the moment."

"And only a Chinaman in the kitchen," Lady Devenish said in horror.

"He's a capable fellow, Lady Devenish," said Henry. "He'll have hot water for you in the morning. I'm afraid it's a matter of making do in the colonies. You don't mind, do you, Celina? You said you like adventure."

"I think it's horrible!" Celina wailed. "Today has been worse than the ship." She ran across the room and flung herself into Henry's arms, nuzzling her face against his shoulder. "Don't mind my bad temper, darling Henry. I'm only so nearly dead!"

Kate turned away. She couldn't stand that foolish beatific expression on Henry's face.

"Come upstairs, Lady Devenish," she said. "I'll lead the way. Come, Emily. I think a bowl of soup in bed is the thing for you."

Lady Devenish followed, hugging her arms about her. "Where is this room with the wonderful view of the Alps? To tell the truth, I hate the mountains. They frighten me. So cold. I suppose I'm a coward. Do they frighten you, Kate? No, of course they don't. Nothing does."

"Kiss me, Henry!" Celina whispered, lifting her blanched face and hungry mouth.

Her mother gave a cry, apparently from shock at her daughter's bad behaviour. But no, it was because an odd little figure had appeared in the doorway. A blue smock, a grinning yellow face, a long outlandish pigtail.

"Dinner velly leddy, boss," Lee Fong announced.

In spite of her desperate tiredness Kate could not sleep that night. The dinner had been good enough, a rich soup made from the red-legged swamp bird, the pukeko, that strutted about marshy ground and creeks, and then the mutton chops served with a savoury rice. After that there was home-made bread and a kind of cottage cheese, which Lee Fong had made, also. He was, no doubt, a useful man, but Sir John promised to find a suitable female housekeeper as soon as he could.

"Not a Maori," Lady Devenish begged.

"These brown girls learn well, I believe," Sir John said. "But I promise you, my dear, if you will be happier with a white woman you shall have one."

"I really only want dear Mary Lodden," Lady Devenish said, wiping her eyes. "I'm sorry to be so stupid, I'm a little over-wrought tonight. It was such a long journey. Nightmarish. I shall never forget it."

"You will when you see the sun shining in the morning."

"I think not," Lady Devenish spoke with finality. She rose. "Excuse me, I really must retire. Celina, you must come up soon. You look like a ghost."

But this was no longer true. Celina, sitting opposite Henry, had become animated, her eyes taking on their lambent shine. Kate wondered involuntarily how long she would stay in her own room tonight.

On retiring, Kate tried not to listen, but found it impossible not to do so. The wretched girl was still her responsibility. Celina's room was just across the passage. She had chosen it because it faced the drive and the poplar avenue, and she would be able to watch whatever comings and goings there were in this lonely spot. Even if it were only a shepherd or a swagman or the vicar from the little wooden steepled church in the village, it would be some kind of company. Celina had got back her restlessness and prowled about opening cupboards, demanding that her bags be brought up, that she at least be able to brush her hair, even if she had had to wash in cold water.

Emily was in the little room next to Kate, and already asleep. She was only a servant's child, Lady Devenish had protested. Was she to live *en famille*?

"Yes," said Sir John. There would be no argument.

The big front bedroom was spacious and almost beautiful, with the long windows that encompassed the majesty of the Alps. But Lady Devenish had drawn the curtains, and had crouched over the fire for a long time before consenting to undress and get into bed. By that time Celina's door was shut, and Kate did not care to spy on her. The wooden floors creaked. She would surely hear if the girl slipped out to find Henry's room.

Then she had decided that it would be humiliating to be discovered by Henry, jealously pursuing her rival, so she buried her head in the soft feather pillow and determined to sleep. She, too, as Sir John had predicted, would feel better when the sun shone in the morning. Poor Sir John, he was so gallantly trying to keep up the spirits of his forlorn women. One must support him. But how achingly different from her anticipation this journey into the wilds had been. If it had been only she and Henry in their new home...

Kate turned angrily in bed. The wind was battering at the windows. She would never hear footsteps on the creaking floor or a closing door. Anyway, she didn't care for Henry any more. After the way he had looked at Celina, what sort of a man was he?

It was different in the morning. The sun did shine, making a pale light over the pastureland, the thin, leafless young poplars, the humped tussocks permanently bent into crouching positions by the relentless wind, the obtruding volcanic rocks and the stiff snow grass. The mountain range was dazzlingly blue and white, with dark shadows running down the vast chasms and ravines. The foothills stretching for lonely miles towards the grandeur of the heights seemed friendly in comparison, sloping gently in their dun colours, low enough for grazing sheep to climb. There was a glimpse, too, of the lake in the distance. A track ran down to it, Sir John had said. There was a small boat shed, and a boat. They could go fishing in the spring and summer, and have lakeside picnics. Swim, too, though he believed the water was perishingly cold even in mid-summer. There were many water birds.

Kate hoped she could have a horse of her own. That would mean a great deal. And later, when Henry came to his senses—already she was forgetting how she had hated and despised him last night—she would ride over to his station to see the progress being made with his house. He must soon realise that it was entirely ludicrous to take a nervous and delicate girl like Celina to a primitive house in the wilderness.

What would she write to Cousin Mabel and to the Irish aunts? How explain Henry's temporary defection? Of course it need not be mentioned. It would all be over before the letters arrived at their destination.

There was going to be no time for letter writing today. Kate put on a sensible working dress and set about the unpacking, a task which was going to take the entire morning since no one offered to help. Of course neither Lady Devenish nor Celina had ever packed or unpacked trunks in their life. Nor had they been expected to do so. They would soon learn differently since it was obvious that ladies' maids did not abound in this country. If

Celina thought of taking her whole wardrobe to the usual type of pioneer cottage there would be no room for herself or her husband. And did she realise she would have to wash and starch the shirtwaists and petticoats and bed linen herself, and hang it on bushes to dry?

Kate scowled and sighed as she shook out the silk and satin gowns and hung them on lavender-scented hangers. There was plenty of room in this house. It really was a fine building according to colonial standards. The furniture left by the previous owners was of good quality and would be enhanced by the fine pieces the Devenishes had transported. The curtains were made of Nottingham lace and the wallpapers showed excellent taste. Obviously the previous mistress had put her heart into this home. One wondered what had made her leave it. Weary of colonial life, Sir John had indicated. But the person who had furnished her house with such care had surely meant to spend many years in it. The garden, too, showed evidence of careful planning. There was a pergola and a path leading to a small summer house, with a thick bank of rhododendrons to shelter it from the constant north wind. Someone had meant to see the roses bloom, and the syringa shed its richly scented blossom. What had happened? Had the lady suddenly become overpoweringly homesick? Had she urged her husband to go home? Or had he uprooted her, taking her back to his English pleasures?

Halfway through the morning Kate was startled at her work by a scream coming from Lady Devenish's room. Lady Devenish had had her breakfast in bed and said that she was still deeply weary and would go back to sleep. Whatever could have awakened her and made her scream?

Kate ran across the passage and into the big bedroom, to find Lady Devenish sitting bolt upright pointing at the window.

"I thought I must have dreamed it in the night when I heard a cat howling!" she babbled. "But suddenly there it was, on the window sill, trying to get in. It must have jumped out of that tree. Look, Kate. See if you can see it."

Kate looked down at the empty garden. The young gum tree

seemed to be empty of life except for a large bird that flew away. A cat on the window sill? Was Lady Devenish, in her weariness, having hallucinations?

"What was it like?" she asked.

"A great black creature. It had a bent ear, and a crooked white stripe down its face. It stared at me. It *demanded* to be let in. It looked evil."

"Not evil, surely, Lady Devenish. Don't you like cats?"

"I abhor them. Oh, a Persian kitten perhaps. But not that great, rough colonial specimen."

Kate was inclined to smile. If they were threatened by nothing worse than a cat, things were not too bad.

"We'll enquire at lunchtime. There are probably stable cats. Jonnie will know."

It was Lee Fong, however, who knew. He gave a broad smile and said, "Oh, yes, missy, that would be Old Bill. He belong Missy Henshaw. He's a velly gleedy animal. Hang alound my kitchen. Want food, food, food, all the time. He velly bossy cat. He must stay outdoors."

"I should think so," Lady Devenish said, with a shudder. "If there's anything I don't want it's a cat jumping on my face when I'm sleeping." The menacing sound of the cat's howls seemed still to be in her ears.

"Then keep your windows shut," said Sir John. "At least until we teach this devil cat manners."

"Mama, what a thing to get upset about," Celina said. "One would have thought it was a wild pig. Henry has told me that those are the animals to be treated with respect. We're going to look for one this afternoon. Can you imagine? Although I think Henry is only teasing me, as wild pigs live in the bush, and unless we can find some bush in these bare hills there won't be any. Perhaps we can find some mountain goats instead?" She gave her brilliant wild smile. "Don't you approve of me for being a pioneer lady, Papa?"

"You're going riding?" Sir John asked.

"You wouldn't expect me to walk over all those rocks and tussocks, would you? Henry is leaving tomorrow, so he wants me to see some of the country first. I really saw more than enough yesterday, but of course it wasn't in his company. Perhaps he thinks he can add some magic to it. I certainly hope he can because so far I think it's dreadful. The end of the world."

She gave a shrug of her shoulders, not looking in the least unhappy. It was all a game to her, Kate thought. Poor, gullible Henry.

After a moment Sir John said, "Get Jonas to saddle the roan mare. She's the quietest. I believe Mrs. Henshaw rode her. There's her side saddle, too. Kate, we'll have to find a mount for you, but we have only one side saddle at present."

"I rode bareback with Irish cousins when I was quite young," Kate said. "I don't think I need a side saddle."

She couldn't fail to notice the gleam of admiration in Sir John's eyes. She had been certain that he would like a sporting young woman. Had they been at Leyte Manor he would have taken her hunting. In spite of her desperate disappointment with Henry and her unhappiness, a twinge of excitement went through her.

She was impelled to go on, "Will you recognise a wild pig, Celina? Or will you mistake a sheep for one?"

"Kate, Kate, Kate, you're jealous!" Celina cried gleefully.

"No, she is not," Sir John said. "Because she is coming riding with me. We'll find our way down to the lake, Kate."

But Kate' had caught Lady Devenish's look of fear. She was in a state of nerves, poor lady. She should not be left in the strange house alone. The demon cat might attack her. The yellow-faced man in the kitchen might wield a chopper. The great wall of mountains might come tumbling down.

"Some day I would like to, Sir John. But I think today Lady Devenish and I have enough to do with the unpacking. And has anyone seen Emily?"

"She's with her brother and that Maori boy," said Celina. "I think, Mama, you will have to take her out of pinafores and put her in trousers. She's going to be a tomboy."

It was Sir John who answered briskly. "Nonsense! She will be decently dressed all the time. Kate, see to it."

"John, I told you, you're going to spoil that child," Lady Devenish complained.

"If bringing her up as an educated young lady is spoiling her, you have a point. I believe there's an excellent girls' school in Timaru. I intend sending her there." Sir John's face was stern. "No objections, pray, Iris. This is my duty. But I also love the child," he added under his breath. Lady Devenish could not let the matter rest.

"She has a brother, John. Shouldn't he be equally well-treated?"

"Jonnie? I've talked to his father. We've both decided the boy is happy where he is learning the skills of farm life. He isn't as bright as his sister. Nor is he so distressed by the loss of his mother. He's a good country lad. But Emily has potential."

"Then if you have Emily you won't mind me marrying Henry, Papa," Celina said boldly.

"Celina!" her mother cried. "Is this true? You must surely be teasing us."

Celina pressed her fingers to her lips, sputtering with laughter. Then she began dancing round the room, her face alight with wild glee.

"It is true, Mama. That is if I say yes. And of course I shall do so if Henry—"

"If Henry what?" Kate asked, her voice ominous.

"If he agrees to certain preferences of mine. Why should a man make all the conditions for one's life? You must agree to that principle, Kate. I am sure you wouldn't be a timid, obedient little mouse of a wife."

"Celina, I can't think what you're talking about," Lady Devenish said distractedly.

"Oh yes, you can, Mama. Do you really think I'm interested in discovering the difference between a wild pig and a sheep? Do I look that kind of woman? Think about it, Papa. If Emily is always to wear silks and muslins so am I. And how can I in a cabin in the hills? Henry has to realise that."

Sir John turned to Kate, as Celina left the room. "What does she mean? Do you know?"

"I think so." Anger filled Kate. "She is not going to allow Henry to live in the country. She is going to tell him she won't be a sheep-farmer's wife."

"Then what is she planning to do? She didn't sound as if she meant to send the fellow packing."

Kate shook her head miserably.

"I think she is going to persuade him to be a city man. Like Mr. Collins and Mr. Fitzgerald and others we met in Christchurch. Living in comfort."

"Ah!" said Sir John thoughtfully. "Captain Oxford behind a bank counter or in the town council offices. I can't imagine it. He's an outdoor man, a soldier, and adventurer. He would be a fool to agree."

"He already is a fool," Kate said. She tried to speak without bitterness, but was unable to do so.

She knew Henry too well to be mistaken. That evening he had the grace to ask to speak to her alone, and said that he was abandoning his plans to buy land in the higher foothills.

"It would be much too hard a life for Celina. She is so beautiful, she must have a proper setting."

"And what is that?" Kate asked with hostility.

"Why, a drawing room, of course. Good furniture. Servants. Plenty of company. She is too delicate and too sensitive for this bleak country." His face took on its maddeningly besotted look. "I want her always to be beautifully dressed and cherished like a flower, a rose."

Kate's face hardened, contempt was her only refuge against tears. And she would not cry before him.

"I never thought to hear you talk such sentimental nonsense, Henry. What good is a rose to a man like you? You needed a prickly thistle like me."

"Not a thistle, Kate," he protested.

"But you have asked her to marry you, I presume. And she has agreed on her own terms?"

"She has made me realise they are eminently sensible."

"For her, naturally, they are. But for you? You never intended to become a soft town man. Won't you find the price too high?"

"For having Celina as my wife?" he asked in astonishment.

She stared back at him. "Oh, Henry, you blind foolish man. You have been caught."

She tried to show the love she had so recently felt for him in her eyes, but it would not be summoned up. At present she could feel nothing but contempt and bitterness.

"You have not been honourable, Henry. But I will try to forgive you because I'm afraid you are going to get your deserts."

"Kate, don't be so hard. I had never met anyone like Celina in my whole life. I daresay I am a lovesick fool, and probably a laughing stock. I can't help it. I must have her."

Kate felt a stirring of sympathy, and of self-blame. She should have told Henry more of the truth before he had become so smitten. But would he have listened even then? He certainly would not do so now.

You may need to lock her in the house. Or even in her bedroom, she wanted to say.

But it was too late. He would only think her consumed by jealousy.

"When do you intend to marry?" she asked formally.

"In the spring. When I have a house ready for her, and work for myself. She will wait here for me until then. Look after her, Kate. Is that too much to ask?"

Kate thought of the long snowy winter ahead, of being, as she had been on board ship, a prisoner of two women of nervous disposition. And with no spring to look forward to for herself.

9

Captain Oxford had scarcely gone, galloping down the avenue of thin poplars and disappearing round the bend of the road, than winter began in earnest.

The mountains disappeared behind a thick grey flannel of cloud. A drizzle that turned into icy rain, driven against the windows by the rising wind, kept them all indoors. The world, with the mountains invisible, grew infinitely smaller.

Lee Fong had taken the bullock cart to Mossbridge for provisions. The dry goods store had plenty of flour, sugar, coffee and tea, rice, dried peas, barley and lentils, and numerous other commodities that might be in short supply if it were a bad winter with heavy snowstorms. In the store-house at Avalon there were smoked hams and venison, sacks of potatoes, wheat for grinding, and sharp-tasting winter apples and pears. They would never lack freshly killed mutton. It was the staple diet of New Zealanders. Even in a snowfall an old ewe could be dug out and slaughtered. There was no danger of starving at Avalon. There were speckled hens that laid brown eggs, and goats for milking if the three cows dried up before the spring. It had been a well-planned, well-run station, which made it all the more puzzling that the young Henshaws should have abandoned it and gone back to England.

Homesickness, said Kate, who had begun suffering a sharp bout of that malady after Henry's departure and the cruel end to her dreams. She was longing intolerably for the soft green hills of Ireland, the dripping trees, the scents shaken out of the flowering shrubs in the evening breeze.

Boredom, said Sir John. Henshaw had been a young man with too much money and sudden enthusiasms that waned. It must have been hard on his wife to be twice uprooted.

No, the wife would be the one who would have wanted to leave, Lady Devenish insisted. She seemed to have worked so diligently at the house, covering the walls with carefully chosen wallpaper, hanging curtains and laying warm red carpets, but she had also lined the walls of the passages with sad water-colours, the lake always grey, the mountains menacing. Obviously she had been unhappy. She would have been the one who persuaded her husband to leave.

Then Lady Devenish made the curious remark that sometimes she thought Laura Henshaw was still there. She had fancied she had heard a baby crying. Her husband said sharply that that would have been Old Bill whose nightly laments everyone had now heard. The animal objected strongly to being shut outdoors. Possibly he should have been kept down at the stables or in the men's quarters, where Jonas, Jonnie, Honi and the shepherds lived; but the stubborn creature craved for luxury, especially the luxury of the best bedroom. Lady Devenish was afraid that one night he would actually break the window pane and come leaping in on her.

Celina, who after Henry's departure had sunk into one of her states of apathy, said that Laura Henshaw, who must have been quite a young wife, would have refused to stay in such a windy, desolate spot if she had had any sense. She was sure that people could go mad here in the winter.

"Well, you are not going mad." Kate could scarcely contain her impatience. Had the pampered girl not the spirit to wait cheerfully for the spring, knowing that then she would get her heart's desire—if indeed Captain Oxford were truly that cherished object, and not merely the only personable man available. One never knew with Celina. The light went out of her when there was no man with whom to flirt.

"We're going to begin a programme of reading French and English, and also painting and needlework and music," Kate went on. She knew that this was what Sir John expected of her. At least she would not be the one to disappoint him. Emily could join in these activities. She must be kept away from the stables where she was becoming too friendly with the Maori boy, Honi. His flashing dark eyes and his black curls fascinated her. He was a nice boy, Emily assured them, even though his father had been a tattooed warrior who had fought the British soldiers. When Honi imitated the savage Maori cries, and made fearsome faces, she trembled with delicious fear.

But she was to go to school in the spring. That was Squire's order. She would wear a uniform and have a satchel of books and sleep in a dormitory with a dozen other girls. Mam would have been pleased about this, never having dreamed of anything but the humble village school for her daughter. But Emily no longer thought so much about Mam, or about poor Willie. She was completely absorbed in her new friends, Honi, funny, grinning Lee Fong, Miss Pugh and solemn Daniel, and most of all Squire with his strong arms and tender smile.

She didn't mind Lady Devenish although she thought her a poor, timid thing, she avoided Celina who scared her in an inexplicable way, she would obey Kate who was kind and pretty. But there was no one like Squire. She would follow him anywhere and do anything he wanted. If it would make him love her more she would go to this strange school and wear an ugly uniform and learn to be a lady.

She would miss Honi, however. He made her laugh. And she needed to laugh for sometimes the crashing wind against the house reminded her of the waves beating against the ship, and then the misery of Mam's and Willie's deaths did come back. This made her seek Kate's company. Kate, unlike Lady Devenish or Celina, had comforting arms and a warm bosom. How could that stuffy Captain Oxford have been so stupid as not to marry her?

It was virtually a household of women, Sir John said. So they must begin going to church on Sunday and making the acquaintance of other families. They must live the "good neighbour" life of pioneers.

There was also another reason. Domestic help was needed in the house, and there was the possibility that someone in the village might be available. Going to church was the way to get to know people.

"Who on earth would there be in that tiny place?" Lady Devenish grumbled. "Trained maids? Housekeepers? Oh dear!"

"We can investigate," Sir John said serenely. "Anyway, there's the excellent Miss Pugh whom we must see again. And her boy, Daniel. He seemed a promising lad. Emily thought so, I'm sure."

His eyes twinkled. He was trying so hard, Kate thought, to get them all cheerfully through this first difficult week, and heaven knew, he must be suffering from the transition from his familiar world as much as any of them. Still, he had brought them here.

"Do we have to dress up for a dozen yokels?" Celina complained. "And go in that dreadful bullock cart?" she suddenly asked in dismay.

"You will travel by bullock cart until the buggy arrives. It is ordered and should be here in a few weeks. Personally, I think it much more friendly to travel as other people hereabouts have to. Don't you, Kate? We are all equals in this country. Didn't Mr. Wakefield say so?"

"But you don't believe a word of that," Celina said shrewdly, the lurking hostility for her father in her eyes again. "That's for others, not yourself. If I go to that dismal church I shall ride."

It ended with Lady Devenish, Kate, Emily, and Jonnie in the bullock cart driven by Jonas, and Sir John and Celina following, their horses at a walk. Jonnie said that he had invited Honi to come, but Honi refused to believe that a God was in the sky. The Maori gods, he said, lived in mountain caves, and lightning-struck trees, and in the lake, or even behind that particularly large boulder on the hillside. That was *tapu*. Which meant you mustn't go near it, Jonnie explained. Honi was a bit scary sometimes.

"Do you believe him?" asked Kate.

"No, but I think it better to do as he says," Jonnie said cautiously.

Lady Iris said in her thin voice, "You must take no notice of heathens. It is your duty to make poor Honi believe in our God. Isn't that so, Kate? Why do the missionaries come here, otherwise?"

"I sometimes think—" Kate began, then stopped. No use to voice the daring thought that no one really had the right to deprive any human being of his own religion. Bishop Selwyn would never have agreed with her, nor any of the other clergy and missionaries. But lately God had seemed awfully far away and remote—if He had not always seemed so to her. She had to admit that she had almost always found His will very hard to accept.

Fortunately it had stopped raining and the little church was surprisingly full. One would have thought there would have been only a handful of people, but twenty or more faces turned to look curiously at the new family which had arrived in their midst.

An important family, it was rumoured. Just the sort needed to leaven the lump of farm labourers and tradesmen and publicans.

They were not the only newcomers today for the English spinster, Miss Pugh, was there, accompanied by her scrubbed and unwilling nephew, Daniel.

Poor Miss Pugh. For all her obvious common sense she was never going to be able to exist in that derelict homestead, helped only by a boy scarcely in his teens. She held her sharp and stubborn chin high, it was true, but she must already have discovered the extreme hardship of her situation.

It was good to hear her cry of pleasure in the hushed interior of the little church when she saw the family from Avalon arriving.

She hastily turned back to her hymn book and gave Daniel a slight cuff to make him do the same. His eyes had been on the little girl in the fur-trimmed blue coat, which she had begun to outgrow.

There was certainly a stir of excitement in the little wooden church with the window over the nave that gave a view of the lake.

The minister was a young man, fair-haired with a correctly devout manner. Clearly he too had not long arrived from England or he would not have kept that fair skin. He did a circuit of small country churches riding his elderly black gelding from parish to parish. But Mossbridge, since it boasted a vicarage, a single-storey building with a verandah, was his headquarters. He rang the tinny bell in the squat wooden steeple every second Sunday at eleven in the morning. On alternate Sundays he visited the more isolated stations, some of which had small private chapels.

Kate had read that information on the notice board in the porch.

> The Reverend Edward Hope will take divine service in this church every second Sunday. Baptisms, weddings and funerals can be arranged at such times as the vicar is not absent at Geraldine, Temuka or Mount Peel.

What a nice but rather fraught young man, Kate thought, looking up at the boyish face above the white surplice—and realising that the Reverend Hope was giving the Avalon party a speculative look before resuming the impartial benevolence of a servant of God. At least they could help him with the singing. She had a good clear voice, so had Celina, and Sir John's baritone could not be ignored.

And it was so good to see dear Miss Pugh. Aunt Tab. One could hardly wait for the service to be over to get outside and talk to her.

This was an inordinately long time later, for the Reverend Hope enjoyed rhetoric and had a surprisingly resonant voice for someone of such delicate appearance. Emily and Jonnie fidgeted, but Celina gave the impression of drinking in the young man's words. Kate thought cynically that his agreeable appearance would mean more to her than his sermon, and wondered what was ahead for them all, this winter in a strange land.

Her apprehension was renewed when the small congregation was outside in the bitter wind. Jonnie and Emily had found a grave, it seemed. Yes, there was a small burying ground, the Reverend Hope told them. He had made a point of welcoming the newcomers and talking to them as formally as if they stood in the porch of a well-ordered English church. Was he hoping to be invited back to Avalon for Sunday dinner—and the opportunity of talking exclusively to Celina, at whom he kept stealing glances?

"But we have not had many interments yet," he said. "Poor Mrs. Henshaw and her baby. That was very sad. Then we give a decent burial to the odd tramp, too, who dies on the road. Swaggers, as they call them. I have only been here a few months so I am still learning the dialect."

He gave a charming boyish smile which nobody noticed, for Lady Devenish was whispering, "Laura Henshaw dead! Why didn't you tell me, John? She must have died having her baby at Avalon. Oh, how dreadfully sad! Oh, I hate this country!"

"That's the very reason I didn't tell you." Sir John had put his arm round his wife's huddled body in a warm, protective gesture. "Because it would have prejudiced you against the house."

"Oh dear, have I been clumsy?" asked the young vicar anxiously. "There were complications, I believe. Mrs. Henshaw would just as likely have died in London with the best doctors, Lady Devenish. Death is as natural as birth, do remember. Man cometh up like a flower..."

"We have had enough of death," Lady Devenish said sharply. "On the ship. Now here." She shuddered violently. "It's so cold. Take me home, John."

"What's this?" asked Miss Pugh, bustling over. Her face already had the reddened look of a country woman exposed to the weather. She had fitted into the landscape immediately, Kate thought admiringly. "Why, poor Lady Devenish looks frozen. Now why don't you all come back with Daniel and me for a hot cup of tea? We're only a mile away. Actually, Sir John, I would value a word of advice from you."

"On what, dear lady?" Sir John asked courteously.

"On Daniel's and my future. I have found the sorriest mess here."

It appeared that Miss Pugh could not afford the passage money back to England for herself and Daniel. Nor did she want to go so quickly. She had a great fighting spirit and was sure this country could be conquered. But not from a primitive sod cottage with a leaking roof and a smoking chimney, nor from a pitifully small holding with little stock. If the river hadn't taken her brother and his wife, sheer despair would have succeeded in doing so. Poor Lawrence had never been a practical man. Daniel had existed on the kindness of neighbours until her arrival. No wonder he was so white-faced and serious.

The two of them were put in the bullock cart and were on their way to Avalon without argument. Sir John could scarcely hide his satisfaction. Here was the opportunity not only to demonstrate the traditional hospitality of settlers, but to solve his own problems. He liked and admired Miss Pugh, a sturdy, strong little woman. He would ask her to remain at Avalon as housekeeper. Daniel was a good lad and could be employed outdoors.

Looking at the ruddy face framed by the brown bonnet, Sir John smiled at Miss Pugh with compelling warmth. She would stay. He knew his persuasiveness.

He had reason to be more relieved each day by the way things were going. Celina's future was decided and he would soon be rid of his troublesome daughter. The sooner the better, judging by the way the young parson had looked at her. Kate was proving to be the greatest blessing, and Emily would take the place of the daughter he now regarded as lost. He was going to enjoy being a station holder. He had superb health and could face all kinds of weather. He could quickly learn about sheep, breeding and mustering and branding and lambing. As for Iris, his abnormally nervous wife, if she felt haunted by the death of a young woman and her day-old baby she could move to another bedroom where death had not occurred. Kate would organise that. He would have the front room himself. It was directly opposite Kate's. That thought slid into his mind unbidden. Yet not entirely unbidden. He had been watching her ever since the defection of Captain Oxford and had admired her good sense and self-discipline.

He must not be over-critical of his wife's nervousness. He knew himself what it was to be in a haunted house. And he also knew that nothing would ever compensate him for what he had had to give up.

Unless—and he encouraged the thought to linger—it was the young Irishwoman, Kate O'Connor.

Lady Devenish must have caught a chill, for on their return home from church she sat in her bedroom, huddled and shivering.

Kate put a match to the fire, and begged her to sit near it.

"Unless you would come downstairs, Lady Devenish. The drawing room is warm. The fire was lit an hour ago. And Miss Pugh would like to talk to you."

"To hear how she, too, is being taken in by my husband's lies?"

"About staying here as housekeeper? Oh no, Lady Devenish, she has seen the house and admires it. How could he take her in about that?"

"In the same way that he took me in." Lady Devenish's face was pinched and narrow, her eyes full of resentment. "He never told me that this was a dead woman's bedroom."

"But, my dear lady—" Kate knelt beside the little figure. "In every room of an old house at home haven't there been deaths?"

"This is not an old house. Far from it."

"All the same—"

"It cries with grief. I hear it," Lady Devenish said starkly. "Oh, I know you think me mad, Kate. Like my daughter. She can be mad, too. My husband blames me. He says Celina has inherited my genes. I have had some strange ancestors, I know. But I myself am perfectly sane. And Celina only uses her—her eccentricity to get what she sets her heart on. She has strong desires."

Did Captain Oxford understand that, Kate wondered. Should one warn him? Or leave him to his deserts.

He would never listen anyway.

"Kate, you're not listening to me."

"Yes, I am."

"I'm telling you that it isn't from me that Celina gets her nature. It's from her father. He will have his way, no matter what. Even submitting us delicate women to such a cruel, lonely life."

"Lady Devenish, Sir John did say you could choose another bedroom where there hasn't been an unhappy circumstance. Where Old Bill doesn't sit on the window sill and bully you, as you say. Indeed I don't care for a cat howling in the night myself. It's worse than the little owls and the keas."

"They say the keas kill the newly born lambs," Lady Devenish said, determinedly gloomy. She was referring to the parrot-like birds with the dun-coloured feathers, the startlingly rosy underwings, and the savagely curved beaks. Inquisitive creatures that gathered round the back door for scraps, waddling about, making their harsh cries, clumsy until they swept into the majesty of their rainbow-coloured flight. Lady Devenish distrusted the new and the strange. She was perfectly right when she said that Sir John had brought them all here for his own selfish reasons. Yet one could not believe that that handsome, genial man was thoughtlessly undiscerning and cruel. His reasons must be very serious and valid ones. The dark brooding never quite vanished from his eyes, even when he smiled.

Perhaps some day he would confide in her, Kate thought. She would like to be his confidante. It would make what Lady Devenish called this cruel, lonely life more acceptable. For she, too, had her moments of bewilderment and intense isolation from all that had been familiar, as well as the crushing disappointment of Henry's fickleness. Already, at only twenty-three, she had had two chances of marriages snatched from her. Would there ever be a third? Or must she be another valiantly cheerful Miss Pugh?

"I am not going to move from the best room in the house just to please my husband," Lady Devenish was saying, her face suddenly spiteful.

"But it wasn't to please him, Lady Devenish. It was for your own peace of mind."

"Does he think I'm a coward? Oh, I am, of course. But I am determined not to be. I get afraid of the winter, I admit. So near the mountains. I am not used to mountains."

"You're still shivering, Lady Devenish. Shall I go down and get you a little brandy?"

"No, no, I can manage very well without stimulants." But a thought had occurred to her. "Kate, have we any of Celina's medicine left?"

"Yes, we have." Kate remembered putting the blue bottles in the medicine cabinet, and Sir John watching her, then locking the cabinet.

"We won't be near a doctor, Kate," he had said. "I will take charge of these powders and potions. I took the opportunity on board ship to get the advice of the ship's doctor on simple ailments such as coughs and fevers and toothache and earache and stomach ache. All the aches we mortals are subject to. You are looking at me oddly, Kate. I should have guessed that you have all that knowledge already."

"Not all of it, Sir John. But my Irish aunts did take me into the peasants' cottages and we administered a spoonful of this or a spoonful of that." She smiled. "Medicine that couldn't harm even if it was the wrong one. We found that as long as something was swallowed it went halfway to a cure."

"Exactly. I see I can trust your intelligence. All the same this small stock of medicaments is precious. We must keep the case locked so that the supplies are only used for genuine illness."

The memory of this conversation made Kate turn back to Lady Devenish.

"Are you expecting Celina to need her medicine?" she asked. "But she is so much better now that she's happy."

"She is always unpredictable. And she won't have Captain Oxford to keep her amused over the next three months."

"To keep her amused! Is that all she expects of him?"

Lady Devenish's glance was sharp and not quite direct.

"Her nature is all too frequently frivolous. Charmingly frivolous, don't you agree?"

"Captain Oxford seemed to think so."

"Exactly. Don't be bitter, Kate. He wasn't your kind of man. John and I both agreed. But what did you think of the minister today?"

The fire was growing bright and Lady Devenish was relaxing, throwing back her shawl.

"He was a good-looking young man, didn't you think?" she went on. "A younger son, I expect. Perhaps not as stalwart as a pioneer minister should be. But at least civilised, Kate. We might ask him back to dinner the next Sunday he preaches. I won't come down today. Have Emily bring me a tray up here."

"Emily?"

"Why not? Her place is in the kitchen. I won't have her ruined by my husband's foolish notions. Miss Pugh will be instructed to train her. She can become as good a servant as her mother was. I intend it. All this talk of equality. It's nonsense. Why should people be different in New Zealand? They're the same the world over. The rich and the poor, the master and the servant. It's the arrangement of society. If that collapsed, can you think of the sorry state we should all be in? And," she added, with her new slyness, "Sir John must remember where his wealth came from. I can't withdraw it, but I can remind him of it."

Goodness, the white mouse has claws and teeth, Kate thought. But she would never really stand up to Sir John for all her threats. She was too accustomed to cringing before him. She could nag him, of course. She could make constant complaints. And reserve this bravado for servants like herself. Kate realised that having pitied Lady Devenish in a sympathetic way she now disliked her. Even distrusted her.

The winter was going to be truly difficult.

10

Apart from wintry gales, cold winds that blew straight from the South Pole, it still didn't snow. The flocks of sheep with their draggled wet wool had been brought down from the high ground to winter in the valley. Their calling had become so familiar a sound that it no longer seemed melancholy. Or perhaps it was that the house was so much more cheerful now that Miss Pugh had installed herself and taken over its management. She had the good sense not to interfere with Lee Fong in the kitchen, apart from tactfully teaching him some traditional English dishes, but the rest of the house was her territory and at last the trunks and boxes brought from England were unpacked. The Georgian silver, the Bristol and Waterford glass, the Derby dinner service and the pictures and books and fine Persian rugs and delicate pieces of furniture were carefully arranged in appropriate places.

Miss Pugh's own modest possessions were brought over from Daniel's wretched place and set out in the smallest bedroom at the back of the house. The room was ample for her, she said. She and her sister had always lived in a spartan way. There was a place for her writing desk. That was the main thing. There were so many letters to write and especially now when she could relate her and Daniel's good fortune. She hadn't been able to bring herself to tell her sister of the way their poor brother and his wife must have struggled to feed their stock and themselves.

Now Daniel rode over every day or so to dole out hay for the scrubby cows and heifers and the handful of ewes left behind until they could be sold together with the small holding. He was always glad to get back to Avalon and what seemed to him its great riches.

"Your father's a good man," he said to Emily.

"Pa?"

"Oh, no, I'm daft, I mean the boss. I keep thinking he's your real father, the kind way he treats you. You living in the big house and all."

"Yes," Emily conceded. "It's a nice house. But not nearly as grand as Leyte Manor."

"Leyte Manor, what's that?" Honi asked.

"A very old and big house."

"How can a house be late? Or early either?"

They all burst into laughter, even silent Jonnie. Honi was so droll.

"It's L-e-y-t-e. I don't suppose you can spell, Honi."

"What's spell?"

"There you are, you see. You're an ignorant Maori boy."

"What's ignorant?"

"Oh, Honi, you're pretending. You know very well. You're teasing me."

"Teasing you, Miss Emily?"

Honi's eyes were limpid, his curls as black as coal. His white teeth flashed in his brown face. Emily thought him astonishingly attractive, much more so than serious Daniel with his spiky hair, and red-cheeked Jonnie.

"You don't have to call her miss, she's my sister," Jonnie said. "It's Miss Celina, Squire and the mistress, but Em's us. Like Aunt Tab and Kate."

"Oh, I made a mistake. I think she aim to be grand lady," Honi's eyes twinkled with mischief.

Emily put her head in the air.

"I do. At least Squire plans it. And I'll do anything to please him."

"As if he is your father?"

"He's not my father," she said crossly.

"Then perhaps he thinking to make you second wife," Honi said slyly. "Big chiefs have two wives, maybe even three."

Emily flew at him, grasping his glossy curls in both hands. They felt resilient and alive, while the skull beneath them was hard and warm. And he was grinning from ear to ear. She blushed and let her hands fall to her sides. She felt uneasy and discomfited, afraid she had behaved like a child. And yet she wanted to touch his curls again, more gently.

"You'd better go up to the house, Emily," Daniel said in his sober way. "Aunt Tab will be wanting you to set the table or something. You're not supposed to be in the stables."

"I'm not supposed to be a housemaid, either! Squire says so."

"But the mistress says you are to be, so you'd be better to obey. Anyway, girls have to learn about housework and things."

Jonnie looked at Emily critically. "Dan's right, Em. You're getting stuck up. Mam wouldn't have liked it."

Emily was scarlet with mortification. She wanted to fly back to the house where Squire would be sitting by the fire smoking one of his long cigars, and to throw herself against him for caresses and comfort. But she also wanted to talk and giggle with the three boys, enjoying their admiring glances at the red ribbons in her hair, and her rosy face.

It was difficult. She sensed she was always going to be in trouble and not only with the mistress who had had her way to an extent, making Emily dust, and polish the silver, and lay the long shining table in the dining room each midday and evening. She realised that she was to have to decide whether she most wanted to be a tomboy or a lady, whether to please Squire, or the mistress and Aunt Tab, or the giggling irreverent boys at their work in the stables and cowshed.

But she had found a way to escape this confusion. When she conjured up a vision of Leyte Manor, calm and unchangeable, as old as the knobbled mulberry trees in the garden and the ancient oaks in the park, her world ceased rocking. She became cocooned in her soothing dream.

Before the constantly threatening snow arrived, by good luck the postman came. He had taken delivery of the mail off the coach in Timaru and had ridden to the isolated homesteads with his precious burden. Avalon was the last stop before returning to Mossbridge to spend the night and rest his horse.

It was a day of great excitement. The first letters had arrived from home for Kate, Miss Pugh and Sir John and Lady Devenish. There were also letters from Christchurch for Sir John, and one slim envelope, sealed with wax for Celina.

Newspapers had come, too, so that they would at last be able to read what was happening in these two small islands, the North Island where Governor Grey had his residence, and Mr. Wakefield lived his chosen solitary life with his elderly, faithful bulldogs, and where there were still sporadic raids by hostile natives on settlers' homes, and the South Island where all the interest was in new arrivals, quarrels over land grants, and the eternal subject of sheep.

Celina disappeared with her letter. It would be from Henry, of course. Kate fixed her attention on her fat missives from Cousin Mabel, and the Mallow aunts. There was a parcel, too. She was longing to open it.

The aunts wrote that they were well though Aunt Dolly had been troubled with neuralgia. It had rained so much, everything was damp, and how lucky Kate was to be in the tropical sunshine. The Fenians had paid a visit to the house late one night, but had been persuaded—"It didn't take much persuading, Kate dear"—not to set fire to it, but to drink several glasses of ale instead. Then they had departed quite peaceably. "At least you won't have trouble from wretches like these in New Zealand. I am sure savages could be no worse."

Cousin Mabel wrote wittily about London life, just in case dear Kate should be homesick.

> But I am sure you have so much to divert you in a new colony. What are the ladies like? And the fashions? If I know females, there will be plenty of parties and balls, no matter how lacking in the right materials and accommo-

dation. I am sending you a package of some new silks and
ribbons from Paris, and I will expect you, my lovely Kate,
to outshine everyone. Also there are some new novels, to
amuse you. We are longing for your first letters. Have you
had an affair of the heart yet? Or is suitable material in
short supply? Giles is convinced that a new colony is mostly
inhabited by wasters, rogues, and opportunists. Escaped
convicts from Australia, also. He does so enjoy his lurid
imagination. I daresay you have encountered nobody but
the most respectable in Canterbury, the elite settlement Sir
John talked so much about. A little dull? I fancy sheep are
dull, too. But at least you have the company of your charming and civilised employer... we are simply burning with
impatience for your first letters.

Which contained Kate's happy and sanguine anticipation of a
future with Captain Oxford. How Kate wished she could call
back those optimistic letters. The thought of them caused her
intense humiliation.

"What is your news, Miss Pugh?" she asked.

Miss Pugh lifted a disappointed face, waving her sheets of
pale blue notepaper.

"This has come so far and taken so long, yet all my sister can
write about is the new curate, a hungry young man who calls
and eats enormous teas. And the plum cakes and strawberry
jam she has made for the church fête, which no doubt will be
mostly consumed by the starving curate. And the garden, of
course. It's nice to picture the garden, the stocks and delphin-
iums and carnations."

"How nostalgic that sounds," Kate sighed. "I have a letter full
of Irish rain. I admit I long for that, too. The softness of it." Kate
turned. "Do you have interesting news, Lady Devenish?"

Lady Devenish pushed her letter into her reticule.

"Nothing of any moment. This is from a cousin. I particularly
asked my friends not to try to correspond with me immediately.
The difficulties are too great." She sighed and Kate could not
help being fairly certain that there were no friends. Poor lady.
She attracted so little attention.

Sir John, riffling through his letters, as yet unopened, said
philosophically, "I seem to have only business communications.

They can wait. Where is Celina? Has she gone to pore over a love letter?"

Before anyone answered it was noticed that Emily was in tears. She was holding a parcel addressed to Mrs. Mary Lodden. Sir John cursed himself. He had meant to hide that parcel and give it to Jonas later.

But Emily was saying, "Mam's dead! How could this come?"

"Let's open it," said Kate. "I expect it's meant for you."

And so it was for there was a letter from Grandpa and books for Emily and Jonnie, and a book of the alphabet for little Willie to help him learn his letters. "He will need them if he is to become somebody in that new country, full of opportunity," Grandpa wrote, and Emily could see him vividly, a stooped figure sitting by the small fire in the familiar parlour. More vividly than she could see Mam, who was at the bottom of the sea. "Come, child," said Miss Pugh kindly. "Share the books with Daniel and Jonnie. Daniel hasn't had any letters at all."

Whatever was in Celina's letter, it had not lifted her spirits. When she returned to the drawing room she wore the despondent look that had been all too familiar on board the *Albatross*. In response to prodding, she said that Henry was investigating the possibility of becoming a stock and station agent, but that was not much improvement on being a station holder, as it would involve his being away from home a good deal. If they had a nice house, he said, and good neighbours, perhaps Celina would not mind too much. He was contemplating, too, a trip to the North Island where there were rumours of trouble with the Maoris. If these became serious he felt in duty bound to offer his services to the militia. Not permanently, of course. The present rebellion should be crushed by the spring, and then he would be coming to claim his bride.

Kate sensed that, away from Celina, Henry was getting back some of his natural good sense. But Celina was pouting in dismay.

"I do care very much if I am left alone," she declared. "Has Henry forgotten how nervous I am? Papa, you must tell him."

"Don't ask too much of him," her father advised. "You've already persuaded him to give up his original plan. That could have been no small sacrifice to him. You must prove you're worthy of it by not being a complaining wife." Sir John gave his wife an oblique glance. Lately Lady Devenish had never ceased to complain about one thing or another.

Celina's eyes were bright with indignation. "You think, Papa, that Henry should risk his life fighting those dreadful savages?"

"He's a soldier. You wouldn't want to make a tame puppy of him."

"He promised his soldiering was over," Celina said sulkily. "Although,"—her strange incandescent eyes went dreamy—"he must look very fine in uniform."

"Some young ladies," Miss Pugh commented, "imagine they can have things any way that pleases them. Others of us have the sense to accept life as it is. Isn't that true, Kate?"

"Well, I intend to have only what pleases me," Celina said. "I can, you know. Men always do what I say."

Miss Pugh snorted. "And fools they are."

"I'm a witch," Celina declared. "Look!" She pulled the pins out of her hair and shook it round her face like a pale cloud. Her dark brilliant eyes shone through it. "Men can go mad looking at me," she said. "Can't they, Papa?"

"Celina!" said Sir John sharply. "Stop that ridiculous play-acting. Put your hair up decently."

After a moment Celina pushed back her hair, her face crumpling childishly.

"Oh Papa, why can't I have some fun? I'm going to go crazy staying in this house all the winter. No company, only things to do that bore me. *Why* did you bring us to such a lonely house, Papa?"

"That is my affair," Sir John was saying shortly.

Emily had crept to his side, and was running her fingers up and down his sleeve, saying nothing. After a moment he took her hand and fondled it. The anger slowly left his face.

"I think I have too many women," he said. "Not that I am complaining."

The *Lyttelton Times* that had arrived contained little news from England. Interest in the Westminster Parliament about the New Zealand colony was minimal. It was too small, too far away, and anyway Great Britain had plenty of colonies already. It was recognised that the settlement in Canterbury might be the finest sheep country in the world, but Governor Grey had said that he detested the class character of the settlement and those "superior people in Canterbury" were excluding genuine settlers.

"Ha!" said Sir John who had been reading aloud. "There's where we have to prove him wrong, and Mr. Wakefield right. Now here is some more alarming news. There is growing unrest in the Taranaki settlement. Te Rauparaha has been seen coming down the river with a full party of war canoes, and small bands of his braves have been terrorising isolated families in the bush. The harassment is slight at present, but Te Rauparaha is reputed to be a mighty chief and these incidents could turn into a conflagration. It is the everlasting land question again..." He folded the paper. "Well—how fortunate we are to be in this superior English settlement far away from the sound of war cries."

After a brief uneasy silence, Kate said, "Doesn't it say more about what is happening at home?"

"Do you mean Ireland? There have been more rebel outrages, of course. The Irish do have a marvellous imagination when it comes to new ways of twisting the English tail. In England— it doesn't seem that anything worth reporting has happened except a late spring snowstorm, but that was three months ago, so it doesn't need to concern us."

"But what is happening here, Papa?" Celina asked. "Do we have to hear about snowstorms in England when we are soon to have one here ourselves?"

"Then these advertisements might amuse you." Sir John settled down to read again.

"Someone is advertising for a little Chinaman to milk cows. I wonder why he must be Chinese. And the Queen's bootmaker—now who can presume to be that?—states he has superior boots and shoes for sale. Now listen, 'Sweep! Sweep! Sweep! R. Cory begs respectfully to inform the residents of Christchurch who are troubled by dirty chimneys that he will be happy to sweep them at reasonable rates. R. Jenkins begs to inform his friends from Wellington that he has commenced business in a boarding house where he hopes to meet with patronage from all his friends.'

"Now here is something for you ladies. 'Thomas Burton and Son have pleasure in announcing that there has just arrived ex *Cresswell* from London a supply of silk and alpaca dresses, umbrellas, stays, ribbons, laces, wool shawls, calicos, flannels, linens, combs, brushes, soaps, perfumes, ladies' bonnets, straw hats, boots and shoes.' They also add that they are expecting hourly off the *Gavalion* a variety of drapery goods. It must be quite an emporium, this Thomas Burton and Son.

"And I wonder, Celina, if Henry has seen this. 'A villa residence on the bank of the River Avon, ten minutes' walk from town.' A villa. How surprising. It sounds like the Italian Riviera. Would that be grand enough for you?"

"Anything would be better than this place," Celina grumbled. "Truly, Papa, you must expect us all to die of boredom."

"And haven't you a trousseau to sew, young lady?" Miss Pugh asked. "Surely that can occupy you for the winter months. I think all that information remarkably interesting, Sir John. It makes Christchurch sound like a metropolis. We won't need to write home for the latest fashions, Kate."

Kate drew her woollen shawl closer round her. In Ireland only the peasants had worn shawls like this. But she didn't mind. In the evening she always put on her good merino wool gown with its Irish lace collar. It was too cold at present for silks and muslins. She was in a strange mood after this wealth of news and letters. Acute homesickness mingled with a desire to shut her ears against news from London or Mallow, to became completely absorbed in her new world.

Lady Devenish, however, wanted to return to her past life.

"Never mind all that newspaper gossip, John. It seems very trivial. Haven't you had any news from Leyte Manor?"

Sir John obligingly looked through his unopened letters.

"Why, yes, here's one in my bailiff's handwriting, if I'm not mistaken." He tore open the envelope. "Let us see what he has to say. He has a fairly florid style. Nevertheless..." He began to read in his animated benevolent voice,

Dear Sir,

I have to report that all is well at Leyte, that is to say as far as the house is concerned. There being no strong gales this spring and not too much heavy rain, I have not had the roof to worry about. I regularly check the locks and the shutters as you instructed. Since nothing has been disturbed I have not gone indoors, as you also instructed, unless I saw anything suspicious, which I have not done. The old house is ready to weather another hundred years, although I venture to hope not unoccupied.

There was one curious event that perhaps I should mention. A man and a woman came to my door, out of the woods, where perhaps they had been picnicking although they had no baskets. Trespassing, I suspect, and I told them so. I doubt they understood because they were foreigners, and nor could I understand them. They seemed to have lost something, a dog, a horse, a child, I couldn't gather. I had to tell them to be off or I would send for the police. The woman seemed distressed. But it made no sense to me. I think—

Abruptly Sir John stopped reading. He folded the sheet of paper and crushed it in his hand. His knuckles were white.

"What, John?" Lady Devenish asked in her soft indifferent voice. "Does he think that they were foreign spies?" She smiled vaguely.

It seemed at first that Sir John was reluctant to satisfy his wife's curiosity. Kate was curious, too. Leyte Manor was changing from an innocent house into something mysterious. The sudden darkness in Sir John's eyes and his cold clipped voice suggested some untold drama.

"Merely that he thought the people were French. They could just as easily have been German or Swiss, as far as Watts's knowledge of languages goes."

"French!" exclaimed Celina. And Sir John abruptly turned and went out of the room.

The incident nagged at Kate. Why should Sir John have been disturbed because two foreigners had called at the Manor? What was it about that house that brought the darkness into his eyes? Something unhappy? Something haunted? Why did he not talk about it?

That evening, when the other women had retired, she lingered by the fire in the drawing room. She sat on the hearth-rug trying to forget the mystery about Sir John and Leyte Manor by conjuring up faces in the flames, Cousin Mabel's, the elderly aunts, ah, there was Dermot, smiling and young. A movement behind her made her start.

Sir John was standing looking down at her, his face gentle and quizzical, the darkness gone.

"Dreaming of home, Kate? Don't get up. I'll sit here." He pulled up a low chair and sat down close enough to touch her. "I confess that I have a touch of the prevalent disease of home-sickness, too." Although something about Leyte Manor had given him that earlier distaste, or even fear?

"But you came here voluntarily," she said, questioningly.

"So did you, I hope. I didn't use coercion on you, did I?"

When his face was soft and a little melancholy she liked him most. He had two sides, this man, one arrogant, quick-tempered, impatient, a little cruel, the other that was bewilderingly tender and perceptive.

Did his wife see that gentle side? Perhaps, at the beginning of her marriage, before too many things had disillusioned and frightened her. She was too timid, no match for a man like this.

How dreadfully sad life could be.

"Of course you didn't use coercion, Sir John. I wanted to come. And I'm not in the least sorry that I did. You must overlook my homesickness. It's only because of the letters today."

"And how shall you answer them?"

"Why, I shall write that everything is tremendously challenging and exciting. Or can be, if one makes it so."

"Henry Oxford wasn't the man for you, Kate."

"Why?"

"He's a decent enough fellow, but I found his views narrow and naive. I'm sure he's splendid in a battle. It'll be just the thing if he drives his sword through a few of those murdering Maoris."

"Naive?"

"He allowed himself to be completely undone by a little feminine guile and wickedness. Of course he'll find out his mistake but by then it will be too late. Put him out of your head, Kate."

"If you think these things of him, why do you allow Celina to marry him?"

"I thought you knew my daughter's determination by now."

"You said guile. And wickedness."

"Of course she's wicked. She's a female devil. Which is irresistible to some men. I admire her myself. Or I always did until—"

"Until what, Sir John?"

"Her waywardness got beyond a joke. Which I'm sure you know by now. She's the kind of young woman who must be married early. But I'm sorry it has been at your expense. Nevertheless, I think you will realise, as time goes by, that this was right for both Celina and yourself."

She felt his hand on her shoulder. When she looked up she saw that he was giving her a look of such intensity that the warm colour rushed into her face. She was both excited and fearful. He had the same determination as his daughter. He also had a complaining wife who would not be like poor Laura Henshaw and find an early grave in a lonely churchyard.

He must be so starved of love.

And yet, if he had married Iris for her money, as she maintained he had, it was in the nature of things that he should pay in one way or another. She must not fall into the trap of pitying him, or comforting him.

"You're far from being wicked, Kate. But I wonder if you know what an exciting woman you are. That combination of docility and strength."

She tried to speak lightly.

"Henry didn't think I was particularly exciting."

"Henry became blinkered."

His fingers pressed into her shoulders. She had to fight an impulse to touch his hand, to take it in hers. The fire was so warm on her, she felt so brilliantly alive.

Ah, he was a seductive devil, like his own daughter. And this was a lonely house, with the bleak sound of the wind day and night. One craved for the closeness of another human body.

"You winced, Kate. Are you afraid of me?"

"Of course I'm not." She moved away and sprang to her feet. "But it's late and I'm going up to bed. I think we are both a little sentimental tonight after our letters from home."

"Is that the reason? Yes, I suppose it is. Then good night, Kate."

And it was over, that disturbing conversation with its too intimate undertones. She, too, was starved of love. But a scene like this must not happen again.

And, although she longed to ask questions, it was none of her business why Sir John had chosen to leave an ancient family home to come to a raw colony, or that something disturbed and haunted him about the home he had left. Did he see himself as a famous pioneer, playing a prominent part in founding a new and ideal society for the Crown? She doubted if he were that idealistic, or indeed that patriotic. The reason was far more likely to be a personal one. She wondered if she would ever discover what it was. She longed to know, but was also determined to put the matter out of her mind.

11

$\Large A$t last the clouds lifted and the mountains literally blazed in their sun-drenched covering of newly-fallen snow. The snow lay on the higher foothills, too, but had not yet reached the valley by the lake. The sheep were able to crop among the tussocks, which were stiff and gleaming with frost. The sky was a deep, dazzling blue.

The austere beauty was admirable viewed from the windows of warm rooms, but outside the wind stung like ice. Emily had chilblains. So had Daniel, whose duty it was to milk the cows night and morning so that his hands were frequently damp. They compared their red, swollen fingers. Daniel's were the worst, they both admitted. Emily said she would knit him some mittens. His solemn face showed its pleasure.

"Daisy will be having her calf soon. You can name it if you like."

"Oh, may I? I'll call it Sweet Jasmine."

"Supposing it's a bull," Honi said.

"Then I'll name it after you."

Honi burst into irrepressible giggles. They all lay in the dry straw in the barn and Emily didn't know whether it was the straw or Honi's creeping fingers that tickled her most. Daniel sat up and watched with his serious eyes, not saying anything but making his disapproval plain. For a little while he had had all of Emily's attention.

Jonas, on Celina's orders, was saddling the roan mare. On such a fine day she wanted to go riding. She stood impatiently watching him tighten the girth and refused to listen to his warnings.

"The fine day won't last, Miss Celina. You see that bank of cloud away in the south, that means a southerly buster."

"Don't be so gloomy, Jonas. There's always a wind from somewhere in this place. Besides, how do you know the weather signs in a strange country?"

"If you live on the land you know them, miss, no matter what country it is. That way," he pointed, "it's the dry nor'-wester over the Alps, and the other way its gales with sleet and snow from the south. Stands to reason, it blows over the icepacks. The whalers go down there and come back with stories of the white blizzards and towering big bergs. It's the Antarctic. You've got to learn this new world, Miss Celina."

"I don't want to and I don't intend to," Celina said, waiting for him to help her into the saddle. "All I know is that it's a sunny morning and I want a good gallop."

"Mind the ruts in the track," Jonas called. "They're frozen hard. The mare could slip and break a leg."

"Jonas, you old crow!" Celina shouted as she rode off.

An hour later the blue sky had vanished, clouds were rolling up from the south and the wind was whining across the thorny manuka bushes and frozen tussocks. The sheep huddled together. The boys drove the cows and goats into the shelter of the cowsheds. The air tingled with imminent snow.

But Celina had been gone an hour and by now would surely be on the way back with the wind behind her.

Sir John had been busy over letters and accounts in the study. As the first flakes of snow began to fall he went to the window to look down the track. He knew Celina had gone out. She had been in one of her smouldering moods and there had been no stopping her. A little freezing air from the Antarctic would cool her down, he had thought. She would soon turn back.

But two hours had gone by and she had not appeared. The snow, beginning so tentatively, was now a blinding flurry. There was great danger of her being lost and attempting to shelter, as the sheep did, in the shelter of an outcrop of rock. But in which direction? Already the track was lost, and no one knew where to go. It would be downright folly to have Jonas or the shepherds lost as well.

Sir John, at first angry at his daughter's foolhardiness, became increasingly anxious. Miss Pugh and Kate were both sure that Celina would have set out for Mossbridge, and having reached there safely would have the good sense to shelter with one of the villagers.

Jonas volunteered to ride to the village. Reluctantly Sir John permitted him to go. Lady Devenish wrung her hands and looked helpless. She was on the verge of another tirade about the wretched uncivilised place to which her husband had brought them all, but controlled herself. Presently she suggested that she might take a spoonful of Celina's medicine. Latterly she had been doing this more and more—when the cat, to which she had such an aversion, crossed her path, when Sir John lost patience with her, or when she became too weary of the claustrophobic life the winter weather forced on her.

She supposed it would be better in the spring. Then she wouldn't need the support of the medicine.

It was almost dark when Jonas returned. He was alone. He was covered in snow and his horse was on the verge of foundering. He hadn't been able to reach the village. The dirt track had been completely obliterated and the snow had covered all tracks of man or beast. When his horse had stumbled badly on a concealed boulder he had judged it too risky to go farther. Miss Celina would have reached the village before the worst of the storm, he was sure of that. They would now have to wait until morning when the worst of the blizzard would probably be over. It was the only sensible thing to do.

Kate was doubtful if anyone slept much that night. The wind had dropped and the silence was uncanny. It was dreadful to think of Celina freezing to death in a snow-filled ditch, her still face guileless at last and as pure as an angel's. All the same, she was certain this would not be so. Celina, for all her apparent fragility, was a survivor. She would live to pursue her wilful way.

As soon as it was halfway possible Jonas would set off to Mossbridge again, this time accompanied by Sir John. Then, if Celina was not found, a search party would be organised.

If she had perished, how was Henry to be told?

Their faces were haggard in the morning. They looked out at a white world, for the wind had dropped, the sky was clear and soon the sun would be dazzling. Had their purpose been anything but a life and death one, it would have been tremendously exhilarating to ride out over the pure frozen snow.

"I surely can't be responsible for another death," Kate heard Sir John saying under his breath as he put on warm wraps.

She responded warmly. "You were not responsible for any deaths. I know you're thinking of Mary and Willie, but you didn't create the epidemic of measles on the ship."

"It was my doing that they were on the ship and in danger. Just as it's my doing that my wife and my daughter are so reluctantly here."

Kate couldn't resist touching his hand.

"It will get better, sir."

"I hope so. Perhaps my purpose is a little shaken."

"You must read Mr. Wakefield's thesis again. It would be such an example to the whole world if it could be proved to work."

Sir John gave her a sideways look. There was the merest glimmer of humour in it.

"It could also be a desperately dull society, don't you think? I've wondered about it lately. A few charming rogues can enliven things. But no, Kate my dear, I won't give it up. The balanced society. The unflawed human beings. I'll write a treatise about it one day. Ah, there's Jonas with the horses. I must go."

They were gone for three hours. Kate and Miss Pugh occupied themselves with household tasks. Emily kept her nose pressed against the window pane for almost the entire time, watching not for Celina but for her beloved Squire to return safely. Lady

Devenish sat in her favourite wing chair by the fire, her narrow hands encased in black lace mittens, a foot tapping ceaselessly on the brass fender.

At eleven o'clock Lee Fong came in with a tray of steaming bowls. "Chicken soup," he said cheerfully. "Missees need hot dlink."

"He's like a woman, that little yellow man," Miss Pugh said.

Kate gave a half smile. "You'd better not let Sir John hear you say that. He thinks the house is too full of women already."

"So it is. But we'll be one less when Celina marries. We have to assume she will be alive to marry, don't we, Kate?"

Kate's own feelings were confused and very private. If she had known the half of it about Celina's character she would never have undertaken the care of such an erratic charge. Now one could hardly wait for her to be out of the house for good. She was far too disturbing an element.

At last Emily shouted, "They're coming! Squire's first. It's all right, Kate, he's not carrying a body. Celina's on Brownie and Pa's following. They're all safe."

"I could have guessed that young woman would be able to look after her own skin," Miss Pugh observed under her breath.

"I wonder where she sheltered," Kate said.

"Is Celina home?" Lady Devenish lifted a wan bewildered face. She had used her anxiety as an excuse to take a spoonful of the soothing medicine and was now dazed and sleepy. (Tincture of laudanum, Miss Pugh had said, on examining the blue bottle.)

"Yes, they're all home, Lady Devenish," Kate told her. "We must ask Lee Fong to heat some more of that excellent soup."

"But I thought she had run away," Lady Devenish murmured.

"No, she only went riding and got caught in the snowstorm. She must have been taken in by one of the villagers. She'll be able to tell you herself in a minute."

They came in, stamping their boots in the hall. Celina's face was flushed and very alive, her father's grim. What now? Kate wondered silently, and Miss Pugh exclaimed, "Tch! Tch! Such a mess!" looking at the snow on the floor.

"John, where has Celina been?" Lady Devenish was clasping

and unclasping her mittened hands. "She doesn't look a bit wet or frozen."

"Naturally not since she was perfectly dry and warm in the vicar's house. I think she found it all a pleasant adventure, having little regard to our anxieties here."

"I did think of you, Papa," Celina protested, lifting her glowing face to him. "But what was I to do? Try to ride home in a blizzard and freeze to death halfway?"

"Don't be so theatrical," Sir John said shortly. "I find your tendency to dramatise very tiresome. I'm sure that poor young parson thought so, too."

Celina's eyelids dropped.

"Oh, I don't think so, Papa. We talked for hours by the fire and he never looked in the least bored. He was a saint to me, Mama."

Lady Devenish's face had become suspicious.

"And what made you choose his door, I wonder?"

"Because he was the reason I rode to Mossbridge. I wanted to talk to him about the meaning of the marriage vows. I have been thinking a great deal about them lately and wondering if I can fulfil them. Papa, you don't believe what I'm telling you."

"I'm simply perplexed as to why you chose to call on a young unmarried minister alone in his house in a small village where by now everyone will know of your arrival and departure. Personally, I am sorry for the embarrassment caused to Mr. Hope. He seems a decent young fellow and shouldn't have to live a thing like this down in what I assume to be a God-fearing parish."

Celina's chin was high, her eyes defiant.

"If you're going to blame anyone, Papa, it has to be God for sending so much snow. Anyway, Edward—"

"Edward?"

"What else would I call him after a night together?"

"I think you had better go to your room," Sir John said coldly. "You'll want to change your clothes after sleeping in them."

For a long moment their eyes met. Kate was less conscious of Celina's defiance than of the look of torture that had come back to Sir John's eyes. What was it that troubled him so deeply?

Then Celina looked away, saying airily, "Yes, I would like to go to my room and rest. I am aching all over from a night on the floor. Edward did offer me his bed, but I refused, naturally, so we both lay on the rug by the fire. To keep each other warm. It was the sensible thing to do. Those squalid houses have thin walls and damp floors. I expect you knew that, Papa, when you brought us to this place."

"Go to your room, miss!" Sir John thundered. He waited until Celina obeyed, dragging one leg after the other in pretended weariness up the stairs. Then he turned to the rest.

"I apologise for that. I lost my temper. Kate, go up to Celina. Persuade her to talk to you. This whole matter must be cleared up. There's no need for tears, Iris." Lady Devenish had begun to sob in a frightened way. "Ah, Emily—" For Emily had come silently to his side and was fiddling with his sleeve.

"You're wet, Squire. Please take your wet coat off. Lee Fong has some hot soup."

That child was getting far too old for her fourteen years, Kate thought. Little wonder, with an example like Celina. And what was to be done with that tiresome creature for the rest of the winter?

Celina had taken off her riding clothes and put on a warm robe. The fire in her room, lit an hour ago, was blazing brightly. Kate stooped to throw another log on, then said politely,

"May I sit down and talk?"

Celina shrugged. "I suppose Papa has sent you. I'm really very tired and my bones do ache."

"I expect the Reverend Hope's do, too."

Celina gave a small giggle.

"He won't mind. It was he who insisted on lying close to keep me warm. He put his arms round me quite tightly."

"Celina, you didn't—"

"Oh, Kate! Don't be so prim. It doesn't suit you. No, we didn't consummate anything, if that is the word. Not that we—I, at least, and I think he, too, didn't want to."

"You're shameless! Really—"

"Don't get in a tizzy, Kate. I'm just being honest. Haven't you ever had feelings like that? When you want to be undressed, naked, with a man touching your skin?"

With Dermot, one sweet, mild night a long time ago. But they had not consummated anything either, much to her regret after Dermot had died. She breathed deeply, not knowing the sound was like a sigh. "How can you say such things? I'm thinking of that poor young man. Facing his parishioners next Sunday when they'll know what happened. I'm afraid you've ruined him, Celina. Don't you care about that?"

"I haven't ruined him. He told me that he hasn't got a vocation for the church, anyway. He was only persuaded to go into it because he was the youngest of three brothers. So he came to New Zealand to add a bit of adventure to a dull clerical life. But he doesn't care for it, he says it's such a lonely country and the people are too narrow."

"Strange words for a minister."

"I told you, he has no vocation. He intends to go back to England as soon as he can get a passage."

Something in Celina's face made Kate say ominously, "Yes?"

"Oh, you've guessed. You know me too well. Yes, he has asked me to go with him. We'd marry first, of course, if Papa will give his consent. Even if he doesn't, we will find a way to marry. The captain of the ship could perform the ceremony."

"But Henry? Your fiancé?" Kate was almost too shocked and angry to speak.

"Yes, I know. It's a pity about Henry. I really did go to see Edward to discuss what marriage vows mean. I wanted to tell him how uncertain I had become, not only about Henry but about living in this country, which I really will never grow to like. It's so dreadfully dull, so dowdy. And I'll never be a practical housewife the way women here have to be. I would make poor Henry completely miserable."

"Why didn't you think of all this before you promised to marry him?"

"When he was with me it was different, it seemed a good thing."

And then you wanted to be undressed, naked, Kate thought silently.

"He is good-looking, Kate. You thought so, too." Celina was quite unashamed. "But so is Edward in a gentler way. He has a beautiful face. I fell in love with it the first time I saw him in the pulpit. And he says he did the same with me when he saw me in the congregation. We think it has all been ordained."

"Don't be blasphemous," Kate said. "And how could all this happen with such amazing speed?"

"It's not speed when you're alone in a house with the snow falling and a fire blazing and no one to interrupt you from talking for hours and hours. It's like a lifetime. Do you know, Edward's beard is quite golden when he needs to shave in the morning. Henry's must be as black as an Indian's."

"I think you're mad."

"No, I'm not, Kate." Celina's eyes had a curious sober intensity. "I know I appear so at times when I can't control my moods. I have very strong urges and when I'm imprisoned, as I am here, and as I was on the ship, and in Leyte Manor, too, after Papa—"

"After Papa what?"

"After he punished me," she said. "Do you know that I only despise Mama, but I hate Papa."

Kate had a sense of pain.

"Whatever he did would have been for your good. He loves you."

"Does he?"

Kate collected her anger.

"All this is outrageous, using men the way you do. First Henry because he happened to be the only suitable man around, and now this very naive young parson because he will take you back to England."

"He isn't naive, Kate. He's quite worldly. But I expect you're right about me. I am wicked. I can't help it. It's so exciting, seeing the way men look at me. I have fun. You could have fun, too, Kate, with those eyes of yours."

"One thing is certain," Kate said vehemently, "I can't have fun with you around. You spoil things for everybody with your selfishness, your thoughtlessness."

Celina laughed delightedly.

"Then bless me and wish me godspeed. Talk to Papa for me. Tell him he'll be lucky to get rid of me. Because honestly, Kate," her eyes darkened, "I do truly hate him. He's not the good man you think he is. He's a hypocrite. As well as other things."

"No!"

"Of course you're on his side. But don't fall in love with him. He would be bad for you. Even I, your bad pupil, know that."

12

The snow melted and the harsh beauty of the landscape emerged.

"Like China," said Lee Fong, pointing to the thin pencils of the young poplars, and the track wandering to the foothills. The coarse snow grass was amber, the distant lake a pale, shining aquamarine.

Whatever comforting familiarity the landscape had for Lee Fong, he wanted his body to be transported back to China. A coffin for this purpose had been stored at the undertaker's in Timaru. It comforted him greatly to know it was there, a stark, unpadded bed in which he would travel to his ancestors. He had come to New Zealand from the Australian goldfields. He had thought there would be gold in New Zealand, too, but so far his only form of riches was his modest quarters at Avalon and his safe job. He was a contented man. Not everyone, he commented, was contented in a strange country. Little Missy was not. Master should let her go or there would be trouble.

Miss Pugh related this philosophy to Kate. Kate sighed. "What sort of trouble? Does he think she's a witch and able to call down curses? I must say I'm half inclined to believe that myself." She was thinking again of her conversation with Celina and the emphatic way in which she had declared her hate for her father. There had been something blood-chilling about that. There were indeed no half measures about Celina Devenish.

Miss Pugh gave her snort of laughter. She saw Celina only as an extremely self-willed young woman with deplorable morals. That poor young parson had got caught in her toils, although with the greatest willingness. Perhaps they were a good pair.

"What will Sir John do?" she asked Kate.

"Oh, he'll let her go. I think he'll be rather relieved. She's been a terrible burden on him. I've seen that. But he won't give in too quickly. He has to punish her a little. And it's embarrassing for him too. Everyone's talking. Captain Oxford will have to be told. There'll have to be some kind of wedding." Even then Kate was fair. "I don't think Celina is deliberately wicked. I suppose she can't help having an unbalanced nature."

"Too fond of the opposite sex, if I may put it bluntly," said Miss Pugh. "She's in such haste to catch one of them. Or even two, if one counts the cuckolded Captain Oxford."

Kate thought of the shameful episode on board ship with the anonymous sailor.

"Yes, I'm afraid you're right. But she does long to be back to England, and this is one way of accomplishing that."

Miss Pugh nodded. "She's too spectacular for this country. Like a fire cracker. I confess I always did wonder what real motive Sir John had for bringing two such unsuitable females into exile."

"They're his family. He couldn't leave them behind."

"Then a great deal of the blame is on his shoulders for not giving up his pioneering dream. What exactly is his dream, if I may ask? He's no farmer and never will be. Oh, a gentleman farmer, perhaps, riding his horse and not soiling his hands or his boots, but that's not the sort wanted here. What was his purpose, Kate? Now you're looking offended."

"You don't know Sir John as I do, Aunt Tab. His dream, like Mr. Wakefield's, is to create a perfect society. Or as near perfect as it can be, taking into account human fallibility. He finds it such an immensely exciting concept. Oh, he might be a little arrogant and demanding, and selfish, too, but underneath those things he has almost the mind of a poet, a dedicated and glowing inspiration."

Miss Pugh's brows were raised sceptically.

"Kate, do you know you sound like one of those blessed Fenians in your own country, with their high-flown language and their impossible dreams. You're a trifle touched yourself, I believe. Though not with the desire to create a new society. With the great man himself, I dare to make a guess."

Kate's flush scorched her cheeks. Miss Pugh was too acute. She was reading Kate's secret thoughts. How dreadful! She would be turning her into someone as immoral as Celina.

But Miss Pugh merely added, "Couldn't he have done something about that concept in England? Goodness knows, there's plenty needing to be done. Or did he require an almost uninhabited country so that he could start at the beginning, as the Lord did? In that case he might be wise to ship his erring daughter home. She'll only be an embarrassment to him here. What does her mother think?"

"Her mother doesn't think of anything much at all most of the time," Kate said. "We'll have to start keeping her medicine from her, Aunt Tab."

"The poor lady should never have been allowed access to it."

"I know, but once or twice, especially when Old Bill frightened her and she got an obsession about cats in general, and then when she found out about poor Laura Henshaw—well she did need calming. I think she feels so lost here."

"It's my belief she'd feel lost anywhere, and always has done. A domineering husband and an unmanageable daughter don't help. But we can't let her ruin herself with laudanum. It's a highly damaging medicine in the long run."

"I know. I'm beginning to see that. The only answer is not to keep any in the house. I'll talk to Sir John about it. Oh dear, Aunt Tab, I'm so glad you are here."

"The perfect society not being quite so perfect?" Miss Pugh queried mildly.

"You know that can't happen all at once. Don't tease."

"Well, let's say it will be a little more perfect with Miss Celina homeward bound."

Sir John said there must be no unseemly haste in making a decision even though he knew he was dealing with two importunate young people.

The Reverend Edward Hope was neglecting his small far-flung parishes and his clerical duties, and appearing at Avalon every second day, his face shining with eagerness and sincerity.

His father had owned a considerable estate in Somerset, which had been inherited by his eldest son. However, substantial legacies had been left to the two younger sons. The two daughters, as was the custom, were left to the care of the eldest son. Edward said that he would not be dependent on any dowry his wife might bring to the marriage. He also assured Sir John that he had got the roving out of his blood, such an activity was far too lacking in comfort, and he would go back to England and settle down. Soon, he said ingenuously, Celina would have a son, and Sir John would then have a male heir for Leyte Manor, something that gentleman must keenly desire.

Sir John privately thought a grandson provided by these two feckless young people was a poor substitute for the son he might have had himself. He was still only in his early forties. Lately, he had been keenly aware of this and had indulged in some forbidden dreams.

However, Edward's arguments were convincing, and one could not help agreeing with their good sense. It was a great pity about Captain Oxford, of course. When, after a decent interval, Sir John announced that the pleadings of Edward and Celina had prevailed, he said that he would journey to Christchurch and break the news to Captain Oxford himself. It was the only honourable course.

As well as the interview with Captain Oxford he had other matters to attend to in Christchurch. He wanted to arrange for the purchase of some pedigree rams for breeding purposes. This was Jonas's suggestion. The flock at Avalon would greatly benefit by cross-breeding. Some trustworthy sheep man who was making a trip back to England or Scotland could be found to carry out this commission.

While he was away he trusted Kate and Miss Pugh to take care of his womenfolk. They could be occupied with the bride's trousseau, couldn't they?

From then on the wedding was a foregone conclusion.

Kate worried about Sir John's long journey in winter when the rivers were flooded and the road treacherous. Also, there was the outcome of his awkward errand to Captain Oxford. Not that Henry was not getting his deserts.

She found Celina's high spirits harder to endure than the familiar pattern of her sulks and depressions, and the amorous behaviour of the young couple intensely irritating. She told herself that this was sour grapes because Celina at nineteen had had two ardent suitors while she herself at twenty-three seemed destined for spinsterhood. What was her future to be when Celina, her charge, had departed? She had not yet discussed this problem. Lady Devenish would only be vague and uncertain, and Sir John was absent.

So they all sewed at the lace-trimmed petticoats and lawn shifts, even Emily who had been trained long ago by her mother and grandmother to hem and backstitch and embroider as neatly as possible. But Emily, too, was restless. She hated Squire being away. The house was full of old women. She constantly disappeared to hinder the boys at their work, until she was roundly scolded by Miss Pugh and told she was becoming a tomboy. Which Squire wouldn't care for, Miss Pugh added slyly.

So Emily pouted and settled to the dull sewing. The wood fires hissed and sparked and Lady Devenish dozed in the armchair and Celina, in one of her states of high euphoria, chattered incessantly. The time passed with excruciating slowness.

Only one small incident disturbed the peace. It was when Lady Devenish found Emily with that disreputable monster, Old Bill, on her lap. Emily had been encouraging Old Bill surreptitiously for some time. She enjoyed his soft weight and his rumbling purr. It had been fun persuading him to trust her, and to feel the heavy nudge of his head against her ankles, indicating that they were friends. The boys had the newborn calves and soon there would be the lambs. She needed something to love, even such a battle-scarred veteran as Old Bill.

She had been careful to make her overtures secretly, knowing Lady Devenish's aversion to the animal. But on this occasion Lady Devenish came on her not only in Squire's study, which was forbidden territory, but with Old Bill curled up on her lap. She had been dismayed and frightened by Lady Devenish's hysterical rage.

"Get that creature outside at once! How dare you disobey my orders, you impertinent child. You know he is to be kept outside at all times. And there you are, sitting in my husband's study, in his very chair. Oh, I declare, if only your mother were to see you!"

The white look of fear and anger on Lady Devenish's face had been alarming. Emily stood up, shedding Old Bill who, with the greatest assurance, strolled out of the room, his tail twitching with what seemed like derision.

"He's really quite a friendly cat," she said placatingly. "You shouldn't be afraid of him, my lady."

"And you should respect my feelings, you thoughtless child. He is a dead woman's pet, and gives me cold shivers. He's so determined, too. I know that one night he will get through my window and attack me."

"Oh, no, my lady. He only wants to be friendly. He wants love."

"Isn't that what we all want?" Lady Devenish said strangely, and went out, clutching her shawl round her thin shoulders.

When she had gone Emily began to cry. She suddenly felt intensely lonely. Squire was away and there was no one to talk to, or to notice her particularly. She had never been able to talk to her father. He was a silent inarticulate man. "Thinks his own thoughts," Mam had used to say. The boys were fun and teased her, but they were just boys. She had liked and admired Kate until lately when she had noticed how Squire watched her when he thought no one was observing him. His face got that thoughtful soft look that Emily had imagined was only for her. She was bewildered and jealous. She hated being regarded as a little girl. She longed to grow up.

Everything had been well at Avalon since Sir John's departure. There had not been any storms or snow, even very little wind. Sharp frosts, and glittering stars, and ice on puddles, Old Bill with cold paws and cool rough fur when he gained access to the kitchen in the mornings, frost patterns on the windows and the smoke from newly-lit fires rising blue and misty against the clear sky. The air outdoors was unbelievably pure. And always there was the immovable majestic backdrop of the shining mountains. The peace seemed as if it might remain permanently unbroken.

But the night after Lady Devenish had discovered Emily with Old Bill on her lap, the house was disturbed by the sound of thin gasping screams coming from the big front bedroom.

Lady Devenish had had a nightmare. She had thought she was suffocating, with Old Bill laying across her face and making her unable to breathe. She thought she had pushed the animal aside violently, then groped for matches to light the bedside candle. But when Kate came hurrying in there was no sign of Old Bill, only the trembling shape of Lady Devenish in her frilled winceyette nightgown, sitting upright clutching her throat.

"It must have been a nightmare," Kate said soothingly. "The cat isn't here. Your door was shut and the window is properly closed. It couldn't have got in."

"It was Laura Henshaw's cat," Lady Devenish whispered in acute distaste. "I wonder if he suffocated her."

"That's nonsense," Kate said, shocked. "You've simply had a bad dream. I'll go down and make you a hot drink and you'll sleep again."

"Oh no, dear, that means lighting the fire in the stove."

"It burns all night, didn't you know? Lee Fong sleeps on his pallet beside it. It's the warmest place in the house."

Lucky Lee Fong, Lady Devenish thought, pulling the eiderdown over her shoulders. It was so cold. John had never told her the winter would be so cold. New Zealand was supposed to be tropical country. In the North Island they said there were palm trees and hot springs. Why couldn't they have settled there? But John had chosen to make her and Celina prisoners in this freezing, lonely place because he didn't trust them, and at Avalon they were far from anybody.

Or was it only Celina whom he didn't trust? She had been so

wild, so wilful. There had been that strange night at Leyte Manor—no, don't think about it. Think of your childhood when Nanny, Mama, Doctor Hunt, everyone, pampered you, saying you were delicate and must be cherished; you mustn't go in the sun without your bonnet; you mustn't play rough games; you must go for gentle rides in the pony cart and play quietly with your dolls in the nursery. Dolls were the substitute for other children whom you never met. But one day you would have children of your own. If anyone would want to marry such a timid, shy creature who cried easily and never spoke up for herself—as Nanny said to the nursery maid, thinking that Miss Iris was deaf as well as having lost her tongue.

But there had been nice things too, the glowing fire in the nursery, the sun on her face when her frilled sun-bonnet blew backwards, the excitement of birthdays and Christmas, the enormous pleasure when Mama spoke gently to her and smiled, the occasional, very occasional bear hug from a bearded Papa, and a "Bless my soul, doesn't this child eat? Has she been having more tantrums?" "Not so often, sir. She's getting more docile. Stronger, too." "Fine. A good healthy husband will be the making of her."

And this had seemed to be true when Sir John Devenish had come along, young and slim and handsome. She couldn't believe her luck that he even noticed her, let alone wanted to marry her.

"A gilt-edged investment, they say." Nanny had observed, mysteriously, to cook. But Iris, the diffident, reserved, very rich young lady, who had inherited, as well as wealth, that unexplained thing called "the Haddow temperament" had had her brief flowering. John had said romantically that she was like a water lily. When, after Celina's birth, and he had been told that his wife was unlikely to have more children, he might have said that his water lily had too quickly grown brown and withered round the edges. There was not to be a male heir. So he saw no reason to go on flattering a wife whom he could never really have loved. Except for her money, of course. His own family, except for his fine house, was impoverished.

Plenty of money and to end up here, in this wilderness, Lady

Devenish thought bitterly, while Celina, with more than her share of the mysterious Haddow temperament, was to be allowed to escape.

When Kate returned with the steaming glass of milk, Lady Devenish was saying wildly. "I don't imagine it, Kate. That cat has my husband's eyes."

Hiding her shock, Kate sat on the bed and persuaded Lady Devenish to drink the milk. She stayed until the poor creature had at last fallen asleep. Then, looking at the thin face on the pillow, troubled even in sleep, she felt deep pity and anxiety. Was the laudanum affecting her brain? It really must be stopped. She would hide the remaining bottle on her own initiative. But what could be done about Lady Devenish's unhappiness? Should she unselfishly hope that Iris's husband came back lovingly to her bed? But that, Kate was sure, was the last thing that Lady Devenish wanted. Or did she only hope that this was so for her own private reasons?

What is happening to us all, she wondered uneasily. Taken so completely from our own environment, thrust into a strange, wild country, none of us is behaving normally.

How do we become the reliable citizens that Sir John envisaged?

At last Sir John returned and at once the house came back to life.

He brought messages from many people. Ada and Hubert Collins had made the most generous suggestion that the wedding festivities should take place in their house. It would be spring, the garden would be in bloom, it would be the greatest fun for everybody after the long winter.

Celina clapped her hands. Her eyes had their luminous shine. "Oh, isn't that wonderful! Edward will be so pleased. He didn't want to be married in his horrid little church and neither did I. Besides, who would have come? Now we can have a proper wedding." Belatedly she asked, "What about Henry, Papa? Was he very angry with me? Will he come to the wedding?"

"He's behaved with much greater decency than you deserve. He's shattered, of course, but he says honestly that he isn't entitled to any pity because of the way he himself behaved to Kate."

"Oh, poor Henry. I shall beg him to forgive me."

"You won't have the opportunity. He has already left for the North Island to join Major Von Tempsky and help to put down the native uprisings in the Taranaki province. He says he will probably settle down there after peace has been made."

And so, Kate thought, he will never dream again of his sheep station in the far-off foothills, he will never make his hopeful list of necessities. One thousand ewes, a horse or two and three or four milking cows, a bullock dray loaded with stores and tools, a shepherd, a bullock driver, labourers for bushwork and fencing, a cook, timber for building a house, and a crow's nest in the highest cabbage tree from which to watch the sheep. And a wife, of course... She remembered vividly the evening they had discussed that list, and her own high anticipation.

Kate listened with deep interest to Sir John's informed account of the latest events in the long struggles with the Maoris. They heard so little news here, they were so isolated. It would be stimulating to have a brief time in civilisation—for that was what the small burgeoning city of Christchurch now seemed.

They would travel to Christchurch as they had come here, Sir John said, except that now they had the comfortable buggy to replace the bullock cart, which would have had to jolt its slow way to Timaru. From Timaru the journey would be by Cobb's coach to Ashburton, and, after the night's rest, on to Christchurch across the endless Canterbury Plains. A long journey, but a merrier one this time, considering that the object was a wedding.

Miss Pugh volunteered to stay behind to mind the house. There was no question of Lady Devenish, who any other time shrank from the arduous distances, remaining behind. She was the mother of the bride. And Kate must go, too, for she must dress the bride and give Ada Collins help.

Kate admitted that it would be nice to see Ada, that cheerful, gregarious, garrulous lady, again. And indeed many other people whether they were strangers or not. There would be news of ships coming into harbour, of new arrivals. People! Avalon had been singularly short of that enlivening commodity. She looked forward to the visit, and to seeing Celina safely married. But when it was over, what then? What was her future to be?

The opportunity to speak of that came that evening. Sir John, although weary from his long ride, wanted to sit on by the fire after everyone else but Kate had retired. Was this going to be a familiar pattern for the future? Kate hardly dared to hope so.

"Stay here, Kate. Talk awhile. Has everything been well?"

"Oh, yes. With Celina particularly. She seems to be happy at last."

"I could see that for myself. What about my wife?"

"Did you think she was looking a little poorly, sir?"

"She always does that. But more than usual?"

"Only after a strange nightmare. A very alarming one when she thought Old Bill was lying on her face, suffocating her. It was hard to convince her that the cat hadn't been in the room. She has an obsession about it. Because it belonged to Laura Henshaw perhaps, or because she is making it the whipping boy for her own—"

"Her own what, Kate?"

"Her discontent, I imagine. She does get very low, sir. And I wanted to ask your permission to hide the laudanum. I think she has been taking it too frequently and it has an effect on her brain. Miss Pugh thinks this, as well."

"Certainly," said Sir John vigorously. "Get rid of what's left. Or lock it up. As you know, we had reasons to administer it to Celina on the voyage. This was on doctor's advice because of her emotional state. But it was never meant for Iris. It has an addictive effect, I believe. Kate, we must pull her round without that sort of help."

"Yes, we must. Although that brings me to the question I wanted to ask. Will you be needing me at Avalon after Celina is married? I mean—" she faltered beneath his sudden intent gaze—"that was why I came to New Zealand in the first place, wasn't it? For her to be my charge."

"Do you want to leave us?" His voice was abrupt and accusing.

"No. I didn't mean that. But what would be my designation in the house after Celina has gone?"

"Your designation. Such old-fashioned language. Why, you would be Lady Devenish's companion. Surely you've been that all along."

"I suppose I have. I had only thought that you mustn't allow me to stay out of the goodness of your heart."

"I could say I wanted you to stay for my own selfish reasons. That wouldn't be fair. There's not much here for an attractive young woman. You should be going to balls and parties, meeting enterprising young bachelors, having some healthy flirtations. Here you have too much on your young shoulders. Disturbing things. Yes, I am aware of that, Kate." Now his hand was lying over hers, his fingers gently squeezing. "I tell myself not to beg you—but I am begging you. Stay here. Stay with me. Give me your support."

"Why, of course, sir." Her lips were dry, her cheeks hot. "If you really wish it."

"In the meantime, at least. Until the summer is over. In the summer we'll get to know our neighbours, no matter if they are fifty miles away. We'll have picnics on the lake, guests for a long weekend. And then you may find it all so agreeable that you'll want to stay for next winter, too."

Her head was bent. "Yes, sir. I imagine I shall."

She couldn't bring herself to tell him that Lady Devenish had thought Old Bill had his eyes. What kind of eyes did Iris see in her husband's face? Gentle ones, loving, even? Or cruel?

"Kate," he was saying softly, "you know that I couldn't do without you."

13

W hen Celina's trunks were strapped and labelled, her wedding dress packed separately and with great care, and just two days before the party were to set out for Christchurch, catastrophe struck Emily. She developed a high fever. She lay in bed, hot and heavy-eyed, declaring she would be better by tomorrow or the next day. She had to be.

On the morning of departure her fever had dropped. She felt cooler and less dizzy. But to her horror she discovered her chest and arms were covered in red spots. So was her face, as she saw when she looked in a mirror. She began to sob loudly, and Miss Pugh came running.

"What is this all about? Oh, my goodness!" Heartlessly Miss Pugh began to laugh. "I declare you've got the measles."

Measles! The disease that had killed Mam and poor Willie. The very name filled Emily with dread. How could Aunt Tab laugh!

"So you won't be travelling anywhere, my girl. There'll be two of us to mind house. Now, now, don't look so upset. There'll be other weddings. Including your own, no doubt."

"Aunt Tab, will I die like Mam and Willie?"

"Heavens no!" Miss Pugh's voice was suddenly deep and warm. "No, you won't die. Emily. You're getting better already. And I'm about to bring you a bowl of Lee Fong's excellent chicken soup. I have to admit he makes it better than I do."

Emily sniffed and hiccuped. "Are they all going this morning?"

"They must. It's all arranged. And I think it wiser for them not to kiss you goodbye. Especially the bride. She wouldn't much care to be covered with spots on her wedding day. So be a good girl and smile, and we'll have a fine time while they're away."

A fine time, Emily thought miserably. Only Squire had the courage to come in her room. He even kissed her brow, his face so kindly above hers that her heart went weak with pleasure. To her disgust she cried again, but he was gone before he saw her tears.

The next day there was a strange sound on the stairs, a frail, high cry like a baby's. Someone knocked at her door.

"Em! Can I come in?"

It was Daniel's voice and when he came in, at her bidding, he had the smallest lamb she had ever seen tucked under his arm. It had tightly curled wool and a pink nose, and the most darling tiny hooves. She wanted to hug it.

"Oh, Daniel! How adorable! Is it for me?"

"If you want it." Daniel's usually pale cheeks were pink, probably from the cold. His voice was gruff, too. How funny. Daniel's voice was breaking. He was becoming a man.

"Where's its mother?"

"She died. The birth didn't go right. It doesn't always."

Like Laura Henshaw's, Emily thought fleetingly. This was what could happen to women. But she was no longer in a sad mood.

"How do I feed it, Daniel?"

"With a bottle, of course. I'll show you how. It will have cow's milk. It will think you're its mother, Em, and follow you about."

"Will it really? What shall I call it?"

"Well, not Sweet Jasmine." They both laughed. The calf, born some weeks ago, had been a bull calf and was called simply Bruiser because it butted so heavily.

"I'll call it—Pearl. It's sort of pearly and beautiful."

"You are soft, aren't you, Em?" This was said by Daniel in tones of admiration.

"No, I'm not. I just have a romantic nature. That's what Squire says. Oh, Daniel, thank you for thinking of me. Oh, goodness, do I look terrible with all these spots?"

Daniel's eyes lingered shyly.

"They don't do so much for your romantic nature," he said in a dry voice that made Emily giggle.

"Now you're teasing. You boys are awful to me." Emily bounced in the bed. "Aunt Tab says I can get up tomorrow, so I'll be able to start feeding Pearl. Won't that be the greatest fun?"

It was strange how after only a week of being confined indoors so much could change in the outside world. Emily saw that a delicate green sheen lay over the rocky ground, the poplars were budding, the tussocks shone like well-groomed cats, and various interesting green shoots were appearing in Laura Henshaw's garden.

There would be daffodils and tulips and primroses, Aunt Tab said. Wouldn't that be nice. They would all feel at home.

Emily felt excitement and happiness rising in her. Perhaps it was only the springtime that gave her this ebullience. She was glad that Celina, that strange, moody girl who was sometimes a little frightening, had gone. If Kate were to go, too... The thought had occurred to Emily several times, for what would Kate do now that she had no difficult charge to care for? To whom would she give French and pianoforte lessons? If she were to go, Emily could have Squire all to herself. One didn't count Lady Devenish, who was noticed so little by anyone, least of all by Squire. But Emily had seen the way Squire lately had looked at Kate and the way he asked for her opinion on various matters. Kate was nice, of course, but if she were not here Squire would be aware of how Emily was growing up, and no longer a little girl to be petted and indulged. She was fourteen, after all, and her body was becoming a woman's. She knew that by the way the boys looked at her, Daniel shyly, Honi knowingly. Honi found too many excuses for touching her, especially her bare arms, as if the pale flesh puzzled him.

All the same, there was school to go to first. She would have to submit to that if she were going to be as clever and witty and cultivated as Squire would expect her to be. Then she could be his loved companion for a long time. She would do anything to please him.

The long, straight road across the Plains to Christchurch seemed more tedious than ever. Lady Devenish thought she could not bear another word of Celina's constant voluble conversation, in the high-pitched voice that was a sign of her euphoria. She leaned back in her corner of the coach and closed her eyes, longing for a spoonful of the contents of the magic blue bottle. Once it had been Celina's medicine, now it was hers. But before leaving Avalon, when she had looked in the usual place for the bottle, it had gone. Miss Pugh said she knew nothing about its disappearance. Neither did Kate, but then Kate was in league with Sir John and would not tell tales. She did not dare to ask John himself whether he had deliberately hidden the medicine so that she would not be dependent on it while away from home. He had said that she must be weaned from it. But what a time to start the process, with this long journey to endure, and the days of social life ahead.

She constantly felt faint and a little nauseous. Kate, who was watchful, occasionally offered smelling salts, and propped her head against a cushion so that she might doze a little. But Celina's chatter went on and on. What a rattle that girl was when she wasn't in one of her silent moods. It would be a distinct relief when she finally boarded a ship and left these shores. Which was a sad way in which to view one's only child.

For Celina the hated adventure of coming to New Zealand had finally turned into a complete success, culminating in the acquisition of a passionately adored husband, and a return to England. But for her mother there was only the prospect of going back to the lonely house in the foothills, to the sound of the wind, and the lambs crying, and the blossoms of that dead woman's garden fluttering down. In the mournful dusk she simply must have her medicine.

A slow tear trickled down Lady Devenish's cheek. She furtively dried it, not wanting Kate to see her weakness. That young woman saw too much. She was a prisoner to them all, and she knew that they all despised her for her fearfulness, her ineffectiveness, her insignificance.

She had seen Miss Pugh looking at her. Also Lee Fong with his sideways slitted-eyes glance. And that unspeakable old ruffian, Old Bill, to whom she had such an aversion. What place was there for her at Avalon now that her husband was seeking self-importance and power, and she no longer had even the doubtful status of being the mother of a marriageable daughter?

She wished uselessly that Celina had been more biddable, more loving, more confiding. But if this had been so the parting would have been so much more painful, instead of being the secret relief that it was. Perhaps everything was for the best. John undoubtedly thought so. He had been afraid that such a wilful and immoral daughter would detract from his status and his ambitions. He was a completely self-centred man. One wondered if Kate knew this. If not, she would find out eventually.

Iris reflected that she was not yet forty years old. It seemed too young to be so hopeless. And indeed too young to dread the nights in Ada Collins's house where she would be compelled to share a bed with her husband. How many nights? How could she bear it?

She dared to voice some of her perplexities that first night in the comfortable bed in Ada Collins's best spare room. Her husband in his nightshirt seemed a more approachable person, almost an ordinary human being. She knew that they would spend the night each carefully on his or her own side of the bed. Indeed, that was what she profoundly desired. But there could surely be some verbal communication.

"John—could we talk?"

"Certainly, my dear. Although I thought you would be too exhausted for conversation. That's a devilish long journey. I won't put you through it again for a long time. But you'll enjoy your change of scene here. Comfortable house, different people, all the fuss of the wedding. You must be as thankful as I am that our daughter has at last become a conventional young lady."

That was a joke. His handsome, confident face smiled down at her.

"Yes, I am thankful, of course. But John—I so envy her going back to England."

"And you were about to ask if we couldn't go, too?" He shook his head. "That isn't possible. I have no intention of giving up Avalon for at least five years, possibly ten, possibly for the rest of our lives."

"No! Oh, no, no!"

Irritation crossed his face, and was suppressed.

"I don't do things by half measures, Iris. You know that. I intend Avalon to be one of the best sheep runs in the country. I have many plans for it."

"But John, you're not even a farmer, either from skill or inclination."

He smiled, humouring her.

"Oh, others will do the hard work, as you have so shrewdly guessed. This useless old man will merely give orders. Isn't that the concept of an orderly society? Those to order, with knowledge and wisdom, of course, and those to obey."

"You're talking those high-flown ideas again. Anyway, isn't that exactly what happens at home? The ordering and the obeying. It's only human beings who get out of hand."

"Yes, I agree that I've simplified the concept. Of course it's much more complex than that. But we begin here with a supreme advantage, a virgin society."

"You mean all these people we've talked to today and will again tomorrow have come here with pure minds? As if they were just born."

He was staring at her, anger stirring in his eyes.

"Of course they can't entirely forget their past lives. But surrounded by a completely new environment, given the chance of a fresh start, indeed as if they had just been born—I'll remember that phrase when I'm speaking to Governor Grey—"

"You're going to see him?"

"I believe so. I have a lot of work to do here, after the wedding and after the happy couple have sailed."

Now he had successfully diverted her attention.

"They have a passage? You didn't tell me."

"On the *Neptune* anchored in Lyttelton harbour since last week. She sails again on Saturday or Sunday according to the time taken in loading supplies. Edward had arranged this before we arrived. He didn't tell you because he thought you were over-tired and distressed."

"And now you have told me."

"You have wrested the information out of me." He was good-humoured again, sitting on the edge of the bed, patting her thigh gently through the bed clothes.

She lay against the pillows, thinking deeply. Perhaps, after all, John's long journey to New Zealand really had been because he had this extraordinary desire to be a sheep-farmer. Although it didn't seem possible.

"Will Edward and Celina go to Leyte Manor?" she asked at last.

He shook his head.

"But why?"

"Because it doesn't belong to Celina and won't do so until my death. If then. As you know, she dislikes the place. Too dark, too old, too cold. You have heard her express her feelings often enough."

"What do you mean by 'if then,' John?" Iris was asking intensely.

"What do I mean—why, the obvious. I know you think it impossible that we might still have a son, but we're neither of us too old. I'm forty-two and you're what—thirty-eight? Thirty-nine? Not forty, anyway. And in this healthy climate, plenty of sunshine, uncontaminated air—who knows?"

His eyes looking at her were suddenly the cat's, the hated cat's.

She pressed her face into the pillow. Not that again, she was thinking. It must be five years or more. And she had always hated it, knowing that on his part it was only duty, the desire to procreate. Although wasn't that the biblical reason? Supposing, if there were a boy, he was like Celina, wild, hysterical, unmanageable. She would be blamed again for her genetic flaw, and there would be all the misery to relive.

"It's too late," she whispered. "If we couldn't before, why now?"

"I want a son for Leyte Manor," he said almost to himself, and she had never heard that longing in his voice before.

Then he startled her by giving his loud jolly laugh.

"Now we've had the talk you wanted, haven't we? More than you bargained for, I believe." He threw back the bed clothes and climbed into bed, sprawling tiredly, not bothering to respect the invisible division down the middle. "Don't wince," he said in a voice audible enough to be carried through the wall into Ada and Hubert's bedroom. "I'm far too tired tonight. Get a good sleep."

"I can't, John," she said wanly.

"You can if you try. You don't really need that medicine. It's not wise to get dependent on it. Give you hallucinations. What about that cat, eh? But if you're in extremes, to get you through the wedding—but go to sleep now, my dear."

He could be kind when it suited him to be. It was she who was the failure. Timid, untutored in the ways of sexual love, a pastime that her daughter shamelessly declared was irresistible, unable to bear a son...But why go through all those shortcomings again? Tomorrow, if he kept his promise to give her a spoonful of medicine from the blue bottle she would be fine.

Ada Collins was as plump and ebullient as ever. Kate found having her cheerful company greatly pleasing after the isolation of Avalon and the strain of the long winter.

On the morning after the arrival of her guests, Ada walked with Kate through the town to see the changes that had been made, the streets of new shops and houses, the recently completed Law Courts, a fine building in the Tudor style on the edge of the river, the foundations of the building that was to be Christchurch Cathedral.

"It's getting to be a city," she said. When she had first come to Christchurch, she had thought it such a straggling pioneer town of mostly shacks and two-roomed cottages, but now, after her sojourn in the empty country, it seemed a complete metropolis.

"Oh, it is, indeed. You know, Kate, it's the greatest satisfaction to see something taking shape under one's very eyes. At home everything was full grown, wasn't it? We came into a completed world. But here we're creating our own, and we're getting mighty proud of it."

"That's what Sir John says. He's tremendously excited about it all. He's talking of roads and railroads and tunnels through the mountain range to reach the West Coast. I wonder if it will all happen in our lifetime."

"We'll see a deal of it. I certainly intend to. New settlers are arriving on every ship. Some of them are the educated kind we need, lawyers and so on. And there are plenty of craftsmen. I have the greatest fun arranging soirées and dinner parties for interesting newcomers. Like Sir John and Lady Devenish and you all were six months ago. Now there's Celina's wedding to give us an excuse for more gaieties." Ada paused in her breathless recital. "But what about you, Kate. Seems to me you've had a poor old time of it, what with that faithless Captain Oxford and all. Now who do I blame for that? The stupid man, or that shameless little flirt, and excuse me for referring to your charge in that way. I simply don't know how men can be so taken in by her. That nice young parson is getting a handful. But what about you, Kate?"

"I'm fine. Really I am. I got over Henry. I made myself. Well, perhaps I wasn't quite so much in love with him as I had thought. Don't look at me like that, Ada. My heart wasn't broken."

"I can see that," Ada said drily. "You look quite blooming. That fool Henry. Oh well, he isn't the only man in the world, is he? I intend that you shall meet others while you're staying with me. Heavens, the town is bursting with eligible bachelors."

"Stop!" Kate begged. "I have promised Sir John to go back to Avalon. I'll be a little out of reach of all these famous bachelors."

Ada frowned. "Oh, dear, must you go back to that lonely place?"

"Yes, I must. For a few months at least. You can see yourself how Lady Devenish is. So worn and sad."

"Fretting over losing her daughter?"

"I think more envious that Celina is going back to England."

"So the poor lady is homesick as well."

"As well as what?"

"Now, my dear, let's be delightfully indiscreet. It doesn't need sharp eyes to see that Sir John isn't the easiest husband in the world."

"Oh, you mustn't think that, Ada. He's awfully patient and kind. I don't know how he manages to be sometimes when she's so drooping and fretful."

"Ah! I see whose side you are on."

Kate flushed.

"Anyone would be on his side, Ada. And I don't care what you make of that admission. I sympathise entirely with Sir John. But need we discuss these things?"

"Not if you don't wish to. I only don't want to mislead any hopeful bachelors who might feel the desire to drown in your blue eyes."

"Ada, for goodness sake—"

"And I shall still do my best to find one who does. It's downright unhealthy thinking of no one but a married man. There! I've said my say. Now shall we go to Mr. Burton's emporium and look at his newly arrived goods. Summer's coming. Even at that end of the world place you're returning to you'll need some new gowns. I daresay you'll manage some sort of gaieties."

"Oh, yes, indeed. We're quite close to a beautiful wide lake. We're planning to have picnics there. And weekend guests. Ada, how wonderful if you and Hubert could visit. Now wouldn't that be a treat for us at Avalon?"

Ada looked doubtful, then the thought of a holiday and new society brought the sparkle to her lively eyes.

"Why, yes. If I can persuade Hubert to agree. He's rather a stick-in-the-mud. But I'll tell him some of those new station holders will be needing a reliable banker. He can make it a business trip. But I'll make it for pleasure. Oh, what fun life is.

Well, it hasn't always been for you, poor Kate, but you must make it so. You really must."

"You'll see how civilised we are at Avalon," Kate said carefully. "It will surprise you."

"No, it won't. I can't imagine Sir John living anywhere un-civilised. He's not a true pioneer, you know that, Kate?"

"Oh, but he is. He's so deeply interested in this new colony."

"A fad." Ada dismissed the idea. "He'll grow tired of it. And then perhaps that poor Lady Iris can go back to England with him. You'll find out that that's what will happen, Kate. So let's enquire about the newest fashions from London and Paris, and keep your thoughts on an interesting young bachelor. You're bound to meet one or two or more at the garden party we're giving after the wedding. Isn't it lucky, the Governor, Sir George Grey, is visiting Lyttelton and Christchurch and has promised to come for a little while, at least?"

"How interesting! Sir John will welcome meeting him."

"And you, too, Kate? Don't underestimate yourself."

"Oh, I don't think I have anything to say to governors."

"What nonsense! You could talk to anyone. You're a very good-looking young woman. Do you know something"—Ada's eyes were mischievous—"I long to see you lose your temper. If I can make a guess, you've kept it under control for far too long."

Kate laughed. "My Irish paddy. Yes, I do have one, but it isn't anything to be admired."

"I don't know so much about that. Anyway, I'm going to per-suade Sir John to stay for a few days after the wedding. There's going to be a dance in the new jail. Can you imagine? It's just been completed and hasn't any inmates yet."

"What fun! Will many people come?"

"Oh, yes, from all over. The ladies will travel in drays on straw piled with rugs, and change into their finery in the cells. Some of them who have too far to go home will probably sleep in the cells, as well. That is, if there's any of the night left. You must be prepared for an energetic evening, Kate. There's always a shortage of ladies so you may have to dance thirty or forty times."

"Heavens!"

"Oh, yes. I know one lady who wore out her shoes in one night."

Kate couldn't help giving a little skip.

"Ada, you're a marvel."

"Oh, no, the jail ball isn't my doing. But I do confess I love parties. Don't you?"

"Yes, I do. At least I always did at home. There hasn't been much opportunity at Avalon."

"That's the trouble. So you're to enjoy every minute of your stay here."

14

Celina, with her pale hair and lambent eyes, and the cloud of delicate white lace and tulle surrounding her, made a bride who was either astonishingly beautiful, or too fey, too unearthly, according to people's tastes.

Her bridegroom looked a little dazed as if he couldn't yet take in the suddenness of his good fortune. His mouth was pursed, as if about to begin a sermon.

The rather handsome wooden church on the banks of the river, with its churchyard gate and its steeple, and its too newly varnished pews and creaking wooden floor, was decorated with trailing clematis blossom and fern.

Lady Devenish's face was the same colour as her pale satin gown. She was very erect, very narrow, her head held high, her neck as slender as a child's. She looked like a fine Chinese ivory carving, even down to her furled parasol and her tiny feet in their laced high-heeled shoes. Surely nothing like her had been seen in this colony. Nor indeed like Sir John in his top hat and tails, his immaculate pale grey gloves and spats. Beside them

Kate felt quite rustic in her simple muslin with its wide yellow sash. It was the first time she had had an opportunity to wear this dress since Cousin Mabel had packed it so carefully months ago in London, and now it didn't seem right for a wedding. Most of the women were dressed elaborately in striped taffeta or French brocade. But what did it matter? Who was to notice her? The thing to be grateful for was that Celina had not lost her determination to be married to her blue-eyed parson, for that young lady could change her mind between one breath and the next. However, up to now her behaviour had been exemplary, even to some gracious thanks to Kate for helping her to dress.

"You're being very polite all at once," Kate said drily.

"Oh, I could be polite to everyone today. I'm so happy. Do you think this will be the grandest wedding the colony has seen? I'm sure no one has ever displayed spats, like Papa, before." She giggled. "Trust Papa to set the correct fashion. But Kate"—now Celina was looking at her with nervousness and anxiety—"look after Mama. She'll need help. I shouldn't be leaving her here with Papa," she added strangely.

"Why ever not?"

"Because—well, I'm an only child and it's really my duty." Kate was sure Celina had been going to say something quite different. What it was she would never know, for just then Ada Collins burst in saying it was time to go down.

"Your father's fidgeting, Celina. Oh, you do look adorable. So slim, so young. I declare, I'm going to have to cry. Hubert will be mad at me. What a lovely wedding this is going to be."

The congregation in the church were an odd mixture. At the back stood a collection of sightseers, women in simple cotton dresses and shawls and plain straw bonnets who clearly loved a wedding and had come to gape and to feel homesick. The lovely young bride, the silks and laces, it was just like a grand wedding at home. The guests who were invited to the church and to Ada's garden party, however, were much smarter. There were not only crinolines, but plenty of bustles beneath less than slender waists, plenty of frills and tucks and braid and lace fichus, and neat little bonnets with jaunty artificial roses or feathers. A tall, thin man with a long, handsome face, grey side whiskers and a thick grey moustache who sat with Ada and Hubert was obviously Governor Sir George Grey, soldier, explorer, Latinist, wise and subtle administrator. When he turned his head to look briefly round the church Kate saw that his eyes were large and pale blue and rather cold.

Sir John was looking at him, pleased that he had had time to come to a stranger's wedding.

The voice that breathed o'er Eden... The hearty voices rang out. Was this little colony Eden, and did such a voice ever breathe over Celina? As the organ ceased, Lady Devenish sighed quietly, with what seemed deep relief. She would not be shedding emotional tears. Sir John, however, lifted his hand to his cheek and quickly smoothed away something. He had idolised his daughter when she had been a little girl, Lady Devenish had told Kate in a surprising confession that morning. She had been so delicately beautiful, like thistledown, and so lively and bright and amusing. But later the liveliness had somehow got out of control.

"Growing up," Lady Devenish murmured, unable to use such a word as *puberty*, "she got so wilful, almost violent. I know a young girl has changes in her feelings as well as her body, but when we had to forbid her things and scold her, she seemed to hate us both. She had such unruly desires and wouldn't be refused. Well, you know how she can be, Kate. I don't need to tell you. We were so afraid she would do something terr—"

"Terrible, Lady Devenish?"

"No, no, not terrible, just beyond mending."

Such as having a baby out of wedlock, Kate thought. That, of course, must have been the great danger. She was already aware of the temptations someone of Celina's nature faced. But, although there had not been a baby, she was certainly no virgin on her wedding day.

Poor Sir John who had treasured his only child must have been deeply disappointed that her growing up had ended with this obscure ceremony in an obscure colony. Kate had the great-

est desire to touch his hand. In that moment she almost understood what it was to have Celina's strong desires. But hers didn't
stray towards all and sundry. They were firmly channelled in
one direction.

And what was to be done about that? It was ironic, Kate
thought, that it was she, the apparently level-headed companion,
and not feckless Celina, who was in trouble. Emotionally, at
least.

The wind was too strong for Lady Devenish's parasol to be
unfurled, but the sun shone strongly, too. Fallen peach and
plum blossoms sprinkled the green lawns, the feathery plumes
of the *toi toi* rustled like the ladies' silk skirts, the air was full
of the scent of bruised grass and wallflowers, and the beautiful
creamy clematis.

Sir John Devenish and Sir George Grey had met. Kate stood
near enough to listen eagerly to their conversation.

"You know that Wakefield is dying? He's a complete recluse,
only his niece Alice is allowed to look after him. The fellow must
have a lingering weakness for young girls. There was that
schoolgirl heiress he ran off with, and then his daughter Nina
who died of consumption when she was only sixteen. He has
his bulldogs, too. Strange fellow, but with some clever ideas."

"Very clever," said Sir John. "It appeals to me to attempt in
some small way to put them into practice."

"You may try. But they're not entirely related to the human
race, eh? I fear we're all too earthy."

"Did the Maori have a paradise here before the white man
arrived?"

"Comparatively. At least he had no one to make him change
his ways. I once met an old chief who described himself as a
retired cannibal! Thank goodness that unpleasant custom has
died out except for a few wild young warriors who smear themselves with war paint and run amok. In the past the Maori ate
kumaras—we call them sweet potatoes—and fern roots and
wild pig and shellfish, and snared birds and caught fish in the
lakes and rivers. Now he has new tastes, not only in food but
in goods like tobacco and gunpowder, clothing and blankets,

/   173

iron pots for cooking, knives, muskets, Manchester goods. You realise, Sir John, that the essence of making New Zealand a good country, and I don't mean just this esoteric Canterbury province, is in proving that we can live with the Maori and he with us. We shall do it in time, I promise you."

"And what are your tastes, Miss Kate? Small birds, little fishes?"

Kate had been so absorbed in the conversation she had been overhearing that she swung round, startled, and found herself only a few inches from the unremarkable sunburnt face of a large young man, with broad shoulders and a thatch of luxuriant brown hair ruffled by the wind. Large hands, too, and immense feet, which Kate couldn't help noticing as her gaze fell nervously.

"To eat?" she said confusedly.

"Cooked, of course. In those iron pots. Mrs. Collins said I was to talk to the pretty lady with the yellow sash. That must be you. If it isn't, I nevertheless intend looking no further. My name's Ezekiel Dryden, ma'am."

One of Ada's eligible bachelors already! Oh dear, how that indefatigable lady kept her word.

"I'm Kate O'Connor." Kate had to take the large outstretched hand and found it surprisingly soft and unroughened. So, for all his size, he was not an artisan. Or he had been taking a long holiday.

She made a guess. "You've just arrived on the *Neptune*."

"Do I look such a newcomer?"

"Yes, I believe you do. You're looking at people as if they're a different species."

He laughed heartily, his narrow, very bright eyes disappearing in layers of wrinkles. He was like a tortoise, Kate thought, and wanted to laugh with him, not for the reason he was laughing but for his nice, plain, intelligent appearance. He had good speech, too, which indicated education. He was obviously the kind of settler of whom Mr. Wakefield and Sir John would approve.

"No, you're not a different species. You're all remarkably English, including the ladies who have a healthy open-air look. That's good. I like it. I'm a trained observer, you might say."

"Ah. A newspaperman?"

"Wrong this time, Miss Kate. No, I'm a lawyer. I'm one of the breed that the New Zealand Company in London has been advertising for. There's a shortage of the professions in Great Britain's newest colony, they said. And since I hear the jail has just been completed I couldn't have arrived at a more opportune time, could I? I shall no doubt have some clients to plead for, or against."

"Did you not have a good practice in England?"

"Now you're thinking that only failures emigrate."

"No, no, you're entirely wrong."

"So I am then, for if that were so such a lovely young lady as yourself would not be here."

"I wouldn't count myself the greatest success," Kate said honestly. "But my employer, Sir John Devenish, is far from being a failure and so are many others here. They're men with vision and a sense of adventure."

"I couldn't have said it better myself. Sir John, now, is the father of the bride? Am I putting my large foot in it again if I suggest that he might have found a husband for such an alluring young lady at home? It's an awful long journey here and back."

"There were reasons," Kate was beginning, then held her tongue. No wonder this young man was a lawyer. With his deceptively soft remarks he could wrest information too easily. "The alluring young lady you refer to has had a breakdown," she said briefly. "I've no doubt, in the future, with sailing ships growing more comfortable, sea voyages will be recommended for various ills. I can only say that Celina benefited greatly."

"And I can only say that I hope never to have you as a witness against me in court. You would be too clever. Also a little devious, I imagine."

"I think that's impertinent, Mr. Dryden."

"Nevertheless, a characteristic of the Irish? I find them an admirable race, even at their worst."

"I am only half Irish." Kate's chin went up. "But I am proud to be so."

"Then shall I admire your Irish or your English side the most?"

*　　*　　*

"Kate! Kate, will you come here. I want you to meet Sir George Grey." That was Sir John's voice, its autocratic tones rising clearly above the general hubbub. The wind was shaking down the perfumed blossom, the ladies' bonnet strings were tossing like streamers, Ada's two faithful servants, Martha and Maggie, were carrying trays of food and drink, and a trio of fantails, like a miniature ballet, flew in and out of the creamy clematis flowers, spreading their tails and flirting. Lady Devenish had managed to put up her parasol, and looked more than ever like some delicate, inscrutable Chinese figure.

But it was Sir John's voice calling audibly to Kate above all the noise that made her colour with pleasure.

The introductions were made. Kate curtsied to the stiff, immaculate man standing before her. She looked briefly into cold, tired eyes.

"We have been talking of the Canterbury settlement, Kate," Sir John said. "And apropos of that, is the young man you were talking to a new arrival?"

"Very new, Sir John. He was a passenger on the *Neptune*. He's a lawyer."

"Perfectly splendid. Isn't that what we were just saying, Sir George? That there's a shortage of the professions here. Can we meet this young man, Kate?"

But when Kate turned, the burly figure of Mr. Ezekiel Dryden in his tweedy jacket (not exactly wedding attire, but how could he have known that, on landing in New Zealand, he would walk straight into a wedding?) had disappeared in the crowd.

Anyway, Sir George said that he must be leaving.

"Captain Oxford," Kate said suddenly, not meaning to. "We knew a Captain Oxford, late of the Royal Hussars, who has gone to the North Island to fight in the latest uprisings."

"Very good. We need experienced soldiers. This is only a small, spasmodic war, you know, waged by a few fanatics. They will soon be stamped out. I wish your Captain Oxford well."

"Oh, he's not mine," Kate protested, but the tall stately figure had moved away and Sir John was saying, "Some refreshment, Kate? You've been having quite a conversation with that young man. Did you find him interesting?"

"Inquisitive. Like all lawyers, he tends to cross-examine. I find it an irritating habit." She smiled at the handsome face above her. She just prevented herself from taking his arm.

"What a lovely wedding for Celina. You must be happy now."

"Indeed I am. Especially," he added playfully, "in the last few moments."

If Kate had wondered whether visiting Christchurch would revive memories of Henry too painfully, she knew now that this was not so. Indeed, she thought uneasily, she could almost understand Celina's habit of faithlessness.

All the same, standing on the hillside above the dusty town of Lyttelton, watching the *Neptune* spread her sails and slowly move across the sparkling blue bay, Kate was filled with poignancy and sadness. As, she imagined, were most of the watchers who waved and called farewells to the frail vessel bound for home, with so many thousands of miles of ocean to be crossed before reaching the calm of Southampton water.

"Goodbye! Goodbye!" cried a woman next to her. She was waving a red knitted scarf and screaming above the wind. "Give our love to Granny and Grandpa. Tell them the little ones are well." These must have been injunctions she had made many times over to the friends or relations while they were still on shore. She was wild and distraught. The faces of the two small children who clung to her skirts were smeared with tears.

It was like East India Docks in reverse, the partings in this far-off land even more painful. One felt so desperately abandoned.

Kate could not ask Celina and Edward to take messages to the aunts in Ireland, although they would post her recently written letters in a London post box. Lady Devenish, she thought, had not sent any messages at all. Perhaps Sir John had done so. He had come with her and Ada Collins to watch the sailing. Ada unashamedly loved sailings. It gave her a chance to have a good weep although she was not in the least unhappy. She simply liked to share in others' emotions, to comfort the distressed and to ask endless, fussy, warm-hearted questions about people's well-being.

It was such a moving event, she declared, those brave little ships setting sail into who knew what seas. And there was always the chance of sighting fresh sails on the horizon. That was the exciting part, when the newcomer dropped anchor. One watched the boats rowed ashore and studied the new arrivals clutching their husbands, their babies, their carpet bags, their family Bibles. Once there had been a red-faced lady hanging on passionately to a speckled hen.

It was the human drama that was so fascinating, she said. Kate must realise that. But Sir John, she said disappointedly, had scarcely seemed upset at all by the event. He had kissed his daughter briskly on the cheek, shaken hands with his son-in-law and then had walked off to examine the town and talk to whatever dignitaries he could find.

"He's behaving as if he's the Squire," Ada said to Kate. "I suppose it's a habit he can't break."

"He does have a naturally commanding manner," Kate agreed. "I admire it."

"You may, but everyone won't. People have come out here to be equal, not to be treated like tenants or servants. But he is a good-looking fellow, I must say. I'm sure he'll go down in the country's history. Is that what he wants, do you think?"

"I don't know what else," Kate admitted.

The wind blew up from the sea, chilly and smelling of salt. The ladies' skirts billowed and a carelessly held shawl sailed away. Clouds came over the sun. The *Neptune*, all sails spread, was making for the harbour mouth and the open sea. Melancholy filled Kate. Suddenly she was near to tears. Did she want to be on the *Neptune* sailing back to the life she had left? No, she thought vigorously. She was more than content to stay. There was no need for sadness, no need to think that human beings were little more than leaves tossed irrationally hither and thither. She at least was going to be in command of her future.

Or was she, she wondered, as she saw Sir John striding towards them up the hill, his hat in his hand, his dark locks blowing in the wind. He looked light-hearted and happy. Her heart lifted in immediate response.

*   *   *

"Is the young man with the puritan name to be at this dance, Kate?" Sir John asked.

"Who do you mean? Oh, the lawyer, Ezekiel Dryden. Yes, it does sound like a puritan name. I doubt if it altogether fits him."

"Why is that?"

Kate hardly knew why Ezekiel had both irritated and amused her. But she had scarcely thought of him since the wedding. She wondered why Sir John had done so. His remark started her looking among the arrivals at the dance being held in such unlikely surroundings as the low-built brick jail on the outskirts of the town.

Not that it looked like a jail tonight. The doors had been decorated with streamers and greenery, and inside, in the temporary ballroom, chairs were placed round the walls, there was a modest dais for the pianist and the fiddlers, and lighted lanterns hung from the ceiling. There were only candles in the small unadorned cells. They stood in china candlesticks on packing cases, on which there was no other decoration but a small mirror. The windows were barred, reminding the excited, voluble young ladies of the grim purpose of these narrow rooms. Perhaps in time some lonely prisoner would hear echoes of girlish giggles and catch a hint of perfume in the air. It would be nice to think so. Kate remembered the graceful Irish bedrooms where she had prepared for balls in the past. The glow of Waterford chandeliers, the Georgian silver hand mirrors, the heavy cut-glass scent bottles, the velvet-covered chaise longue for any lady who might feel a little faint or over-tired.

However, tonight she was in no mood for nostalgia. She found the austere cells perfectly adequate and rather amusing. At least there was a great deal of giggling going on and a great scattering of clothing as working dresses were discarded and starched petticoats and low-cut, beribboned muslin gowns were donned. There would be no particular style here tonight. The dancing would be too strenuous for delicate silks and satins. The young ladies seemed almost to be preparing for battle.

Although there was some formality, too, the older men leading their partners on to the floor, Hubert with Ada, Sir John following with Lady Devenish. Kate sat at the end of the row of chairs, which surely must have been provided only for tired matrons and the plainest wallflowers. There was a solid phalanx of young men at the doors. As other young women joined her tentatively on the chairs like prisoners in the dock, she thought, the music began and there was suddenly a concerted rush of hopeful males for partners.

She would have to accept the first one who asked her. She couldn't hurt his feelings even if he were the gawkiest of young men. After all Ada did warn her that the girls would be snatched up like prizes.

"And how is my Irish lady tonight? May I have the pleasure?" An arm was held out to her, the broad shoulders loomed.

"Why—"

"Ezekiel, ma'am. Don't say you forgot."

Kate rose, relieved that she had been rescued from the onrush of young farmhands and shepherds. An educated lawyer would surely know how to dance, which would preserve her toes for the time being.

"Of course I didn't forget. We didn't really finish our conversation the other day."

"We'll finish it tonight. That is, if it ever can be finished. I can foresee it being a lifetime occupation."

"Are you a flatterer?"

His eyes, deepset in crinkled flesh, were merry.

"When it suits."

They moved on to the highly polished wooden floor. He could dance. She knew that at once. For herself, it was a pleasure she had sorely missed.

"I expect, being a lawyer, you manipulate people with words."

"You wouldn't be too far behind in that yourself, Miss Kate."

"Sir John wanted to meet you the other day, but you had disappeared."

"There'll be time enough for that, I expect." He looked across the room. "He doesn't look too happy, your grand Sir John."

"Oh—that will be because his wife is very frail. I think they are going to sit down."

"Done his duty already?"

180   /

"I knew you were an impertinent young man," Kate said stiffly.

"I look for the truth in people. It's my vocation, you could say."

"And then speak it aloud?"

"It's possible to be impartial. Perhaps a thoughtful man wouldn't keep his delicate wife on her feet for too long, as you yourself were charitable enough to imply."

He had such penetrating eyes. They were asking her to laugh, and she found she had to respond. The dance was so beautiful. They were whirling and floating.

"Tell me, Mr. Dryden, did you not have a successful law practice in England when you came out here?"

"Now, Miss Kate. A barbed tongue in that soft mouth? I believe you think I have been struck off the rolls, for embezzling my clients' money."

"I meant it as an honest question."

"Then I will answer it as such. My father and my two uncles have the oldest established law firm in Bristol. Dryden, Dryden and Dryden. I was meant to be the fourth Dryden, but I chose to get experience in the most famous law courts in London. Then, when I decided to go to the other extreme and emigrate to the colonies, my father and my uncles were shocked and dismayed. They said I would be defending no one but escaped convicts from Tasmania and Botany Bay, and similar riff-raff. My father always preferred cases with more subtlety. He enjoyed and even secretly admired a cultivated criminal. So do I. But nevertheless I came and so far I have no regrets. Kate, couldn't this important conversation be continued in the fresh air and quiet?"

They were at the open doors and he was urging her out into the cool night. The unfamiliar stars were very bright. As always the mountains shone whitely above the roof-tops, across the plain.

Kate had been reluctant to stop dancing, but she also wanted to hear the end of his story.

"And so?" she queried.

"I have a younger brother to take my place at home. I can go back if I want to, but I fancy I'll leave that until middle age, or longer."

"You've decided so quickly?"

"Oh, yes, Miss Kate."

She admired his certainty.

"There are a lot of things you'll have to get accustomed to. A shortage of comforts, a great isolation from the rest of the world. And you have to be able to live with the natives."

"Do you think those things are going to worry me? My grand-mother had a black slave. I remember him well."

"A slave!"

"Indeed. From darkest Africa. The wretched black men arrived in chains on the slave traders in Bristol. You've heard of them? Or are you too Irish?"

"But we're speaking of the Maoris. They'll never be slaves. You don't imagine it, surely!"

"You haven't heard the rest of my story. My grandmother who was a most admirable old lady rescued one of these miserable slaves, a boy, he can't have been more than ten years old. She made him her blackamoor and he rode on the back of her carriage and waited on her in the drawing room. He learned to love her deeply, and she him. He died at the age of more or less eighty. I remember him as a grizzled, wise old man with a lot of humour in his eyes. He was a cherished friend to us all. Now he's buried in consecrated ground in Bristol, the first black man to be buried in a white man's cemetery. It was quite a triumph for Grandmother who began the process of friendship, and for my father and I who completed it when we buried Horatio. Oh yes, I can live with the natives, Miss Kate." He paused. "Can you?"

"We have a Maori boy called Honi at Avalon. He is treated the same as the white boys. He can be a little devil, though. You should see him performing the *haka,* the Maori war dance. Sometimes he is so naughty I could take a whip to him. But so I could to the other white boys. So you see, Mr.—may I call you by your strange, biblical name?"

"Ezekiel. That would please me very much."

"Manners are so much less formal in this country. I like it. Now I think, we should go in. Anyway, I want to dance again. I do so love to dance."

"Then let us dance. But I don't regard it as fair that I have told you everything and you have told me nothing."

"About myself. That's trivial enough. It can wait." She looked round. "Indeed, it must. Here's Sir John looking for me."

"Does he have the right—"

"He's my employer."

"There you are, Kate." Sir John was looking distinctly put out. He was frowning heavily. "Lady Devenish is feeling unwell. We must take her home."

Not my wife, not Iris. Lady Devenish, with formality. Which showed that he was annoyed. But with his wife, or with her for so obviously enjoying the dance?

"What a great pity, Sir John! I will come at once. Are Ada and Hubert coming, too?"

"There's no need. I'm quite capable of driving the carriage. They will get a lift back with the Fitzgeralds. Will you see to Lady Devenish's wraps. I think she has a chill."

"Sir John, may I introduce you to—"

"Another time." An imperious wave of the hand and Sir John was gone into the darkness towards the hitching rail where the horses were tethered.

"I'm sorry, Ezekiel," Kate said sincerely. "I did want another dance. However Ada had told me I would wear my shoes out in one night, so at least I will save some foot leather."

She laughed wryly. Ezekiel leaned towards her. "You don't need to be a slave, do you? Like poor Horatio?"

"Horatio sounded remarkably happy," she retorted. "Or did I hear you wrong?"

The next day, Sir John said that their packing must be done for he was going to obtain seats on Cobb's coach for the following day. They had stayed away long enough. He found the continuing festivities rather frivolous. He wanted his home, his flocks of sheep, his servants.

Of which she was one, Kate acknowledged to herself. But

willingly. So much more willingly than Ezekiel Dryden would have wanted to believe.

Ezekiel Dryden. What a ridiculously solemn name. But quite a suitable name for a barrister-at-law. Or a Queen's Counsel, perhaps. Judge Ezekiel Dryden? That would sound well. But one would have to grow old first. She couldn't imagine Ezekiel old.

"Kate, I'm perfectly well," Lady Devenish said in her plaintive voice. "John is being extraordinarily fussy today. Last night he thought I looked pale and might have a fainting spell. It's simply that I am unaccustomed to dancing. We shouldn't be behaving like young things at our age. You, of course, have the energy and the youth. I must say you and that young man danced very well. Will you be sorry to leave him?"

"We've scarcely met, Lady Devenish."

"Oh, haven't you? You seemed so at ease with one another. But friendships ripen very quickly in the colonies. Look at Celina and Edward, met and married all in a few weeks. Did anyone find out how poor Henry Oxford is faring?"

"I don't think anyone had heard. But he's very capable of taking care of himself. And I'm not sorry to be going home, Lady Devenish."

Lady Devenish gave a faint laugh. "You said home, Kate."

"I meant it, too. I'm almost as attached to Avalon as Sir John is."

"Good gracious. Can that be true?"

"Of course I didn't have a lovely old home like Leyte Manor."

Lady Devenish's face went chilly. "Leyte Manor is not lovely. It is dark and gloomy and very sad. Oh, very sad. I never want to see it again, and neither does Celina. It is only my husband who is sentimental about it. He will go back one day."

Kate thought of leaving a note with Ada for Ezekiel. To wish him success in his planned career, and to hope that all his clients would not be potential occupants of the cells in the jail, where the candles in their china holders had flickered and the young ladies with their tumbled hair and bare white shoulders beneath sunburned necks and freckled faces had twittered like a hundred birds in a tree.

In the end she did nothing about it. She was too busy getting Lady Devenish steeled for the journey, and trying to dispel the moodiness that had settled on Sir John. He must be missing Celina after all.

15

Henry Oxford could not have said how long he had lain in the ditch outside the Maori *pa*. He kept drifting in and out of consciousness. The pain was less now. He guessed this was because he had lost so much blood and was becoming dangerously weak. His nerve ends were numbed. It was daytime, he knew, possibly about mid-afternoon by the slant of the sun through the forest trees. They had attacked the *pa* at daybreak, surprising the inhabitants and putting them to flight, though not without a fierce battle.

The Maori was a brave and fearless fighter.

On our side, when defending British colours, Henry thought fancifully, sometime in the future, he could dance his earth-shaking *hakas* and put superstitious fear into all enemies of the British Crown.

But not yet. We're still the invader, the pale-faced *pakeha*. So our wives and children have to be tomahawked; we, the soldiers, have to be slain and possibly ceremoniously cooked and eaten. It was true that some cannibalism had been revived.

The cannibal islands, Kate had said, but laughing, because

she didn't believe it. Her blue eyes were beautiful when she laughed.

He should have gone back to Kate after Celina's treachery. Perhaps one day he would do so when he could swear he had put Celina's strange, luminous face out of his mind, when he no longer had dreams of her lying beside her smooth-cheeked parson. A parson, of all people! What was he to make of that unscrupulous, bewildering, wanton young woman?

You shouldn't criticise other people for being untrustworthy, Henry. Think what you did to Kate.

Lovely, honest Kate... It's growing dark... I'd like you here beside me...

I wonder why those dogs are barking in the empty *pa*. Is there some of the enemy left, Te Kooti's warriors, 'the notorious *Hau Hau*? Or is it only we, the British, who are all slain? Or about to die...

Henry tried to raise himself, but acute pain struck through his chest. He felt a warm gush of blood and immediately grew chilly. Cold and shivering. If only he had one of those rather fine though no doubt rank-smelling kiwi feather cloaks the *rangatiras* wore to wrap round themselves. He had had only one glimpse of his attacker, a head rising above the palisade and a dark tattooed face, with lips drawn back in ferocity, showing a moment before the musket was raised and aimed with deadly accuracy.

He had fallen while still thinking what superb fighters these brown men were.

Our brothers, that idealistic priest, Bishop Selwyn, had said... He had also declared that he himself was neither a *pakeha* nor a Maori, he was a half-caste. "I have eaten your food. I have slept in your houses, I have talked with you, journeyed with you, partaken of the Holy Communion with you. Therefore I say I am a half-caste. Let us dwell together with one faith, one love, one law." But hadn't the bishop realised how the British hated the natives for what they did to white women, scalping them, smashing their children's heads against tree trunks, and how the natives hated the British for taking their land. Grabbing it too greedily and without proper payment. Her Majesty ought to be informed. There are faults on both sides. There were in India, too. The British expected too much salaaming, always too much of the bended knee.

They were not going to get salaams from these proud warriors. Or from their women, fearsome, revengeful figures who savagely mutilated the blood-drained faces of the *pakeha* dead with their tomahawks. It was only three weeks since he had joined the Forest Rangers organised by that strange, brave Austrian soldier and mercenary, Major Von Tempsky.

Manu-Rau—"Many Birds"—the Maori called him in admiration. Because he moved as swiftly as the birds of the forest.

It was said that the old chief Titokowara ordered funeral pyres to be built for his most fearless enemies and made orations over them. The Maori had a strong sense of poetry.

It was unlikely that there would be an oration for Captain Henry Oxford, an unknown British soldier, scarcely initiated into the ways of these desperate forest skirmishes. The mist was gathering in his eyes again. He attempted to wipe it away. It was getting so damned dark. He mustn't fall asleep. It wasn't wise to do that. He might not wake again. He had seen such a thing happen in India, when the alternative to dying from wounds was dying from sunstroke. The heat slamming down like a red-hot iron from a pale pale sky. He could have done with a bit of that heat now. It was shiveringly cold in this rich green undergrowth. Dear God, why didn't someone come? Were they all dead?

He thought he could hear a rustling like a woman's taffeta petticoats. Suddenly he thought he saw Celina walking slowly down the aisle in her stiff wedding dress, looking about her to make sure that all eyes were on her, wanting her constantly-sought admiration and applause? And physical contact. Her kisses—how she could kiss the senses out of man.

Henry blinked bewilderedly. The vision of Celina was turning into a tiny blob in the distance. It was a sheep. A torrent of sheep pouring down the lonely hillsides that he had dreamed of.

Stupid! Stupid! You allowed Celina to spoil your dream. What were she and her pale mother and that tall, autocratic, vain man, her father, doing in this scarcely fledged country? They were not the right kind of people to be pioneers. Not by one half, no matter what Sir John Devenish, in his conceited fashion, thought.

Lucky to have escaped having a man like that for a father-in-law. Henry gave a wry laugh that turned into a groan. The pain returned unendurably. Oh, God, he had come so far only to die... He could hear a chorus of birds, as pure as a heavenly choir. The glossy black tui, the magpies with their liquid warblings, the chimes of the bellbird, the flurry of fantails that flirted their tails and screeched like impish children. He was only getting to know the strange and wonderful birds in this country. There was so much to discover. Mountains, lakes, forests, fertile plains... A remarkable jewel of a country.

Instead, he was dying, a ball from a musket, which had probably been a gift from an Englishman to a native in unequal exchange for a piece of land, penetrating his chest. They are our brothers, the saintly bishop had said. Irony. Double irony.

The swishing of starched petticoats, Kate's, please God, grew louder. A twig snapped, ferns were pushed back. A shadow stood between him and the slanting sunlight.

"Kate!" he tried to say, in a terrible gleam of hope.

There was a rank smell of oil. A face bent low over him. A strangely majestic face, black from its intricate tattooing, and daubed with red paint for battle. A white-tipped huia feather, mark of a *rangatira*, a chief, was stuck in the dark hair, the naked brown shoulders shone with oil, a greenstone *tiki*, the natives' magic charm, hung round the strong column of the neck.

Henry made a vain attempt to clear his vision. This is the savage who shot me, he was thinking. He has come to deliver the *coup de grâce*.

But confusingly the mouth was not drawn back in the familiar ferocious snarl, it was curiously gentle, the liquid brown eyes full of compassion.

"*Pakeha*... My Brother..."

Henry wondered if he had heard the last words correctly, or whether they were not echoes of the bishop. But he had no time to ponder, for the rushing darkness would no longer be delayed.

He had only time to think how good it was to lie back on the soft, green, alien grass, and let himself drift away. Surprised that dying was not nearly as appalling as he had imagined it would be, he raised one eyebrow into a permanent question mark.

In the South Island of New Zealand, in Canterbury, the elite settlement, the lanterns had been extinguished in the new jail, and the debris of the dance cleared away. From now on the jail would be used for its real purpose, that was if there were enough prisoners to be sentenced in such a carefully planned society.

16

To be back in her bedroom at Avalon, sitting at her writing desk, really was coming home. Kate looked around the familiar room, with its pleasant furnishings, the white crocheted bedspread and the fat pillows in their lace-trimmed linen pillow cases, the chintz-covered sofa, the Nottingham lace curtains billowing in the pure mountain wind, and drew a deep breath of satisfaction. Christchurch had been fun, but hectic and a considerable nervous strain. Keeping Lady Devenish in reasonable health, getting Celina, the unpredictable bride, safely to the church and into Edward's arms, and then watching the sails of the homeward-bound *Neptune* disappear over the horizon. Not least, endeavouring not to displease Sir John who had been in a strange mood, both brooding and irascible.

On the whole she had not been sorry to leave Ada Collins's comfortable house, or the entertainments Ada provided. The latter were too distracting, especially the encounter with Ada's most eligible bachelor, Ezekiel Dryden. Had she been wholehearted she would have enjoyed that encounter. She dearly liked a witty tongue. She thought that Henry's defection must have damaged her confidence more than she had realised. Now she wanted to attend only to the well-being of her employers. It was a safe course. Kate frowned. When had she been so concerned for safety? And was it really a safe situation when it mattered so much that she could coax a smile into Sir John's melancholy eyes.

Was she playing with fire, she asked herself as she sat at her desk preparing to write to Cousin Mabel in London? Once bereaved, once jilted, had she not the courage to trust another man? Not counting Sir John, of course, who was married and for ever out of her reach. All the same she wanted only to be under the sheltering umbrella of his protection. Besides, hadn't he begged her to stay?

She began her letter.

My dearest Cousin Mabel,

We have just returned to Avalon after what to us quiet country folk was hectic activity. I can hardly describe to you how everything here has changed although we have been away only two weeks. Fine mild spring weather has made the grass grow and the blossom, both on native and transported English shrubs, is burgeoning. The Alps have completely lost their cloudy menacing winter look and rise, splendid and shining, into the blue sky.

The mild weather has been fortuitous for lambing, and the shepherds report an exceptionally healthy crop of white and woolly little beasts, noisy and droll. Next year when Sir John's pedigree rams from Scotland have arrived we will have a flock that will be renowned for the quality of its wool.

Are you smiling at the thought of me, your feckless Kate, being a farmer? Perhaps I am not actively one, but I am becoming deeply interested in all the processes of lambing, tailing, branding, shearing and dipping—this last for scab, a disease which can be disastrous but which Avalon luckily has not yet seen. Also I have been visiting the lonely man in the high look-out in the cabbage trees who watches the flocks, as a sailor might watch for ships at sea. Mostly the boys have this task, Daniel or Jonnie. Not Honi who is lazy like all the Maoris, and inclined to fall asleep in the hot sun.

When the season's wool is in bales it will be taken by dray to the little seaport of Timaru and shipped. Eventually you may find yourself sleeping under blankets made from our good New Zealand wool. I find that a romantic thought. But do I bore you with these practical details? Then let us return to personalities.

Emily, who could not go to Celina's wedding because of her measles, was highly delighted to have us back, especially Squire for whom she has a little too much adoration. I admit that he has been exceptionally kind to her, blaming himself unnecessarily for her mother's death. She is an attractive child but in need of discipline, so it is a good thing that she is to begin school. She is inclined to regard herself as almost grown up, which is ridiculous at the tender age of fourteen. Daniel brought her a lamb whose mother had died, and I must admit it was pretty to see them running to meet the buggy as we returned, Emily in her red woollen skirts and her buttoned boots, and the lamb gambolling at her heels.

It was from that moment that Sir John began to look his old, calm, happy self. He had not enjoyed his trip to Christchurch, being away from Avalon as well as watching his only child being married and departing for England. Although he did have the pleasure of talking to interesting people there, including the Governor, and as a consequence is now more firmly than ever attached to this country. I fear this will be a disappointment to Lady Devenish, who has never taken kindly to Avalon and seems so lonely here, poor creature. I am afraid she would be lonely anywhere, being so timid and reserved and seemingly incapable of making friends. It is a pity, because this house is big enough for entertaining, it has spare bedrooms and handsome reception rooms, and now Miss Pugh is in charge it is quite a model. We intend to have Ada and Hubert Collins here in the summer, and I predict that Ada won't allow us to be idle. She will be searching for all the bachelors around for me, for that is her passion!

I have to admit that I caught a tinge of Lady Devenish's uncanny feelings about this house myself the day after our return home. A "swagger" came to the door, with his swag and his old tin billy-can. He had a black beard and was very dirty and his teeth were badly rotted, but when he saw me he gave a great grin and asked if he could see the babby.

"Babby?" I said, and he rocked his arms as if with an infant
in them. Then I realised that he had mistaken me for poor
Laura Henshaw who died with her newborn infant. He
must have seen her in her pregnant condition the last time
he had called.

For a moment I had the chilling feeling of being a ghost.
Just as I imagine Lady Devenish has when Laura's cat, that
determined old ruffian, insists on trying to share her bed.

So in two different ways we both temporarily became a
dead woman, and this did seem to be a house with death
in it, as Lady Devenish insists it is. But I quickly got rid of
that morbid feeling, though I do confess, dear Mabel, that
I wondered if I ever would be in the condition that Laura
Henshaw was.

I have lost two fiancés, one through death, one through
faithlessness, and I have yielded to Sir John's request that
I should stay here and look after his sickly wife. So I am
growing apace into an old maid. I know Ada Collins thinks
so, and so does Miss Pugh (who is, I may add, most contentedly an old maid). But it is my wish to stay here even
though I now have no pupil. I did not mean to be a companion to an ailing woman. I am sorry for Iris Devenish but
I do not love her or even respect her. I do admire and respect
Sir John, however, and it pleases me to try to make his life
more agreeable, even though this postpones my thought of
marriage for myself. So I have given him my promise and
here I will stay until the first of his wool is on the way to
England and Avalon is truly established.

Poor Sir John has been so unlucky with his women, his
weak wife and his shamefully immoral daughter. (This is
for your eyes only.) I feel he has been preyed upon and
unable to reach his potential as a clever, thinking, humane
man and a fine administrator. I shall be honoured to help
him, if that is within my ability. At least we can talk together
in the long evenings. Lady Devenish retires so early. She
had got into the habit of taking tincture of laudanum, but
Sir John, now that the strenuous trip to Christchurch is
over, says firmly that she must give it up for there will be
no more in the house. That is the only way to cure her, for
she hasn't the strength of mind herself.

So I play the piano a little while Sir John sits in his
favourite chair listening or reading. If Miss Pugh comes in
we sing jolly songs. But mostly we are alone, and we talk
about all manner of things. I cannot imagine ever having

this kind of wide-ranging conversation with either poor Dermot or Henry Oxford, supposing I had married either of them. But of course, as you are thinking, I am not married to Sir John.

I did meet a newly arrived lawyer from Bristol in Christchurch and I think I could have sharpened my wits on him. But our sort of fencing with words was essentially flirtatious. There is nothing like that between Sir John and me.

I am letting my pen run away with me. Do I sound old and staid and a little too superior? You will be saying that that isn't your Kate. I promise you that your Kate, a bit rebellious, a bit inclined to reckless behaviour, a bit of a dreamer, and who dearly likes to dance, is still alive. But she is much more disciplined in her ways, which does her no harm at all. She is also very happy.

Two weeks later the letter came from Ada Collins. It contained distressing news.

Dear, dear Kate,

You will probably not have heard, but Captain Oxford is dead. Slain when Von Tempsky's troops were storming a Maori *pa*. I know you will be as upset as I am. He was a brave man. If his death was a direct consequence of that flibbertigibbet girl, Celina, jilting him, I suppose one could say he got his deserts for jilting you. But surely the punishment was too severe. I cried for hours until I couldn't see, and Hubert scolded me for my foolishness. A soldier risks death every day, he said. It is his profession, and lucky he didn't fall long ago in a battle in India. All the same, to come so far only to die. How sad.

This tragic event happened nearly four weeks ago, and no one had heard. To think we were dancing in the new jail and being so merry.

Worse still, I have news that will upset Sir John. Mr. Wakefield is also dead, though he passed away tidily in his bed, cared for by his devoted niece. She has said that in his last hours he was dreaming of the past. Once he called the name Eliza, that was the heiress he so shamefully eloped with. Then he thought he was in Newgate jail, and he talked of the wretched prisoners with no hope at all in life, especially of the little chimney sweeps, undersized boys of seven or eight, put in jail for stealing from rich houses as they emerged from those horrid sooty chimneys and faced the temptations of treasures in beautiful drawing rooms. He murmured pieces out of his treatise, things about building roads in new colonies, and houses, churches, schools, libraries. There must be books, he said, plenty of books. He asked for a map of New Zealand to study where the wastelands were, so that they could be appropriated by decent white settlers. But his failing eyes were incapable of reading it. The last name on his lips was that of his dead daughter Nina.

How much of this is his distraught niece's imagination, no one knows. But the poor man is at rest now, and for ever to sleep in his ideal colony. I have no doubt a statue will be erected to him some day, no matter what his faults. I think we are all of us part good and part bad, part dreamers and part sinners.

Am I not sounding like a philosopher? Hubert says this role is not at all suited to me, and he can't look at my doleful face any longer. Indeed, all of this has brought me to the suggestion that Hubert and I should make our promised visit to Avalon at Christmas.

You will remember that Christmas here takes place in mid-summer, the best time for setting out on long journeys. If this should seem suitable would you be so kind as to drop the suggestion to Lady Devenish and Sir John. It would be idyllic to share your picnics on the lake, perhaps with the Christmas turkey in the hamper.

And for a lighter note, and to make you jealous, if that is possible, it is reported that our most illustrious newcomer, Ezekiel Dryden, has been calling on two or three different young ladies. Sophia Harrison, whose father owns the brick kiln; Amy Martin, who arrived as a child on one of the first four ships, this being a criteria of social standing; and Clara Settle, who has no especial qualifications except that she has an ambitious mother. But didn't Mr. Wakefield once write that in the colonies, with such a disproportionate number of men to women, even a drudge is better than no wife at all? At the risk of your displeasure, I will say again that you should have stayed in Christchurch and taught in a school or organised the new library, or any other of several suitable occupations for a person of your intellect. It distresses me that you should bury yourself in the country. I admire you so much, Kate, and count you my dearest friend.

*   *   *

Ada's suggestion about a Christmas visit was greeted with enthusiasm by everyone except Lady Devenish, but this meant little for she was seldom enthusiastic about anything. Lately she had become so quiet and dreamy that one would have thought she was secretly taking spoonfuls of her medicine again. This couldn't be for there was none in the house. The blue bottles had been banished from the medicine cupboard.

Without her participation, preparations for the first guests at Avalon were discussed and rediscussed. It helped to pass the time pleasantly. Miss Pugh said that more help would be required in the house, and took it on herself to go to Mossbridge and engage the eldest daughter of the blacksmith, a rather stout, stolid girl called Hannah, who would benefit from working in what was to her a fabulously rich house. And also, in the weeks before Christmas, Emily had to go to school.

Sir John took her himself. He handed a quietly sobbing child dressed in the hated grey flannel school uniform into the buggy and they set off at a brisk pace. Everyone left behind waved farewell, and Honi, who had long, swift, brown legs, ran ahead to open the road gates. He stood there making fearsome faces, a talent he possessed that had never before failed to make Emily laugh. This time, however, she hardly raised her head to look, much less to giggle.

She was too old for school! Couldn't Squire realise that?

"Come on, Emily, cheer up," he said. "Someone will visit you quite often. Myself, or Kate, or Miss Pugh."

"But why must I go to school?" Emily implored, fixing her reddened, woeful eyes on him.

"I've told you many times, Emily," Sir John answered patiently. "I want you to learn the accomplishments of a lady. You're a pretty child, and with a suitable education you can be someone very special in this small country. You could never have had an opportunity like this in England, so I beg you to appreciate it and make the best of it."

"I only want to see Leyte Manor again," Emily said mournfully. "That is my only ambition."

Sir John was surprised. "Do you, child?"

"If I go to school and learn to be a lady, could I see it proper some day?"

"You mean to be a guest in it rather than work in it as your mother did?"

Emily clasped her hands fervently.

"That's exactly what I dream of. Or even to live in it, if that isn't rude. Oh, Squire, please, couldn't that happen? I think of putting on a silk dress and jewels and going down to dinner and sitting at one end of the table—even as the mistress," she finished daringly. She looked sideways nervously to see if Squire were offended, but he gave a small indulgent smile which delighted her.

"And who would be at the other end of the table?" he asked.

"That I don't know, sir. But my Mam always told me about dinner at night with the candles lit and the silver shining and the servants bringing in the food, hot and steaming, and people laughing, and wine in the glasses."

"You seem to be having what is known as a fantasy, Emily. Don't worry. Many people have them. I do myself."

"About being back at Leyte?" Emily said eagerly.

"No. I have another one. Shall I tell you? Yes, I shall for we're alone and it might dry your tears. I dream of not myself but of my son sitting at the head of that table."

"You haven't got a son, sir!"

"No, not yet. But I'm not an old man, you know." He looked at her playfully. "Do you think I'm too old to watch a son grow up?"

"Oh, no, Squire. You're a fine figure, Pa always says. But where's the baby to come from, that's what I want to know."

Sir John put back his head and laughed heartily. "I confess I don't have an answer to that question, Emily. It is, however, a very practical one. We must wait and see what life has in store."

"Then will it be Miss Celina sitting at that table? She'll have got there first, won't she?"

"No, she won't be in the dining room or anywhere else. That's one thing that isn't fantasy, Emily. My daughter won't be living at Leyte Manor. Not after the *Neptune* docks, or ever." The playfulness had gone from his face. It looked hard and bleak and troubled. "She has no desire to live there. Neither does Edward. My bailiff has orders not to open the house until my return, and those orders have not been changed." Then he whipped up the horse and said more easily, "I think this is a ludicrous conversation. I only began it to make you stop crying. We won't refer to it again. You just attend to growing up nicely. That will please me most of all."

Emily didn't care to breathe her next thought. She simply hugged it close to her heart and determined then and there to endure school and do her best to turn into the gracious young lady Squire hoped for. Because then he would marry her and she would give him a son to sit at the head of the table at Leyte Manor. Of course, Lady Devenish would have to vanish in some way. With all the dying that went on, Mam and Willie and Laura Henshaw and her baby, nice Captain Oxford, and Mr. Wakefield, whom Squire admired so much, and with Lady Devenish being so poorly most of the time, that didn't seem an impossibility. No one would really miss the poor sad lady.

As Sir John and Emily were departing, Lady Devenish stood with her nose pressed against the window pane, like a child. She hadn't gone downstairs to wave with the rest of the household. Why should she wave to a servant's child? What John was doing was quite wrong. It was all very well for him to preach equality in this new society, but she was well aware that he didn't include himself in such a fine scheme. He could not imagine anyone being equal to him.

All this posturing was done for the admiration of others and perhaps for more obscure reasons. Was he attempting to turn Emily, a bright enough child, into what he had hoped his own daughter would be? Was he making amends for Mary Lodden's death? Or was he simply showing people what a fine, broad-minded fellow he was?

One had to admit the two in the buggy made an attractive picture, the erect figure of her husband in his casual tweed jacket and rakish tweed cap, and the little girl with her pigtails hanging over her ugly school uniform.

But the little girl was the daughter of his cowman, and this was entirely unsuitable. Now she would never learn her proper place and there would be trouble. One did not alter the order of society so easily. It would take two or three generations, and who could say it would be an improved society even then.

Lady Devenish moved the lace curtain a fraction and saw that the mountains had almost dissolved in the bright sunshine. They had retreated into a pale mirage. How strange! Was the summer going to be endurable after all? Would that nasty cat Old Bill stay outdoors in the warmer weather, and would John cease to spend such late evenings downstairs with Kate? Thank goodness he seemed to have forgotten his intention of trying to conceive a son, and had not come to her bed.

Yet that slender thread of power over him would have had its own satisfaction. However, if she remained barren, things would be worse than ever. He would refuse to realise that he had been indulging in the fantasy of a middle-aged man, and would blame her, as always. And give Kate as the only attractive young woman around more openly admiring glances.

Was there no way she could get some revenge?

Ada and Hubert were coming for Christmas. Why not invite others whom she had met in Christchurch? There had been a newly-appointed judge, Mr. Justice Harmon, and his wife, a little, brown-haired, quiet person. There would not be too much work for the judge in the absurdly small Supreme Court, but as he had come to New Zealand for reasons of health, not too many strenuous court trials must be fortuitous. There was an occasional murder, she had been told. One didn't need to be reminded under what stress uprooted and homesick emigrants lived. There were also the unscrupulous fortune hunters, the gamblers and rogues.

Ada had told her that that new arrival, Ezekiel Dryden, who had taken a fancy to Kate, was likely to be appointed Crown Prosecutor. If this were so, why not invite the Harmons and the new barrister to Christmas on a sheep station? It would be a novel experience for them. She was sure that they would accept.

AN IMPORTANT FAMILY

Miss Pugh would have to find another maid. Hannah was obedient and eager to learn, but slow and stupid, and hopeless at waiting on table. A quick, intelligent girl must be found, and Lee Fong, excellent cook that he was, must be kept out of sight. His grinning oriental face round the dining-room door would no longer be permitted. The girls must be dressed in proper uniforms, too. That was something Kate could organise. She was an excellent seamstress.

There was the question of how much Kate should be permitted to mingle with the guests. But of course she must if she were to entertain and amuse young Mr. Dryden. Anyway, Ada would expect it. Ada was a tiresome, ill-bred woman, but full of warmth and friendliness, which one supposed could not be discounted in this community.

Lady Devenish's mouth had turned down. She was beginning to think of the difficulties. This hotchpotch of people didn't amuse her. But she could make the best of it and show that she was mistress of her house. She had allowed herself to be put aside for too long, and now that she hadn't the constant anxiety of Celina, things would be easier.

If only she had the physical strength. She had felt dreadfully ill since being deprived of her medicine. But she was slowly conquering that malaise, and with the summer heat and the garden flowering, and the mountains retreated to distant, shining castles in the air, she would feel infinitely better.

Her daring plans were invigorating her already. She had always managed to be an adequate enough hostess at Leyte Manor and this colonial house was not a shadow of that. Besides, she had the breeding. No one else in this end-of-the-world place had. She might actually enjoy herself. And if such a thing secretly annoyed her husband she would be glad. He had only been taunting her about wanting a son from her. He would much prefer one from a healthy younger woman. What he expected of his wife was that she be permanently in the background, silent, uninterfering and virtually invisible. He must be shown that although she was meek, she was not compliant, or invisible, or without social skills.

The buggy had disappeared in a cloud of yellow dust. The

landscape was empty of life except for the eternal sheep, like blobs of dirty cotton wool and just as interesting. Lady Devenish gladly retreated from the window and went to her writing desk. It was the first time she had used it since coming to Avalon. She was about to establish her identity here.

The postman called a week later on his long country round, not only delivering mail but collecting the postbag. When Lady Devenish was quite sure that her letters were on the way she announced her plans.

They were received first with surprise and incredulity, then, belatedly, with approval.

"Why, Iris, what a splendid idea to have the Harmons here," Sir John said in his courtly way. "I liked the judge very much. An admirable fellow with an excellent record. I only met his wife briefly, but I'm sure she's an agreeable lady. What do you think, Kate?"

"It would certainly make a much more interesting party."

"Although I don't know, Iris my dear," Sir John continued, "why you had to include young Mr. Dryden. We've scarcely met him."

"He's a protégé of the judge's, John. And I thought that hospitality was already a tradition of this country. Anyway Kate knows Mr. Dryden."

"If you are inviting him for my sake, Lady Devenish," Kate said quickly, "then I think you may be a little late. Ada writes that he has been pursuing several young ladies."

"Then this will give you the opportunity to distract him." Lady Devenish was actually smiling. "We don't want this party to be composed of only elderly people like ourselves."

"Speak for yourself," Sir John said sharply. "I don't regard myself as in the least elderly, and neither, I am sure, do the Collins or the Harmons think themselves approaching the bath-chair stage. What do you think, Miss Pugh?"

Miss Pugh's plain face was amused.

"I'm quite sure Ada Collins would be horrified at the idea. She is quite the youngest middle-aged lady I have met. I haven't met Mr. Dryden so I can't comment on him. But for my part I think the whole idea is splendid. I shall ransack Timaru for a suitable maid. Mossbridge has nothing more to offer and I doubt if I'll ever train Hannah to lay a dining table properly. She had never seen good silver and crystal in her life. But she makes excellent butter, if anyone has noticed, and is a good laundry maid. Well, Sir John," Miss Pugh concluded, with satisfaction, "your Avalon is coming into its own."

17

The weeks went by so quickly, Christmas had arrived before anyone was quite ready, especially Lady Devenish. That lady had had time to reflect on her impulsive invitations, and was now in a state of acute nervousness. She didn't know these people. Why ever had she asked them? There was so little formality in the colonies, and she had been trained only to be completely formal. What did she say to guests who arrived tired and dusty and wind-blown and sunburned, climbing stiffly out of a bullock dray and wanting only to collapse on a sofa or a bed? Who would unpack for them and prepare hot baths and generally minister to their comforts?

Kate, she thought, with a touch of malice. Let that superior person be a ladies' maid. It would do her no harm and keep her from idling away her time in the drawing room as if she were a guest and not a servant.

But there was no one remotely suitable to be a valet. The men would have to brush the dust out of their clothes themselves, and bravely have a cold bath after the ladies had used up all the meagre supply of hot water. The plumbing in this house, no doubt marvellous for the colonies, still left much to be desired. Ada Collins would laugh hilariously. One didn't know how the judge's wife would behave.

But Lady Devenish did know how she herself would behave if she couldn't overcome her fits of nervousness and trembling. She would burst into tears or have one of her fainting spells. She had so much wanted to carry off this visit with verve and confidence. But she hadn't counted on the hot nor'-wester that had raged all day and had sapped her energy so disastrously. In winter it had been the southerly gales and the snowstorms; now, in summer, it was the hot, dry, violent wind that scorched the pastureland and uprooted trees and filled the house with dust.

No one else seemed to be affected by it as she was. Kate and Miss Pugh tied on their bonnets more securely and laughed at the mischief played with their skirts. Emily, who had come home from school for the Christmas holidays, and thankfully discarded the hot flannel uniform, showed very little improvement in her hoydenish manner and went romping about the garden with that overgrown lamb at her heels. At table she sat stiffly upright and spoke in a low, polite voice, obviously parading her training in genteel behaviour for John's approval. She was a little ridiculous, putting up her hair and behaving as if she were seventeen and out in society. Which all proved that John's experiment with a working-class child was absurd and a little dangerous. Lady Devenish had seen him looking at that thin young neck, exposed too early. He was susceptible to young women. She had always known that. Having what he regarded as a highly unsatisfactory wife he had quite certainly always sought other women's company. He had probably had a succession of mistresses but, being John, he had been excessively discreet. She had been thankful for that. However, in this uncivilised country, there were no cosy houses in unfashionable areas where a man's mistress could be accommodated. So his desires had to be restricted to glances, tender smiles, or, with Emily, quite blatant caresses. Emily, after all, was only a child, and motherless, and no one would misinterpret his affection as being anything but paternal.

Kate was another matter. Lately Lady Devenish had suspected that that young woman, probably suffering from the painful end to her affair with Henry Oxford, was returning her husband's flirtatious overtures. That would be disastrous, and she would be genuinely sorry. She was fond of Kate who, until now had been capable, cheerful and always kind. She had even been glad when Kate had agreed to come back to Avalon after Celina had gone. One couldn't imagine the house without her.

But she was a grown woman and deprived of male society, except for rough, bearded and inarticulate farmhands. She must have impulses, for she had wanted to marry Captain Oxford, and had no doubt been kissed and fondled by him. Also, hadn't there been someone else in Ireland? Oh yes, she undoubtedly had impulses, if not the wild, deeply embarrassing ones Celina had manifested.

But surely she was too well-bred and too sensible to risk her chances of marriage by having an unfortunate liaison.

All the same, juxtaposition was dangerous, as Lady Devenish realised on the evening before the expected arrival of the Christmas guests.

She had gone up to her room to retire for the night, and after her ritual examination of the windows to see that Old Bill could not gain entry—the persistent animal had never given up trying—she realised that the wind was rising again and the nudging on the window panes could be scraping branches or that demon cat demanding entry. She knew that she would never sleep and in the morning she would be a pale, exhausted wreck.

It was useless to go to the medicine cupboard in the hope that there might be a blue bottle overlooked on a previous search. But there were other palliatives such as cough mixtures—if one drank enough of them one could become drowsy—and headache powders. Perhaps a headache powder stirred thoroughly in hot milk would calm her. She should have rung for Kate, but was reluctant to do so. Also, she didn't want to disturb Lee Fong sleeping on his pallet behind the stove in the kitchen by asking for milk to be heated. She would get water from the bathroom instead. Suddenly she felt secretive and guilty. She didn't even light her candle, but crept down the stairs in the last glimmer of fading yellow dusk. She reached the small storeroom at the end of the hall without being seen. Safely inside she did light the candle she had carried downstairs, and opened the cabinet to disclose the array of bottles and tins. Iodine, castor oil, rhubarb pills, mustard, rheumatism salve, linseed for poultices, several bottles of cough mixture... Where were the headache powders? At the back of the cupboard? No, no, it couldn't be! Lady Devenish's hand trembled so much that she nearly dropped the candlestick. For there, concealed by the other medicines, was a blue bottle, a miraculous blue bottle, full to the top.

It must have escaped John's notice. And hers, too, when she had last come here in despair. But there it was. Tincture of laudanum. All ready to be opened and hidden in a hatbox in her wardrobe upstairs. Oh, bliss!

But she must be careful. Only the smallest spoonful tonight, the rest to be kept for emergencies. For she mustn't give any sign that she had found her comforter, otherwise the bottle would be searched for and confiscated and there would be no more.

Tucking it inside her robe against her breast Lady Devenish made her silent way through the hall, past the dining room, which was in darkness, past the open door of the drawing room, where there was a murmur of voices but strangely no lamplight. Why were people sitting in the dark? Involuntarily she paused and heard a sound that could only be stifled breathing, then a gasp, then the audible breathing again. Kissing! She knew that instinctively. With her ear to the door she listened to the treacherous voices.

"No, Sir John. Please! This is wrong..."

"Kate, my darling, must we wait for ever?"

"But there isn't any other way. Oh, dear, now I shall have to leave here."

"Never! Never! You must stay. At least we can see each other and smile, talk, even hold hands. For a little while, please. My lovely Kate. A little while won't ruin your life, will it? Although I mustn't be selfish."

Selfish! Lady Devenish gave a suppressed snort.

"I'm thinking of poor Lady Devenish upstairs. She's so lost, so miserable. She hates it all so much. And you did bring her here, you know. You have to make amends for that. Poor lady."

"Kate, I dislike you when you're moral."

"You're moral, too, my dearest. You have to be, don't you realise? You're an important man out here. That matters a great deal to you, doesn't it?"

"Yes, I admit it does. You're too clever."

"Well, then—"

There was a movement in the dim room. Lady Devenish started and almost ran up the stairs, clutching the blue bottle, fearful of being seen, breathless with rage and indignation.

Poor Lady Devenish upstairs… How dare that Irish hussy speak like that? Was that what everyone said of her?

Her husband's voice called sharply, "Who's that?" And then, in lower tones, "It must have been Miss Pugh going up to bed."

With violently trembling hands Lady Devenish shut her bedroom door. She could scarcely take off her robe, scarcely get the cork out of the bottle. She mustn't spill any of the precious liquid. It had to numb her anger, her hurt, her loneliness, her bitter sense of failure. Particularly her failure.

But she must be awake tomorrow for the guests. She had to be a successful hostess, if not witty and scintillating, at least courteous and attentive. She would wear her cream lace gown and carry her parasol as she walked down to the garden gate. She would be the epitome of civilisation, a charming figure not one whit less important than her husband.

With her simmering fury and her determination, and a little help from the blue bottle to quiet her raw nerves, she would never be an object of pity again.

Pity! And she a lady and that girl, with her mixed Irish breeding, and nothing else but a pleasant face. And youth, of course.

Later, as she began floating into a blissful sleep, she thought with great clarity. He deliberately did this to Kate tonight because that young Mr. Dryden is coming tomorrow…

"You're stuck up, Em," Jonnie said. "Pa said you were. He said Mam wouldn't like it."

"I am not stuck up."

"Then why do you sit up so straight as if you had a poker down your back?"

"That's the way ladies sit."

"That's what I mean. You're pretending to be a lady and that's stuck up."

Honi was stroking her arm with his warm, brown fingers. She snatched it away.

"Don't do that. It's rude."

Honi grinned, showing his white teeth.

"It's like stroking a little cat. That's not rude."

"Old Bill," said Jonnie.

"No, a lady cat. A very very lady cat."

Daniel watched solemnly, saying nothing. He said so little, but he never missed anything. And he had given her Pearl. Though Pearl was large and bossy now and liked to butt her and knock her over. She really had to try hard to remember Miss Macdonald's precepts when she was with these rough boys. It was very difficult to keep her dignity.

"Daniel, you're to be in charge of the picnic hamper when we go down to the lake. That's what Aunt Tab says."

"Do I have to come?" Daniel asked in dismay.

"Don't you want to?"

"I don't know all those grand people."

"Don't be silly, you've stayed in Mrs. Collins's house."

"I didn't enjoy it."

"Well, you don't have to talk to them. When you've unpacked the hamper you can go and sit on a rock by yourself."

"You could sit with me, Em. We'll be the only young ones."

Emily tossed her head.

"I'm not that young. And I'll be needed to help entertain people, Squire said. He says it will be an opportunity to show what I've learned at school."

"Ugh!" said Jonnie.

"*Pi korry!*" said Honi, using his habitual Maori expletive.

Emily got up, prepared to flounce off. "You're all just teasing me. I think you're just too ignorant for words."

Pa didn't tease like the boys. He looked at Emily with his sad, serious eyes and slightly shook his head. His hair, since Mam and Willie had died, had gone quite grey and he looked like an old man. Yet he wasn't any older than Squire, who had thick, glossy brown hair and alive, sparkling eyes. Emily didn't like to think of them being the same age because then it seemed embarrassing to want to have Squire's baby. This desire had not just been a passing fancy. She wanted it more and more. She could hardly bear him out of her sight and mooned about the door of his study until Aunt Tab told her sharply to help Hannah in the dairy, or help Myrtle, the new girl, a small, deft person who had been trained as a parlour maid far away in England, and whose husband had deserted her to go to the Australian goldfields. Myrtle would teach her how to lay a dinner table for five courses, and how to serve tea to company in the drawing room. Emily thrust out her lower lip mutinously. What did she want with those skills? She was learning to be a lady. One day Myrtle with her superior half-smile would be waiting on her. Aunt Tab was simply reminding her of what she thought was her right place. Just as Lady Devenish did, and now Pa.

Pa said, "It isn't what your Mam would have liked, Emily. It's giving you wrong notions." He added ponderously, for he was not an articulate man, "I think Squire's having a game with you. He has high-flown ideas. That's what Mam always said."

"Ideas about me, Pa?" Emily asked with feigned innocence.

"About what he can do with people. The same as breeding sheep, in a manner of speaking. He's importing these pedigree rams to get better wool. You're a nice-looking lass so he's thinking of raising your station in life, so you might get an educated husband and have clever children."

It was the longest speech Emily had ever heard her father make. She pretended to listen carefully but all the time she was crying triumphantly inside, "It's to make me the right mother for his son, Pa!" But she had to keep completely silent about that. Hadn't Squire told her that it was a great secret.

"He's a good boss," Pa said fairly. "But Mam would never have let him interfere with her family. She'd have said it was wrong. You think on that, Emily child. Mam watches you from heaven,

210 /

you know. Ah, dear. If we'd known all this we'd never have come to New Zealand."

Emily couldn't prevent herself saying joyfully, "But I'll go back to Leyte Manor one day, Pa. You, too, and Jonnie," she added belatedly, and stopped herself from saying that she would then be the lady of the manor. With his eyes on her, in some bewilderment, she held herself straight and folded her hands quietly in her lap, not fidgeting. She deeply disliked her stubby fingers, which would never have the narrow, ivory perfection of Lady Devenish's, but determined never to roughen them by work in the dairy or the kitchen. She would pass tea cups to the guests and converse with them, as Miss Macdonald had instructed. She would put up her hair for the whole of Christmas. Oh, oh, oh! She narrowly prevented herself from skipping with excitement.

18

The travel-worn party arrived at dusk on Christmas Eve. Ada Collins tumbled out of the dray, shedding an armful of small packages as she held out her arms to Lady Devenish, who was advancing sedately down the garden path.

"Oh, my, Iris, you do look such a lady even at the end of nowhere. What a vision you make in that lace gown, as perfect as if you were at a garden party. And that house—Hubert, do you see that house? It's twice the size of ours, and in this wilderness!" Ada shook her head wonderingly. "We always did say your husband was never a true pioneer, but just a sybarite. No offence intended, we need cultivated, amusing people here, and I couldn't be more glad of real comfort after that horrendous journey. So could poor Maud, I'm sure. The men, of course, could go on for ever, great, strong brutes. But we poor ladies— oh, there's my dear Kate looking a picture. And the garden! Smell those lilies, Maud. We call them Christmas lilies here because they bloom at Christmas. And look at the climbing roses, and the sweet peas. Someone was clever in making this garden."

"Laura Henshaw," Lady Devenish at last had an opportunity to speak. "It was her garden. We're just tenants of it."

"She's the lady who went home?"

"She died, in fact."

"How sad! Isn't that sad, Maud? But at least she's left something to be remembered by, which is all any of us can hope for. A kind of footprint in this vast wilderness."

Lady Devenish, still a little drowsy but quite calm, brought Ada's spate of words to a stop by moving on to greet Mrs. Harmon, a small lady dressed in brown, and, one guessed, like herself almost always overlooked. She had no difficulty in putting warmth into her voice.

"Dear Mrs. Harmon, you must be worn out. Have you ever made such a long journey before?"

"No, I haven't. But I think we have survived very well." Mrs. Harmon had attractive, twinkly brown eyes, which appeared to be her only good feature. But they were enough to ease Lady Devenish's anxiety. Maud Harmon would not be a difficult guest. Neither, one imagined, would her husband be. He was a squarely-built, grey-bearded man with a long nose and a formidable, rounded forehead. But his bow was courtly and his smile friendly. Mr. Dryden behind him was carrying some sort of cage. It had a woollen cloth over it and seemed, by his careful handling of it, to hold something breakable.

Hubert Collins, dry and peppery, might just have stepped out of his bank. There was really nothing about his neat, sparse figure to be ruffled.

Sir John had appeared, hastening down the path, hands outstretched in one of his flamboyant gestures.

"Welcome! Welcome to our mountain fastness. Now just leave all your baggage where it is. The boys will bring it in."

"Boys, Sir John? You sound very grand," said Hubert Collins.

"Only the lads on the farm. I haven't a personal servant, alas, but we didn't come out here expecting to be valeted, did we?"

"My wife is better than any man I ever had," Judge Harmon observed.

"Yes, I believe we women were just brought out here to be

slaves," Maud Harmon said drily. "Starching and ironing His Honour's shirts, brushing his lapels. Well, I quite like it, you know. Makes one indispensable. Don't you agree, Lady Devenish? Ah, but you do have servants."

"Won't you all come indoors?" Lady Devenish said. She didn't want to see Ada Collins's amused grin at the thought of poor Lady Devenish ironing her husband's shirts. Poor Lady Devenish..."We have cold lemonade. Or something stronger if the gentlemen prefer it. Mr. Dryden, what is that extraordinary object you are carrying?"

The long journey, eyes squinted against the wind and the bright sunlight, had made Ezekiel Dryden's face more curious than ever. A most unusual face with the narrowed blue eyes always half-puckered into a laugh, and the slightly cherubic, sunburned cheeks. He, too, had a bulging forehead—was this a characteristic of the law?—but his thick, brown hair tumbled attractively over it, where Judge Harmon's protruded beneath sparse locks without disguise.

"What do I have here, Lady Devenish? It's actually my Christmas present for Miss O'Connor. It will announce its presence quite soon, I am afraid."

Ada Collins was laughing helplessly.

"The fun we have had, especially in Mr. Turton's hotel in Ashburton. And then those people in the coach yesterday. But no, I mustn't give the secret away. Oh, dear me, look at my hair falling down. I must be a scarecrow. How do you look so immaculate in these hot winds, Iris?"

"I haven't ridden for miles in a bullock cart. Such a barbaric method of transport, don't you agree?"

"Oh, I don't know. It gives one plenty of time to look at the country and to see that it isn't all tussocks and snowgrass. Look at those mountains, Ezekiel. Do you still want to climb them?"

"Some day. That's why I was so happy to come here." He moved nearer to Kate. "At least, that's one reason."

"Are you a mountaineer?" Kate asked politely.

"I've done some climbing in Switzerland. But I haven't got any gear yet. And if that peak is the famous Mount Cook, I doubt I'll be attempting that. What a beauty! Perhaps the next time

I come I'll go further into the foothills, and get within striking distance of a glacier, at least."

Providing you are invited again, Lady Devenish thought silently. She had seen at once that her husband was not going to be over friendly with Mr. Dryden. He represented youth. As Kate did. That invaluable asset that once lost never came back. She found herself repressing a smile. She believed her small act of revenge was going to be effective.

They had just entered the house when a sepulchral voice behind Kate said "Terrible weather we're having!" She jumped in alarm, and Ada Collins doubled up with laughter. Little Maud Harmon smiled and the men grinned broadly.

"Come on, Ezekiel, the secret's out," the judge said. "Unveil the creature. But Miss O'Connor isn't going to thank you for having to harbour such a misanthrope. Can't he say something more cheerful?"

Ezekiel whipped the covering off the cage and displayed a white sulphur-crested cockatoo. It was clawing its way up the cage, its yellow crest raised, its head tilted inquisitively.

"For me?" Kate cried. "What a strange present. Whatever does one do with a parrot?"

"Love it," said Ezekiel. "It's a very long-lived species. It would be rather unfortunate if you disliked it."

Kate went down on her knees to examine her gift more closely. "Does it bite?"

"Only its enemies."

"Is it male or female?"

"Now that I confess I don't know. Parrots keep these matters to themselves. If one day it lays an egg you'll know it's a lady, otherwise I'm afraid it will keep its own counsel."

"Then I'll have to be very careful in naming it. Or is it named already?"

"The man I got it from called it Whitey, which is hardly dignified enough for such a superior bird. He brought it from Australia. He had no idea of its age, either. But I personally think it's quite a young bird. So you must be careful that what you teach it will make suitable listening for your grandchildren, Miss Kate."

"Heavens, you're plummeting me into old age!" But Kate was laughing and saying she would call the young fellow something grand like Caesar or Mephistopheles. "What do you think, Sir John?"

"I think that if he's to be a permanent guest in my house he had better have good manners." There was the faintest tetchiness beneath Sir John's affability. "Take it away, Kate. It will amuse Emily, perhaps. Now, gentlemen, I have some Napoleon brandy I've been saving for just such an occasion as this. Would you like a tot before you freshen up?"

"I think the ladies would like to go upstairs at once," Lady Devenish said. "Kate, will you show them to their rooms? And tell Myrtle to take up tea trays. We dine at seven, but please don't attempt to make a grand toilette after your exhausting day. Kate will put out your things for you."

Kate had listened in some surprise and relief to Lady Devenish being a good hostess. She was quite happy to take over the task of ladies' maid, but before she went she had an inspiration.

"Why, we'll call the parrot Napoleon after the brandy! Do you think it needs some refreshment now, Mr. Dryden? If you were to find Lee Fong in the kitchen—yes, Lady Devenish, I am about to take Mrs. Collins and Mrs. Harmon upstairs."

"Why, I believe you like that bird," Ada said. "You're quite flushed with pleasure. I'm so happy. Mr. Dryden was very anxious to please you. He has such an original mind. Hubert says he will go a long way. I admit he isn't as handsome as Captain Oxford was, but he has a much more lively personality. Dear me, what a charming room this is."

"It was Celina's," Kate said. "Yes, it is one of the nicest in the house, although Celina never appreciated it, as you can imagine. Nothing ever pleased that girl except personable young men."

"There won't have been time to hear from her yet?"

"No. Sir John thinks in another eight or nine weeks there should be some news. But really, Ada, I can only say this to you, but it's so peaceful here without her. Sir John is so much easier in his mind."

"And Iris?"

"Oh, she, too, I'm sure. But she doesn't have the ability to be completely happy, poor lady. She has a sad nature. All the same, she has been looking forward to this visit, and has cheered up a great deal since you arrived."

"I thought she was looking exceptionally well," Ada said. "Really quite splendid for her."

"Yes. She was excited. It's given her some colour. Now, Ada, don't get the idea that I suggested Mr. Dryden be invited. I didn't. It was entirely Lady Devenish's idea."

"No matter. He's here. And being rather a lonely young man he'll enjoy it enormously. I hope you will, too. After all, Judge Harmon is a dear but a little prosy, and you know Hubert. If that man ever says an amusing thing I'll die of shock."

"You say the amusing things for both of you."

"Exactly his argument. Don't encourage him. But my, that parrot! Ezekiel has been trying hard to teach it some more words, but so far he says it is as stubborn as a witness who won't open his mouth in court. You'll have to coax words out of it, he says. He's sure it has quite a repertoire. Kate, I hope you were not too grieved for Captain Oxford."

"I was very grieved. It was tragic. He was far too young to die."

"Well, if he had been a sensible young man he would never have been in that forest. He would have been here in Canterbury preparing to marry you. That's something I can never forgive Celina for." Then she looked at Kate slyly, "But perhaps it's all for the best."

"Whatever it is, it can't be changed. And I had got over being in love with him. Or imagining that I was."

"Well," Ada said philosophically determined to pursue the subject, "there was one young man wanting to breed sheep beneath the mountains, and now there's another wanting to climb them. Which aspiration do you think the more romantic?"

"Neither, as it happens, has anything to do with me. Henry passed me over, and I have never been anything to Mr. Dryden, nor him to me. So will you please, Ada, stop this embarrassing match-making?"

"If that's what you call it," said Ada. "Of course. Willingly. On the principle that any young man worthy of his salt is capable of doing his own. Now then, I'll wear my amber silk. Iris said not to dress up, but I'm certain everything in this house is going to be so perfect, that I must match it. I mustn't disgrace my hostess. Or my host. Dear Sir John. Such a handsome man..."

They sat round the dining table, the candles wan in the yellow sunset. Emily, against Lady Devenish's and Miss Pugh's wishes, had been allowed to join the grown-ups. She was behaving with the utmost decorum, trying to conceal her pleasure, and also trying not to squeal with excitement at the antics of Napoleon in his cage. Oh, why didn't someone think to bring her such an adorable present? Would Squire ever? No, he would give her jewels, a dear little tiara of sparkling diamonds and pearls, or some rings for her fingers, as soon as they grew less stubby.

But she would dearly love a parrot.

She sat between Kate and the judge with his grey beard. Mr. Collins, Mrs. Harmon, and Ada Collins sat opposite. Mr. Dryden sat on Lady Devenish's right, which Emily had learned from Miss Macdonald was an important place. They were not an even number. To be correct, Aunt Tab had said, if Emily were to sit up to dinner every night, Daniel should partner her. Daniel, imagine! He wouldn't say a word, and he would never know what to do with the cutlery for five courses, much less the wine. Though to her chagrin, Squire, who opened the bottles and poured the wine, ignored her glass. However, she was growing up. Fast.

The conversation was mostly between the judge, Squire and Mr. Dryden. They were talking about criminal cases. Squire had raised the question of murder.

"I don't imagine you have many such serious cases in your small court, judge, and in this orderly community."

"You would be surprised, Sir John," the judge answered. "There is plenty of crime. But not, I admit, many first-degree murders. That is murder with malice aforethought," he explained, looking round the table.

"A wonderful phrase," murmured Sir John.

"A very telling phrase, wouldn't you agree, Ezekiel? Let me

explain it to the ladies. Murder with malice aforethought is a crime planned in cold blood. As a punishment, if he is found guilty, the accused will hang. But a second-degree murder such as one committed in the heat of the moment—supposing in an ungovernable rage a man kills his lover, the French call that a *crime passionel*—is dealt with more leniently. Ezekiel, what about that sailor who found his wife *in flagrante delicto*. He had been away at sea for a long time and she likewise had been deprived. Ah hum! So the poor, crazed fellow picked up the nearest weapon to hand, a brass candlestick in this case, and dealt the fatal blow. I must say one's sympathy could be brought to bear on both criminal and victim in cases of that kind. The letter of the law is sometimes flexible."

"We now have the first occupant of that fine new jail, Miss Kate," Ezekiel said. "For ten years, no less. No dancing for him, poor fellow." His narrow brilliant eyes dwelt on his host. "Don't imagine, Sir John, there is little crime in a new colony. On the contrary, it can be a breeding ground. Most people are living here in conditions of stress. They have left their loved ones, they have had a long and trying sea voyage and are probably suffering from weeks of an extremely poor diet. They find they have to build their own house before they have a roof over their heads, perhaps their wives are ailing or unfaithful or just desperately homesick." He paused. "Everyone is not as fortunate as you, Sir John, arrived into ideal conditions."

"I regarded it as my duty to my family to ensure that," Sir John said stiffly.

"Everyone hasn't the means to ensure it. Those are facts." Ezekiel smiled good-humouredly. "But I assure you the judge and I among others will administer the law fairly. Just don't make the mistake that it is dull or inconsequential because the number of inhabitants of this colony is small. On the contrary I have a belief that these new New Zealanders, so far from home and often so emotionally distressed, may have a penchant for bizarre murders. Not," he added lightly, "that that was what drew me here."

Lady Devenish had pushed back her chair.

"I think we ladies might retire to the drawing room. I have

never regarded murder as a suitable dinner-table topic, which perhaps proves your point, Mr. Dryden. We are all suffering from isolation, and the inability to reason calmly. I know that after the nor'-wester has blown all day I am in an extremely nervous state." She endeavoured to smile. She was desperately tired and longing only to get upstairs where she could take a very small teaspoonful of her comforter. If ever she had earned it, it was tonight.

The other ladies, Ada and Maud Harmon, were not in the least disturbed, but perhaps this kind of conversation was more familiar fare to them. Kate was frowning a little, and Emily, too wide-eyed, and quite out of her depth, was dispatched to bed.

"Those men love dramatics," Ada said. "Now they'll sit over their port for hours. Maud, how does the judge feel when he has to don the black cap?"

"I don't really know. He would never discuss it with me. But I imagine the way a surgeon does when he has to amputate a leg. It is for the patient's good."

"Hanging!" exclaimed Ada.

"He has to pay for his crime, doesn't he? He has to meet his Maker with his guilt removed, just as if it were a diseased part of him."

"This is *not* a topic for Christmas!" Lady Devenish exclaimed, on the verge of hysteria. "I can't think how it began. I really think—we are all very tired—if you would like to retire. We have a busy day planned tomorrow..."

"The most sensible idea I've heard yet," said Ada. "Come along, Maud. We can snatch an hour or two of sleep before our husbands are dragged away from their port. I must say, Iris, your husband has thought of all the comforts. He's a truly re-markable man."

"Oh, yes," Lady Devenish was swaying with weariness. "He always determines to have his comforts."

Kate had just come back from seeing Emily to bed.

"I was just saying, Kate, that my husband likes his comforts."

Their eyes met in a brief question.

"Were you, Lady Devenish? But all men do, don't they? Perhaps some are more clever at getting them than others. I think we should wish them luck."

Whether it was because of the macabre dinner-table conversation, or the fact that, in her weariness, Lady Devenish had forgotten to close her window and Old Bill had got in, no one was quite sure. But in the early hours Lady Devenish woke the house by her screams.

Kate was the first to her door. She lit a candle and found Lady Devenish sitting on the side of the bed clutching her throat.

"That cat! He nearly suffocated me! I woke up and couldn't breathe."

A breeze was blowing gently through the half-open window. If Old Bill had come in, he had disappeared. Ada, holding her wrap round her plump figure, swore that she had seen a great animal leaping down the stairs.

"Was I dreaming, Hubert?"

"No, dear. But it wasn't a great animal. It was only a normally-sized cat. At least that was my impression."

"There you have the unreliability of witnesses," Ezekiel Dryden said in his dry, legal way. "Ada thinks it a Himalayan bear, Hubert sees a domestic animal."

"Whatever it was, my wife is very distressed." Sir John, never anything but immaculate, had appeared in his brocade dressing gown. "She has an unfortunate phobia about cats, this one in particular, because it was a great pet of its previous owner who is now deceased. The cat has taken a fancy to Iris, or more probably to a familiar bed. We have had this problem before. Pray, all of you, go back to bed. Kate knows how to take care of my wife. You will find her quite recovered in the morning. Though I think perhaps we will talk of more congenial matters at the dinner table in future." His brows rose in gentle reproach. "Anyway, we are all going to church in the morning so we can repent of our sins of omission or thoughtlessness or whatever they are. I have planned on this being a completely English Christmas for you all. Except for the quite unfamiliar weather, of course."

*　　*　　*

On a balmy Christmas morning, full of sunshine and bird song, Lady Devenish seemed quite recovered. Indeed, she only vaguely remembered what had happened and was most distressed to hear that she had disturbed the household.

"I fancy I thought I was being suffocated, but it surely was only a dream. I have had these dreams before, as my husband may have told you. I have a terribly nervous disposition. But now I am quite well again."

When the parrot squawked loudly she was able to add calmly that Old Bill, that dreadful renegade, now had a rival, and would perhaps stay outdoors.

"Terrible weather we're having," the parrot announced, and Emily burst into fits of giggles. She was longing for Jonnie and Honi and Daniel to see this comical creature.

But Squire was saying in a tight voice, "Get that bird out of here. It has a voice like a hacksaw. I can't think why you find it amusing, Emily."

He was dressed for church, which partly accounted for his air of severity.

"The horses will be round at ten thirty. The ladies will ride in the buggy, and the gentlemen will go ahead on horseback. This afternoon I plan to take anyone interested round the estate. We can amuse ourselves by counting my flocks—different from the parson's, eh?" He was getting back his humour and his equanimity. "I believe my housekeeper will have Christmas dinner ready in the late afternoon. Tomorrow, if the weather is kind, Kate and I have organised a picnic by the lake."

"Is Iris not coming?" asked Ada.

"I doubt it. She says sitting on rocks and getting sunburnt isn't her idea of pleasure. The wind prevents her from holding up her parasol. She isn't an outdoor person, Ada."

"What a pity!" Ada exclaimed innocently. "Since almost everything here is outdoors. There's so much of it. Hadn't you envisaged that when you came here, Sir John?"

Sir John smiled gently.

"Since the rest of us have grown to love it, I am praying that Iris will do the same. In time."

222

19

Kate had longed for one of the gentlemen to prefer the buggy so that she could give up her place to him and ride beside Sir John. She hadn't had a moment alone with him since the evening before the arrival of the guests when he had so surprisingly drawn her to him and kissed her. She realised that she had been longing for him to do that, and now that he had done so a desperate hunger had awakened in her. She wanted to be near him all the time. The impulse to touch him, on his sleeve, his hand, his thigh, was intense. Now and again she succumbed, even in company, which made it unbearably exciting. She would pass him a cup and saucer and her fingers would linger a moment. Or she would find a book for him and point to some passage, leaning slightly against him. Or encounter him in a doorway and brush by him.

That secret kiss had given her this freedom. It had made her bold in a way she had never been. She longed for the guests to be gone so that they could be alone again.

Nevertheless, she had an acute feeling of guilt. She knew that she would have to overcome this terrible turmoil inside herself. How much of her feelings did she show? Ada was no fool, and those sharp observant eyes of Mr. Dryden were frequently on her. He was a nuisance, that young man. If not cross-examining her with words he was doing so with his eyes. It would be a relief when the visitors had gone and she could relax and enjoy the supreme pleasure of her emotions, all the more intense for their being forbidden.

What was to happen? There could be no future for herself and Sir John. Yet all her usual good sense had flown away and she could live only in the radiant present. Let it last a little while, perhaps a few months, perhaps a year. She was ashamed to admit that now she had a far greater understanding of Celina. She had thought her behaviour shameless, immoral and unforgivable, yet now she had a suspicion that Celina, by refusing to be shackled by prim conventions, had known how to live.

She was secretly dreaming of being put to the ultimate test. Flesh against flesh. Sir John's fine, grave face above her.

The Reverend Salt, a middle-aged minister of the Church of England, who had come to New Zealand as a missionary and had spent several years converting the Maoris to Christianity was standing in until a younger and more energetic man could be found for the long round of small parishes. The little church, decorated with ferns and the heavily sweet Madonna lilies, was packed on Christmas Day. Kate suspected the villagers of coming more to see the ladies and gentlemen from Avalon, in their fashionable attire, than to listen to the Reverend Salt's ponderous sermon.

After the service was over Mr. Dryden asked Lady Devenish to walk round the small churchyard with him. "Why must we so determinedly bring our culture with us to a foreign place?" Kate heard him saying, "Even the graves are conforming, by growing ivy decently over the tombstones."

Lady Devenish, her ruffled silk parasol shielding her from the hot sun, looked more than ever like an ivory carving.

"There's Laura Henshaw's grave," she said. "It's so sad. Perhaps you will understand my abhorrence for that cat when you know it was her pet. I think I associate it with churchyards. And yet,"—Kate thought that she couldn't be hearing correctly—"its face has a look of my husband." She gave a high nervous laugh. "Is that an absurd thing to say?"

Mr. Dryden took her arm with gentleness. "One of my aunts looked exactly like a sleepy barnyard owl. She had large round eyes and blinked a great deal, and certainly could see out of the back of her head."

He's making that up, Kate thought, half amused, half irritated. He had scarcely looked at her or spoken to her all morning. Not that she minded. It was nice that someone should pay attention to Lady Devenish. That lady was actually laughing.

"What was her name?"

"My aunt's? Persephone. All our family has high-flown names."

"Mr. Dryden, I don't believe a word you're saying. And you just have attended church. For shame!"

Nevertheless there was a faint glow in Lady Devenish's face. She looked quite pretty. One suddenly saw how she must have appealed to Sir John looking for a bride and finding this shy, young, malleable creature. But the glow must so quickly have faded and the maddening timidity taken over.

Clever Mr. Dryden. He had a way with women. She must ask him about Sophia and Clara and Amy in Christchurch. No, she wasn't in the least interested. She wouldn't give him the satisfaction.

The heat increased during the afternoon, the outcrops of rock glittering in the sun, the wind smoothing back the tussocks and sending up small spirals of dust. It seemed absurd to sit down to a meal of roasted turkey and plum pudding, Sir John said, but unthinkable not to do so. One kept to one's country's customs, or one lost one's identity. It was an important precept for emigrants.

"Like growing ivy on tombstones?" Mr. Dryden commented, but no one knew whether or not he was being mildly satirical, so no one laughed.

"I must say I wouldn't care for that creeping thorny manuka, which is the local shrub," Lady Devenish said presently. "You wouldn't recommend that, Ezekiel?"

"Certainly not, dear lady. For you I would plant a white rose bush. But not for at least half a century from now."

Lady Devenish's high, soft laugh was so unfamiliar that everyone looked at her.

"Ezekiel, what a flatterer you are."

Sir John was frowning slightly.

"We seem to be starting another unsuitable dinner-table conversation. Kate, tell us an Irish story. Make us all laugh."

"Not all Irish stories are funny, Sir John. But after dinner, if you wish, I'll sing some Irish songs."

"Now that would give us all great pleasure. After we have distributed the presents from the Christmas tree. The men are coming up from the yards, the boys, too, of course. I am going to ask Emily to hand out the presents. I hope that no one has been forgotten."

"John, you didn't tell me—" Lady Devenish was beginning.

"No, I arranged all of this when I was in Timaru collecting Emily from school. She was sworn to secrecy. She was a great help because she remembered the names of all the shepherds and farmhands. Not forgetting Lee Fong, of course. We found him a brass gong so that punctuality at meals will be much improved, and the house will sound like a Buddhist temple."

"Sir John, I think you're remarkable," Ada exclaimed. "Why, this will be just like a baronial hall, with the servants gathered round."

"It's what Squire did at Leyte Manor," Emily said primly. And she was to behave like the lady of the manor, handing out presents. Sir John meant her to get into practice. She was so happy she could burst.

They even sang carols in the hot, windy evening, the shepherds bashful and grinning and clutching their presents, mostly tobacco and bottles of ale. Jonas Lodden, as befitted Squire's oldest servant, unwrapped a fine briar pipe, and Jonnie and Daniel both had books of New Zealand flora and fauna. It was not the value of the gift but Squire's thought for every last man that counted. They suddenly began clapping and demanding a speech.

Kate watched Sir John standing very straight, his kindly gaze bent on his servants whom, he declared, had worked hard and well during the whole cycle of that famous and important beast, the sheep. Next season he hoped to be working with them, but he still had to learn his trade. He held up his hands. "I shall have honest callouses on these next year. There's not going to be room for idle people in this country. We must all work. I hope Avalon will set an example in this respect."

"The beggar didn't even build the place," Kate heard Hubert Collins whisper to his wife at the back of the room, and Ada's louder whisper, "But he has such style, he carries you away."

The crowd broke up and Ezekiel came to speak to Kate for the first time that day.

"Amazing fellow, our host. Do you think New Zealand is going to appreciate him?"

"Of course it will."

"You say that very confidently, Miss Kate."

"I've known him for a much longer time than you have. I should be able to speak confidently."

"I won't quibble. Though it's rather a pity that this occasion has been only for us. I have the feeling that there should have been a newspaper reporter here. A journalist from the *South Canterbury Times*, perhaps?"

"Yes, isn't it a shame there was not," Kate answered serenely.

"I'm not a bad hand at a pen myself," Mr. Dryden added proudly. "I intend writing an account of Christmas in the Antipodes for English journals."

"Do you?"

"You sound surprised. Is it that you do not expect me to be flattering? I have a high regard for our host and hostess, you know."

"I had noticed you getting on well with Lady Devenish. You have a talent with ladies, Mr. Dryden?"

"I believe I do. At least, I have persuaded her to come on our picnic tomorrow."

"Oh, but—"

"Leave her alone in the house, Miss Kate? When she has all these nervous fears about prowling cats. And other dangers."

"It was only that she can't sit in the sun for long. Her complexion is too delicate. Someone will have to take her home early." Kate paused. "What other dangers?" she added hesitantly.

"Oh, one or two, Kate. I had the feeling, quite erroneously I hope, that she might be under the influence of some drug. Does she take a sedative?"

Kate looked startled. "No. At least not now. She took a little laudanum when she was suffering from the strain of Celina's wedding, but since then Sir John has forbidden it. He has refused to bring any more bottles into the house. Whatever makes you think that, anyway?"

"I had noticed the pupils of her eyes. But perhaps they are their normal size. After all I've had a very brief acquaintance with her until this weekend."

"Surely I would have noticed something like that."

"I imagine you would have. But she did have an hallucination last night."

"That wasn't an hallucination, that was real. I'm afraid the cat did get in her room. Ada and Hubert both saw it run out. I will particularly remember to see that her window is closed tonight, even though it is so hot. No, Ezekiel, I think you merely have an over-suspicious lawyer's mind!"

"What an indictment you make that sound, Miss Kate. Then I suppose I must accept your superior knowledge of the circumstances."

Lady Devenish was the first to retire, when the long festive evening of singing and talking was over. She was quite exhausted, she said, but no one must disturb themselves on her account. It was only Kate who slipped into her room half an hour later and found the bedside lamp still alight, the curtains blowing in the warm wind, and Lady Devenish fast asleep, her narrow face turned into the lace-trimmed pillow slip. Kate bent over her. She seemed so deeply asleep. But she had been very tired. It did not mean that she was drugged. It was a pity to shut the window on such a warm night, but the door could be left open for air. She did not think there would be a repetition of last night's alarm.

* * *

The following day was less windy, and consequently hotter, with the sun blazing down out of a blanched sky, and all the gentlemen preparing to swim, no matter how cold the snow-fed water of the lake might be. The ladies would find some shade, Lady Devenish beneath her parasol, Kate, Ada and Maud with firmly anchored straw bonnets, Miss Pugh in a large gardening hat, and Emily braving the heat with nothing but a wide hair ribbon holding back her hair. She would get sunburnt and freckled. Christmas was being so wonderful that today she had forgotten about being a lady. Hannah and Myrtle, who were permitted to leave their caps and aprons behind, had come to lay the table-cloth on a flat piece of ground and set out the cutlery and plates and glasses.

The picnic hamper was packed to the brim with cold turkey and ham, freshly baked bread, slices of plum pudding, lettuces, and tender young onions, and some small rather hard green apples. It was too early for plums and pears to have ripened.

Bottles of wine were put in the lake to cool. Sir John said that no picnic was worthy of its name without some good French Chablis, no matter that his precious stock was getting small. There would be another consignment arriving before too long. He had had the foresight before leaving London to arrange with his wine merchant for continuing supplies.

Daniel was in charge of the billy-can full of water. He would make a fire later and boil the water and put in a lavish handful of the strong, invigorating tea that was so popular among outdoor workers. He had also brought a fishing rod and asked Emily to come with him while he attempted to catch some blue trout.

There were no nibbles in the shining expanse of water, but it was so peaceful sitting on the warm rocks with their feet in shallow water that they didn't mind their lack of success with fish. Daniel's face was a raw red against his mop of tow-coloured hair, his eyes the blanched blue of the sky. He was just as solemn as ever, but for the first time Emily found herself able to talk easily to him.

"Are you happy at Avalon, Daniel?"

"Now you sound just like Squire's wife. Don't get too grand at that school, Em."

"Me, grand! Sitting here barefoot like a Maori!"

"It's the way you talk sometimes. Not always, though. Not when you're excited about something like you were about Pearl. You look pretty when you're excited."

"Well, I'm not excited now because you haven't caught a fish. I'm just peaceful and happy. Do you think of your parents in heaven, Daniel?"

"Aye. Sometimes."

"I think of Mam, too. And Willie. Willie was not very strong so he wouldn't have been good for hard work on a farm. He was meant to learn his letters and be a parish clerk like Grandpa. It's funny, isn't it, writing all those names in church registers and having them sort of live for ever. They're born, they get married, they die, and their names are written for people to read centuries later. Only Mam's and Willie's didn't get written anywhere. But Squire said that wouldn't stop them going to heaven."

"Mine are buried in the churchyard in Timaru. Aunt Tab had a little cross put up with their names. So God will know where to find them if He goes looking. It beats me, though."

"What beats you?"

"How He can keep account of everyone all over the world."

"Not heathens, Daniel. I should think He only speaks the English language."

"You mean not the Maoris? Not Honi?"

"Honi has some funny old gods. All those *tapu* things. I expect they'll look after him. Oh, Daniel! You've got a fish! Look, it's nibbling your bait. Oh, quick! You can land it."

With an expert flourish Daniel swung his line and landed the small flopping fish.

"Oh, well done, Daniel! You are clever!" Spontaneously Emily flung her arms round him, and he dropped the line and returned her embrace. For a moment his warm, slender body surprisingly hard and muscular was pressed against her, his sunburnt face shone rosily above her, and she could feel his warm breath on her cheek.

"Hey, you two!" called Sir John.

They sprang apart, startled, half guilty.

"Look, Squire!" Emily cried. "We've caught a fish. At least Daniel has. Come and see."

"Dum him!" Daniel muttered.

"What did you say, Daniel?"

"I said the miserable fish is too small. I'm going to throw it back. It's got to do some growing. Like you, Em." He was scowling, his happy mood gone. Emily didn't know why except that Squire, tall and easy and handsome, was advancing towards them, and Daniel was a bit soft about liking to have her to himself. He also, she decided, had a lot of growing to do.

When the sun was directly overhead the wine was lifted out of the lake and opened, the food was laid out on the snowy table-cloth, and people sat on rocks or on the ground. Ezekiel sat a little way off on a tussock. It had looked like a soft armchair, he said, but it was devilish uncomfortable. Lady Devenish sat primly on a flat boulder, and presently Ezekiel got up and began finding some tender slices of turkey for her and a fresh green lettuce leaf. Hannah giggled a good deal and was clumsy, as always, but Myrtle was as neat as if she had been indoors waiting on table. Everyone ate heartily and there was a great deal of laughter about Daniel's fish. He had recovered his good humour and said he would come back to catch it in a few weeks' time.

Lady Devenish's cheeks were a pale japonica pink beneath her lacy hat. She looked so much better, Kate thought, with a strange twinge of jealousy. Ezekiel now sat at her feet, and was really making a ridiculous fuss of her. Even Sir John noticed Iris's frail blooming and went to sit on her other side. Was he shamed into that?

Would he be whispering to Kate to linger downstairs after everyone had gone to bed, as he had done last evening? Then he had wanted to tell her how charmingly she had sung. He had held her hand a moment, then followed her upstairs and at her bedroom door had given her the briefest kiss on her cheek. Whenever she woke in the night she touched the cheek that had been kissed.

But today she was expected to sit with the other ladies, conversing politely and seeing that they had sufficient to eat and were not too hot or too bored by the placid expanse of water and rocks and scrub and bare hillside.

"At least," Ada Collins said contentedly, "there are no wasps to torment us. That's almost sufficient reward for living in New Zealand."

Maud Harmon, an inveterate journal keeper, suddenly read aloud what she had written.

"Unknown birds are singing, all too familiar sheep are calling, the snowpeaks are mirrored in the glass-clear waters of the lake. This must be a small paradise."

"And now," she added, "I am about to sketch you all to illustrate my antipodean picnic. So please don't move for a little while."

Everyone clapped, and Sir John said warningly, "If you think this a paradise, you must never visit us in the winter. Must she, Kate?"

His face was relaxed, his eyes gentle and benign.

After lunch a walk was proposed. Everyone except Lady Devenish sprang up. She said she would just rest quietly in the shade of her parasol. Ezekiel sat down again, electing to keep her company. He would doze with his hat over his eyes, he said.

"Not too far," said Ada. "I haven't the shape for it."

It was agreed that they should go to the spot where the lake curved round an outcrop of rocks. It was not far. But when they returned Lady Devenish and Ezekiel had gone.

Sir John was mildly annoyed. "Iris was looking so well in the fresh air. She should have waited for us to come back."

"Well, I imagine the heat got too much for her and Mr. Dryden took her home," Ada said. "He's a very thoughtful young man. Charming manners. He has a way of drawing out the shyest people."

"Then I think we'd better pack up and follow them." Sir John had overcome his brief flash of annoyance and was looking jovial again. "Before all the secrets of the Devenish family are disclosed."

"Secrets, Sir John?" Ada enquired archly.

"You said that young man had a way of making people talk."

"Ah, his habits in court," said Judge Harmon. "But he should learn to quell them in private life."

What secrets? Kate was wondering involuntarily. Were there more than the embarrassing history of Celina?

When they arrived back after the mile-long walk Ezekiel was playing cricket with Jonnie and Honi in the stable yard. He had an old bat and ball and an upturned packing case for a wicket. He was the bowler, Jonnie was the batsman and a bewildered Honi kept wicket.

"Is my wife all right?" called Sir John.

"Perfectly splendid, sir, except for being a little tired. She went upstairs to rest before dinner. I promised to teach the boys cricket. Daniel, come and join us."

"So that's all right," said Ada cheerfully. "You worry too much, Sir John. Iris is much stronger than she looks."

"Perhaps. But Kate, go up and see her, will you?"

Upstairs Kate leaned over the bed, listening. Lady Devenish had lain down in the muslin dress she had worn to the picnic. She hadn't even taken her shoes off. She was deep in sleep. She must have been quite exhausted to sleep so profoundly. Or there had been some agent to help her. Tincture of laudanum? How could one know? At least she was breathing deeply and evenly, and a little colour had stayed in her cheeks. It was still daylight and so warm that Kate was tempted to leave the window open. On such a mild summer day Old Bill would surely not be seeking a haven indoors.

She would come up again in an hour or so and rouse Lady Devenish to dress for dinner.

"Terrible weather we're having," said Napoleon in his grating voice from his cage in the hall, and everyone laughed hilariously at the absurdity of the pronouncement. Presently Ezekiel came in and said that Jonnie had been out for a duck, but Honi had made one terrific hit for six over the stables.

"Cricket's important," he said. "It teaches discipline as well as sporting skills. I believe the Maoris may be quite good athletes." Then he sank into a chair, wanting nothing but a long, cold drink.

"Time to dress for dinner," said Sir John. "I'm afraid I'm going to regret giving Lee Fong that gong. He will shatter our ears. Don't worry about Lady Devenish, Kate. The gong will wake her."

It must have been half an hour later that his cry resounded through the house. "Kate, Kate, come quickly! Oh, my God, my wife is dead! That cat has suffocated her!"

20

The nearest doctor was twenty miles away in Timaru. He could not be there until the next morning, even though Ezekiel set out at once to ride the long dusty miles. Sadly, there was no need for haste. Lady Devenish had stopped breathing.

She must have been so deeply asleep that when Old Bill had curled up on her face she had not been able to wake sufficiently to push him off. Kate had been the first to share the tragic discovery with Sir John. He had shown her the hairs from the cat he'd found on the pillow, and told her how he'd seen Old Bill leap off the bed and sit glowering beneath a chair. But by then it had been too late to arouse his wife.

The cat escaped through the window while he was still shaking her, and drenching her with cold water from the bedside carafe. The mystery was how she could have been so deeply asleep that she could be suffocated without a struggle. There was surely more to it than weariness. She must have had some drugging agent.

After Ezekiel had set off, a search was made and the nearly empty bottle of laudanum was found concealed in a hatbox in the wardrobe.

"Ah!" said Sir John, the bones prominent beneath the flesh of his cheeks. His eyes were tragic. Kate wanted to weep. She couldn't bear seeing either of them, Lady Devenish in her deep, permanent sleep, her face as small and pallid as a sick child's, and Sir John with that haunted look on his face. Not of surprise, not even of grief, a look of retribution, as if he had always known this would happen and as if it were in some way his fault.

"Your guess is right, Sir John," said the doctor, a burly Scotsman called McTavish, the next morning. "The puir wee lady has been suffocated. You said it was the cat. Aye, a heavy animal could do that, but the victim would have had to be vurry sound asleep, otherwise the instinct would be to struggle and get rid of the offending object. Does she take a wee drop of alcohol, may I ask?"

Sir John, grim-faced, held up the blue bottle. "This is the cause, doctor. We found it hidden in my wife's wardrobe. I'm afraid she had developed an addiction to laudanum as a result of certain family problems. It had got to the stage where I had forbidden any in the house. But when we were on a recent trip to Christchurch to see our daughter married she must have obtained a supply. And this—" he looked at the sheeted figure on the bed—"is the result."

"The cat? Is it a large, heavy animal?"

"Very large. And my wife had an aversion to it. It had belonged to the previous owner of Avalon and obviously had always slept on her bed. When we discovered its habits and how it disturbed my wife we kept the window shut. But last evening was very warm and in any case it was hardly seven o'clock. We thought she would be dressing for dinner. It has been the greatest misfortune, Doctor McTavish."

"Aye, that's it, sir. That's what the coroner will certainly say."

"Must there be a coroner's inquest?"

"I'm afraid so, sir. The lady's not my patient and I haven't her medical records. We have to follow the law. But don't worry, sir. I'll make the arrangements. The post mortem can be done immediately, and the body released for burial after that. Would you like the funeral here, or in Timaru?"

"In Timaru certainly. Don't bring her all the way back here.

She was never happy in this place, I regret to say. She didn't like the mountains or the loneliness." Sir John breathed heavily. "Nor that cat. She saw it as a fiend. Now I believe she had some uncanny kind of intuition. We should have paid more attention to it. Shouldn't we, Kate?"

Kate, who at Sir John's request had been present at this discussion said sadly, "It was my fault. I left the window open last evening. It was still so early and I hadn't thought Lady Devenish would sleep so soundly."

Sir John touched her hand.

"You mustn't blame yourself, Kate. Miss O'Connor has been the most loyal of friends to my family, doctor. She is the last person to be blamed."

But in spite of Sir John's reassuring words she would never forget that narrow, bone-white face on the pillow, eyes closed, mouth drawn downwards. It would haunt her all her life.

"Kate, I can't believe Iris would have bought that laudanum herself. She wouldn't have had the courage," said Ada, her plump face a mottled red from tears.

"She would if she wanted it badly enough. I hear that is what people addicted to drugs do."

"Well, she did, as I recollect, go for a walk alone one morning when she was staying with me. Perhaps past the apothecary's. But did she really need the medicine that badly?"

"I'm afraid so. As we now know."

"Then it may have been the drug that killed her and not the cat at all."

"It may have been. Her heart may have stopped, the doctor said."

"From the drug or from fright?"

Kate winced. "We don't know. Oh, Ada, it's so terrible. You and Hubert will stay for the funeral, won't you? It's to be in Timaru, so you can go on to Christchurch from there."

"And you intend to stay here, Kate?"

"Of course."

"With neither pupil nor mistress?"

"Ada, how could I desert Sir John now? He's so tortured."

"Why?" asked Ada bluntly. "He hadn't the happiest of marriages, now had he?"

"No-o. But he could never never have expected it to end in this way. It's the most terrible shock to him."

"I grant you that. It is for all of us. But although you may not believe it possible of a chatter-box like me, I'm the greatest one for facing facts. And it isn't the best thing for you, a young unmarried lady, to stay here and comfort the bereaved husband. Such a handsome one, too."

"Ada! I refuse to believe what you're saying."

"I have your interests at heart, Kate. You've always known that."

"But I won't be here alone. Miss Pugh is here. And Emily."

"Emily has her father whose duty it is to look after her. She also has a sensible woman like Miss Pugh. She'll be all right. That's no excuse, Kate."

Kate pressed her hands to her burning cheeks.

"I can't talk of these things now, Ada. We must all have time to recover from the tragedy." After a pause she said steadily, "I will go to the funeral and afterwards come back with Sir John. That is definite. So let us say no more about it."

Unexpectedly, it was Ezekiel, that very contained young man, who showed the most grief. After returning from his all-night ride, accompanied by the doctor, he sat in the kitchen drinking the strong tea Miss Pugh had made. Suddenly he buried his face in his hands and wept.

"The poor sweet lady," he said in a choked voice. "I tried to amuse her and cheer her up. But she was so disorientated, so overwhelmed." And then, "How could he do that to her?"

"Do what?" Kate asked sharply.

"Bring her here, of course. It's a place for strong, self-reliant pioneer women. Not for hothouse plants." He raised his wet, brilliant eyes and stared penetratingly at Kate. "What did you think I meant?"

"I don't know. You sounded so accusing."

"So I was. So I shall remain. And I must leave you, Kate, to

238 /

plant the white rose on her grave on my behalf. Will you do that?"

She nodded, hating him. Yet a moment earlier, with his face buried in his hands, he had looked so boyish, so disarming, that she had wanted to comfort him.

Two days later they came back from the small quiet funeral, a much diminished party, Sir John, Miss Pugh and Kate.

It had been established that Lady Devenish had died from a heart attack brought on by the combined effects of a recent large dose of laudanum, and suffocation from some muffling object on her face which she had not had the strength to throw off. It was tragic and bizarre. Old Bill would have to be destroyed. No one could bear to see him about.

As for Ezekiel's strange present, the cockatoo, that bird was permanently ensconced in its cage in the drawing-room window. It was a comical creature, swinging by one claw and tilting its head sideways with a quizzical look, not unlike Ezekiel's own. Its comment on the weather had never changed, but on the evening of their return from the funeral it had climbed to the top of its cage, ruffled its yellow crest, and said in a caressing voice, uncannily like Ezekiel's, "I love you, Kate." It had been uncanny and disturbing, and Kate had nearly jumped out of her skin. She was thankful that there had been no one else in the room to hear, and prayed that Napoleon would exercise discretion in the future. Sir John would not find that pronouncement pleasing, and she couldn't bear to have him hurt any more. Yet she was almost smiling. "Haven't you the courage to tell me so yourself, Ezekiel? Must you send messages by birds?" She felt a moment of light-heartedness, as if normal life had been resumed.

Apart from Napoleon's quirk, life at Avalon went on as usual. It was quickly realised that the mistress's absence would not be too noticeable. She had been so quiet, so unobtrusive, almost invisible, a pale shadow walking beneath her parasol in the garden, a face at the window, a quiet form with idle hands in the chair by the fire. A lonely lady who had never confided her thoughts to anybody.

21

All Lady Devenish's personal belongings had been gathered up and packed in the trunks in which they had arrived from England. Kate and Miss Pugh hadn't known what else to do with them. They had wanted to remove them from Sir John's sight but not to distress him by asking what his wishes were regarding their eventual disposal.

One item, however, had been overlooked. The ruffled cream silk parasol that had been left hanging behind the front door where outdoor wraps and heavy boots were kept. Emily found it and took it into the garden. Holding it over her head she walked up and down with short mincing steps, just as Lady Devenish had done. She hadn't put her hair up or pulled on long white gloves, but she was sure she felt exactly as a well-groomed lady did. Her skirts swayed and she imagined she was teetering on high heels.

"Emily!" The voice was Squire's, and it was hard with anger. "Whatever do you think you are doing, you impertinent child? Come indoors and put that parasol away at once."

Swift hurting tears filled her eyes. She hadn't thought she

was doing any harm. Just practising being a lady as Squire wanted her to be. With Lady Devenish so sadly dead, the time to learn had grown much shorter. She would have to cram all her learning into two years, for she was sure that was the least time Squire would wait to get his son. She would be sixteen then and old enough. Some girls had babies when they were only fifteen. But sixteen was safer. That was what the older girls at school said.

"Kate, will you take care of this?" Squire was continuing. "I wouldn't have thought Emily would be so unfeeling, so insensitive." He had his hand on Kate's arm. They looked well together, Kate in her starched gingham and Sir John standing tall and straight beside her. Emily blinked at her tears. It would never do to burst into sobs. But to be scolded in front of Kate who really was only a servant was too unfair.

"I'm sorry, Squire, I didn't think. Did I look like Lady Devenish?"

She wanted him to say yes, so that she would know that her posture and her mannerisms were improving. But he said harshly, "How dare you ask me such a thing? Are you trying to torment me?"

Now she could only hand the furled parasol to Kate and flee indoors before her trembling lower lip and her scarlet face betrayed her anguish.

I didn't mean it, Squire. I was only trying to look nice for you. To show you how fast I am growing up. To stop you being lonely. Don't be so cruel to me...The muddled impassioned words wanted to burst out of her. She could only crouch on the floor behind the sofa in the drawing room, stifling her sobs and praying that no one would find her.

"Terrible weather we're having," said Napoleon conversationally.

That made her begin to giggle in wild hiccups, and Kate found her.

Kate was brisk and kind.

"Come along, Emily, don't be so upset."

"I was only practising how to walk... to be a lady... I didn't mean to hurt Squire."

"Yes, I know. He does understand. But he's got rather raw nerves at present. So no more parasols, promise?"

Emily nodded hard. Nevertheless, she couldn't help thinking that Kate was looking very pretty nowadays. Squire must notice. Should she be jealous?

"He's never been angry with me before."

"No, I'm afraid he's spoiled you a little. But never mind, you're going back to school next week. When you come home again you'll find him much more his old self."

"Will I?"

Kate nodded. She seemed to be blushing.

"I think so. Grief takes time, you know. But you were always his favourite."

Emily's tears were dry, her face suffused with delight.

"Was I really? Then I can wait for him to get over his grief. I can wait and wait and wait."

"That school plurry bad, Em," Honi said. His sparkling eyes rested on her longingly. "You hurry home, see." He suddenly gave her a kiss, Maori fashion, rubbing her nose, then followed the buggy to the road gates, as usual, running gracefully on his slim, brown legs, which seemed to have grown inches longer every time she came home.

Emily had looked forward to the long drive with Squire, but this time he was almost completely silent, his face stern and sad. He hated Timaru now, Emily guessed, because his wife was buried there.

The long-awaited letter from Celina arrived at last. It was addressed to Lady Devenish. Kate would have liked to open it and conceal from Sir John anything that was antagonistic or hurtful to him. But she didn't dare. His moods had become unpredictable, swinging from explosive anger to silent brooding, and, less often than she longed for, to a tender affection and concern for her. She was afraid the letter would plunge him into a brooding state again.

It was written in Celina's schoolgirlish hand.

My dearest Mama,

Edward and I arrived safely in England ten days ago. We had quite a merry voyage in good company, with singing and dancing most evenings, and deck games at all times. So different from that horrid *Albatross* where Papa kept me from people as if I were a leper. Edward could hardly believe his ears when I told him this. All the same I am finding that he, too, has a jealous nature and is upset if I so much as smile at another man. We had many small quarrels but always kissed and made up and it was highly delightful. Now we are living temporarily in his brother William's Mayfair house, quite a small place, but perfectly suitable until we find our own home. Edward, after his monkish life in the church, is enjoying enormously going to parties and the theatre. So am I. It is all so exciting after that awful snow-bound Avalon. Poor Mama! Are you still finding it dreadfully boring?

Will you tell Papa that although he has not given me permission, I intend taking Edward to see Leyte Manor. Although I never never want to live there it is my family home and I have an added reason for wanting to show it to Edward because we are to be parents in about seven months' time. If our child is a boy I am sure Papa will want to make him his heir. He had always wanted a boy, hadn't he?

I send my regards to Miss Pugh and dear, good Kate, and to Mr. and Mrs. Collins if you should see them. And to Captain Oxford who I hope has forgiven me. I am no longer such an outrageous flirt! Edward will not allow me to be. If Mr. Watts, because he has orders from Papa, will not allow us into Leyte we shall find a way in. I don't think I need to remind Papa that I am quite clever at that!

Edward and I entertain people with stories of life in the Antipodes. Much love, dear Mama, and you would be surprised at how good and respectable your bad daughter has become...

As Kate had anticipated, Sir John's face went stony on reading the letter.

"How dare she!" he muttered. "Against my explicit request."

"But what—"

"It has nothing to do with you, Kate. This is a family matter."

However, he allowed Kate to read the letter, and when she handed it back to him he reread it, his face set in that stony look. What could be so bad about Celina taking her husband to Leyte Manor? Was Sir John expecting them to have wild scandalous parties? A merry life on board ship, she had said. Surely that was harmless enough. Edward was jealous if she looked at another man. Did Sir John think that she would indulge in something more than an outrageous flirtation when all the empty rooms in that large house were available? Was it that kind of behaviour that had so deeply offended him in the past? She could never dare to ask.

Nearly three months had passed since Lady Devenish's death. The evenings were getting shorter, and there was a tang of frost in the air. The great peaks were frequently enveloped in cloud, and emerged to show fresh snowfalls, the white blanket edging down to the foothills. Soon the ewes would have to be mustered and brought to lower ground. The water of the lake had lost its deep azure blue and had faded to a colour that was steely and cold in the late afternoon light. The poplars glowed golden before the next violent wind would strip them of their leaves. The gooseberry and blackcurrant bushes had been stripped and bottles of preserves, made by Miss Pugh, filled the larder shelves. Apples and pears and quinces were stored away and winter supplies of flour and sugar and cereals brought in from the village store.

It was like stocking a ship, Kate thought. But were any of these passengers going to have a merry voyage? It seemed unlikely. She wrote long letters home, expressing a cheerfulness she didn't feel. She also wrote with determined optimism to Ada in reply to that lady's garrulous missives. No, she had no intention of leaving Avalon. No, she hadn't any particular interest in accounts of that lively young man, Ezekiel Dryden's latest conquests, although she did wonder if he was teaching another parrot to talk. Yes, they were all well, except that Sir John was still apparently inconsolable. She couldn't bear to admit that she seemed unable to comfort him. Nor did she tell Ada that he had held her at arm's length for too long. She felt that she was withering like the leaves in the first winter breath.

Strangely, Celina's letter proved to be the catalyst. After receiving it Sir John maintained his black silence for another week, then one evening at dinner he drank a good deal of wine, followed by brandy by the fire, and some tight knot of pain seemed to ease inside him. He began to look mellow and relaxed.

Miss Pugh had gone upstairs, as had Myrtle and Hannah. Lee Fong would have curled up on his pallet in the kitchen. Kate and Sir John were alone.

He beckoned to her to sit on the hearth-rug at his feet, as she had used to do when Lady Devenish was alive. He turned the lamp low, and then let his fingers run through her hair and caress her neck. Her skin began to tingle. The warm firelight on her face made it glow. She breathed deeply in a great sigh of contentment, leaning against him. Then, without warning, his fingers on her neck were replaced by his lips.

"Ah, Kate! Ah, Kate!"

The kisses became more vigorous. He pulled her face round and lifted it towards his, covering it with hard, desperate kisses as if he had been starving for the feel and taste of her.

"Kate, will you marry me?"

She held her breath.

"Now, no protests. No foolishness about my being too recently a widower. Life is going by and I've loved you for a long time. Long before Iris died. You know that, don't you?"

Kate bent her head in acquiescence.

"And I've loved you."

"Bless you, my dearest. We could be married in six months. In the spring. That would surely not offend any puritan sensibilities."

Must they wait so long? Must they worry about other people's sensibilities? Kate wanted to be reckless, urgent, even immoral. She had never forgotten Celina's words which for all their immodesty had seemed to contain the essence of life.

"It will be a long winter," she murmured.

"Yes, it will. But it must be this way. We'll be married quietly in the church in Mossbridge. No fuss. A big wedding would hardly be in the best taste. You do agree with me, Kate?"

Of course she did. He had always wanted to set an example of culture and education and gentlemanly behaviour to this raw province, and she would firmly support him.

But the long, dark winter in this house with all these quiet evenings together, touching but not really touching, creating hungers that were not fulfilled... Wasn't it foolish to waste so much time?

"And then,"—he was kissing her again, stopping her words—"we will have our son. The dream of my life." Celina, too, was waiting for a son. The thought flicked through Kate's bemused mind, and was forgotten.

"I don't mind telling you that that was the great disappointment of my marriage. I began to think it was a dream I could never realise. But now it's going to happen at last. You can give me sons, can't you, Kate? One to inherit Leyte Manor and another to follow me and be an important figure in this wonderful new country, to make it a worthy part of our Queen's possessions."

He's so vain, Kate was thinking adoringly. But I love him to be like that. Confident and articulate and arrogant and so good-looking that I want my hands on him all the time.

"Kiss me, Kate. You kiss me."

His breath smelled of brandy. She thought it had made her a little drunk herself. She pressed her breasts against him and parted her lips on his. The sensation was so wild and sweet that she lost all sense of discretion and began to say urgently, "Yes, yes, we'll be married in the spring—for convention. But need we wait so long for the rest? Need we?" She looked at him boldly. "It gets very tiresome being a virgin."

At once she knew she had made a mistake, a terrible mistake.

He stiffened, pushing her away. It was surely not possible that his face could change so quickly from desire to stony coldness. But it had.

"I don't like that kind of talk, Kate. It doesn't become you."

"But you—but I—" she was almost crying, "why can't we be natural?"

He stood up. "Being natural, as you put it, applies to matrimony only. I hope you will never forget that. Indeed, I know you won't. You're just a little carried away. Don't mistake me, I do want your response, but at the right time. Do you understand?" He gave her a light kiss on the forehead, scarcely brushing her skin with his lips. "Now be a good girl and go up to bed. Tomorrow I'm taking Emily back to school, and while I'm in Timaru I'll visit a jeweller and select a ring for you to wear. Perhaps that will help you through the everlasting winter?"

His eyebrows were raised quizzically, in the way she loved. Although he had made her feel like a chastened schoolgirl, he was smiling with that tenderness that completely disarmed her. She wanted only to please him.

And, of course, fool that she was, her behaviour had reminded him of Celina's, and all the consequent suffering it had given her parents. It had disgusted him. Yet she would never apologise. And when she was his wife she would make her feelings plain about everything. There would be no pretence about emotions, and she would never consent to be just a figure in his shadow. Even if she failed to give him a son...

But it was humiliating to be rejected. Humiliating, humiliating, humiliating... Much as she would love him, she doubted if she would ever forgive him for that moment.

The next morning, for the second time in her hearing, Napoleon raised his startling yellow crest and said in Ezekiel's voice, "I love you, Kate."

What a terrible sense of timing that bird had.

The ring was quite modest, a half hoop of sapphires and diamonds. There had been nothing better to be obtained, Sir John apologised, but when next he went to Christchurch, or to Wellington when he received his expected invitation to visit Governor Grey, he would find something more important.

Kate wasn't sure that she cared for that word in this context. She wanted her engagement ring to be simply a token of love. But it fitted her finger perfectly and she felt deeply happy. Nevertheless, her response was inhibited.

"Come, Kate, that's no way to kiss me."

"I thought it wiser—after last night—" Her voice was prim.

"Good heavens, do you mean to say you're cross with me?"

She was laughing lightly.

"A woman spurned? There's a dangerous animal for you. Perhaps it's better not to tempt me. Remember that I'm Irish."

His eyes gleamed. "You're teasing me."

"You deserve to be teased."

"As long as you love me—"

"With discretion?" she said. "As you wanted me to."

If she were to keep this up she would be playing with fire. But it might make the winter seem less long. It might even be quite amusing. Like Celina and Edward, they could quarrel a little, then kiss and make up. It sounded a delightful way of passing the time.

Ada wrote, "Kate, my dearest, are you really sure you're in love with that man? Hubert says it is the inevitable result of propinquity, but as you know, my husband is a great deal better informed about money than women. Of course we wish you well, but I am glad you have decided not to marry until the spring. It is better in all respects..."

The next line had been crossed out. With difficulty, Kate deciphered the words. Perhaps Ada had meant her to.

"In such a small community people talk..."

About Lady Devenish's death? What else?

For once Ada didn't mention her favourite, Ezekiel.

Miss Pugh, her plain, wise face puckered with sincerity, said virtually the same thing later that evening.

"I'm glad you're not rushing into marriage, Kate. It needs to be thought about very soberly. Sir John is a great deal older than you, and a very worldly man. I have always thought your greatest charm your natural warmth and simplicity."

"You think that will eventually bore him, Aunt Tab?"

"He'll be a fool if it does. No, I don't mean that. I just wonder if you know him well enough."

"Surely I do. I've been living in close proximity—propinquity,

Ada calls it—for more than a year." She saw Miss Pugh's frown. "I didn't say I entirely understood him, but that makes it all the more exciting."

"Does it?"

"Of course it does."

"By the sound of that you're telling me that I'm an elderly spinster who has never experienced these unruly emotions. Perhaps that's true. But the onlooker does see a great deal, and I'm a fairly sensible old lady."

"I know you are, Aunt Tab. But I'm so happy. How can I be wrong about my feelings?"

"Provided they're durable. Aye, well, the house does need a mistress. Now what do we tell Emily? She's devoted to Sir John, you know."

"In a childish way, I grant you. She's just fifteen."

"An ardent age."

"But she thinks of him as a benevolent parent."

"That should be the way of it, I agree. But even as a parent, she definitely regards him as her property. You may have some jealousy to contend with."

"But that's absurd. Emily and I are good friends."

"If you think it's absurd you don't understand adolescents. We'll just have to see. But handle her carefully, Kate. One way or another, she's been rather pushed into maturity."

So nothing was said to Emily. On her next school vacation she was desperately disappointed to find that her father had come for her.

"Where's Squire, Pa?"

Jonas whipped up the horse. "He has other things to think of now he's getting married and all."

Emily was appalled. She couldn't speak for several moments. She chafed her cold hands and tried to stop the shivers that suddenly ran over her body. The wind was chilly, but not so cold that she should be freezing.

At last she managed to say, "Squire—m-married!"

"Not yet, Em. In the spring."

"Who to?" It was a desperate hope. Did Squire mean to surprise her with his offer when she got home?

"It couldn't be anyone but Miss Kate, could it? It was to be expected. She's a bonny young woman and as there aren't many ladies of quality in this country she'll do very well, I don't doubt." After some thought Jonas added, "I do grieve for the mistress. It did seem wrong that she should die like that. But your Mam would say it's God's will and I daresay it is. We haven't got anything else to believe, have we?"

After a while he said, "What's the matter, lass? You're awful quiet."

The tears rolled slowly down Emily's cheeks.

"I was learning to be a lady. To p-please Squire."

"You can still do that. Miss Kate won't interfere. Mind you, I don't hold with all this palaver myself. You should be learning to be useful like your Mam was, cooking and making butter and milking cows and sewing on buttons. This is a country where women don't sit about fanning themselves and sipping tea. They work. Being a lady might be fine enough back home, but here it seems to me she's a bit useless, a bit of a burden. Miss Kate could have been a fine pioneer woman. Now Squire will spoil her, too. It's a shame. But don't tell anyone I said so. I suppose I should have minded you a bit more, Em, but to tell the truth I was fair addled by your Mam's death, and I thought it was fine someone else was giving you attention. Now I'm not sure about that. You look right peaked to me. And someone else's little girl, not a good honest Lodden. I don't know what Grandma and Grandpa would say."

She had never heard her father make such a long speech. She wanted to stop her ears because she didn't like what he was saying. Hadn't he known she would have that dream of being mistress of Leyte as well as being the mother of Squire's son? If he hadn't known he didn't understand women very well.

And she was a woman now, not the little girl he imagined her to be. She had been a grown woman for over a year and there had been only kind Miss Pugh to give her care and advice. Miss Pugh had said, "This is what you have to endure if you're to have children, Emily. And you want children, don't you?"

Oh, she did! She would cheerfully put up with the worst inconvenience to be able to have Squire's son. Romantically she had thought it something like being the mother of Jesus. But now the dream had gone. Kate had killed it. Squire, smiling and treacherous, had killed it.

When they reached Avalon Emily climbed out of the buggy and made straight for the stables.

"Em, where are you going? Squire will be waiting."

"I want to see the boys," she answered over her shoulder. She was no longer crying. Her eyes had been reddened by the wind, she would say. She had already taken off her silly hard-brimmed hat, and undone the buttons of her long school coat. As soon as she could change, she intended never to wear that horrid uniform again.

But she couldn't go into the house because she would be expected to smile at Squire and Kate. It was simply too much for them to expect.

Honi was alone in the little room beside the horse boxes. He was polishing some saddle leather and singing to himself in a deep rich voice, a song with Maori words. It sounded nice, both sweet and sad.

Emily slid into the room.

"What's that song about?"

"Hi! Em! When did you come?"

"Just now. Where are Daniel and Jonnie?"

"Mustering. I was up the look-out but the wind got so strong I came down." He was looking at her with pleased dark eyes. His cheeks were reddened from the wind. He looked like a red and brown berry, hair tousled, strong brown throat bared. When he put out his hand to stroke her cheek Emily let him. Usually she forbade his cheeky advances.

Now his fingers felt soft and strangely comforting, and suddenly she began to cry.

"Em, what's the matter?"

"N-nothing."

"They hurt you at that bad old school?"

"No."

"Didn't you want to come home?"

"Of course I did. Except that Pa told me—" He was watching her with such wide-eyed concern that she blundered on clumsily, "I can't bear for Kate and Squire to be married."

"You're not *jealous,* Em!"

"I am. I am so!"

"But they're old people and you're only a little girl."

She stamped her foot. "I am *not* a little girl. I'm grown up, too. I am. I truly am, Honi."

He looked at her with very bright eyes. Then he began to smile joyfully. "I'll marry you, Em. If it's just being married you want."

"Kiss me then," she said.

He started to put his nose softly against hers.

"No, no, not that way. The *pakeha* way."

Honi began to giggle. "You mean it? Like this?" His lips were tentative, unbelievably soft. Then he stopped giggling and pulled her against him, nuzzling at her throat and trying to undo the buttons of her blouse.

Emily was a little breathless, also secretly shocked, although she tried to hide that.

"I think—actually I think that's a bit rude. If you're going to do that we'd have to go where no one can see us."

Honi gave a whoop and leapt in the air. For a moment she thought he was going to begin his weird Maori war dance, the *haka.*

"Let's run away! I've got a cave. I've got some things there. We can light a fire. If you don't want to see Miss Kate and Squire—"

"I don't, I don't."

"Then serve them plurry right. You be my *wahine.*"

"What's that?"

"My woman. My first wife."

"Your *first!* You mean you are going to marry other ladies."

He was instantly shrewd. "Not with you for my wife, Em. You'll be my lady in the moon. That was the song I was singing."

"What does it say in English?"

"I'll sing it to you."

> *Rona, Rona, sister olden,*
> *Rona in the moon.*

AN IMPORTANT FAMILY

You'll never break your prison golden
Never late nor soon...

His deep throbbing voice sent a thrill through Emily. He sounded just like a grown man. Responding, she exclaimed excitedly, "Well, I have broken my prison golden. That's Squire's house. That's Leyte Manor and everything. So take me to your moon, Honi."

The cave, beneath a large, jutting rock, was shallow and dark. It was a mile or more from the homestead. Emily had left her hat and coat lying on the floor of the tack room. Now she shivered, half from cold, half from nervousness, as she peered into the gloom.

"Wait until I light the fire," said Honi. "You'll see it's cosy and dry. I've got a piece of candle, too. And look—" he had lit the candle stuck in a bottle and held it up. "We've got a rug, too."

The so-called rug was a feathered cloak, very old and dirty, the once proud black and white feathers that had been fashioned into a cloak for some Maori chieftain looking thin and tattered.

"Where did you get that, Honi?" She was so nervous that she wanted to keep on talking.

"Stole it. Long time ago. From an old Maori lying drunk behind a shed. Stole his hat, too, but I lost that. He had a tattooed face like this—" Honi scowled and pulled his mouth into a fearsome snarl. "Too many Maori getting plurry drunk."

"Will you, Honi? When you're grown up?"

"I'm grown up now. And I'll get drunk when I need to."

"You must have looked funny wearing that cloak, when you were a little boy, when you came to Avalon."

"I wrapped it in a bundle with my knife and my spear. When old Billy Castle brought me here. He was a shepherd and I looked after his horse. When he fell off his horse one day and died they let me stay. Then you came, Em, and I was very happy. Now I'll light the fire."

He did that by thrusting the candle flame beneath a pile of dry twigs. They were quickly crackling and blazing, and the light showed Emily that there were no rats or bats lurking in the corners. She relaxed a little and sat on the spiky feathers, letting the fire warm her. It was better now. She almost liked it here. She liked Honi, too. When he sat down close to her she could see his wide grin, his gleaming eyes.

"I speak good *pakeha,* Em?"

"Yes, you do. Sometimes you use bad grammar."

"What's that?"

"Just the wrong words. They don't matter."

"You like me, even with my bad grammar?"

"Of course I do, silly."

He moved closer, his shoulder touching hers. "You like me to show you how to make baby?"

The too new pain surged inside her again. But now it was anger as well. She turned to Honi fiercely. "Yes, I do. I have to learn, don't I? I have to show Squire."

Honi burst into his irrepressible giggles. "You don't show Squire this, Em. That's why we've run away."

She was silent. Suddenly her heart was beating too fast. He became silent, too, as he pushed her backwards on to the rather musty-smelling cloak. If she had been with Squire for this purpose they would have been in a real feather bed, she thought mournfully. But the beating of her heart was choking her throat, and she could think only of Honi squeezing against her and breathing in her face.

"You have to take your clothes off, Em."

"All—of them?"

"Just the ones down here." He dragged at the legs of her pantaloons. Her face went fiery red. She hadn't actually thought of doing this—well, not of doing it in reality. Showing herself, looking at him.

He had got her pantaloons tangled round her ankles and was hastily pulling them off. Then he seemed to lose patience altogether and threw her petticoats up over her face so that she thought she would suffocate like poor Lady Devenish. Before she had emerged breathless from the flurry of flannel his strong hard hands had pulled her legs apart. She winced and clenched into herself and tried to lie still.

It hurt badly. She bit her lips, then let herself scream, louder and louder.

"Oh, Mam! Mam, help me! Mam, come and save me!"

"Shut up," Honi growled angrily.

But she continued to scream, and then she began writhing and wriggling, pitting her strength against his. She got a handful of his thick curls and tugged them unmercifully. Then his ear came against her lips, and she caught the lobe of it and bit it hard.

He thrust his head backwards.

"Em, you hurt me!"

"Serve you right for hurting me. You're being a beast."

"I am not." His eyes had a wild gleam. He looked ferocious. Suddenly she was afraid. "Honi—"

"You said I could. And then all you do is call out for your Mam." His breath was coming fast. He was too strong to be thrown off her body. He felt like a young tree lying across her. She knew intuitively that she had somehow to stop him being angry, to quieten him.

With an enormous effort she made herself say calmly, "Is this really how you make a baby?"

"Of course it is."

With that throbbing thing between her legs? She curled up smaller inside, retreating.

"Will the baby be brown?"

"It just better be."

"Then, Honi, I don't think it would be right." Her voice was very prim. Very slightly she could feel him subsiding. "I should have a white baby. Since I'm a *pakeha*."

There was a long silence, a stillness. Then he flung himself off her.

"You should have thought of that at the beginning."

"I know I should have."

"If you weren't a baby yourself I wouldn't have stopped."

"I am *not* a baby."

"Well, you certainly don't know about this." He was sulky and aggrieved. "A Maori girl would."

Emily found that she could sit up. She was hot and rumpled and half naked and immeasurably older. But quite calm.

"Then I expect you should find a Maori girl, Honi," she said gently. "That would be best for you."

"I will next time. I tell you I will."

He kicked at the fire, sending twigs blazing and expiring. She was truly sorry for him. He really was very young, she thought indulgently. Even younger than she was. They would go on being friends.

She patted the floor beside her.

"Let's go to sleep," she said.

22

It was Jonnie bursting in with a lantern who woke them up. He had known that Honi used this cave when he went to snare birds. When Emily hadn't been seen in the big house, and everyone was looking for her, he found her school hat and coat in the tack room and instantly guessed what had happened. Jonnie was growing up, too.

He didn't want to tell Pa, who would be mad. So he took Daniel with him and while everyone else was searching the attics and the garden and the cowsheds he and Daniel found Emily and Honi fast asleep on that filthy old feather cloak in the dying firelight.

Daniel went very white.

"Do you think—" he began, then stopped.

"I don't know," Jonnie said furiously. "But my sister can be crazy enough for anything. We'll take her home. Better leave Honi here. For his own good."

So the three of them stood before Squire and Miss Kate, Emily nearly falling over from tiredness, Daniel very erect with his hand protectively on her arm, Jonnie fidgeting nervously as he said, "Please, sir, I didn't want to tell my father in case he killed her."

"Killed her? Surely that's a bit extreme." Squire's voice was calm, but distant, as cold and distant as the mountain peaks. He behaved as if he had never seen this rumpled and grimy little girl before.

"Because Honi was there, you think?" he enquired. "But surely they're too young—Kate, you'd know more about this. Emily's an innocent child. Honi, of course, is probably as shrewd as they come, but even he wouldn't dare—with such a young girl, and white. He'll have to leave Avalon, of course. We'll have to decide about Emily. What do you think, Kate?"

"I think a bath and bed," said Kate unhesitatingly. "She isn't fit for another thing tonight. We can have a long talk in the morning, preferably with Miss Pugh. You said I'd know about this, John, but Miss Pugh will be much wiser."

"You not wise, Kate?"

"Not always."

Kate was uncomfortable about the way the two boys were watching her with solemn curiosity. She didn't care for her own private feelings, either. It was true that Emily was only a child, but had the little minx already learned more than she, Kate, knew? Could she be suffering from pique and jealousy, and not least her own unsatisfied hunger?

If only the spring would come quickly...

The next morning, neatly dressed, her hair in pigtails because she had stopped wanting to be grown up, Emily sat with the two women, Aunt Tab and Kate.

Kate was asking carefully, Aunt Tab bluntly, what exactly had happened with Honi.

"Nothing happened," Emily said uncomfortably. She was feeling desperately ashamed.

"But you ran off with him. And there you were sleeping side by side." Aunt Tab was uncompromising. "Jonnie said your clothes were very mussed about. Emily, can you swear on your honour that nothing happened? Or must we have a doctor to examine you?"

Emily fought back tears of distress. She hated having to remember that awfulness in the cave. But Aunt Tab would be answered, that was certain.

Reluctantly she began, "It was my fault. I was wondering about having babies. The girls at school are always talking about it. And Honi said he would show me. But then—when he was going to—I got scared and screamed. It *hurt!*" she said indignantly.

The complete silence from the two women went on for so long that eventually she realised that they were waiting for the final disclosure. Their faces were anxious. They cared about what had happened, Emily thought with sudden gratitude. Perhaps just as much as Mam would have done.

So she was able to say simply and earnestly, "I didn't let him. And he got cross. I thought he might hit me. But I managed to get him quiet, and then we were tired so we went to sleep. That truly was all that happened."

Miss Pugh leaned back. "Thank God for that."

"You believe her?" Kate asked.

"Oh, yes. She's a truthful child." In a lower voice, as if she thought Emily wouldn't hear, she went on, "It's as I said, Kate. She was jealous about you and Sir John. He has spoiled her and she has regarded him strictly as her property." She raised her voice, "Is that right, Emily?"

"No one told me," Emily burst out aggrievedly. "I didn't know Kate had Squire's ring and was going to have Leyte Manor and all. That was my house, Aunt Tab. Mam and me looked after it with ever so much love. I wanted to go back to it. I thought Squire would take me. When I knew he would take Kate instead I got mad." She bit her trembling lips and tried to revive her anger. "Anyway, he's *old!*" she said with unaccustomed spitefulness.

"Emily, that isn't like you," Miss Pugh scolded.

"He's not old," Kate said, anger in her own voice. "He's—do we have to talk to a child like this, Aunt Tab?"

"She's proved she's no longer a child, I'm afraid."

"Are you going to send me away?" Emily asked apprehensively.

"Oh, no. We have other plans for you." Now Aunt Tab was smiling mysteriously, and was no longer severe. "You're not going back to school, however."

"Truly? Aren't I really?" Emily shouted.

"Now don't get so exuberant. You should be punished for your behaviour and you may well think this is punishment we're proposing. But we both think it wrong that you should be taught to be merely idle and decorative. That school has been a mistake. Hasn't it, Kate?"

"Oh, yes," Kate agreed. "Sir John agrees, too. He blames himself. He was trying to make it up to Emily for losing her mother and perhaps—experimenting a little. He's such an idealist."

Miss Pugh gave her a sidelong look, then turned to Emily again.

"Do you want to hear what has been planned for you? Now that your rebellion is over."

"Yes, please, Aunt Tab," Emily said meekly.

"This is your father's wish. He thinks it best for you, and he is your surviving parent, after all. You're to keep house for him and your brother. You're to live in the old sod cottage that was here before this house was built. It's quite clean and dry and comfortable. It has a room downstairs, and a loft with a ladder that leads to two bedrooms under the roof. There are plenty of cooking utensils so that you can learn to cook and do the housework and wash the linen and help Hannah in the dairy. Of course you may come up to the big house whenever you wish but you're no longer to be waited on. You're to learn to be a good respectable working woman such as this country needs, and then you'll make a good wife."

Live with Pa and Jonnie? Get their breakfast and pack their lunch and make their meal at night? Polish the hearth and sit in the rocking chair by the fire as Mam would have done?

In some ways Emily liked the idea. Her fantasies had suffered brutally of late. It would be nice to be mistress, even of a cottage, and she only fifteen. But married? When? And to whom?

"Daniel has spoken for you," said Miss Pugh as if she had heard Emily's unspoken question.

"Daniel! Oh, but—"

"You think he's only a boy? He'll be eighteen when you're sixteen, and that's time enough. He'll wait. He has a nice nature. He had a hard time losing his parents so he has learned to be understanding. He doesn't mind about your adventure yesterday. He says that growing girls get into a state sometimes— goodness, the wisdom of the boy. You'd go a long way to find anyone more generous, Emily. So"—Miss Pugh leaned forward—"what do you say?"

Emily was aghast. Yet half pleased. As if she had found a haven after all the desolation and the fright and the exhaustion.

"He gave me Pearl." She was thinking aloud. She remembered, too, how he had held her at the lakeside after he had caught that ridiculous little fish. He had been warm and strong and his freckles had looked like dust on his face.

Miss Pugh looked at her kindly.

"He's a kind lad. And he says—if telling you won't go to your head—that he'll never love another woman. Now that's a gift of rare value, Emily. You should cherish it."

"Should I, Aunt Tab?" Muddled emotions made her head swim. "I'm too young to know."

"Well, that's something to admit, after yesterday. Shall we just let time take care of everything? Sir John will be happy with that solution, Kate?"

"Oh, I do think so. It seems so right." Kate tousled Emily's hair affectionately. "I do think we know best, Emily. Especially Aunt Tab. Honi is being sent back to his tribe. They live in the bays near Lyttelton harbour. They weave baskets, and catch fish and grow sweet potatoes and take them to market. It's probably time Honi found a nice little brown-skinned wife."

"You make her sound like a hen!" Emily cried, and suddenly they all began to laugh.

"Sir John would enjoy that," Kate said. "I believe that school has taught Emily to be witty after all."

*   *   *

Emily liked the sod cottage. It was dry and in good order. She would sweep the floor and put down rush matting and make curtains. The deep oven was for making bread, the kettle would hang over the fire, and the teapot be always ready on the hob. She could make a small flower garden at the door. In the evenings she would light the lamp and sit by the fire knitting or sewing. Mam would have liked this cottage, she thought. And suddenly felt peaceful, as if no more difficult demands were to be made of her. Perhaps Squire would visit. She didn't really care whether he did or not.

The first night Pa carried a wooden trunk with brass locks into the downstairs room.

"I've had this put away, Em," he said.

"What's in it, Pa?"

"Your Mam's things. I think you're ready for them now." He opened the lid and there was a faint scent of lavender. They took out, one by one, the stored treasures.

A quilted bedspread and linen sheets. A red crocheted shawl, some finely sewn lawn shifts and petticoats. One grey watered-silk dress with a ruffled neck and a tiny waist, a bonnet with a crushed yellow rose and yellow ribbons. A pair of highly polished black buttoned boots with little heels, and some long white kid gloves. A bead reticule lined with black silk, but disappointingly empty. A painted fan. And, at the bottom of the trunk, crushed and a little yellowed, a lace veil. A wedding veil.

"Hers," said Pa briefly.

"And now for me, Pa?"

"That's what she must have intended. Bringing it all this long way."

Emily touched the things softly.

"They're nice. I'll take care of them."

"You better." Pa cleared his throat. "It's what she had when she came to me. I thought she was a well-dressed lass, and bonny."

Emily slid her hand into one of the gloves. It clung, like Mam's fingers holding hers.

"There's the Family Bible, too. I've put in it about Mam and Willie, died at sea. Later we'll put in it your wedding. Married in Canterbury, New Zealand. That'll be a happier thing. Daniel is a good lad, Em. He'll make you a good husband."

Leyte Manor had faded into a misty dream, a fairy story. This was reality, Grandpa's beautiful script on the marbled paper, recording the Lodden names. Thomas, Samuel, Martha, Jonas, Mary, Emily, Jonnie, Willie... Her family. Real people. Daniel Pugh and Emily Lodden, she thought. She could imagine the careful, spiky, black writing setting out their names and it was suitable. She would never be a silly girl obsessed with dreams again. And that was right, too.

"She's quite got over that foolish behaviour, John," Kate said. "You don't need to worry any more about her."

"I'm very glad to hear it."

"You mustn't blame yourself."

"I don't." His confidence was supreme. But his fine, deep-set eyes still had that underlying pain. "I was only upset because her behaviour reminded me of Celina. If you had known how much my daughter made me suffer when she was little more than Emily's age, you would understand."

Kate nodded, her head bent because she was blushing a little. He had been referring to loose behaviour. He had been shocked when she also had attempted to indulge in it. His precepts were so high. She should not have criticised them, and determined never to do so again.

When she was his wife everything would be different.

Even if he had not been able to make his first wife happy. But that poor, drab, timid woman's nature had been the reason.

The house seemed lonely that winter. Lonelier when the sky was dark and heavy with incipient snow, and the gales from the Antarctic rattled the windows and sent chilly draughts swirling. Kate was now mistress in all but name. She ordered fires to be kept alight in the drawing room, the dining room and the study by day, and in the bedrooms at night. Now that they were such a small household there was not too much work for Myrtle and Hannah. They could well attend to cleaning grates and filling the log baskets.

Last winter had been spent sewing Celina's trousseau. This winter it was her own. Yet, although she had had an exciting parcel from Cousin Mabel with the latest French silks and satins and striped taffetas with braids and lace for trimmings (intended for her wedding to Captain Oxford, of course, since the parcel had been posted so long ago), she somehow found sewing alone, or with Miss Pugh, dispiriting. It was strange to realise that she missed Celina's disturbing presence. The house had been full of chatter then, comings and goings and a certain amount of enlivening strife. Even Lady Devenish had been another person in the room, if a silent and almost invisible one.

Now for most of the time there was only herself and Ezekiel's comical parrot. It had taken to nibbling at her hair with every evidence of affection. It made an amusing companion. She found herself listening for its more outrageous statement, made in Ezekiel's voice, but to her knowledge it had not said those words more than twice, and never, fortunately, in John's hearing. She occasionally wondered what Ezekiel was doing, how many prisoners he had successfully prosecuted, fixing his bright intimidating gaze on them, how many young ladies he had escorted to balls and parties. He was a lively young man. He would not be idle.

However, all this reflectiveness and vague nostalgia would pass when she was married, and, by good fortune, expecting a child.

Long ago Jonas, who was an excellent rifle shot, had been chosen to administer justice to Old Bill. The cat had been elderly, bad-tempered and stubborn, and it gave one cold shivers to think of it leaping into a baby's cradle. It was entirely right that it should suffer the death penalty for its crime.

There had been further family letters, brought by the sailing ship, the *Clara Jane,* sixty days out of East India Docks but nothing from Celina. Kate fancied Sir John was relieved. His antipathy for his daughter was very strong. But she intended to persuade him into more forgiving ways. She would point out that it was no more possible to make a perfect family than a perfect colony. Human nature was so perverse, and genes from generations back could not be stamped out. Perhaps Celina had had a promiscuous great-grandmother. Although it was difficult to believe that there had been any such ancestor in prim Lady Devenish's family. Nevertheless people could not be blamed for the seeds borne inside themselves. This was already evident in the crimes committed by seemingly respectable emigrants. There were too many, Sir John said disappointedly, after reading the latest newspapers. People would be better behaved when they were better fed, and lived comfortably, and had plenty of work. This was all possible in a fine, fertile country. One must not be deterred.

He was so good. Perhaps an idealist could never be entirely happy. But Kate hoped that when he held his son in his arms she would never see that dark, brooding look in his eyes again.

Maud Harmon had sent her the sketch she had done on the day of the picnic at the lake. It was like a piece of history now, the ladies sitting on the tussocky grass, their skirts spread about them, Daniel in the process of landing his fish, Sir John standing tall and graceful, his finely shaped head turned to watch Daniel and Emily. Most nostalgic was the little oriental figure of Lady Devenish beneath her tilted parasol, Ezekiel stretched at her feet.

Kate shivered a little. It all seemed so happy, so serene. So much happier than it was today. She could not understand her feeling of oppression.

23

At last the first lambs were gambolling in the evening light. The pale spring sunlight showed their comical sideways leaps and their flicking tails. It was a mild season, excellent for lambing. A week ago Sir John and Jonas had gone to Timaru to take delivery of the three fine pedigree rams brought from Scotland. The fourth, unfortunately, had died on the voyage, but the three survivors were prime animals and would show their effects on the flock with their progeny next spring.

It seemed odd to be thinking of the following spring when this one was surely the most important. Although it was possible that it would not only be the lambs that were eagerly awaited at Avalon next September.

If I don't give him a son, will he still love me, Kate worried. She had become altogether too anxious. Her face was sharpened, her eyes too large. Sometimes during the long winter, with rain, gales and snow, and always the looming mountains, she had thought longingly of Lady Devenish's soothing medicine. She now understood that poor lady's temptation. She would like to have blurred her mind a little to the never-ending dark days, the boredom of sewing and reading and passing time, and always behaving with exacting correctness when Sir John was in the room. Almost as if Lady Devenish were still watching them. It was Sir John's fault for showing none of the light-heartedness of the affianced man, but tending to grow more quiet and withdrawn. Was he haunted by his late wife, or his absent daughter, or both of them?

Kate thought longingly of being able to escape for a period from Avalon, much as she loved the house. Perhaps, when they were married, she and John could have a honeymoon visit to Wellington and present themselves at Government House. When the postman arrived, muddied and weary from his long ride, she welcomed him warmly. Just to see a fresh face, she thought, quite apart from receiving what he carried in his leather bags.

There were letters for everybody, for Miss Pugh from her sister, for Emily and Jonnie from their grandparents, for John from his agents, his financial advisers, his wine merchant, his tailor, and for her from the Irish aunts.

> Our dear Katharine, *they wrote. It was, of course, Aunt Esmeralda who was writing, but they spoke with one voice.*
>
> How very terrible about poor Captain Oxford's death, which we have just heard of in your last letter. But didn't we warn you about the cannibal islands and what fate might meet you there? Poor Kate, first Dermot and now Henry. Do you not think it better to come home? Surely the desperate Fenians are not as bad as murdering cannibals. Nevertheless we go about as usual, morning and evening service on Sundays and a great dinner party last Saturday evening at the Donnellys', the Marches and the O'Hagens there, and we two elderly ladies. A good deal of talking and eating, not to mention the amount of good port that vanished.
>
> Daffy has had her calf, a fine heifer. The chestnuts are in bloom and the stream, as usual, jammed with marsh marigolds, and buttercups and a wilderness of water weeds. The newly fledged ducklings get tangled up. We have heard the first cuckoo. We miss you, dear Kate.

/   267

Disappointingly there was nothing from Cousin Mabel, but Ada's bold, sprawling writing was on the next envelope that Kate opened. Her mouth fell open as she read. It was impossible to take in Ada's meaning.

Dearest Kate,

I have not the time or the mood to write you general news today. I am sending you this on Ezekiel's behalf. By the time you receive it he will be on his way to Timaru. He intends putting up at the Victoria Hotel and requests that you meet him there about midday on Thursday. (*That is tomorrow, Kate realised.*) He has matters of great importance to discuss with you. It is *most* important that you meet him. But alone, or with Miss Pugh. Yes, take Tabitha Pugh with you, but *not* Sir John. These matters are not as yet for his ears. I can only say that to be forewarned is to be forearmed. You can trust Ezekiel absolutely. Make some excuse to Sir John about women's matters, shopping for your wedding or some such. But I beg you to go.

Your loving and sincere friend, Ada.

"What is it Kate?" Miss Pugh asked. "You look shocked."

Wordlessly she handed the letter to Miss Pugh. Better for that wise-headed lady to read it rather than attempt to explain. How could she explain what she didn't know?

After a long moment Miss Pugh said, "You must go, Kate. Of course I'll come with you. Can you arrange it with Sir John?"

She nodded. "I'll ask for the buggy. He may want to come, too."

"Then he must be persuaded against it." Miss Pugh was brisk, and practical, as always. "What time shall we set out?"

"I think about eight o'clock. If we are to be there by midday. But Aunt Tab—what can this be about?"

Miss Pugh shook her head.

"I haven't the foggiest notion. But I trust Ada Collins, and I trust that young man, too. An honest young man. But cheer up. These mysterious matters can't be as bad as your expression suggests. I think Lee Fong might make us a good, strong cup of tea."

At dinner Kate found herself able to speak quite calmly to Sir John, who fortunately was looking relaxed and at ease. He had been out all day with the shepherds.

"May Miss Pugh and I have the buggy tomorrow, John? We have suddenly decided on an expedition to Timaru. I have found I have many deficiencies in my wardrobe." She leaned over to touch his hand. "I don't want to be anything but a well-equipped bride."

He looked surprised, and not altogether pleased, she fancied.

"Couldn't these things wait until after our wedding when we go to Wellington? There will be a much better selection in the shops there. May I ask what these important articles are?"

"Important matters," Ada had written.

"No, you may not. This is women's business. Isn't it, Aunt Tab?" She attempted to look roguish. "Anyway, I have to give you notice, sir, that with or without your permission we are going."

"Ah! Rebellion already? That can't be allowed." If he had felt displeasure it was over. "Of course you may have the buggy. It sounds a delightful expedition." He looked more closely at Kate. "A day away will do you good. You've been looking pale lately."

She was afraid his tender concern would have her breaking into tears.

"I would accompany you myself but every hand is needed with the ewes. Importunate lambs make no account of other engagements."

"Is all going well, Sir John?" Miss Pugh asked in her quiet, normal voice.

"Excellently. We have several pairs of twins and one of triplets and only a few difficult births so far. Of course the mild winter has helped. I am finding my first lambing season enormously exciting. I shall be an experienced hand next spring. I believe Daniel has already found two orphans to delight Emily. He pampers that young lady."

He smiled indulgently as if he had never done any such thing himself.

"That's nice," Kate murmured. When Sir John was like this she loved him so dearly. What matters had that mischievous

Ezekiel to impart? She knew that she would be unlikely to sleep that night.

She did fall asleep in the early hours of the morning, but then was awakened by a nightmare in which she thought Old Bill was mewing furiously at the window demanding admittance. Not Lady Devenish's window but hers. As if he had designs on her as well.

In the morning, Sir John, stooping to kiss her goodbye, pressed some sovereigns into her hand.

"Don't stint these matters, Kate. I'll be looking forward to seeing your purchases tonight. And be careful of riff-raff in the streets. They say there are disappointed gold-diggers arriving from Australia with rumours that gold might be discovered in the Otago hills. I would suggest some luncheon at the Victoria Hotel. It's the most respectable place."

"Yes, we had planned that, Sir John." Miss Pugh had seen Kate's guilty face and quickly answered for her. "We'll need a rest, too, before setting out for home. Don't expect us until late."

Darkness would be best, and candlelight, in case Kate had been crying too much. But what could there be to make her cry?

The tall figure of Ezekiel was striding up and down outside the Victoria Hotel when they arrived. He hurried forward to help them alight from the buggy, and beckoned to a boy to tether the horse and feed and water it. Then he took a lady on each arm and climbed the wooden steps on to the hotel verandah.

"I have asked for a quiet table. You will want to freshen up." He was serious-faced and had not once smiled. "I will be waiting at the table when you are ready."

"I don't believe I can eat anything," Kate said, looking at her fatigue-smudged face in the mirror over the modestly equipped dressing table. "Whatever can Ezekiel want? He looks so serious."

"Best to find out as quickly as possible." Miss Pugh had splashed her face with cold water and was ready. "Pinch your cheeks, child. How can you look so pale on this warm day?"

"My appearance is the last thing I'm worrying about." Kate tucked away a wandering curl. "I'm sure that the trouble will be Celina. How am I to tell John that? He had thought his trials with her were over."

"If that is the worst of it, I don't think it should entirely spoil your appetite. Come along."

There was a long table down the centre of the dining room, with benches on either side. These were already occupied by diners, mostly men, although there were two buxom ladies who looked like farmers' wives. Ezekiel was at a side table by the window. He had drawn out chairs for Kate and Miss Pugh, and asked them to be seated.

"There is only mutton, I am afraid, either hot or cold. And will you have something to drink? A light ale, some kind of fruit cup which I wouldn't recommend, or very strong hot tea."

"I would like a glass of water," Kate said. "I'm far more thirsty than hungry. The road is quite dusty although summer hasn't begun. It's a long way, Ezekiel. I hope this journey has been made for a sufficiently important reason."

"Oh, yes, it's important. I'd hardly have made my own long journey otherwise."

A plump young woman with large red hands was setting down plates of food

"Perhaps we should eat first," Ezekiel said.

"Oh, please, don't keep us on tenterhooks. It has been bad enough worrying all night. And later I have to shop for wedding finery. That is imperative since it's the reason I gave John for coming."

"It may not be as imperative as you think. But eat a little while I begin. It has to do with Lady Devenish's death."

Kate's mouth was suddenly dry with an unexplainable fear. "Not Celina?"

"Celina, too. But we come to Lady Devenish first. Do you remember how we discovered the nearly empty bottle of laudanum in her wardrobe, and, since Sir John had forbidden that there be any in the house, we imagined that she had secretly acquired it herself?"

"Yes. We remember that," Miss Pugh agreed, since Kate did not answer.

"The assumption has proved to be wrong. It was Sir John who

acquired it on his last visit to Christchurch. At the time of Celina's wedding."

Kate's head jerked up.

"That can't be so, Ezekiel. It was then that he became so stern about his wife having it. She was growing too vague, too distrait, he said. It had to be stopped."

"If you swear those were his instructions, I believe you, Kate. However, he didn't carry them out. For it was he who went to the chemist and purchased the laudanum. The chemist remembers him well. He watched him sign his name in the Poisons' book."

"But—"

"So," said Ezekiel, his eyes hard and direct, "he brought the medicine back to Avalon and put it where his wife, in her state of nervous depression, would find it. Which, as was to be predicted, she did. From then on she was drowsy, not herself. You must have noticed that, Kate. I did, and I was only a visitor, not at all well acquainted with the lady. You may have observed me watching her."

"I have Maud Harmon's sketch," Kate said irrelevantly. "You lying at her feet by the lake that day."

"Exactly. So you will remember that I took Lady Devenish home early and she collapsed on her bed and instantly fell asleep. Too much sun and exertion, too much poison..."

"Poison!" whispered Kate.

"Indeed, yes. Taken indiscriminately, tincture of laudanum is very dangerous. As it proved to be."

"But she didn't die of it!" Miss Pugh exclaimed. "Surely it was the cat?"

"Or some other means of suffocation? Did anyone but Sir John see the cat? I believe he has no supporting witness?"

"He saw it under the chair. He said so," Kate declared.

"Yes. He said so."

"He found its hairs on the pillow," Kate remembered triumphantly.

"The animal sheds hairs, I believe. Not difficult to gather some up."

Kate was staring at Ezekiel in amazement.

272   /

"And put them on the pillow! You are accusing John of doing that! And then—oh, no, I can't say it, he couldn't have used some other means, a p-pillow—"

"You are saying it, Kate," Ezekiel said inexorably. "You have pondered on this quite a lot, I believe."

"No, I have not. Not until you put these wicked thoughts into my head. Why, Sir John has had Old Bill destroyed."

"Naturally. Although the poor creature would have been unable to prove its innocence or guilt. So who does it seem had the guilty conscience?"

Kate started up. "Ezekiel, I will not listen to another word of this terrible nonsense."

Miss Pugh took her arm and pulled her back into her seat.

"You must, Kate. But quietly. We don't want all the town hearing this extraordinary conversation. Ezekiel, as a criminal lawyer, you must have strong grounds for these accusations. Otherwise I must say your theory sounds far-fetched, and I sympathise with Kate's indignation."

"Oh, yes, I have strong grounds," Ezekiel said grimly. "I remember that we discussed murder in its various guises at dinner at Christmas. With malice aforethought, by criminal negligence, accidental."

"Then I must have been criminally negligent in not waking Lady Devenish, in not seeing that her window was shut," Kate said belligerently.

"Hush, Kate. I have more to say, and this is going to shock you. There is a strongly held theory that once having successfully committed a murder—and by successfully I mean in not having been apprehended—a murderer, in provocative circumstances, will have an overpowering temptation to commit the crime again. We know that Sir John Devenish had a semi-invalid wife who could not bear him a son, that he had fallen in love with you, Kate, or perhaps had been obsessed with the thought of a healthy young woman giving him a son—"

Kate was clenching her hands in despair. He knew that part of it too well, too well. But what else was there?

"Judge Harmon has had a communication from Celina."

"Celina had written to the judge!"

"Yes. She met him at her wedding. She thought him to be the correct person to write to after her discovery."

"What discovery?" Kate cried. "Why are you talking in puzzles?"

"In riddles? No, this is all very plain fact. How am I to tell you over your meal? No one is eating."

"You began," Kate said coldly, "so you had better finish. But be careful what you say for shortly John and I are to be married. It will be my husband you have maligned."

"We'll see," said Ezekiel equably. "However, let me be as brief as possible. Celina has taken her husband to see her home, Leyte Manor. Natural enough—"

"Except that her father expressly forbade it."

"Why?"

"I don't know why, Ezekiel. For some reason he didn't want her to go there. He loved his ancestral home and she had been a great trial to him in it."

"More than a trial. She writes that one evening he discovered her *in flagrante delicto*—you understand my meaning—with a young French student she had met in Oxford and brought home. His name was François. She didn't know the rest of it. Anyway, her father, finding the lovers in this very compromising situation, lost his temper and dragged the young man from the bed and threw him half-clothed into the passage. Then he locked the door so that Celina was a prisoner and could do nothing to help her unlucky lover. She says she heard some thuds, then a scream, and then a dragging sound. Much later, her father returned to unlock her door and tell her that he had sent the young villain packing. She would hear no more from him, he said. And if by some happy chance she had not conceived a child, he would see that he got her to the other side of the world out of reach of scandal. There she might find a husband who would be only as good as she deserved. She was mentally sick, he said, and would have to be confined as much as possible. This last you know, Kate. Only too well, I imagine." After a long pause he said, "Do you know the rest? Can you guess it?"

"You have mentioned murder," Kate said dully. "So I suppose Celina and Edward have found a decomposing body—" she began to shudder realising from his expression that she had spoken the truth. "Oh, dear God!"

"In the priest's hole. Did he tell you that that fine old mansion, Leyte Manor, has a priest's hole?"

The memory of the letter from Mr. Watts, Sir John's bailiff, was vividly with her, the French couple looking for some lost object—their *son!*—and Sir John's haunted look on reading the letter. Sir John's insistence that Celina should not visit her childhood home, for fear of what she might find, of what she had found!

Kate had wanted an answer to the mystery, and now, heaven help her, she had it. She began to speak her horrified thoughts aloud.

"So that's why—he hated Celina so much. And she him. I could never understand. He is such a good man. He wanted to set the tone out here. No emigrants escaping a guilty past..." She was laughing in dry, mirthless gasps. "It is all so—satirical. Celina called him a hypocrite."

"I think a little brandy would be a good idea, Ezekiel," Miss Pugh suggested. "Kate needs it. And I, too. The waitress must be told we are not hungry. But may I ask, what has this to do with Lady Devenish's death?"

"This is a legal matter, Miss Pugh. There is not yet any extradition of criminals from this country. If there were, Sir John would undoubtedly be taken home and charged with murder. Under the circumstances, Judge Harmon thought, and I concur, that Lady Devenish's death warrants further investigation. I am afraid we have to take a member of the constabulary to Avalon with us."

He suddenly looked very tired, his eyes receding into puffed flesh. His face was quite plain when it was not smiling or animated.

"This is all highly unpleasant, Kate. As I hope Ada warned you. She wants you to return to Christchurch with me. And I hope to persuade you to do so. But you'll be needed here for a short time for the purposes of the investigation."

"What will happen to him?" Kate somehow dragged the words out. "That jail—we danced in?"

"That, yes. But don't let us reach further conclusions yet. I have Sergeant Murphy waiting with fresh horses. We'll begin the journey when you feel able to." He gave a half-smile, completely without humour. "But no wedding finery, I'm afraid."

Sir John was waiting on the verandah. The overhanging light shone on his high brow, his handsome face.

He went to help the ladies out of the buggy. Miss Pugh, for all her weariness, neatly sidestepped his arms. Kate stumbled and fell into them and instantly stiffened. He could not fail to notice.

"My dear! You're tired out. It's been too long a day for you. Where are all your packages?"

"We—could find nothing," Kate mumbled. "Nothing suitable."

It was almost dark and Sir John hadn't noticed the approach of the two riders, Ezekiel and Sergeant Murphy, their horses slowed to a walk.

In the hall the gong rang with a resounding clang. Lee Fong's merry face peered out into the night.

"You people just in time for dinner," he announced. "Food velly leddy."

The house looked warm and welcoming, the lamps lighted, the pictures glowing on the walls, the well-polished furniture gleaming. A most desirable house for an important family in this very young colony. Kate thought she saw a shape move at the end of the hall, a pale glimmer, a little oriental figure, secretive as always.

She shivered in fear and distaste, understanding now the oppression of the house, and found herself welcoming the sound of horses' hooves, and the two men, Ezekiel and Sergeant Murphy, appearing out of the darkness.

24

After a startled enquiry, and then an accusing look at Kate and Miss Pugh as if they had arranged the whole business, Sir John's presence of mind was admirable.

He welcomed Ezekiel as an old friend, and acknowledged Sergeant Murphy courteously, though with a query in his voice.

"I hardly know what your interest in Avalon is, sergeant. Were you escorting the ladies safely home? Is the road threatened by brigands? Swaggers run amok, perhaps? Homesick cadets gone mad with drink? No, I am joking. I can see your visit is meant to be a serious affair. But shall we dine first? My cook doesn't like his excellent food to get cold. Now we have given him a gong to strike, the authority it implies goes to his head. Miss Pugh, Kate. I know that you must both be exhausted, but I would be grateful if you could find enough strength to entertain our guests."

He was so dignified, so in command of himself, despite whatever his inner feelings were, that Kate's heart ached unbearably.

How could those terrible things Ezekiel had told her be true?

Yet Sergeant Murphy had a warrant to search the house, although one didn't know what he was looking for. He also had the authority to question Sir John at length. But this would be done in privacy after they had eaten.

For some reason Sir John, who had never said a formal grace, elected to do so this evening. He stood with bowed head saying in his grave, cultured tones:

> Be present at our table, Lord,
> Be here and everywhere adored.
> Thy creatures bless, and grant that we
> May feast in Paradise with Thee.

Kate feared that she would cry and be unable to stop. When Sir John filled everyone's glass with some of his fine French burgundy she lifted hers and drank deeply. She thought the wine would help her to get through the dreadful evening and turn it into nothing worse than a blurred and lunatic nightmare.

Whatever John had done, he had been driven to.

Even to putting a pillow over his wife's unconscious head?

"Come, Kate. You're not eating. How was your journey from Christchurch, Ezekiel? Were the rivers in flood?"

"The Rakaia and the Ashburton were, after a high nor'-wester. But not too disastrously. I had a good horse." Ezekiel's voice was polite but cool as if he were speaking to a stranger. "It's a devilishly long ride, however."

"It is. You must have had a very good reason for coming." Sir John's eyebrows lifted questioningly. "It was to see Kate, of course."

"Yes, sir, it was. Though in part only. It was to see you, too. And the sergeant isn't here merely to protect us on the perfectly safe ride from Timaru."

"I hadn't imagined so. But I think we agree to postpone the explanation of his interesting presence until after dinner."

Sergeant Murphy gave a suppressed snort. He took a mouthful of wine and shook his head slightly, as if the dry taste puzzled him. His host obviously puzzled him, too, judging by his guarded but disapproving looks. He was a fierce-looking fellow with his black beard and his small, sharp, black eyes. He had been extremely kind to the ladies on the journey.

"I've had a hard day myself," said Sir John. "We're having a most successful lambing. Very heartening. But those little murderous parrots, the keas, create havoc among the newborn lambs. Peck their eyes out. I'd like to shoot the lot of them."

Then he turned his dark, hollow gaze on Kate. "So am I to take it that you performed part of your purpose in going to Timaru? Even if you have appeared to have forgotten your approaching wedding."

Kate flushed.

"I'm sorry to have deceived you, John. But as Ezekiel will tell you later, it was important. Quite important."

She laid down her fork. It was useless to pretend that she could sit at the dinner table, so civilised with its silver and crystal, and continue this meaningless and macabre conversation.

"Would you excuse me, John. I really am tired—to the point of collapse. I think Miss Pugh, too—"

Miss Pugh was making no bones about it. She stood up and came round the table to take Kate's arm.

"Personally I can't wait to find my bed. We'll bid you all good night, gentlemen. Then you can settle down to talk. I'll tell the maids not to come in disturbing you."

Tired as she was, Kate knew that there was no possibility of falling asleep for a long time. The scene at the dinner table would not leave her, the two visitors and Miss Pugh and herself dominated by their host whose good manners and composure never left him despite what must have been his deep, inner anxiety. She would never forget Sir John's grave, considerate glance on her as he observed her exhaustion. The memory of it made her begin to sob.

What was going on downstairs at this moment? How could she be such a coward as to leave him to face Ezekiel's accusations alone? She should be at his side, giving him her love and support, most of all making plain her belief in him—if she still had that belief...

What was she doing lying here as limp and ineffective as Lady Devenish had used to be? The comparison conjured up Lady Devenish's white, frightened face, which suddenly seemed to hover in the darkness in mute appeal. Distraught, Kate threw back the bed clothes and reached for her dressing gown. She had to know what was happening. And she had to either stand by Sir John, wholly on his side, or to move over to the side of the law, to Ezekiel and Sergeant Murphy. Reality had to be faced. She could never live with herself as a craven coward.

She went downstairs silently, in her slippers. The last light had died out of the sky. She had to feel her way in the dark, guided by the shaft of lamplight from the partly open dining-room door. As she came near she could hear Ezekiel's voice. Emotionless, direct, demanding, yet oddly conversational, Kate was almost deceived by the nature of his words. Surely he couldn't be asking such terrible questions in such a polite voice?

"And did you have difficulty in removing the body, Sir John? Once the young man was unconscious, as you admit he was? Was he too heavy to be carried, and therefore had to be dragged? Did you realise at once that he was dead?"

"No!" came Sir John's voice, thick and heavy and almost unrecognisable. "No, I did not."

"Nevertheless, you somehow, by dragging or carrying, put him in the priest's hole. If he were not dead, were you going deliberately to leave him to starve to death?"

Kate was impelled to the half-open door. She had to observe Sir John, to see the horrified repudiation of Ezekiel's monstrous suggestion in his face—or alternatively to recognise his guilt. She had to hear every word he said.

"You can't be expected to understand now, Mr. Dryden," he was saying slowly in his unfamiliar thickened voice. "But if you ever have a daughter like mine—and God forbid, my dear fellow—I think you will understand the uncontrollable passion, the rage that overcame me when I found that young man taking advantage—of her weakness."

His head was sunk into his shoulders as if it were too heavy to hold upright. Perhaps it was a trick of the lamplight, but his figure seemed shrunken, his skin yellowed, his eyes as hunted as a common criminal's.

In contrast, Ezekiel seemed immensely tall and upright, oddly noble, as if he were growing in stature in his quest for the truth, while Sir John was diminishing.

"I imagine the door to the priest's hole would be of exceptional thickness, made so, of course, to muffle sounds from within. You would be aware of this, Sir John, since this was your family home and you would be familiar with all its quirks, so to speak. Was the door easy to unlock, did its hinges squeak, did anyone ever come near that room? Or possibly not for years on end? In other words, Sir John, I am asking you again if the unfortunate young Frenchman was dead, or if you were deliberately locking him into that small, hidden, virtually forgotten room to starve to death."

So that, Kate thought numbly, is how prosecuting counsel breaks a witness, by asking intolerable questions, by summoning up unbearable visions... In an almost detached way she saw Sir John cover his face with his hands, saw, with an aching heart, his proud head go down.

"He was dead," she heard him mutter. "Oh yes, I admit I was quite sure of that. Pray don't think me a torturer, Mr. Dryden. I was not that. Nor with my wife—who I swear didn't suffer. In both cases some madness seized me. Who will ever understand?"

Kate could not listen any more. Her loyal desire to stand by the man who had so nearly become her husband had turned to revulsion. It was all madness, madness. As Sir John himself had just confessed.

The only sanity in that dreadful scene had come from Ezekiel with his courteous, probing, impersonal but relentless voice, his almost holy seeking for justice.

And now what would happen?

She lay huddled in bed, longing for the morning and yet fearful of its coming. What could the day possibly hold but more horror? What was being done with Sir John, the guilty man, tonight? Was it his turn to be locked up, Sergeant Murphy standing guard? It was like snaring a splendid animal that had run amok, she thought dazedly, and suddenly fell asleep.

The birds twittering in the early morning made her realise in astonishment that exhaustion could bring unconsciousness for a few blessed hours. She sat up in bed, listening. She had heard another sound, that of a door closing downstairs, of footsteps on the verandah, and then crunching on the gravel. In a flash she was out of bed and at the window, looking into the pearly light of the dawn. A tall figure was moving swiftly into the distance, a rifle over his shoulder. Sir John! Not guarded by Sergeant Murphy after all, but striding free to go out shooting!

Where was he going? What was he planning to do? In the distance she heard the faint mewling cries of newly-born lambs. Ah, he was going to attempt to shoot the keas, those cheeky birds with their iridescent underwings and their savage, hooked beaks. He had talked of them last night. Even the mists of exhaustion had not made her forget that.

Then was life to go on as usual in spite of that desperate confession she had overheard? Or had she dreamed the astonishing scene? Surely not.

Filled with a terrible apprehension that must be communicated to somebody, she put on her dressing gown and went along the passage to Ezekiel's room.

In the dim light she could see his sleeping face, his tousled head. He must be very tired, after his long journey from Christchurch, and then the events of the night. He had been so splendid, so quietly implacable, so skilled with his lethal questions, yet it must have been deeply distressing for him. Now it was a pity to wake him. But there was no alternative.

She shook his shoulder. "Ezekiel! Wake up!"

He opened his eyes and saw her and was instantly wide awake. "What is it, Kate? What's happened?"

"I've just seen John go out with his rifle. To shoot keas, I imagine, but I'm not sure. We must go after him."

"I think not, Kate." Ezekiel's voice was calm and unsurprised.

"But supposing—"

"I'm supposing what you are, and I say, do nothing. Sergeant Murphy has my instructions to that effect, also."

"But even if—"

"Even if."

As she stood unbelieving, he took her hand and pressed it to his cheek, as if it gave him comfort.

"If a man has the courage to face his own fate, I say it is the best way. I'd like that to be a law in this colony. Sir John Devenish did care about the colony and his ambitions were genuine. He could have made a fine statesman. Unfortunately, like too many of us, his own life was flawed. But in many ways he was a good man. Remember that, Kate. You were not to be blamed for loving him. Do you know what Mr. Wakefield said when he was dying—how quickly people are forgotten when they are dead. Not very profound, perhaps, but true." He looked at her steadily. It was growing daylight so quickly. How was she to face this day?

"So you must do some forgetting. My darling."

She caught her breath on a sob.

"I have had to do a great deal. Already."

The distant shot rang out almost before she had finished speaking. It was not followed by another.

Later in the morning, when the sun was high in the sky and the mountain peaks shining in their immense purity, Jonas and one of the shepherds carried the body of John Devenish, Baronet, late of Gloucestershire, England and Avalon, South Canterbury, New Zealand, on a five-barred gate from the bottom of the lambing paddock.

He was destined to lie for ever in an obscure graveyard beside the wife he had despised.

But he must have remained clear-headed to the end, for he left a letter in his study saying that his only child, Celina Hope, was now his heir. He hoped that she would listen to the advice of her husband "a respectable and honest young man" and care for Leyte Manor in a suitable way. Also, that she would allow Avalon to be managed by Jonas Lodden and his son Jonnie. This

he owed them, for their loyalty to him at the greatest cost to
themselves. He would like Jonas to arrange for the transport of
Lee Fong, "now quite an old man although one would not have
guessed," when he died, to his ancestors in China, since that
was his great wish. As for Emily, she would marry Daniel Pugh
and the two young people would take care of that fine lady,
Tabitha Pugh, in her old age.

A final sentence read, "I would earnestly recommend that
Miss Katharine O'Connor, whom I loved, should return to England to the bosom of her loving family. This country has not
been kind to her. Farewell, my lovely Kate."

In a less certain hand was scrawled the last line of the grace
he had said at dinner, *That we may feast in Paradise with
Thee...*

"The colossal nerve of the man!" Ezekiel exclaimed. He was,
of course, referring to that last line. But the whole letter had
upset him.

"Have you no compassion?" Kate asked sadly.

"Of course I have. I don't always enjoy administering the law.
Neither did good Sergeant Murphy. Nor Judge Harmon. But
this is a society of human beings, Kate, not theories. Something
that man didn't see in the round. We all have flaws. His biggest
mistake was not to recognise his own."

"Perhaps he did," Kate said. Her face was stricken. "More
than anyone knew."

"Ah, Kate! Don't look at me as if I'm a heartless stranger."

She was not doing that. She was remembering, with reluctant
admiration, his commanding presence at that terrible inquisi-
tion.

"I hadn't ever seen you go so long without laughing."

He made a grimace. "I would laugh now to please you, if I
could."

Later he said, "You must begin packing." He was taking her
to Ada in Christchurch immediately after the funeral was over
the next day. In Ada's loving and garrulous company she could
come to a decision about her future. It would be sensible to

284   /

follow Sir John's wishes and return to England. But did she want to leave this country yet, in spite of the hurt it had held for her? Suffering was part of being a pioneer. Everyone said so. In the North Island young mothers and children were still to be killed by the ferocious *Hau Haus*, tomahawked, scalped, burnt alive. Young husbands were periodically drowned in flooded rivers. Disease, without available doctors, or medicine, struck suddenly and was fatal.

Was grief an excuse for leaving? Was it not more a lack of courage?

Referring obliquely to the tragic death of the English baronet, the *Lyttelton Times* wrote, "We must beware, in our endeavours to create an honest and as near perfect society as is possible in this sinful world, a society which is to be an example to our beloved Queen's great Empire, of those whom we welcome to our shores and trust too completely. We must beware of the serpent in our midst..." It might have been Mr. Wakefield, that other great idealist, speaking.

"Shall we take Napoleon, Kate?" Ezekiel asked. "Perhaps Miss Pugh would like to keep him. Or Emily. He's such a dumb rascal. Has he never delivered that message I sent?"

To her surprise Kate felt a faint warmth in her wan cheeks.

"Once. No, twice. I thought him—you—"

"What, Kate?" His face had that great gentleness that was now inclined to make her weep. This was another Ezekiel, and she was glad to know him.

"Impertinent."

"Oh, dear! What a pity! After all those hours of lessons. Could you perhaps teach him to give me an answer?"

"Well—I imagine *impertinent* would be a difficult word to learn."

"Then it must be modified."

"Perhaps." She turned away. But not before she saw the leaping hope in his face.

*   *   *

Ada cosseted her endlessly. It was a programme of hot syllabubs, endless cups of strong tea, occasional sips of brandy, long invigorating walks, and enough deliciously cooked food for dinner at night to deaden any thoughts.

Would she buy a passage home? If she hadn't enough money Hubert would gladly give her some. Give, mark you! And Hubert was a man who valued money above all else.

Certainly it would be wise to go home, but not entirely wise. In London or Ireland she would be that unsuccessful creature, an unmarried woman of twenty-four with no dowry.

Here, there were many opportunities for a young woman of spirit, and Kate had plenty of that. And many entirely suitable young men to marry, one in particular whose name should not be mentioned, but on whom that lady had set her heart. Kate did like the country, didn't she? Wouldn't she be desolated never to see it again?

Kate's monosyllabic answers were becoming monotonous, but she hadn't the strength or the desire to conduct a lively conversation, or a lively argument, which was what Ada wanted. Although the thoughts were growing beneath her skin, inside her skull.

A ship had come inside the Lyttelton heads that morning. Imagine, Ada said excitedly, it was the *Albatross*.

"Shouldn't we go to watch the people disembarking? Or would that revive too many painful memories? No, really, Kate, you have brooded for long enough. You must now begin to face things. Put on your bonnet and we'll have Hubert drive us to Lyttelton. Hubert likes to meet new colonists. There are always some in need of his services. Banking services, of course. Just wait until we have the railroad. And the cathedral is built."

But she would not be here to see those things, Kate thought, the eternal dilemma pressing on her.

She would like to see Daniel and Emily married. She would like to see dear Tabitha Pugh again. She would always admit that Ada Collins deserved to be known as her dearest friend.

But scents of a wet Irish garden lured her. Cousin Mabel's

witty, informed chatter was something she had sorely missed. The buildings here were so miniscule, so trivial, compared with those in London. Old remembered faces and voices would blur what had happened on this opposite side of the world, and make it a dream.

But the grandeur of the Alps, the brilliantly blue sky, the clarity of the air, the space, the plans, the hopes. Could she now live without these?

They stood on the quayside watching the familiar sight of the long boats coming ashore. Standing out to sea, the *Albatross* looked small and weather-worn. Kate knew that she would never want to board that ship, with all its memories, again.

Nor any ship!

As she watched the eager, hopeful faces looking up from the boats, anxious to be on dry land, the women tumbling over their skirts as they clambered ashore, the children tossed up and caught by good-natured watchers, the baggage flung on to the hard ground and sometimes spilling open, the words came unbidden into Kate's mind. Nor any ship!

She was part of this scene with its intense, lusty life. She was an experienced settler waiting to help the timorous, the sorrowful, the homesick. She was a legitimate part of the great adventure of developing a new land. What did she want with old countries, old institutions? She had crossed the barrier. She was permanently a part of the new world.

She wanted to help the stumbling, perplexed women, pale faced from the poor food and the long weeks at sea, with their babies, their baggage. To ask them about the journey, the London fashions, the Queen and Princesses, the Prime Minister and the Foreign Minister, and their plans for this latest colony, supposing that they had any plans, supposing that they had heard of the colony... That last mattered little for this colony was now the rightful possession of the new settlers. They would take care of it.

It was Kate O'Connor's as well.

"Ada," she said, in a calm but decisive voice. "I'm not going home. I've just made my decision. No matter what you say, I won't change my mind."

Ada gave a loud cry of joy.

"I've no intention of making you change your mind, you dear idiot. Oh, Kate, I'm so glad. I did so want you to stay. You're the kind of person we need." The wind was blowing her words away. But in her delight she was still the same incorrigible lady. She shouted above the wind, "We must tell Ezekiel at once!" And dared Kate to be cross with her.